THE WHITE SHEPHERD

THE WHITE SHEPHERD

An Oxford Dogwalkers' Mystery

Annie Dalton

This first world edition published 2015
in Great Britain and the USA by
SEVERN HOUSE PUBLISHERS LTD of
19 Cedar Road, Sutton, Surrey, England, SM2 5DA.
Trade paperback edition first published
in Great Britain and the USA 2015 by
SEVERN HOUSE PUBLISHERS LTD.

Dalton, Annie author.
  The White Shepherd.
  1. Murder–Investigation–Fiction. 2. Dog walking–
  England–Oxford–Fiction. 3. Suspense fiction.
  I. Title
  823.9'2-dc23

ISBN-13: 978-0-7278-8521-0 (cased)
ISBN-13: 978-1-84751-621-3 (trade paper)
ISBN-13: 978-1-78010-674-8 (e-book)

All Severn House titles are printed on acid-free paper.

Severn House Publishers support the Forest Stewardship Council™ [FSC™],
the leading international forest certification organisation. All our titles that
are printed on FSC certified paper carry the FSC logo.

Typeset by Palimpsest Book Production Ltd.,
Falkirk, Stirlingshire, Scotland.
Printed and bound in Great Britain by
TJ International, Padstow, Cornwall.

ACKNOWLEDGEMENTS

Many thanks to Jane Darby and Tim Couché for their useful advice; also grateful thanks to Fiona Ferguson and her niece, the real life Kirsty, and to Jeanette Johnston, for helping us out with Anna's job-share at Walsingham College. Finally, a big thank you to Sue Chapman for telling us about Lord Dunsany's story *Dean Spanley,* from which Laurie Swanson quotes to Anna. Any glaring mistakes are, of course, the sole responsibility of the authors.

PROLOGUE

When Anna saw why her dog Bonnie had half-dragged her on to the bright-green spongy ground beyond the trees, her heart started to beat so fast that she was afraid she'd choke. The peaceful sweep of Port Meadow, the nearby allotments with their fading bean flowers and the railway track blurred out of focus along with all their ambient sounds; for a moment she thought she was going to pass out. But Anna had never been much of a fainter so was denied that mercy.

Random, shocking details jumped out. A single running shoe soaked almost black with blood; more blood welling out through ripped and gory running clothes and streaking the honey-coloured hair that was still pulled back into a ponytail; the trickling little streamlet a metre or so from the bloody head; the contorted features, an agonized mask scarcely recognizable as human.

A name formed inside her head. *Naomi*. She instantly recoiled from the thought. How could that mutilated emptied-out thing be Naomi?

Anna continued to stare down as she tried and failed to make sense of what she was seeing, to understand how this lovely lucid autumn light, which she'd always associated with crisp school uniforms and fresh starts, could be illuminating Naomi's corpse.

Then some internal wall dissolved and there were two Annas: the thirty-two-year-old woman, gripping on to Bonnie's lead with bloodless fingers, and the stoned, terrified sixteen year old, stopped in her tracks by this same slaughterhouse reek.

A scream exploded in her head. It felt like all those times she had screamed for help in dreams, help that never came, because she could never make her stupid vocal cords work, though inside she was howling like an animal.

Bewilderingly, help did come. Two women came pushing through the trees, their two dogs straining against their leashes. Anna had seen both dog-owners before, walking separately over Port Meadow. The older woman's hair was a startling mix of jet black and snowy white, loosely wrapped in one of her collection of gypsy scarves. The younger woman – just a girl, really, Anna thought – had once asked Anna jokingly if she was sure that Bonnie wasn't a wolf.

'God, oh my God, oh *shit*!' the girl whispered now, then shrieked, 'Buster! *Leave*!' frantically reeling in her retracting lead as her tiny apricot poodle went to sniff at the blood pooling around the corpse. Just in time she turned aside, vomiting into the grass.

The older woman had pulled out her phone. 'Get me the police! Yes, my name is Isadora Salzman.' She had one of those actressy voices, the posh side of middle class. Anna saw little tremors running through her.

The girl straightened up, fumbling for a tissue. Her skin, normally delicate cinnamon brown, had turned ashy with shock. 'Sorry, I never thought I'd have to see something like this.' She pressed her hands to her mouth, fighting off another bout of retching. 'This is exactly why I didn't want to mind Nick and Leo's dog,' she said shakily. 'I told them, "It's always some poor bloody dog walker who finds the body, *every* fucking time." And now I have.' Her eyes skittered back to the dead woman, then away. 'Are the police coming?' she asked the woman who had phoned.

She nodded. 'We've got to stay until they get here.'

No one had bothered to check Naomi's body for a pulse. Everyone knew she was dead.

Bonnie had settled at Anna's feet, calmer after their frantic dash. Keeping her eyes watchfully on Anna, she keened softly, a sound Anna had never previously heard from her rescue dog, and the only sign of her continuing distress.

'I'm Isadora,' the woman was saying. 'And this is Hero.' She reached down to soothe her dog, which was shivering and trying to hide behind her legs. Some type of highly-strung spaniel, Anna thought, its wayward fringe scraped back from its eyes with a bright-pink clip.

'I'm Tansy,' said the younger woman. 'This is Buster. This is nuts,' she said, almost to herself. 'Why are we introducing the dogs?' Her eyes veered back to Naomi. 'Oh God, her *poor* face,' she moaned.

Isadora began untying the knot at the back of her scarf. Today's headscarf was made of shimmering blue silk. Stooping down, she laid it tenderly over the once-lovely face, and Anna tried not to see the scarlet stains that immediately bloomed. 'There, my darling,' Isadora said in the tones of someone settling a child for the night. Anna couldn't tell if she was trying to comfort the freaked Tansy or the no-longer living Naomi.

'Should you have done that?' Tansy said anxiously. 'Isn't that, like, disturbing the body?'

'Her name was Naomi Evans.'

Anna only knew she'd said the words out loud when Tansy said, dismayed, 'Oh my God, she was your *friend*! I'm so sorry!'

Anna had wondered if she and Naomi might become friends, but she just shook her head. 'We spoke a couple of times, that's all.' Her voice seemed to be coming from somewhere weirdly distant.

'I used to see her out running,' Tansy said.

Isadora nodded. 'She always seemed so vibrant. So—' She quickly checked herself, but Anna knew what she'd been going to say. *So alive.* Instead, she said, 'What a cruel waste.'

Tansy was pacing now. She was ridiculously pretty, Anna thought. In her boyfriend jeans and well-washed sweatshirt she could be an off-duty model. 'I wish I still smoked,' she said abruptly. 'Damn it, I wish I had a spliff.' She gave Anna an anxious glance. 'Sorry if I'm babbling.'

'I'm half-Russian. I'm genetically wired to babble.' Isadora was delving in her bag as she spoke. 'Would this help?' She handed Tansy a small silver flask.

Tansy looked anxious. 'Are you sure? I've just been—'

'Quite sure,' Isadora reassured her.

Tansy unscrewed the top, releasing steam and fumes fierce enough to make her eyes water.

'I put a shot of vodka in it,' Isadora said unnecessarily. She saw their expressions. 'Hero is an early morning girl. I need a little help to get going.'

Tansy hesitated. 'I haven't touched coffee for months.' Using a small quantity as mouthwash, she spat it into a bush, then took a grateful gulp. 'Thanks,' she repeated more hoarsely before offering the flask to Anna, who took a deep swallow of the joltingly alcoholic contents.

'I can't look at her, but I'm scared not to look,' Tansy almost wailed. 'Could we move away? It feels disrespectful chatting over her body like this.'

Anna returned the flask to Isadora, who knocked back a serious slug before she said, 'Also, if we get away from these trees it will be easier to see when the police get here.'

They couldn't seem to move. They looked down at the dead woman, taking in her delicate wrist bones, the ruined flesh.

Tansy said, 'She's not wearing her bracelet.'

The persistent *tink-tink-tink* of Naomi's charms as she ran had been like her signature soundtrack.

'She *always* wore it,' Tansy said.

Isadora started peering at the marshy ground around Naomi's body. Unbound from her scarf, her hair made a tangled cloud around her sharply intelligent face. 'She *was* wearing it.' She pointed into the grass where silver charms lay scattered, winking in the sun like tiny fallen stars.

They fell silent, not wanting to imagine the final struggle that had caused the links of Naomi's bracelet to snap. Still in silence they led their dogs a little distance beyond the trees. It was just possible to glimpse the awkward sprawl of Naomi's legs, her bare and bloodied foot. They could have turned their backs, but no one did. It wasn't morbid fascination or superstitious fear, Anna thought. It was like they *owed* it to her.

Tansy was partly hugging herself, looking young and vulnerable in a way that Anna couldn't remember feeling. 'Another *person* did that to her,' she said almost to herself. 'Someone I could have just walked past in the street.'

Isadora said sombrely, 'That makes three now.'

'Three?' said Anna.

'Fatal stabbings,' Tansy said. 'A girl was stabbed to death in Magdalen College Gardens a couple of months ago. Then a few weeks later they found that other girl – in South Park, wasn't it?'

Isadora gave a bleak nod.

'You seriously hadn't heard?' Tansy asked Anna.

Anna couldn't tell her that it took all her energy to deal with the personal day-to-day. Other people's tragedies dimly registered on her radar, but not enough that she would notice an emerging pattern: three young women, three open-air stabbings. 'I only recently moved back—' she started to say, but Tansy was already talking.

'They need to catch him before the new term starts and the students come back.'

Isadora joined in, echoing Tansy's worries, but Anna had stopped listening. A late butterfly fluttered past. The heat of summer looked to be carrying on into September, and Anna could hear bees buzzing. Cows grazed placidly nearby. How much better to be a cow or a bee, she thought, oblivious to the ugly human drama playing out in a corner of this beauty spot.

Bonnie sat up suddenly alert, one flawless white ear swivelling to identify a new sound. As the first squad cars streaked into view, blue lights flashing, sirens blaring, Anna had to force herself not to run, to keep breathing out and in, all the time feeling as if she was trapped in a recurring bad dream – a dream she was powerless to change and from which she was never allowed to wake.

ONE

The windowless interview room at St Aldates Police Station had that airless feel that Anna recognized from before, and the same tang of disinfectant. Isadora and Tansy had separately given their versions of the discovery of Naomi's body. Now it was Anna's turn to sit at the bolted-down table across from DI Chaudhari, a stocky, weary-looking man in his forties with thick glossy black hair. 'Apologies that we're having to talk to you in here. You're obviously not a suspect. All the care suites are currently in use.'

The young detective sergeant seated himself next to the DI and flipped back the cover of his notebook.

At the exact moment Anna had handed Bonnie over to Tansy before she went in, she'd felt herself break into a cold sweat. Possibly, Tansy had noticed, because she'd whispered, 'That Sergeant Goodhart is annoyingly hot!' in a misguided attempt to cheer her up. Anna thought that Tansy's hazel-eyed sergeant looked far better-rested – and far better toned – than the world-weary Inspector Chaudhari. But tired or not, there was no doubt whose show this was. Behind the inspector's oddly old-fashioned gallantry Anna felt a sly intelligence that put her on her guard.

She could feel her nerves trying to take over as she told them that her name was Anna Hopkins, that she was thirty-two years old and currently lived in Park Town. This mention of her prestigious North Oxford address sent a faint flicker across the inspector's features, and Anna felt stung into adding, 'It was my grandparents' house. I let most of it out. I live on the ground floor.' She explained that she had lived away from Oxford since leaving school, but had returned six months ago to take up a part-time post at Walsingham College. 'I came back because of my grandfather,' Anna added before the inspector could ask. 'My grandmother died last year, and he was becoming increasingly frail. He's the only—' She stopped, then continued more carefully, 'He's my only close family now. I wanted some time with him while I still have the chance.'

'Your grandfather doesn't live with you?' the inspector said.

'He lives in a retirement home. He hated the idea of me having to do – personal things for him.'

The inspector briefly rubbed at his face. Anna had noticed dark pouches of exhaustion beneath his eyes. Maybe he was coming to the end of a long shift, or perhaps he had young children who woke him in the night. 'So if you could just tell us in your own words what happened this morning when you found the body of Naomi Evans.'

Anna flashed back to earlier that morning at Coffee on the Green. Sitting at an outdoor table, with Bonnie at her feet, she'd managed to spin out her skinny latte for twenty minutes before she'd decided that Naomi wasn't coming.

'Ms Hopkins,' the inspector prompted.

'I'm sorry. I'm not quite sure where you need me to—'

'Start wherever it makes sense for you to start,' he reassured her.

'OK, well, I just recently acquired a rescue dog. She's a White Shepherd. She's still young and needs a lot of exercise. I take her to Port Meadow. It's the nearest place that I can let her off for a good run.' Anna felt herself suddenly short of oxygen, as if she'd been running. She made herself take a steadying breath before she said, 'She normally waits for me to unclip her lead. But this morning as soon as we walked into the meadow she seemed unsettled. She started whining – not normal whining, it was a really harrowing sound. I've never heard any dog make that sound before. Then she took off with her lead still attached. It was all I could do to hang on. It's like she knew exactly where she had to go and what she was going to find.'

'And what did she find?'

'She found Naomi lying by this little stream.' Anna tried to swallow, but her throat couldn't seem to remember how. 'She'd been stabbed over and over. There was blood everywhere. It was still flowing from her wounds.' She glanced across at the inspector. 'That means it had happened quite recently, doesn't it?'

He didn't answer, just waited. Anna took a sip from her glass of water with its slight aftertaste of dust, while she steeled herself to tell the worst part. 'Her face was – terribly damaged. Hardly recognizable.' Noticing that she was unconsciously touching her own face, she forced both hands down into her lap.

'But you still recognized her?' said the inspector, gently steering Anna's narrative. 'You knew Ms Evans, is that right?'

She saw Isadora tenderly laying her scarf over Naomi, the scarlet stains blossoming on the silk.

'I'd seen her out running, when I was walking my dog. One morning she stopped to admire her, and we just got talking.' Anna had found it alarming, this unlooked for consequence of dog-ownership; the way total strangers would see her and Bonnie together and feel entitled to start a conversation. British people were supposed to be reserved, but apparently if you added a dog to the mix, reserve went straight out the window.

Naomi had taken things one step further. She had dropped to her knees beside Anna's dog. And Bonnie, normally shy with people she didn't know, had pressed her snow-white forehead intensely against Naomi's, as if they were old soulmates who'd been reunited.

Anna had felt childishly jealous. She and Bonnie were still in the early stages of getting used to each other. Certainly, Bonnie had never yet leaned adoringly against Anna. But then Naomi had said in a tone of awe, 'This has to be the most beautiful dog I have ever seen in my life! Actually, the two of you look like you've just stepped out of a fairy-tale!' and she had smiled up at Anna with such innocent delight that Anna had felt all her carefully maintained defences melt. She registered that the inspector had asked a question. She forced herself back to the present. 'I'm sorry?'

'I said, do you remember what you and Ms Evans talked about?'

'We talked about my dog. I said I'd only had her a few weeks and that she was almost spookily well-behaved. For the first couple of weeks it was like having a ghost dog. I thought maybe she was grieving for her previous owner. The Rescue Centre told me she'd been brought in after the old lady who owned her died. Naomi agreed with me that Bonnie didn't seem like the kind of dog an old lady would normally have, and I said I wished I knew more about her background; Bonnie's, that is.'

'Were there any subsequent occasions when you spoke to Ms Evans?'

'I saw her again about two weeks ago. Naomi told me that she was a researcher and that if I wanted she'd do a bit of digging around for me, try to find out some more about how Bonnie ended up in the rescue centre.' At this point the rain clouds that had been piling up over Port Meadow had decided to empty themselves. Anna, Naomi and Bonnie had rushed to the car park through the near-tropical downpour, to shelter in Naomi's sporty silver Audi. Bonnie had performed her magic trick of gracefully folding her snowy limbs small enough to fit exactly inside the footwell, while Naomi scrolled through her phone, trying to find a mutually convenient date to meet up.

'We decided on an early breakfast at Coffee on the Green,' Anna told the inspector. 'So she could tell me what she'd found out, if anything.' She remembered Naomi's breezy confidence that she'd be sure to have some info for Anna by then.

The inspector moved fractionally in his chair. 'You and Ms Evans had arranged to see each other? When?'

Anna felt her mouth go dry. 'This morning. It's my day off. But she didn't show up.'

'She didn't call or text to let you know?'

Anna shook her head. 'I left the house in a hurry. I didn't have my phone. I didn't sleep very well last night.' She hadn't slept at all until, finally, at around five, she'd fallen into one of those pitch-black sleeps that always left her totally exhausted. She'd barely had time to throw on some clothes and grab Bonnie's lead.

'She had your contact details?'

'Yes, she said she has – had – to put everything in her phone, because she had such a bad memory.'

'Did we find a phone?' the inspector shot at his second in command.

Sergeant Goodhart had been so quiet that Anna had genuinely stopped noticing he was there. She wondered if it was something they taught in police training. One to talk and a second, invisible, cop to watch.

He shook his head. 'We didn't find a phone with her body, and so far one hasn't turned up at her flat.'

Absorbing what they'd told him, Inspector Chaudhari was

tapping lightly on the table-top, as if accompanying some internal soundtrack.

Anna pictured Naomi leaning out of her car, her face shiny with rain, wet hair plastered to her head. 'I'm so sorry I can't give you and Bonnie a lift,' she'd called. 'I've managed to land an interview with this guy, and I need to rush home to change first.' Then she'd driven away, out of Anna's life forever.

The inspector had stopped tapping. 'If I could just take you back to the moment you discovered the body. You say your dog led you there. But you were still alone at this point?'

'Yes,' said Anna. 'It was just me and Bonnie.'

'Can you remember when you first saw the body – did you maybe cry out or call for help?'

Anna shook her head. She didn't tell him that finding Naomi's body had totally robbed her of her voice; something that had previously only afflicted her in dreams.

For the first time Inspector Chaudhari looked sceptical. 'You didn't make any sound at all? That's unusually controlled given the circumstances.'

Anna felt stung. Did women invariably scream when they found bodies? Yet another epic fail for her unconvincing attempt to impersonate a human being. She settled for a half shrug. Let Inspector Chaudhari think what he liked.

The inspector resumed delicately tapping his fingers. 'I just want to be quite clear. You don't think that you cried out or made any kind of sound, yet nevertheless Ms Salzman and Ms Lavelle came to find you? And you hadn't previously met either of these women before?'

Anna took another sip of dust-flavoured water which, if anything, left her feeling more dehydrated. 'I'd seen them both separately walking their dogs, but I'd only spoken to Tansy.'

The inspector frowned, and DS Goodhart obligingly became visible again. 'Ms Lavelle, sir.'

'Actually, Tansy – Ms Lavelle – spoke to me,' Anna said, correcting herself. 'She asked me if Bonnie was my pet wolf. That was the only time we'd talked until – until today.'

'And though the three of you didn't know each other, Ms Salzman and Ms Lavelle elected to come to your aid, until the emergency services arrived?'

'Yes. I think they thought I shouldn't have to handle it on my own.' Now they were minding Bonnie while Anna was being interviewed. Anna's grandfather had dubbed the twenty-first century the 'walk on by era'. But these unknown women had given up their entire morning to help her. Anna should feel grateful, but she found their kindness claustrophobic. It implied that the three of them had some kind of connection, but after this morning she didn't want a connection with anyone ever again.

The inspector asked a few more desultory questions, but Anna had the feeling that he was gradually winding things up. He had toyed with her a little, mainly for form's sake, she thought, but now his fatigue was winning out. When Sergeant Goodhart handed her a card with the name and number of Thames Valley Support Services, and smiled at her, with a smile that reached his eyes, she felt herself start to breathe more easily. 'So is that all?' she asked, trying to keep her voice even.

'That's all for now,' Inspector Chaudhari said, placing a slight emphasis on the last word. He ran his hands through his hair. 'You probably know that two young women were recently stabbed to death in Oxford in a similar manner to Naomi Evans? It's too early in our investigations to know if we're dealing with the same killer. Either way, we are dealing with an extremely dangerous individual, someone who isn't afraid to strike in broad daylight in a public place. So until he or she is caught, I'd advise you to take extra care in your day-to-day movements.'

He pushed back his chair as the cue for everyone to stand up. 'Well, thank you for your cooperation,' he said in an almost cheerful voice. Anna heard his stomach give a prolonged gurgle. 'Was that you or me, Goodhart?' he asked, straight-faced.

'I couldn't possibly say, sir,' Goodhart said, equally dead-pan.

Their jokey exchange felt like final confirmation that her ordeal was over. Anna felt light-headed with relief as the inspector opened the door, politely moving aside to let her go through.

She already had her back to him as he said casually, 'You don't remember me, do you? Of course, I was a lot younger then. I was with the first-response team that night. It's not something you easily forget.'

Behind her, the sergeant softly cleared his throat. Anna had gone rigid with the effort not to react. Inspector Chaudhari had known all along. He'd known exactly who she was, and he'd waited until she thought she was home free before he showed his hand.

Somehow she found her way back to the concrete stairs with jaunty blue-painted handrails, along institutional looking corridors, past noisy open-plan offices. By the time she arrived back at reception she was frantic to get out into the air. She had just reached the external doors as two burly male police officers came through with a shaven-headed youth in handcuffs.

Isadora and Tansy were waiting with the dogs outside. Isadora was cuddling Hero. Tansy was loosely holding Buster's and Bonnie's leads in one hand as she talked on her phone. She gave Anna a relieved smile. 'And obviously I would have done,' Anna heard her say, 'but I genuinely thought we'd be finished by now. I'm sorry, Julie, but in my world a murder counts as an emergency.' She pulled an apologetic face at Anna. 'Yes, I've already said I'll be in tomorrow. Look, I've got to go now.' She ended her call. 'Unfeeling bitch,' she said, shaking her head. 'Unbelievable.'

'Sorry if I've caused problems,' Anna said stiffly. 'It was good of you both to wait.'

'Of course we waited!' Isadora said, over the top of Hero's curly head. 'We wanted to make sure you were OK.'

'Don't you worry about Julie,' Tansy said. 'She's a passive-aggressive vegan; not a good mix.'

They were trying too hard. There was something different in their faces. Anna didn't want to identify it. She just needed to get away. 'Well, thanks for everything. I'd better get going.' She moved to take Bonnie's lead, knowing she was being totally graceless, but too frantic to care.

Isadora laid her hand on Anna's arm. 'The desk sergeant told us someone would drive us all home.'

Anna felt a flash of naked panic. 'No, honestly! Bonnie didn't get her run, and I could do with some air.' She was ready to scream with the need to escape, but Isadora didn't seem to notice.

'I'm supposed to be going to a book launch tonight,' she said, her hand still lightly detaining Anna. 'Kit Tulliver, an old student of mine, has written a rather well-received biography of Owen

Traherne, but I simply can't face going now. Anyway, Tansy and I thought we'd meet up later for a drink. Perhaps you'd like to come?'

'I can't, sorry. I'm really not in a very—' Anna began when Tansy fervently interrupted.

'I shouldn't think you *are*, sweetie!'

Anna was horrified to see tears glittering on her lashes.

'Inspector Chaudhari told us all about your family. I'm *so* sorry. This morning must have just brought it all—'

Anna coldly cut her off. 'Thanks again for all your help.' Gripping Bonnie's lead with whitening knuckles, she hurried away, not bothering to say goodbye. In her mind, the women and the game-playing detective inspector had now become equally threatening. Inspector Chaudhari had exposed her – *betrayed* her – to these women. He had done it as a form of shock tactics, or maybe just to test their claim that they had never met Anna until that morning. Whatever his reasons, she hated him with a white-hot hate.

She had just reached the gates of Christchurch College when Tansy caught her up. She pushed a wilted business card into Anna's hand. 'It's from the cafe where I work,' she said breathlessly. 'I've written my number on the back. I just thought, in case you ever—' She registered Anna's stony expression and pulled a face. 'You probably never want to set eyes on us again, right?'

Anna shoved the card into the front pocket of her leather messenger bag, gave a curt nod and kept walking. The autumnal light touched the ancient buildings with gold. Somewhere bells rang, the clangorous medieval sound mingling with the hum of traffic.

Throughout the interview she had longed for the moment when she could go back to her safe solitary existence, not having to monitor her expressions or explain herself. But Inspector Chaudhari had shattered her illusion. *I was with the first-response team. It's not something you easily forget.* With those brutally casual words he had shown her that she would never now know any peace of mind.

As she passed Carfax Tower a trio of teenage girls hurried past, laughing, talking, flicking back their glossy hair. She watched them rushing headlong into their unknown future, girls every bit as self absorbed and silly as she had been.

Anna began to walk faster, and Bonnie obediently matched her pace. *She mustn't think.* It felt like if she could just keep moving she could put actual distance between herself and the rising tide of horror. Without slowing down, Anna fumbled one-handed for her ear-buds, plugging herself into a talk radio podcast. She needed impersonal voices; voices, and the physical rhythm of walking.

There had been a dark period in her life when mindless walking was the only thing that had held her together, and so she had walked and walked. Sometimes she'd walked all night. When exhaustion finally stopped her in her tracks, she'd slept – in doorways, on park benches, at the bus station in Gloucester Green – while her grandparents were frantic with worry. Once she'd gone missing for two weeks. The police had eventually picked her up on a street just off the Cowley Road. Her grandparents had begged her to tell them where she'd been, but she only knew that she'd been walking. Her grandmother had cried over Anna's grubby emaciated state. She ran her a bath, put plasters on her blisters, tried to persuade her to eat. For her grandparents' sake, Anna had made a superhuman effort to behave like a normal sixteen year old: breathe out and in, chew and swallow, even go to school, until the next time the furies in her head drove her to walk out of the door and keep on walking. Twice she'd been caught trying to let herself into her old family home with her grandparents' house-key with no memory of how she'd got there.

That lost, driven teenager suddenly felt dangerously close. Anna could feel her grief and terror. She remembered how something from the external world would occasionally break through the muffled undersea sensations that had enclosed her – the smell of mown grass from a college garden, a cafe door opening to let out a babble of voices – before she was sucked back under. She had walked so as not to feel, not to remember. But sometimes, like today, memories would rise up, more disturbingly vivid than when they were really happening. In her memories, everything was burnished, glowing, hyper-real. Whole scenes played themselves out before her eyes. All the times she'd screamed at her mother for being so stupid, for being so unfair, while her little sister looked on, stricken. Worse than Anna's shameful memories were the ordinary good times; like the time she and her brothers had attempted to toast marshmallows on a beach in Cornwall in a near gale while her dad tried to catch fish for their supper. The marshmallows had refused to melt, then turned ominously black and finally burst into flame. The fish had stubbornly evaded their father's hook and line. Her dad had ended up buying everyone fish and chips, which they ate in the fish-smelling car with the heater turned up high. Yet Anna recalled it as a day of pure unalloyed happiness.

If she could just bring them all back for one hour, just one hour . . .

Anna found herself sitting on a stone step. She could feel the chill of the stone rising up through the denim of her jeans. She was soaked through with cold perspiration. Tiny black specks danced before her eyes, and for a moment she didn't know which Anna she was supposed to be. Then she became aware of the solid warmth of her White Shepherd pressing firmly against her hip, pulling her back into present time, back into her body. Anna dimly heard a passer-by say, 'That's the most fabulous looking dog I have ever seen.'

And she remembered Naomi smiling up at her, her arms wrapped around Bonnie's neck.

Anna had offered to pay her for her investigations, and Naomi had laughed. 'Are you kidding! Finding out stuff is like my drug of choice! I'm so lucky,' she'd told Anna as rain battered the car windows. 'I actually get to do what I love every day!'

Bonnie continued to press insistently against Anna. It felt as if she was saying, 'Are you OK? If not, I will *make* you OK.'

Properly taking in her surroundings for the first time, Anna saw that she was sitting on the bottom of the flight of steps at the base of the Martyrs' Memorial, just across from the Randolph Hotel. All she had to do was cross over to the Banbury Road, keep walking, keep breathing out and in, and eventually she'd reach her front door. She pulled herself shakily to her feet.

TWO

Anna's grandparents had lived at the far end of the graceful Georgian terrace for as long as she could remember. She had loved visiting their house as a child, but then for a time in her teens it had felt like her prison. Now the bottom two floors of this house, with all its mixed memories, was Anna's home. But this afternoon she felt only exhausted relief that her sanctuary was finally within reach.

She unlocked the door, disabled the alarm and hustled Bonnie inside, quickly resetting the alarm.

The hallway looked exactly the same as when she'd left it this morning to meet Naomi: the faded scarlet and blue of the antique kelims against the softly gleaming wood floor, the swirling colours of the abstract painting on the wall, a faint scent of her grandfather's favourite roses coming through the open door of her sitting room. But nothing was the same. Dazed and disconnected, Anna bent to unclip Bonnie's lead. 'Basket,' she said. At that moment even a dog's undemanding presence was too much.

Bonnie gave Anna one of her soulful looks then took herself off downstairs to the kitchen. Anna heard her toenails clicking on the polished wood stairs followed by the sound of a thirsty dog gulping water.

She slipped out of her socks and trainers. Gathering them in one hand, Anna looked down at them with mute horror. There was no blood, nothing that she could see, yet she felt contaminated inside and out.

She fled into her bathroom, dropping both trainers and socks into the dirty linen hamper. This action tripped an internal switch, and Anna began shedding the rest of her clothes in a frenzy, feverishly bundling them into the basket on top of the rest. Then she walked into the shower, shut herself behind the sliding glass doors and stood under the scalding hot water, soaping and shampooing and rinsing herself over and over until it finally ran cold.

She emerged into a fog of steam. Wiping her hand across the

steamed-up mirror, Anna regarded her flushed, shiny face. *I'm like a different order of being to Tansy*, she thought. Tansy's delicate heart-shaped face instantly registered her emotions, like weather chasing across the sky, where Anna's was habitually guarded. Her eyes, a dark, almost navy, blue, were the untrusting eyes of a survivor. Her gaze dropped to the neat, faintly-puckered scar below her navel. For the millionth time, she saw the flash of the blade, felt it slice stinging into her flesh, saw herself run, stumbling, bleeding, into the dark.

In her bedroom Anna carefully blow-dried her shoulder-length hair – a similar honey-brown shade to Naomi's, she realized. She dressed in her favourite slouchy trousers and a long, loose T-shirt. Her reflection looked back from the full-length mirror, a thirty-something young woman ready for yoga or Pilates, some holistic activity not involving bloodshed.

She heard herself make an incoherent sound and saw her eyes, reflected in the mirror, turn pleading, but it was no use. Naomi's murder had dragged her back to the bad place, the mad place, and she only knew one way to stop the madness from overflowing.

She snatched up a black scrunchy, painfully yanking her newly-washed hair through it as she hurried across the landing to her study. It was the only room she kept shut. Turning the handle she slipped inside, closing the door behind her. It was the smallest room in Anna's flat. Inside it she kept her somewhat esoteric reference library, her desktop computer and printer, and a running machine. All these objects had been crowded awkwardly into one corner. It was the only way Anna could fit in her giant antique cupboard.

She'd found the ancient French armoire in a street market. She'd loved the way its double doors were hand-painted with an elaborate floral design. Over time the pattern had faded, and in some places only a faint gold and cobalt-blue stippling remained. Anna had thought her street-market find was beautiful once. Now she wished she could chop it up and set it on fire. If the day ever came when it had served its purpose, she would.

The key lived in the top drawer of her desk. Anna fitted it into the lock, turning until she felt the telltale click. She could feel the blood drumming in her ears as she pulled the two doors apart.

Inside was horror and chaos. It filled the top two-thirds of the cupboard, extending on to and totally covering the backs of both doors; layers of yellowing news clippings, photographs large and small, typed lists of names and questions, timelines, witness statements, scrawled arrows, printouts of floor plans, pink and yellow Post-its, and Anna knew the exact position of every single one. Over the top, taut criss-crossed strings ran back and forth, forming a dense spider-web of connections. The bottom third of the cupboard was stacked with tatty cardboard files, so swollen with documents that they seemed about to burst their seams. Gasping now with a mix of emotions so explosive that it felt like they surely had to blow her apart, Anna blindly groped for a marker pen, writing furiously across one of the clippings.

Dead End, she scrawled, in jagged black letters, before she hurled the pen away.

For a long moment she stood where she was, fists clenched, taking great sobbing breaths. She wouldn't cry. She hadn't cried then, and she wouldn't cry now. Instead she forced herself to reread the screaming headlines, forced herself to remember why she had to keep on keeping it together and why she'd come back to live in this city after so many years.

Calmer now, Anna picked up a different marker from the jar on her desk, running her finger along one of the strings until she found a blurry photo of two amiably smiling generic-looking young males. Frowning, she printed a thick blue question mark above one of the faces. Underneath she wrote in a more legible script: *Where are you?*

She relocked the doors, shutting all the murder and madness safely inside. Like always when she'd added something to her cupboard, however small, she had a childlike sense of being forgiven.

Outside her study, Anna was suddenly shaky from lack of food. It was late afternoon, and all she'd consumed, not counting the life-saving gulp of coffee-flavoured vodka, was her skinny latte while she was waiting for Naomi. The idea of food or cooking still felt indecent though, so she set off downstairs to her kitchen to make herself a smoothie.

The room was half kitchen, half conservatory. A pair of French doors looked out on to a pretty courtyard garden. The afternoon sunlight poured in through the glass, glinting off the gleaming copper pans hanging from their hooks and the open shelves where Anna still kept her grandmother's beloved Limoges china. In her heightened state the delicate cups and dishes seemed to glow as if lit from within.

Anna opened the French doors, letting her eyes rest on the pots of herbs and flowers. A late-flowering clematis had been allowed to ramble unchecked over a wooden pergola, creating a leafy roof starred with enormous white, green-veined blossoms.

Bonnie had retreated to her basket in its alcove. She looked cautiously up at Anna, unsure what was required. Anna clicked her fingers. 'Bonnie, good dog, come here!'

Bonnie stepped out of her basket, allowing Anna to scratch her between her ears, her eyes narrowing with pleasure. With her fingertips, Anna gently searched for and found the tiny mysterious ridges beneath the snowy white coat. Bonnie's inexplicable scars were part of the mystery that Naomi had been going to try to solve. 'So you're not just beautiful, but you've got a secret past! You're like the canine Mata Hari!' Naomi had told Bonnie.

'Well, maybe some mysteries aren't meant to be solved,' Anna told her dog softly. 'And that's just how it is. So I am going to make a green smoothie which will hopefully turn me into a whole new woman, and when it's ready we'll go out into the garden and enjoy some of this sun. What do you say?' As Anna went on talking sweet nothings, Bonnie cocked her head first to one side and then the other, seeming appreciative of Anna's efforts at communication.

She went over to her fridge and pulled out a packet of baby spinach, an avocado, a cucumber and other ingredients for her smoothie. Then she plugged in her juicer, found a sharp knife and chopping board and set to work. Bonnie wandered over to the open French doors, sniffing the air before she lay down in the sunlight, positioning herself so that she could keep a watchful eye on Anna. Surprisingly, the high-pitched whine of the machine, which always set Anna's teeth on edge, only induced an occasional ear-twitch in her dog.

Noticing that Bonnie's water bowl was empty, she wiped her juicy hands on some kitchen towel and refilled the bowl before she went back to juicing. Anna still felt like a novice as a dog owner though Bonnie was really so little trouble. Whoever trained her had done a stellar job. But Anna was starting to wonder exactly what kind of life the White Shepherd had led before she turned up in the rescue centre, because she had a bad feeling that Naomi's was not Bonnie's first ever dead body.

Having methodically processed her fruit and vegetables, Anna poured the juice into a blender, threw in half the avocado, added the squeezed juice of half a lime and whizzed everything together. She was just pouring her smoothie into a tall glass when her iPad, which was lying on the kitchen table, surprised her with a friendly *ping*. She'd had an email from someone she'd never heard of, a guy called Jake McCaffrey.

Anna collected up her tablet and her smoothie and, with Bonnie following at her heels, carried them out to the little bistro table and chairs under the pergola's dappled shade.

Dana, the woman who rented the top-floor flat, had her Velux windows standing wide open, and Anna could hear the all-too familiar opening chords of Van Morrison's 'Moon Dance'. In between shifts as a trauma and orthopaedic surgeon at the John Radcliffe, Dana somehow found time to conduct a string of love affairs with a series of unattainable men. Since she only played the bitter-sweet 'Moon Dance' when she was in the throes of a break-up, Anna had to assume that Dana's latest man, a Dutch banker called Rene, had proved as disappointing as the others.

With Dana's break-up music for her soundtrack, Anna slowly sipped at her drink. Warm sunlight filtered down through the clematis flowers, casting patterns on her skin. Bonnie had come to lie with her head resting on Anna's bare feet, something she'd only recently taken to doing. Anna felt ridiculously touched each time. It suggested that Bonnie was starting to trust her, making Anna feel as if she might after all be a halfway OK person.

'OK, shall we take a peek at Mister Jake McCaffrey?' she asked Bonnie after she'd finished her smoothie.

Dear Ms Hopkins,

Naomi Evans has given me your contact details. She seems to think there's a chance that you might have adopted my godmother's dog from the Oxford Dog Shelter. Bonnie was originally my dog, but circumstances made it impossible to keep her. From Naomi's reports though she's happy and healthy, and you're obviously doing a great job of taking care of her. I'm attaching a photo for purposes of identification.

I'm flying in from Washington on the 10th and have to be
in Oxford the following day to talk to lawyers about my
aunt's estate. Would you be available to meet me that day?
If it's not imposing, I'd like to see Bonnie again, and perhaps
you'd like to hear more of her history.
   Regards,
   Jake McCaffrey

After the initial shock of seeing Naomi's name, Anna's next thought
was that Naomi had kept her promise. Not only had she succeeded
in tracking down Bonnie's previous owner, but she'd also gone
the extra distance by putting the White Shepherd's past and present
owners in touch. Anna could maybe have done this herself. But it
seemed that Naomi had liked Anna enough to make her a present
of her special expertise. It was the kind of thing you might do,
Anna thought, if you wanted someone to be your friend.

Then she reread the email and found herself resenting Jake
McCaffrey's attitude. Bonnie was *her* dog now, and this guy,
whoever the hell he was, had no claim on her whatsoever. Anna's
finger hovered over her Trash icon, but then her curiosity kicked
in. She'd wanted to find out about Bonnie, hadn't she? It couldn't
hurt to look at a photograph.

Anna clicked on the attachment and felt a prickle of shock to
see a gangly White Shepherd, still just a half-grown puppy, but
instantly recognizable as Bonnie. In a strangely human, upright
pose, she sprawled against the shoulder of an exhausted American
soldier who was sitting propped against a crumbling piece of
wall. Presumably, he was Jake McCaffrey. Dressed in desert
fatigues, he had cornflower blue eyes, startling against his
sunburn, and looked in serious need of a shave. With a pang,
Anna thought that he and Bonnie seemed like affectionate
comrades in arms, their heads so close that Bonnie was unable
to resist licking the helmeted soldier's jaw as he fended her off,
laughing.

She reached down to find the hidden striations in Bonnie's
skin. 'Is that how you got hurt?' she asked her softly. 'Some
idiot meatheads took you into a war zone?'

Bonnie seemed to pick up on a new tenderness in Anna's tone.
Her tail gave a friendly thump, then she unexpectedly flipped

over on to her back, all four paws playfully pedalling in the air, exposing her vulnerable belly.

That's when Anna saw it. The rusty speck of blood on the underside of Bonnie's forepaw.

Naomi's blood.

For a moment Anna went deaf and blind.

Then the horror flooded back in. She had tried so hard to live a background life, a harmless life, yet still the darkness and blood had followed her home.

Grabbing Bonnie by her collar, she hauled the startled dog to her feet. 'Bath! Now!' she screamed.

In her distress, Anna had forgotten that 'bath' was the one word that caused Bonnie to baulk. Worse still, her new human, who she had just begun to trust, was now yelling at her as if she'd done something wrong. Bonnie was an impeccably behaved dog, but she had a strong streak of self-preservation. Planting all four paws firmly on the sun-warmed bricks, she politely refused to budge.

Panting with effort, Anna had to push and pull her into the house, up the stairs and along the landing until they reached the alcove where Bonnie's lead hung next to the coats. Anna was close to hysteria by this time, and it took several bungled attempts to attach the lead. Even then she virtually had to half-drag her still firmly resisting dog into her bathroom. Somehow she managed to heave eighty pounds of White Shepherd over the side of the old claw-footed tub, accidentally clonking Bonnie's head against its cast-iron side on the way.

Once she was actually in the bath, Bonnie made no further attempt at resistance, even after Anna had removed her collar and lead. Tail tucked between her legs, carefully avoiding all eye contact with Anna, she submitted to her ordeal, enduring two applications of shampoo followed by a long, thorough and, by this time, freezing cold rinse.

Too freaked to remember dog shampoo, Anna had to resort to her favourite bottle of Aveda. When she let out the water, she realized she'd also forgotten her old dog towels. She grabbed an inadequate hand-towel from the rail and quickly blotted the shivering Bonnie where she sat in the empty bath, head bowed, emanating reproach.

'Bonnie, out!' Anna told her.

Bonnie didn't need telling twice. She sprang out of the bath, scattering water droplets and sending out expensive wafts of mint and rosemary. For a moment she seemed poised to bolt downstairs, and Anna felt belated shame at having scared her lovely dog. 'Bonnie, come,' she repeated, and after a moment's hesitation, Bonnie followed her a little warily into her bedroom.

Apart from a few small changes, Anna had kept her rooms much the same as they'd been when her grandmother was alive. Only her bedroom had a haphazard unfinished feel. Framed pictures leaned against walls that she had stripped back to the bare plaster. A carved wooden screen, in need of repair, had been arranged to camouflage a pile of unpacked boxes. Anna's bed, with its silky hyacinth-blue sheets and pillows, supplied the one note of sensual luxury in this otherwise Quakerish room. A battered cube of metal, a flea market find, stood in for a bedside table. On its dimpled surface, next to her mobile, a single dark-red rose in a small fluted vase was dropping petals.

Anna turned away to plug in her hairdryer. 'I'm going to dry you off,' she told her dog. 'Then we'll go downstairs and I'll find you something *totally* dogtastic to eat, and I promise I will do my absolute best not to scare you again, OK?' Then she caught herself talking nonsense to her dog and was glad no one was around to hear. Turning back, she saw Bonnie about to launch herself into an apocalyptic shake. Anna barely managed to snatch her phone out of reach of the watery shock-wave created by a post-bath White Shepherd.

'Should have seen *that* one coming,' she said breathlessly. 'You're a super-civilized dog, Miss Bonnie Hopkins, but at the end of the day you're *still* a dog!'

Her phone had been left switched off, and Anna immediately switched it back on, hoping her grandfather hadn't been trying to get hold of her while she was at the police station. The mobile's screen lit up, and she saw the tiny whirling symbol announcing her reconnection to the outside world. Anna would always remember how she'd felt a prophetic clutch of dread even before she saw that she had voicemail. 'Hi, Anna,' said the light warm voice, immediately recognizable after only two conversations. 'It's Naomi Evans.'

THREE

Dusk was closing in as Anna drove through Summertown. It was more than two hours since she'd heard Naomi's message, but she still felt shaky and unreal.

Waiting at some traffic lights, she found herself watching a young family at the window table of an upscale bistro. A flickering candle on the table illuminated their intent faces as the parents helped their small children consult menus almost as big as themselves. For a fleeting moment Anna saw her younger self, her brothers and her little sister inside that charmed circle. Heard her father saying, exasperated, 'Just *try* it, Will! You'll never know if you like it until you try.'

Anna heard a driver's impatient hoot and belatedly noticed the lights had changed. She briefly considered stopping off at Xi'an, the Chinese place her grandfather loved, to get them both takeaway, but decided against. The thought of food still made her stomach muscles clench.

She turned off the Banbury Road into an avenue of detached Victorian and Edwardian houses and soon saw the familiar sign for Bramley Lodge. The tyres of her Land Rover Defender scrunched on gravel as she swung into the drive. The car park was empty except for the few vehicles which belonged to the night staff. Anna went to let Bonnie out of the back, and she sprang down, her snow-white coat glimmering in the twilight.

Bramley Lodge was a handsome three-storey villa which had been converted to look more like a boutique hotel than a retirement home. Inside it smelled of good coffee, lavender polish and the faint scent of the tasteful floral arrangement on the reception desk. The night receptionist bookmarked her place in her kindle and gave Anna a warm smile. 'Hello, have you come to see Mr Ottaway?'

Anna was hastily slipping off her leather jacket. Summer was apparently over at Bramley House, and the thermostat had been cranked up to near-greenhouse levels. 'Sorry, Gita, I know it's a bit late for visiting.'

'I'm sure he'll be thrilled to see you,' Gita said. 'Not to mention Bonnie here.'

Anna's grandfather lived in one of the coveted ground-floor apartments at the back. In the distance she could hear what sounded like a swelling soundtrack from one of the communal sitting rooms. Monday night was Movie Night, she remembered. Bonnie padded silently at her side over the thick-pile carpet. Her tail gave a happy swish as they reached George Ottaway's door. Like most people who met her, Anna's grandfather had fallen in love with Bonnie at first sight and kept a stock of treats for her.

Anna knocked, and when no one answered, she called, 'Hope you're decent!' and cautiously peered around the door. As she'd guessed, he'd taken out his hearing aid. She could see it lying on a side table, the supposedly flesh-coloured earpiece trailing wires. 'It would be flesh-coloured if I was some gruesome plastic doll,' he'd joked to her once.

Her grandfather was sitting with his back to her beside the open French windows, thoughtfully studying an unfinished painting on his easel.

His hair needed cutting again. The fine white tufts grew straight up like a mischievous little boy's. A rush of feelings took her breath away. Like an ark, this room contained all that was precious in Anna's world. Yet for the first time in her life she felt as if she was intruding.

'Hey, Grandpa,' she said, but he went on obliviously contemplating his canvas. His latest painting showed the remains of a simple meal for two; crumbled yellow cheese, a loaf with its crust torn away, ripe strawberries on a dishevelled white cloth. One long-stemmed wine glass still held an inch or so of red wine. A second glass lay on its side surrounded by a spreading crimson stain. Everything vibrated with the untold, perhaps untellable, story of the mysteriously absent diners. Why had their meal been interrupted? Was it love, lust or something darker?

Anna swallowed. A few months shy of ninety, at an age when most people resigned themselves to crocheted lap throws, George Ottaway was finally becoming the artist he had always longed to be. She had no right to still be bringing her troubles to him.

She was turning to leave, when Bonnie unexpectedly took charge of the situation, trotting up to Anna's grandfather and shoving her nose forcefully between his knees. He gave a startled grunt, turning round in his chair. Anna saw his expression transform into surprised delight. 'Anna, how lovely!'

'Sorry about the cold nose,' she said. 'Bonnie decided it was time to alert you to our presence.'

'You're a wise, wonderful dog!' he told Bonnie. He reached down to scratch her in one of her special spots on the back of her neck, just below her collar.

Anna went over to her grandfather, bending down to kiss his cheek, faintly scratchy with stubble. He patted her on the back, and she inhaled the familiar notes of his Penhaligon aftershave. For Anna, this woody, citrusy scent was the smell of home.

Her grandfather reached for his hearing aid, fixed it into place and gave her an impish grin. 'Right, now I'm fully wired for sound! So, to what do I owe the honour of this unexpected visit?'

'Does there have to be a reason?' In fact, Anna now felt totally confused as to why she was here. To cover her moment of awkwardness, she glanced around at the clutter that had accumulated during her grandfather's few months at Bramley Lodge: jars of brushes, half-squeezed tubes of paint, a tangle of rags stained all the colours of the rainbow and emitting a strong smell of turpentine. And everywhere his growing collection of paintings; some in stacks, larger ones leaning up against the wall. 'Grandpa, seriously,' she teased. 'This looks more like an artist's garret in Montmartre every time I come.'

Her grandfather was still petting Bonnie. 'Shall we find one of your special treats,' he asked the dog, 'while my other favourite girl makes us both a cup of tea?' Bonnie immediately came alert. 'You've got a smart dog here,' he said, laughing.

'So I'm learning,' she said, going into the tiny galley kitchen. Perhaps that's why people had dogs. When you didn't know what to talk about, you could always talk about the dog.

She spooned a mix of Darjeeling and Lapsang into the familiar brown teapot, one of the few things her grandfather had taken from his house in Park Town, and found cups and saucers. Her grandfather disapproved of mugs almost as much as he disapproved of tea bags. Anna carried everything in to him on a tray and saw Bonnie noisily demolishing her disgusting pig's ear or whatever he'd given her. 'Should she be doing that on the carpet?'

'She's a dog,' he reminded her. 'She won't leave a single crumb, believe me.'

Looking around for a clear space to put the tray, Anna eventually set it down on the floor. Her eyes kept being drawn back to his paintings. 'Did you think any more about Art Week?' she asked. 'Last time I was here you and Desmond were talking about entering.'

He suddenly looked vague. 'Remind me when Art Week is again?'

'Next May. As you know perfectly well,' she said, not remotely fooled. 'You should start thinking about which paintings you want to show.'

'I don't think so, darling. Nothing's properly finished.'

'I don't think artists ever feel their work is finished, do they?'

Her grandfather made a dismissive noise. 'I don't know if I'd really call myself an artist.'

Anna gestured around at the thirty or so vibrant canvasses. 'You know what, Vincent,' she said, half laughing, 'I'm not even going to dignify that with a response!'

Lifting a pile of art books from a sofa to make room to sit down, she placed a faded paisley cushion behind her back and suddenly longed to just close her eyes, forget the troubling message Naomi had left on her phone and sleep until morning.

Her grandfather had turned to watch the last of the twilight fading beyond the windows. 'Just say if you want me to shut the doors,' he offered after a while.

'Lord, no!' said Anna. 'I was actually thinking of shedding another layer!'

He laughed, got up from his chair with a little grunt of effort and hobbled over to join her. 'I'm afraid they cosset us frail old sticks as if we were rare orchids.'

'Well, I'm glad,' she said, patting his hand. 'Not that anyone could convince me that you're a frail old stick, but I think you've earned a bit of cosseting. Do you think this tea is fit to be poured?'

'I think we could risk it,' he said.

As Anna passed him his cup he said quietly, 'Are you going to tell me what's happened?'

For a moment Anna couldn't speak. Her childish longing for her grandfather's guidance had been overruled by a new need to protect him. But now he'd opened the way, she felt her old longing rise up. At last she said, 'It's been a – a hard day.' She had to clear her throat. 'Remember me telling you about Naomi?'

'Yes, of course! Your young researcher who is going to find out about this girl's mysterious past.' He reached down to give Bonnie an affectionate pat.

'Was,' Anna said bleakly. 'Bonnie found her body this morning on Port Meadow. She'd been stabbed.'

She felt his hand quickly move to cover hers. After a while, she risked looking up and saw only pained understanding in her grandfather's eyes. 'That must have been particularly awful for you,' he said. 'My poor girl, and of course you had to call the police?'

She shook her head. 'Actually, I didn't. Two women saw Bonnie dragging me across the meadow and came to see what was wrong.' For the first time Anna pictured this from Isadora and Tansy's point of view. What had made them hurry after her? Was it pure animal instinct like Bonnie? Or just a chilling intuition?

She frowned, her mind suddenly blank. 'Sorry, what was I saying?'

'You were telling me about the two women,' he said gently.

'Yes. One of them was a typical North Oxford type. She took charge and called the police.' Anna closed her eyes against the sight of Isadora covering Naomi's face. 'The other was just a girl.' She remembered Tansy's coltish beauty, her face ashen with shock. 'I think she said she was a waitress. Anyway, they both waited with me until the police came.'

'I'm glad!' her grandfather said forcefully. 'I'm so glad you didn't have to go through this ordeal completely on your own. And then presumably you all had to go down to the station and tell them everything you knew?'

Anna gave a tight nod.

He passed his hand over his face. 'I would have given a lot for you to have been spared all that.'

'I know,' she almost whispered.

'And how did they treat you at the police station?'

He meant: how did they treat you *this time*. Anna pulled a face. 'It turned out the police inspector was with the first response team that came out to – to our house. You can imagine the rest.'

'He thought this was too much like a coincidence?'

She nodded. 'He toyed with me a while, because he could, then admitted they thought it was the work of some serial killer, and I should be careful until he's caught.' She picked up her cup, then set it back in its saucer. 'Grandpa, I didn't realize, but I'd had my mobile switched off all last night. Then, after I got back from St Aldates, I switched it back on and I found – there was a message from Naomi.'

'Oh, my dear girl!'

Until this moment, Anna had been telling herself that she wasn't going to involve him, but now that it came to it her need was too strong. 'The thing is, she said something and I need to know if I'm just being paranoid.' She took out her phone. 'Would it – would it be too disturbing if I play it to you?'

He drew a sharp breath. 'You found her body, and you're worried about disturbing me – with a recorded message! You really *do* think I'm a frail old stick!' He sounded hurt and angry. 'Of course you must play it!'

'I'm sorry,' she said, 'that didn't come out how I meant.'

'Play it,' he said fiercely.

She found the message, and suddenly Naomi's voice was with them in the room. 'Hi, Anna! I'm so sorry this is such short notice, but I'm going to have to cancel our breakfast. I interviewed someone last night and something – something absolutely mind-blowing, actually – came up. I've been up till stupid-o'clock typing up my notes, but oh my God, this is going to be a total game changer, Anna! Oh, yes! And I also wanted to let you know that I absolutely haven't forgotten about your beautiful Bonnie. In fact, I might have some solid info for you very soon. OK, really have to dash now, bye!'

Anna switched off her phone. For a few moments neither of them spoke.

Then her grandfather said, 'Was your friend as lovely as she sounds?'

She didn't correct him about Naomi being her friend. 'She really was,' she said huskily.

'What a terrible, terrible waste.' He shook his head. After a while, he said, 'And you wanted me to hear this because you think you might be overreacting?'

'Yes. Because I don't know if I'm just reading something into this that isn't there.' *Again*, she added silently. Aloud, she said, 'She finds something out, something huge, a "game changer". The very next day she's dead. Is that suspicious, or is it just coincidental? She finds something out, goes for a run and meets some random nutter with a knife. It happens!'

'Exactly!' He set down his cup with a clatter. 'I don't know if this message is significant, and nor do you, but if there's the slightest chance it could lead the police to the killer, you owe it to that poor girl and to her devastated family.' His voice shook, and Anna saw him give an involuntary glance at a photograph on the wall. She had the identical family picture at home, but hers was locked inside a cupboard of horrors. When her grandfather turned back she was horrified to see him close to tears.

'I'm sorry, Grandpa,' she said. 'It's just – I've spent my entire adult life, you know, thinking about the kind of stuff that most people never go near. I can't always tell when I'm being rational and when I'm being—'

'Crazy crackers,' he supplied, a jokey phrase of her dad's that had passed into their family's repertoire.

She nodded, biting her lip.

He quickly took her hand, squeezing it hard. 'Given what's just happened, I think you're commendably rational. You are also exhausted. Go home, darling. Try to sleep. And first thing tomorrow, call the police.'

She shook her head. 'I'll go down to the station when I've finished work. I'm only working half a day tomorrow.'

Driving back to Park Town with four of her grandfather's paintings stashed in her boot, Anna kept hearing his last words to her as he saw her to the door. 'I want you to promise me something though, Anna. Once you've given the police this information, leave them to deal with it as they see fit. You don't need more darkness and suspicion in your life, my darling. You're still so young; you should be out in the world, falling in love and having fun.' His words had left her feeling exposed and ashamed. Her grandfather didn't know that he had seen only the smallest glimpse of the dark obsessions that ruled her life. She prayed that he would never find out the full extent of the damage.

FOUR

At six a.m. Anna gave up trying to sleep. Throwing on a hooded sweatshirt and jeans, she took Bonnie for a fast walk around the University Parks, breathing in the peppery, loamy scents of early autumn and trying to calm herself. She walked as far as the River Cherwell, where early-morning mist rose in curling wisps from the water, then headed home.

Back in her flat, she quickly showered and dressed in her deliberately nondescript work clothes. (Anna regarded her job as the least significant part of her life.) Her fridge was almost empty, so for breakfast she made do with a small tub of natural yogurt and an overripe banana, most of which she had to throw away, washing everything down with two mugs of strong coffee. Bonnie watched all these preparations for departure with close attention.

'Not this time, beautiful girl,' she told Bonnie.

She left the house just as Dana, her lodger, was getting into her car. Deathly pale in designer sunglasses she managed to look simultaneously hung-over and fabulously glamorous. 'Isn't it terrible about that poor girl? Do be careful, won't you?'

'I will,' Anna said. 'And you be careful too,' she remembered to call over her shoulder.

Waiting at the bus stop on the Banbury Road, hollow with hunger, she told herself that after she'd been to the police station she'd stock up on groceries at a supermarket. Then she'd come home and cook a proper meal. *Make that two meals*, she decided as her stomach growled, then felt guilty because it seemed so trivial to be thinking about housekeeping when Naomi was dead.

When the bus finally came it was packed. Anna had to stand all the way to the Cornmarket. As she hastily made her way to the exit, she saw the front page headlines on someone's copy of the *Oxford Mail*: 'New Murder Victim Found In Port Meadow.'

Walsingham College was situated just off the High Street. Like St Edmund Hall, its nearest neighbour, some of its buildings dated back to the eleven hundreds, though they'd been added to or modified throughout the centuries. Walsingham was one of the smaller colleges, but the philosophy department was regarded as one of the best in existence. Students came from all over the world to study. Yet the college still retained the homely intimate atmosphere of an old manor house.

All access to the college was via the porters' lodge. As usual, Anna stopped at the counter to ask if there was any mail. Built like a nightclub bouncer, Mr Boswell wore his sombre regulation suit and bowler with the ponderous dignity of an old-style gangster. 'Not many letters for you today, Miss Hopkins,' he said. 'Isn't it terrible about that other young woman—?'

'Sorry, Mr Boswell, I'm running late!' Anna fled through the eleventh century archway and out into the college gardens. The traffic noises immediately faded behind her, as if she'd stepped back in time. She'd tried to tell herself that it was the thickness of the ancient stone walls that created this muffling effect, but was never completely convinced.

If Walsingham reminded Anna of a medieval manor house, the ecclesiastical-style arched windows and gracefully proportioned buildings which surrounded the gardens on all four sides suggested a monastery. A covered stone walkway added to the impression of an enclosed and dedicated community. The atmosphere would be completely different once the new term began, with students and academics rushing everywhere. But this morning, with no one else around, Anna was super-aware of her footsteps echoing on the cobbles, and of all the ghostly scholars who had walked here before her through the centuries.

Next week the philosophy department was hosting a conference, which Anna had helped to organize, and the college would fill with chattering academics of all nationalities. Then, apart from a few resident fellows and research students, it would empty out again until the undergraduates returned at the start of the Michaelmas Term. Anna hadn't acquired her degree at Oxford, but she had lived in this city for the first eighteen years of her life, and the peculiar rhythms of its academic comings and goings were as familiar to her as the seasons.

Anna turned right through another of Walsingham's ancient archways. This one was signposted to the Old Library. A second right turn brought her to the foot of the nondescript twentieth century staircase that led to the college's equally unimpressive administrative offices on the first floor.

The college had three assistant administrators; Nadine, a hyper-efficient older woman, job-shared with Anna, and Kirsty worked full-time. Anna had immediately taken to stocky, forthright Kirsty with her copper-coloured curls and English rose complexion. But this morning the thought of being cooped up in their hutch-like office with Kirsty, or indeed any other human, filled her with dread. Naomi's murder was now common knowledge. Kirsty would be sure to bring it up, and if she didn't, Paul, the senior administrator, would. Anna would have to tell them, singly or together, that she'd been first on the scene. She'd have to cope with their horror, and worse, their sympathy. Resolutely closing her mind to her rising claustrophobia, Anna forced herself to continue climbing the narrow stairs to her office.

The door was open. As usual Kirsty had arrived first, having dropped off her little boy at his nursery. Anna walked in, dumping her bag and her letters on her desk. 'Hi.' She gave Kirsty a neutral smile, then did a double-take as she saw the daunting blizzard of Post-its Nadine had left pasted on to their shared desk. 'Oh, what? *Seriously*?'

'Nadine's been a busy bee,' Kirsty commented.

'I can see that,' Anna said, stunned.

'Paul's off sick, by the way,' Kirsty said. 'So it's just you and me.' She pushed back her chair. 'I'm going to make some coffee. Want some?'

Anna shook her head. 'No thanks.'

Kirsty took the office kettle into the tiny cloakroom across the corridor. 'I'm going to need a ton of caffeine to get me through today,' she said, coming back. 'Charlie kept waking me up with nightmares. I think he might be going down with something. Please God let it not be that projectile vomiting thing that's going round.' Kirsty kept a photo of her three year old on her desk, blond and mischievous, clutching a toy truck. She didn't obsess about him in that tedious way so many mothers did; nevertheless, Anna had the impression that it was dynamic little Charlie, rather than Jason, her husband, who was the love of her life.

'Quite sure you don't want a cup?' Kirsty asked again, spooning coffee granules into her mug.

'Positive,' said Anna, who loathed instant coffee with a passion. She settled down to read her messages, all concerning actual or potential glitches that might disrupt next week's conference. Thanks to Nadine, Anna would have to keep her head down till lunchtime fine-tuning next week's arrangements. Hopefully, that meant that any mention of the Port Meadow stabbing could be avoided, at least for now.

She logged on at her computer to email the caterers the latest update on the delegates' increasingly complicated dietary requirements. Years ago, before the sky fell in on her life, Anna used to imagine all kinds of exotic futures for herself: an intrepid medic with Médicines Sans Frontièrs, or an eloquent human rights lawyer. She had never once imagined admin. She'd taken the job share as a way to structure her days, to help her stay sane while she pursued the real, secret business of her life, but some days, like today, she felt a sapping despair. Was this to be her life from now on?

'Would it cheer you up at all to know that I have cake?'

Startled out of her thoughts, Anna looked up to see Kirsty watching her. 'Sorry, was I looking very suicidal?'

Kirsty gave her a sympathetic grin. 'Just a little bit!' She continued to look at Anna with an expectant expression. She had something on her mind, but Anna didn't think it was the murders. 'Don't you want to know *why* I have cake?' Kirsty persisted.

'It's not your birthday, is it?' Anna said dismayed.

Kirsty attempted a seated curtsey. 'Actually, it is!' She waved away Anna's apologies. 'You didn't know because I didn't tell you! I hate those office traditions. Except the cake part, obviously! I stopped off at Patisserie Valerie on the way here.' She lifted a beribboned patisserie box on to her desk. 'Look what else I bought, in Blackwell's. This is my birthday present to me!' Kirsty passed her a glossy hard-backed book. 'I was just having a sneaky flick through when you came in.'

Anna glanced at it. '*The Boy in the Blue Shirt*. Oh, this is that new biography of Owen Traherne. Someone told me about it just recently.' She had spoken without thinking and felt her body flood with adrenalin as she remembered that this someone was

Isadora Salzman. Kit Tulliver, the author of the book that Anna was holding in her hands, had been one of her students.

'Everyone's talking about it,' said Kirsty. 'Owen Traherne is seriously hot property just—' She broke off, concerned. 'Are you OK? You've gone really pale.'

'I'm fine,' Anna fibbed. 'I just forgot to have breakfast.' For a moment her grip on reality was so shaky, she was afraid that Isadora and Tansy might actually materialize in their airless little office, trailing small dogs, vodka fumes and murder.

Dreading the onset of a full-scale panic attack (she hadn't had a really bad one for years), Anna forced herself to breathe slowly and calmly while she pretended to be taking an interest in the blurb on the back of Kirsty's book. There was a photograph of Kit Tulliver taken against a backdrop of leafless branches, a woollen scarf looped around his neck. Apparently, there was a tiny remnant of Anna's psyche that wasn't totally consumed by the need to stave off terror because she was still able to register that Isadora's former student was remarkably good-looking. She gave the book back to Kirsty, hoping she wouldn't notice how much her hand was shaking. 'I don't think I've ever read any biographies.' She couldn't tell if her voice sounded normal. She wasn't entirely sure what she'd just said.

'This is not *biographies*, Anna. This is *the* biography that's just been green-lighted for a Hollywood movie. Michael Fassbender is going to play Owen. That's how hot this biography is!'

'Why did they launch the book in Oxford though? I thought Owen Traherne was Welsh,' Anna said, to keep up her end of their conversation.

'He might have been born in Wales,' Kirsty said in a dismissive tone, 'but he did his degree and postgrad studies here. He and Audrey made Oxford their home, brought their son up here, and he wrote all his best known poems here. He was Oxford Professor of Poetry for a while. And now he's buried here. Naturally, Oxford's literary mafia is going to claim him for their own!'

To her relief, Anna felt the fog of fear dispersing as she recovered from her shock. 'You seem to be doing a fair bit of claiming yourself,' she pointed out.

Kirsty laughed. 'Can you blame me? Owen Traherne was

seriously fit – if you like your men sexy and dishevelled!' Flicking to the middle of the book, Kirsty showed Anna a photo of a big bear-like man in a rumpled cord jacket. 'I mean, look at those eyes! I'm talking about back in the day, obviously, before poor Audrey committed suicide and he started drinking so heavily, not how he was at the end.'

Anna frowned at the picture. 'Maybe, back in the day,' she admitted. 'He does have amazing eyes.' Amazing, but not very kind, she thought as she looked at that ferociously intelligent face. You would need a lot of courage to love and be loved by a man like that. 'I actually remember one of his poems,' Anna said to her own surprise. 'I had to study it for A level.' Her recall of her two years in the sixth form was imperfect to say the least. She'd been absent more often than not. But for whatever reason the Traherne poem had stuck. Anna thought for a moment, then recited, '"I have passed through the six gates; the gate of black ice, the rust red gate of shame, the shadow gate, where nothing has a name." I can't remember the rest,' she said hastily to cover the fact that she had suddenly remembered the last passionate lines all too well.

'He wrote that for Audrey in the last years of their marriage,' Kirsty said. 'Can you imagine any man baring his soul like that after you've been together that long? I've been married less than twelve months, and I'm lucky if I get a hot cup of tea out of Jason.'

She looked wistfully out of the window then brightened. 'Since you forgot to have breakfast, shall we bring elevenses forward and have my birthday cake now?'

The sugar rush from Kirsty's cake helped Anna to keep func-tioning until lunchtime. Emerging on to the busy street she quickly put on sunglasses, shielding her eyes from the dazzling September sunlight. She hurried past the Grand Cafe, forcing herself to ignore the savoury smells that wafted out.

How was Kirsty going to feel when she found out that Anna had spent her morning methodically working her way through Nadine's Post-its (not to mention a sizeable portion of Kirsty's birthday cake), while somehow never getting around to mentioning that it was Anna who had found Naomi's body? Kirsty was going to think she was inhuman.

Anna was afraid that might be true. She supposed she'd been born with normal instincts, but then the sky had fallen in and they'd been supplanted by this new imperative to camouflage and conceal. And now she was voluntarily going back for yet another uncomfortable encounter with DCI Chaudhari. She had to do it, because of Naomi.

That was the real reason she'd told her grandfather, Anna thought with a guilty pang. Not only because she'd needed him to reassure her that, in this matter at least, she was sane. She'd needed him to uphold her shaky inner knowledge that this was the right thing to do.

She noticed two stressed-looking young women consulting a street map. Anna recognized them as Walsingham undergraduates. The tall shy one had been sent home with glandular fever at a time when all their friends were hunting for rented accommodation for their second year. She guessed they were belatedly looking for somewhere now before the Michaelmas term started. On a nearby news-stand Anna saw a new headline: '"Oxford Ripper Will Strike Again," Police Chief Warns.' She imagined being nineteen years old and living outside college with a possible serial killer on the loose.

Curling her fingers tightly around her phone, Anna turned towards St Aldates, determined to see this through. She didn't want to be that driven impostor, that Anna lookalike who no longer knew what was right. She would march into the police station like a normal concerned person, and she would ask to see Inspector Chaudhari and make him listen to Naomi's message.

But when she arrived Inspector Chaudhari wasn't there. The desk sergeant said he'd been called out a couple of hours ago and she couldn't say when he'd be back.

With every atom of her body urging her to bolt while she had the chance, Anna was surprised and impressed to hear her voice saying firmly, 'In that case I'll just wait here until he comes back.'

She went to sit on one of the bolted down plastic seats. For forty-five minutes, she played phone solitaire and did crosswords while the life of the station went on around her. After an hour and a half, Anna was so hungry and bored that she drifted into a kind of trance.

When Inspector Chaudhari eventually walked in with his sergeant, they appeared to be in the middle of an intense discussion. Their expressions were set and grim.

'Sir!' the desk sergeant called. 'This lady's been waiting to see you, sir.'

Anna unpeeled herself from her seat and stood up.

'Ms Hopkins,' the inspector said, surprised. 'How can I help you?'

She quickly explained about Naomi's message. 'I don't know if it's relevant to your investigation, but I thought you should at least hear it.'

He gave her a polite nod. 'Much appreciated, but as it turns out, things have moved on since we last spoke.' He glanced sombrely at his sergeant.

Anna felt sick. 'You found another body.'

The inspector sounded more than usually weary. 'Yes, unfortunately. In Christchurch Meadow. Same MO, as far as we can tell. We can't tell you any more than that at present, obviously. But please, yes, give your phone to Sergeant Goodhart here, and he'll record your message for our records.'

Anna numbly unlocked her phone and handed it to Goodhart, and he hurried away up a flight of stairs.

'I'm actually glad to have this opportunity to talk,' the inspector said. 'Perhaps we could sit down?' He gently steered her back to the seating area and took the seat beside her. 'I wanted to explain something about yesterday,' he said. 'We're trained to try to get to the truth. One method for achieving that is to deconstruct people and situations. It's not personal; it's just a method that works, or mostly works,' he amended.

Anna felt herself tense. 'You had a job to do. I understood that,' she said coolly.

'A bloody job and a half it's been these past few weeks,' he agreed. He looked down at his hands, so that Anna noticed them for the first time – strong square hands with blunt spatulate fingers. 'All these women. Everyone getting on edge. The local media demanding to know why we hadn't caught the "Oxford Ripper" yet. But after I got home I found myself trying to imagine things from your point of view. Well, I didn't feel too proud of myself to be honest. And I realized I'd forgotten . . .' He took a breath. 'I'd forgotten how hard it must have been for you being here in this station. It must have brought back some really bad—'

'It was a very long time ago,' she said, cutting off his apologies, which she found almost more upsetting than his faux CSI tactics.

To her horror he hadn't finished. 'I used to have to drive past the house every day on my way in to work,' he added in a low voice. 'You probably know it's been torn down now.'

'I do, actually. It was my house after all,' she said childishly.

She saw him register the snub. After a while he stood up. 'Well, if you'll excuse me, I'll go and grab a sandwich. Hopefully, my sergeant won't be much longer. And thank you once again, Ms Hopkins, for all your help.'

He set off a little wearily up the stairs just as Sergeant Goodhart came hurtling down with her phone.

To Anna's surprise he lingered as she slipped her phone into the front pocket of her bag.

'We're going to get him, you know,' he said abruptly. 'We're going to get whoever murdered your friend and these other women. I can't tell you any more than that at this stage, but I just thought you deserved to know.'

She swallowed. 'Thank you.'

Anna walked out through the automatic doors, telling herself that she'd done what she came to do. A totally pointless gesture, as it turned out, but she could tell herself that she had done her best for Naomi. Now Sergeant Goodhart had as good as told her that the net was closing in around Naomi's killer. They'd catch him soon, and the city could go back to normal.

So why didn't she feel as if it was over?

FIVE

B arefoot in her long T-shirt and only half-awake after her usual restless night, Anna drew back her curtains. The sudden movement caused a startled blackbird to take off into a flawless blue sky. Those first few days after she'd found Naomi's body, Anna had barely registered what seemed like perversely lovely weather. But now, almost two weeks later, she couldn't help her delight at yet another golden autumnal morning in what was starting to feel like an endless Indian summer.

Anna was especially grateful for the continuing fine weather since this was the morning she'd arranged to meet Bonnie's previous owner, Jake McCaffrey, in the University Parks. Though they had emailed several times now and spoken on the phone, and Jake seemed like a pleasant guy, she wasn't comfortable with the idea of some strange man just turning up at her house. Meeting him in a public place had seemed the wisest solution. However, she wanted Jake and Bonnie's open-air reunion to be a success – something which would be that much harder if it was chucking it down with rain. Despite living through bomb blasts and terrorist attacks, her white wolf was comically averse to getting wet.

Typically, Anna thought, mentally rolling her eyes at herself, as soon as everything had been finalized, she'd started having extreme misgivings about meeting this American who had been such a big presence in Bonnie's life. For one thing, she felt as if she and Bonnie were finally starting to bond. Seeing Jake might just confuse her all over again. Also, apart from the fact that he had once owned her dog, she doubted they'd have much in common. Jake had told her he'd spent most of his adult life in the US Navy and was now helping to run some kind of inter-national security business. He'd fought in Afghanistan and Iraq, and Anna had a horror of violence of any kind. Last but not least, he had grown up in the American South, not exactly famous for its liberal views.

Jake's slight but unmistakable southern drawl had taken Anna by surprise the first time they'd talked. Other things had surprised her; he was better informed about the world than she'd privately expected a former US marine to be – better informed, in fact, than Anna herself – but he didn't seem to feel the need to impress. She'd noticed that he always tried to say exactly what he meant, even if this took a while to formulate. Once or twice when they were on the phone he'd lapsed into such a long silence that she'd begun to wonder if he'd accidentally wandered out of range.

When she'd told him of Naomi's death, he'd been speechless for so long that she did eventually say questioningly, 'Hello? Are you OK?'

And he'd said huskily, 'Excuse me a moment. I think I need to take that in.' After another long pause, he'd said, 'Do they know who did it?'

She'd explained about the other murdered women and that the media seemed confident that the police were closing in on the man they insisted on referring to as the 'Oxford Ripper'. She could feel Jake still trying to come to terms with the untimely death of the woman who had solved the mystery of what had happened to his beloved dog.

'And Bonnie found her?' he said. 'This sounds really dumb, but I'd had this idea I was sending her to live in some kind of English haven. I never envisaged dead bodies.'

During his most recent phone call Jake had confessed that though he'd visited his aunt Mimi in Oxford a couple of times, he'd never properly explored the city she'd adopted as her home. To her dismay Anna heard herself politely offering to show him around. He'd texted her from London between meetings saying that Mimi had once mentioned a restaurant in the Cotswolds called the Black Bear Inn, and would Anna allow him to take her there for lunch as a thank-you for being his tour guide?

Anna had heard good things about the Black Bear so she allowed herself to be persuaded.

She showered and dressed in skinny jeans and a light cream-coloured Breton sweater. She couldn't decide on shoes, eventually opting for short biker-style boots with buckles, which she thought looked stylish as well as being reasonably comfortable to walk in.

Too nervous to eat, Anna made a pot of coffee in lieu of breakfast. While it brewed, she cleared out the old receipts and crumpled up tissues that had inevitably accumulated in her messenger bag over the past few days. In the front pocket she came across a card advertising a local vegan cafe with Tansy's mobile number scribbled on the back. Anna had intended to throw it away with the rest of the rubbish, but at the last minute she'd returned it to her bag; she couldn't have said why. She had liked Tansy and Isadora, but in that way you feel an affinity with appealing strangers on a train. She couldn't seriously imagine getting in touch with either of them.

The horror of that morning on Port Meadow hadn't faded so much as gradually become absorbed into that catalogue of other horrors that Anna had been forced to accept as her reality. Whether she wanted it to or not, the sun continued to rise and set and life went on. There had been no new murders, the conference she'd helped to plan had been and gone and the feedback so far had been favourable. As the days passed, Anna had felt herself slipping gratefully back into her old routine: going to the gym, spending time with her grandfather, taking Bonnie for walks in Oxford beauty spots, working her way through Nadine's obsessive-compulsive Post-its.

From the outside Anna's life must look oddly middle-aged for someone in her early thirties, but she rarely gave this much thought. Her days were structured so as to leave the maximum energy for her real secret pursuits and minimum room for surprises of any kind.

And yet here she was, she thought, getting ready to meet a strange American. 'Sometimes I confuse even myself,' Anna told her dog as she fastened on the smart blue collar she'd bought so Bonnie would look her best. She had brushed her dog's coat until it was silky and shining and, though Anna knew she was biased, she thought she looked beautiful. For some reason though her White Shepherd was uncharacteristically restless, going back and forth between her usual favourite spots, immediately rejecting them as unsatisfactory and jumping up again before casting herself down somewhere else with what sounded like a loud huff of impatience. It fleetingly crossed Anna's mind that Bonnie could actually feel her former owner somewhere in the vicinity, until she noticed that she was doing similar restless pacing. The poor dog was just picking up on her own nerves.

Anna walked into the park with Bonnie on the dot of nine. Jake had wanted plenty of time for sightseeing before lunch. She'd just spotted a man sitting on a bench, apparently enjoying the early morning sunshine, when Bonnie came to a shocked standstill. Anna saw a quiver run through her like wind through corn. Next minute the White Shepherd ripped the lead out of Anna's hand as she went hurtling down the path towards the man on the bench. Even before she had reached him, Bonnie started uttering broken sounds, frantic whines and whimpers. The man was suddenly on his feet. Anna heard him say, half laughing, 'Hush, hush! It's all right, you crazy puppy. It's all right.' Bonnie seemed to be actually levitating now, leaping into the air again and again, so as to be level with the man's face, letting out little cries and moans of rapture as she tried to lick any part of him she could reach. 'OK, honey, we're gonna sit down,' he told her firmly, 'before you injure us both.' Dropping to his haunches on the still-dewy grass, he gathered the dog up into his arms. 'I know. I know,' he murmured. 'I've really missed you too, puppy.' As he soothed her, he smiled apologetically at Anna over Bonnie's head, and she saw tears shining in his eyes.

The intensity of Bonnie's reaction had made introductions redundant as the dog continued to press herself, whimpering, against her former owner. *She's been missing him all this time*, Anna thought. *She's had all this grief – this love – inside her all this time*. The quiet well-behaved animal that Anna had believed to be Bonnie's true self had simply been enduring, waiting for her real owner to return.

'Well, as you've probably realized, I'm Jake!' the man said at last when Bonnie had calmed down enough for them to make themselves heard. Jake McCaffrey looked older than in his picture, less sunburned, far more rested and with slightly longer hair. He wore a nut-brown leather jacket over a grey T-shirt and faded blue jeans.

She gave a nervous laugh. 'And obviously I'm Anna.' She was still looking down on him as he sat, apparently oblivious of the wet grass, with his arms wrapped around a now blissful Bonnie. With her head resting on his shoulder, she had her eyes closed as if she was afraid to open them and find it was all a dream.

'It's very good to meet you, Anna.' His eyes were tired and

faintly wary. He smiled at her, and she saw that his front tooth had a very slight chip. For some reason this tiny imperfection only made him more appealing. Anna distrusted instant attractions and was dismayed to find herself so irrationally drawn to this unknown American. She was also struggling to deal with the obvious bond between Bonnie and Jake. She had understood, in theory, that her dog and this former marine had a shared history, but actually seeing them together made her feel childishly left-out. 'Tell you what,' she said coolly, 'why don't I leave you to spend some time with Bonnie, and I'll come by and pick her up later?'

For a moment he looked thrown, then he firmly shook his head. 'I liked our original plan better. For one thing, Bonnie can't show me the sights. For another, I've booked us a table for lunch, and from what I remember of this puppy's table manners I don't think they'd go down too well at the Black Bear!'

Anna was surprised into a laugh. 'She is a really messy eater,' she agreed.

Jake didn't smile a great deal, but when he did it lit up his face. 'Does she still do that thing where she walks away from her bowl with her mouth full and casually dumps it wherever?'

She nodded. 'One time she spat drooled-on kibble into one of my grandfather's new shoes. He adores her, luckily, and we managed to clean the shoes, but . . .' She left the sentence dangling.

'Your grandfather never felt quite the same about them?' Jake suggested.

'Not really, no!'

Jake got to his feet. 'What do you say we give this puppy a walk before we take the tour?' Now that he was standing beside her, she saw that he was a couple of inches taller than she'd thought. His eyes were a clear warm blue. His face had the slightly crumpled look of someone suffering from jet lag.

'I think Bonnie would appreciate that,' she said.

It was still early for an Oxford Sunday morning, and apart from the occasional jogger or dog walker, they had the peaceful space almost to themselves. The leaves were starting to change colour now, and though most of them were still on the trees there were drifts of fallen leaves scattered across the park. They set off strolling along one of the walks. Calmer now, Bonnie trotted between them, occasionally glancing up to reassure herself that Jake was still there.

'What is it that makes the air here smell so good?' Jake asked abruptly. 'It's kind of *spicy*, almost.'

Anna shrugged. 'I don't know. This is just how autumn in England smells.'

'I guess it's like the smell of springtime where I come from,' he said. 'I could break it down into honeysuckle, night flowering jasmine, river mud, but really it just smells like Carolina in the spring.'

As they walked, Jake began to explain the circumstances in which he'd had Bonnie shipped over to the UK. He'd been due to leave the military a few months after he'd finished his tour of duty in Afghanistan, but then ended up being sent to join an emergency relief team in the Philippines. 'I didn't want to just leave her there with the guys with the risk that they might abandon her. I didn't have a place to go back to, unfortunately, so I couldn't send her home.'

Jake didn't expand on this mysterious homelessness. Maybe he was divorced and his parents were dead, or maybe they were the kind of people he preferred not to associate with. 'Mimi was the nearest thing I had to a relative,' he said. 'So I wrote and asked her if she'd take care of Bonnie until I knew where I was going to be living. But then . . .'

'Then she died,' Anna said.

He nodded. 'Exactly a year to the day after her husband had a massive coronary. She fell in love with him when he was working in South Carolina – that's where I'm from – and followed him back to Oxford. She was a wonderful woman, so full of life. I thought – well, I *hoped* she still had years left. After some real hard times, she'd finally found some happiness.'

A jogger went pounding past. Jake's eyes followed the gradually diminishing figure until it was out of sight, but Anna sensed that he was really seeing Mimi, who was not apparently a real relative, but a sufficiently significant person in Jake's life that he had shipped his beloved dog thousands of miles to live with her.

'Anyway, I just wanted you to know how Bonnie came to end up in a rescue shelter,' he said awkwardly.

'It wasn't your fault,' she said.

He gave her his wry grin. 'I don't feel so bad now seeing how things turned out.'

'So you've explained how Bonnie ended up in Oxford,' Anna said. 'But I don't know how she came to live with you.'

'I found her,' he said simply, 'guarding the body of a little Afghan kid. A little boy. Couldn't have been more than five or six.'

It was an unseasonably warm sunny morning, but Anna felt herself go cold.

'An IED went off in the street. Improvised Explosive Device,' he explained, though Anna had guessed the explosive part. 'Left a bunch of innocent Afghanis dead, including this little kid. Lord knows how Bonnie came to be with them. She wasn't much more than a puppy, skinny as a rail and jumping with fleas. She'd been hurt in the blast – that's how she got those little scars. She was scared witless. Her eyes kept rolling up, showing the whites. But when we tried to get close, her lip peeled right back and she let out this evil growl like she was going to rip all our throats out if we even laid a finger on that kid. It was getting to be a bit of a situation, starting to get dark, weeping relatives wanting to take the bodies for burial, and Bonnie here snarling and baring her teeth.'

It was hard to believe Jake was talking about the same Bonnie. Anna had never even heard Bonnie growl. Then her heart gave a lurch, and she thought, *But I've seen her track down a dead woman.* She had to clear her throat before she asked, 'How did you get her away in the end?'

He shot her his crooked smile. 'Chicken sandwiches. She was half starved, and she was just a pup. It took a while, but me and the guys managed to coax her away in the end.' He looked down at Bonnie, as if comparing the feral, flea-ridden pup he had rescued with the beautiful adult dog walking composedly now at his side.

'Does that happen often – soldiers just adopting stray dogs?' She was thinking of the photograph of Jake and Bonnie as exhausted comrades in arms.

'More often than you'd think. Men far from home, jumpy, despised and detested by the people they thought they'd come to save. Having a dog helps you feel like an OK human once in a while. I remember when we got back to our base, and I'm lying on my cot, thinking of all those bodies, and that poor little kid, and I'm like, well, at least we saved the damn dog!' He gave a rueful laugh. 'I don't know how this got so deep so fast, but I could really do with a strong cup of coffee about now!'

Anna didn't know how they'd got so deep either. 'Luckily, in this town you're never too far away from a cup of good coffee,' she told him.

They walked down Parks Road into Broad Street. As they passed Blackwell's, Anna caught a glimpse of the window display in which copies of *The Boy in the Blue Shirt* had been arranged in piles along with other hotly promoted new books.

They stopped at a cafe that had tables set out on the pavement. When they were seated with their coffee he said, 'Before you take me on your grand tour, I just want to get something out of the way, so there aren't any misunderstandings.'

Some protective instinct told Anna that this 'something' had to concern the White Shepherd now lying under their table in her alert sphinx pose. Did he want to take Bonnie back to the States? She set down her cup harder than she'd meant. 'OK.'

Jake took a breath. 'I just want to make it crystal clear that I haven't come here to kidnap your dog.' He shot her a cautious grin. 'I'm not even looking for joint custody. I'm just glad to see Bonnie so happy and healthy.' Hearing herself talked about, Bonnie came to lean against Jake, and he stroked her absent-mindedly, as he must have done so many times before.

Jake's startlingly direct statement of his position left Anna open-mouthed. She'd had no intention of giving Bonnie up, yet his generosity took away her breath. Looking at her dog, now shamelessly soliciting for Jake's affection, she said guiltily, 'But she loves you so much.'

Jake didn't deny it. He just nodded. 'And I love her. And we've been through some major stuff together. But anybody can see she's your dog now. A city-dwelling, cafe-visiting dog,' he said teasingly to Bonnie. Tilting her head to one side, she fixed him with perplexed but adoring brown eyes that said, *I have no idea what you're saying, mysterious human, but I will follow you through FIRE.*

He turned to Anna. 'So are we all square? I didn't want to just leave it all hanging and spoil our day together.'

She managed a tight nod. Once she was fairly sure she wasn't going to embarrass them both by bursting into tears, she said, swallowing, 'Thank you for saying that. And now, if you've finished your coffee, I think we should get started before the sun brings out too many tourists.'

She had planned a simple circular tour starting with the Sheldonian Theatre and the Bodleian library. Jake was blown away by the Bodleian and stood admiring its ancient entrance blazoned with coats of arms from various Oxford colleges until she asked slightly impatiently if he wanted to take a photo. He shook his head. 'I was just thinking of all that incredible knowledge inside. You can almost *feel* it. The Bodleian is the oldest library in Europe, right?'

'Yes, I think it probably is,' she said doubtfully, hoping he wouldn't ask her for too many facts and figures that she couldn't supply. Then she brightened, remembering something her grandfather had told her. 'I do know that all new Oxford undergraduates still have to take a vow before they're allowed to use it.'

'A *vow*? Seriously?'

'At the start of every Michaelmas term. They used to have to say it in Latin, but these days they're allowed to use English.'

'What do they have to vow?'

Anna could see Jake wasn't sure if he should believe her. 'You have to swear not to take volumes out of the library or damage them or anything else belonging to the library. Oh, and you mustn't bring into the library "or kindle therein any fire or flame",' she finished with a grin.

Jake looked as if he'd fallen down Alice's rabbit hole. 'Taking flames into a library! What kind of library user would do that? Attila the Hun, maybe!' He looked genuinely horrified.

'I suppose they just want to impress on them the preciousness of books and learning.'

He gave her a sideways look. 'Is that fancy Oxford type talk for "scare the living shit out of them"?'

'Basically,' she said, laughing.

'I feel like we could be in medieval Italy,' he said later as they stood in Catte Street, looking up at the bridge popularly known

as the Bridge of Sighs and which connected the two halves of
Hertford College.

'You seem extremely interested in history,' she said.

Jake must have caught the note of surprise in her voice, but
he didn't seem offended. 'You have to remember I've spent a lot
of time in war-torn countries where almost everything ancient
has been blown to bits. But in Europe past times feel so close.
Just standing here, it feels like you could easily slip into another
time and see William Shakespeare getting wasted in a bar or
whatever.' He smiled at her. 'I don't know if William Shakespeare
was ever in Oxford, but I like to think of him just round the
corner in a bar.' He sighed. 'Mimi was always on at me to go
to college.'

'But you didn't want to?'

'Left home the bare minute I was legally allowed,' he said,
'and joined the Marines, like a lot of tough kids from the south.'
He saw her expression. 'You didn't think I was a tough kid?'

She shook her head, not knowing how to answer.

He gave a short laugh. 'I guess time has mellowed me some
then. I'd have been a helluva lot worse if Mimi hadn't taken me
on. She knocked a few of my rough edges off, luckily, or I probably wouldn't be the civilized person you see today—' He broke
off. 'Catte Street?' he said, glancing back at the sign. 'That's not
named after actual cats?'

'No, it really is!' she said, catching his enthusiasm, 'because
I happen to know that at one point they changed the name from
Kattestreete to Mousecatchers' Lane!'

He broke into a delighted smile. 'You're kidding! *Mousecatchers'*
Lane?' He stretched out his arms and sang out, 'I LOVE this
city.'

They stopped to admire the Radcliffe Camera, now a reading
room belonging to the Bodleian, and went from there into the
High. 'Would you like to see the college where I work?' she
asked impulsively.

She took him into the Porters' Lodge, where Mr Boswell was
gruffly charmed by Bonnie and agreed to look after her for a
few minutes while they walked around the college grounds.

'He seriously has to wear that hat and suit to come to work?'
Jake whispered as they went through the arch into the gardens.

'All the college porters do,' she explained.

'And *nobody* laughs?'

She smilingly shook her head. 'I suppose I grew up here so I forget how weird Oxford must seem to outsiders.'

'You haven't ever lived anywhere else?'

She gave him her neutral smile. 'I've lived in several places. Look, if you stand here you can see my office!'

Jake dutifully admired the poky little upstairs window then wandered back along the deserted cloisters looking up at the creeper covered walls. 'We are still in the twenty-first century, right?' he asked her, half-laughing at himself. 'I mean, we're standing just a few yards from a busy street, and it's like the modern world has just – *gone!*'

'I think you might be suffering history overload,' she said, laughing. 'What time did you book lunch for?'

He pulled out his phone. 'I get so jet-lagged with all this air travel I have to put everything in here. Twelve thirty.'

'I'll drive us,' said Anna, who always preferred driving to being driven. 'My car is just parked on St Giles.' She saw his amused look. 'It makes more sense for me to drive,' she pointed out. 'That way you can admire the scenery.'

The Black Bear where they were having lunch was a few miles from Banbury on the edge of the Cotswolds. They didn't talk much in the car. Anna was concentrating on driving, and Jake seemed content to look out of the window, enjoying the gently rolling landscape, occasionally asking questions about places they passed.

The Black Bear turned out to be a Virginia creeper covered medieval manor house set in several acres of farmland. Inside it was every bit as sprawling and atmospheric as it had looked from the outside. 'I could live here!' Jake said at once.

The dining room was organized so the guests could eat looking out over the orchards and gardens where much of the fresh ingredients for the kitchen were grown. It was too early in the year for there to be a fire burning in the enormous old fireplace, but a whiff of ash and woodsmoke still lingered, contributing to the sense of times and lives gone by.

As usual Anna spotted what she wanted within thirty seconds of scanning the menu. 'I'm going to go for roast sirloin with

Yorkshire puddings,' she told him. 'And if you've never had a traditional English Sunday roast I advise you to do the same.'

'I consider myself advised,' Jake said with a grin.

Anna chose crostini of smoked mackerel for starter, and Jake went for smoked salmon. When the wine waiter arrived, Jake said he didn't drink these days but Anna must feel free to order wine. She smilingly shook her head. 'I'm driving, remember.'

The food, when it came, was simple and good, and they were both hungry. Jake ate his food the American way, using his knife to cut everything patiently into small pieces then eating it with his fork. He looked up and caught her watching. 'What? Oh, you're observing my alien eating habits!' he said with a grin.

'I was actually thinking that I'm too greedy to be an American,' Anna told him.

He laughed. 'You don't think Americans can be greedy? That's refreshingly novel!'

After they'd finished their main courses, they politely waved the dessert menu away; Jake because, he said, he never really got the point of desserts, and Anna, despite a yearning look at the puddings on offer, because she didn't think she could squeeze in another mouthful.

'You know, I still haven't heard your side of Bonnie's story,' Jake said.

'My side?'

'Sure.' Jake's blue eyes briefly lit up with his here and gone again smile. 'What made you decide to get a dog?'

It was an innocent question, but her mind refused to go there. It wasn't that she couldn't remember those first weeks after her grandfather had moved out, more that she couldn't bear to relive them – not here, and not with Jake. So she gave him the shorter, saner version. 'I hadn't long come back to Oxford,' she said. 'My grandmother had become very ill, and I helped my grandfather care for her. After she died, my grandfather decided that he was going to live in a rather wonderful care home in North Oxford. So he signed over the house to me. It was converted into flats a while ago, and I only occupy the bottom two floors, but it's still a big space.' She felt her breath catch.

'Kind of lonely all by yourself,' Jake suggested.

She pictured herself wandering sleepless through all those

rooms that she now officially owned, jumping at every creak, every shadow and being furious because, despite years of therapy and self defence classes, she was still that terrified sixteen year old, running, running through the dark, too traumatized to scream.

But it hadn't just been Anna's pathetic need to have another beating heart beside her own, or even the decision to get a large dog for protection that had sent her to the rescue shelter. It was because, when she was alone in the dark, Anna wasn't always clear exactly why she had to continue to exist. But if she had a dog that needed her to get out of bed and feed it and take it for walks, she thought that her life would have some small but nevertheless real purpose.

'Also I had always wanted a dog when I was growing up,' she told Jake truthfully, on safer ground now. 'And then I saw Bonnie and . . .'

'And you fell in love.'

'I did,' she said, smiling, then was embarrassed to feel her cheeks go pink because she suddenly felt as if they were having two simultaneous conversations, only one of which was about Bonnie.

If Jake noticed any holes in her story he didn't mention them, just as he hadn't asked any follow-up questions about her family. Nor had she asked for any details about his.

He beckoned the waiter to bring him the bill. 'So, shall we get Bonnie and explore some of these Cotswold lanes?' he asked her. 'I mean, assuming you don't have to rush back.'

'I don't have to rush back,' she told him. 'Also, I *really* need to walk off that Yorkshire pudding!'

They walked for over an hour, often in companionable silence, up and down the hilly lanes past rough fields of pasture divided by ancient stone walls. There were sheep grazing in some of the fields, and they set up a nervous bleating at the sight of Anna and Jake with their suspiciously wolf-like dog. Once a pony trotted up to have its nose rubbed over a wooden gate. 'Why is it you never, ever have an apple with you when you need one?' Anna said regretfully. 'Or a carrot?'

'I think that's just one of those natural laws, isn't it?' Jake said, laughing.

At the top of a steep hill, the breathtaking view of the valley below stopped them in their tracks. Sandstone cottages were dotted about here and there. In one of the gardens a man was tending a bonfire. Anna could hear the snap of burning wood mixed with the cawing of rooks above their heads. They hadn't seen a single car since they'd started walking. She looked down at Jake, who was pretending to growl at Bonnie as they play-wrestled on the grass verge. It had never occurred to her to play wrestle with Bonnie. She must have missed this kind of rough and tumble, Anna thought, noticing how the sun showed up the tiny fair glints in his hair. He glanced up at her. 'Walked off that Yorkshire pudding yet, kid?'

'*Kid*? What am I, Huck Finn?' she said in mock outrage, trying not to notice the pleasant confusion that his deep southern voice had set off somewhere in her midriff.

'I think you'd make a great Huck Finn,' he said with a grin. 'But you didn't answer my question.'

'I must have walked it off,' she said, suddenly shy, 'because I was just wishing we had more time so I could take you to this Chinese restaurant where my grandfather and I like to eat.'

'I have time,' he said at once. 'I'm in no hurry to go back to my hotel, believe me. And by the time we've walked back down that long, *long* lane to your car I'll be up for three Chinese meals!'

She felt a flash of panic. They'd have to drop Bonnie off first. That meant taking Jake back to her flat, something she'd been determined not to do. *But we're having such a great day together*, she thought. She didn't want it to end, and she sensed that Jake didn't either. 'So you'll get to see my flat,' she said, as if she invited people to her home every day.

'I could live here,' was Jake's instant response when she let him into her hallway. She showed him around, swiftly bypassing her study, enjoying seeing everything through his eyes. He wanted to know about her lodgers, and so she told him about Dana and her taste in break-up music, and also Tim, who was in international finance and spent most of his time travelling overseas, only occasionally using the Oxford flat for his base. She fed Bonnie, and then unbelievably they were both hungry again, so she drove them to Xi'an in Summertown. On the way she found herself talking about her grandfather and how he was finally, in his late eighties, discovering himself as an artist.

'You want to invite him to come eat with us?' Jake asked at once.

She shook her head. 'He's out visiting a friend tonight. I'd like you to meet him though if you come again. I think you'd get on.'

They hadn't booked ahead, but Anna and her grandfather were regular customers at Xi'an, and they were immediately ushered to a table. Jake looked around him with approval. 'This is a good place.'

'I'm starting to think you think everywhere is a good place,' she teased.

'Not everywhere, but most places,' he said. 'I've travelled a fair bit, and I've reached the conclusion that most places have something interesting about them if you know where to look.'

'Home is where you hang your hat?' she suggested.

'Mimi used to say you could throw me out of a plane and wherever I landed I would make myself at home!'

They ordered a lot of food, including a fish dish with ginger and chillies that Jake especially liked. While they were eating, Anna remembered something she had meant to ask. 'Why did you call Bonnie "Bonnie"?'

'You want some of this fish?' Jake asked.

She nodded, and he helped her to a portion using his chopsticks.

'Mimi used to have a dog called Bonnie,' he explained. 'I started walking her some days after school. That's actually how I got to know Mimi. My Bonnie – *our* Bonnie,' he corrected swiftly, 'looked nothing like Mimi's Bonnie, who looked more like a big old dish mop on legs than any kind of serious pooch. But she'd get this look in her eyes, sometimes, like she was channelling the dog wisdom of ages, you know? And, even as a pup, this Bonnie had just the same look.'

'I know that look,' Anna said before she'd thought.

Their eyes met in a moment of such complete understanding that Anna found herself holding her breath. The atmosphere couldn't have been more intimate if he'd kissed her.

Jake's mobile started to beep. 'Excuse me.' He took out his

phone, frowned at the caller display but didn't answer. 'Where were we?' he asked Anna, smiling.

They returned to their meal, but it was obvious that something had changed. A few minutes later, Jake's phone went again. Again he checked the screen, and again he didn't answer. The fourth or fifth time this happened, sensing that he was getting stressed, Anna said, 'I honestly don't mind if you answer. Someone obviously needs to get hold of you.'

He shook his head. 'I'll call her when I'm back at the hotel.' He picked up his chopsticks then laid them back down. 'My ex fiancée just split up with the guy she left me for.'

Anna kept her face carefully neutral. 'Oh?'

'She's in a bad place,' he explained. 'Everything seemed to be going really well for her. She started a new job, signed a lease for a new apartment – she's a real high-flyer – finally found her ideal guy, but then the new guy turned out to be a real piece of work and she's just in pieces.'

Anna thought Jake's high-flying ex sounded like quite a piece of work herself.

'I think I should take you back to your hotel so you can sort things out,' she suggested in her best admin assistant's voice.

She wasn't angry with Jake, who after all had never made her any promises. She was furious with herself. *Brought together by a dog*, she thought bitterly. And she had almost bought that whole ridiculous Disney fantasy.

As she drove him back into the city centre she knew she was acting cold and hostile, but it was the only way she knew to deal with the collapse of her hopes; hopes she hadn't let herself know she'd been entertaining until Jake's phone call brought them crashing down. After she'd repeatedly stonewalled his attempts at conversation, Jake gave up and stared silently out of the window. When she dropped him off at the Randolph where he was staying, they both got out of the car, and he said tentatively, 'I'll be coming back to Oxford quite soon. I've got some legal stuff to sort out with Mimi's estate. It'd be good to spend some time with you and Bonnie.'

You and Bonnie, she thought, gritting her teeth. 'I'll look forward to it,' she said coolly. 'That's assuming I'm around, obviously.'

There was a moment when she thought he might try to kiss her; and then, when he didn't, she knew for sure that it had all just been in her head. Any attraction had all been on her side, she thought numbly as she drove back to Park Town. It really had been just about Bonnie.

Letting herself into her flat she went straight to the drawer where she kept the key to her cupboard of horrors. She was about to unlock the doors, when her desktop computer pinged with a new Google alert. Anna felt her heart jump into her mouth. Sweet as it had been, her day with Jake had only ever been a fantasy. What had happened to her family was real. Now after all these years the search engine had finally found fresh information.

It was only when she feverishly clicked on the link that she remembered setting up another, more recent, alert for Naomi Evans.

She buried her face in her hands. She knew it was insane to keep on hoping, but the disappointment was always so savage it was like a lightning strike.

'*It will pass, it will pass*,' she whispered, as she had done so many times before.

With an enormous effort of will she made herself turn back to see the latest update on Naomi's case and felt the last of her hopes unravel as she read: 'No DNA. Police reach dead end in Port Meadow Murder.'

SIX

It was almost eleven thirty in the morning, and Anna was still sitting at her kitchen table. She had got as far as putting marmalade on her toast, but like her coffee it remained untasted. She had showered, dressed, walked Bonnie, but back at home she'd been overwhelmed by a growing sense of futility. Like an aimless fly, her thoughts went round in fruitless circles as she stared unseeingly into space. Anna had battled depression in the past, and this disgust at her own uselessness felt frighteningly familiar.

Bonnie had come to sit at her feet and was gazing at her with the kind of intense expression normally reserved for marrow bones. Something told Anna that her White Shepherd had been sitting there watching her for some time. Bonnie still maintained a tactful distance between her and Anna, preferring to be invited before she entered Anna's space. They were still a little shy with each other, Anna realized. On impulse she knelt down, and Bonnie immediately bowed her head so that their two foreheads were lightly touching. Anna's throat closed as she remembered Bonnie performing this exact tender manoeuvre with Naomi.

'If it was a work day I could go into the office,' Anna told her, swallowing. One of her therapists had told her that whenever she felt like this it was always better to do something, however mindless.

'Scrub the toilet. Pull up weeds,' Miriam had told her. 'Something that won't set your panic sensors screaming. Try it! You just might find out what it is you think you're not supposed to do, and if you don't – well, at least you'll have a clean toilet!'

But it wasn't a work day, and Anna didn't want to clean her toilet. She sat back on her heels. She had to do something or she'd go mad.

She jumped up. There was something she could do. She could keep her promise to take her grandfather's paintings to the framers. 'Won't be long,' she told the dog.

Grabbing her jacket and car keys, Anna ran upstairs to find her grandfather's portfolio case and flew out of the house.

Someone was backing out of a parking place on St Giles just as she pulled up. She shot into the space, fed coins into the machine and stuck the ticket inside her windscreen. Only as she walked away did she allow herself to wonder why she had paid for two hours' parking, when it would probably take less than half an hour to get to the framers and back.

It took five minutes to walk to the framers in the Covered Market. In another ten Anna was retracing her steps to St Giles. But at the last minute, she found herself walking right past her car, turning down Little Clarendon Street and then right into Walton Street. *You just might find out what it is you think you're not supposed to do.*

She was now on the fringes of Jericho, once an infamous red-light district before the arty media crowd took it over. Anna slipped Tansy's wilted little card out of her bag, checked the address and kept walking.

Tansy's cafe occupied a prime position close to the Phoenix Picturehouse and had recently been revamped. Anna had known the building in its former incarnation as Beryl's, a popular greasy spoon, where hung-over students breakfasted on bacon and eggs. Now the frontage was painted a chic Farrow and Ball blue-grey and the name had changed to Cafe Marmalade. In the window an earthenware jug held jaunty sunflowers. Inside, a woman behind the counter leaned down into the chill cabinet, refilling the salad bowls.

Anna pushed open the door and went in. The brightly lit space inside smelled of fresh salad stuffs and good coffee. She wondered what Beryl would think of the galvanized bins filled with organic produce and the farmer's market style baskets piled with artisan breads. At a table by the window, two young men in big boots and skinny jeans had their heads together over a MacBook. A youth in a Pink Floyd T-shirt at the table next to theirs briefly glanced up at Anna then went back to reading a battered copy of *Slaughterhouse Five* while he sipped his latte, his slightly-squashed pork pie hat tilted towards the back of his head.

She anxiously scanned the cafe. She didn't even know if this was Tansy's day to come in.

A teenage boy wearing a Cafe Marmalade tea-towel tied around his narrow hips for an apron was taking a complicated order from two girls. From what Anna could hear they were being sternly specific about their menu choices. One wore a retro floral frock with ankle boots. Her friend had opted for ripped lace and faded denim over wildly patterned leggings. Marmalade's customers generally seemed to be aiming for a too-cool-to-bother-with-a-consistent-style style: mismatched layers, ironic eyewear. If she hadn't been so freaked about being here at all, Anna might have appreciated the ambience more.

'Can I help you?' The woman behind the counter finally straightened up, having finished with the salads. Her androgynous hairstyle was dyed fuchsia pink. Anna wondered if this was the passive-aggressive Julie.

At that moment a door opened at the back of the cafe and Tansy came out balancing her tray on her hip. She looked as ridiculously young as Anna remembered, wearing a baggy sleeveless white T-shirt over her skinny jeans, her curly hair pulled up into a careless topknot. She spotted Anna, and Anna saw instant shocked comprehension in her eyes.

Anna never knew which one of them moved first, just that next minute she and Tansy were standing face to face in the middle of the cafe. 'It's not just me, is it? They've got it wrong,' Tansy said in an anxious whisper.

'No, it's not just you,' Anna whispered back.

'I mean, *shit*, there wasn't any DNA.'

'I know! That's why I had to come.' Anna felt dizzy with relief at being able to share her nightmare with someone at last.

'Look, don't go anywhere, Anna, OK?' Tansy said.

Anna found an empty table and waited. Tansy finished serving her customers then slipped behind the counter to confer with the pink-haired woman. A few minutes later she came back carrying two tall foaming mugs and a plate of glossy little pastries. 'It's almost my lunch break. If we get a sudden rush, Brendan can pull his weight for a change.' Tansy pushed a mug towards Anna, giving her a close-up of the dozen or so bangles around her wrist. One consisted of a tiny silver Buddha charm dangling from a knotted red thread. Around her neck, she wore at least five necklaces of different lengths and provenance. Her fingernails were bright turquoise. Looking at her, Anna felt as colourful as an old-style movie flashback.

'These are soya lattes, by the way,' Tansy added. 'You knew this was a vegan cafe, right?' She planted her elbows on the table, suddenly businesslike. 'OK, so tell me how you've been?'

'Actually, I have kind of a dilemma.' She took a sip of her coffee, trying to hide her nerves. 'After I got back from the police station I found a message on my mobile from Naomi.'

'Fuck,' said Tansy. 'What did she say?' Her eyes widened as Anna quickly filled her in. 'Did you take it straight to the police?'

She nodded. 'They made a copy. But by then they'd found the fourth body.'

'What difference did that make?'

'All four victims were young blondes. All stabbed several times in a public place.'

'So they decided the same nut-job did all four,' said Tansy.

'You can see why that would be a really tempting theory,' Anna said. 'If you're the police.'

'A really lazy theory!' Tansy sounded as frustrated as Anna felt. 'I was doubtful when I read about the DNA, but that message – how can they not see that it brings up serious doubts! God, the police can be so – *rigid*! Their minds get set in a certain groove, and they can't even entertain another possibility!'

Anna nodded. 'I agree.'

'I haven't been able to stop thinking about it, have you?' said Tansy.

'I *think* I've stopped,' Anna admitted, 'then I find it's still kind of running along underneath.'

'Same here,' said Tansy. 'It's like feeling sick. It comes over you in waves.'

'I can't really eat either.'

Tansy gave her a rueful grin. 'It hasn't affected me that way. I'd have to be dead, myself, not to eat.' She fiddled with her bracelets, distracted by a new thought. 'I guess it isn't fair to paint *all* police as lazy fuckers,' she said, half to herself.

Anna couldn't remember having had such an unguarded conversation with another woman for years. She and Jake had also got on well at first. Encouraged by her unexpected success as a social being, Anna risked a sisterly joke. 'Your dreamy sergeant was really kind to me when I went in the other day.' She was dismayed to see a flash of real annoyance in Tansy's eyes. 'Yeah?' she snapped. 'Well, let's face it, with a name like Goodhart he was pretty much doomed from birth to be *someone's* knight in shining armour.'

Anna had a too-familiar feeling of having lost a crucial page in the script. First Sergeant Goodhart was 'annoyingly hot', now he was 'doomed' to be a knight. She wondered what it was about him that pissed Tansy off and if she would ever find herself on the same wavelength as another human being for longer than five minutes.

'*Anyway*,' Tansy said a little too emphatically, letting Anna know that this subject was now closed, 'since Thames Valley police have gone selectively deaf and blind, what are we going to do about it? We have to do *something*.'

Anna opened her mouth to agree just as Tansy added, 'I think we need to talk to Isadora.'

Anna looked down at her latte. There was no point trying to explain. Tansy would never understand what it was like to be Anna, how many internal prohibitions she'd had to break to get here at all, the ridiculous amount of nervous energy it was costing her right at this moment.

And it had been worth it, she thought. It had been like healing balm to know that Tansy felt exactly as Anna did. But though Isadora seemed like a perfectly pleasant woman, Anna found it challenging enough even to be relating one to one. Involving a third person was totally out of the question.

'I don't mean to be rude,' she said, feeling that she was just about to be, 'but I'm – an extremely private person. I don't particularly see myself as part of a—'

'A female detecting trio?' Tansy shook her head. 'No way!' She pulled a face. 'I would be like the world's first ADHD detective! I have the attention span of a hyperactive five year old, seriously. But Isadora was there with us on Port Meadow. You haven't seen her since the day we found Naomi, but I have, and I know this has badly shaken her up. Plus . . .' Tansy left her sentence hanging.

'Plus?' Anna said, all her defences suddenly alert.

Tansy deliberately met her gaze. 'We've both been wondering

if you're OK, because, please don't take this the wrong way, Anna, but we couldn't really see how you could be.'

Experience had taught Anna to dread certain expressions that came unbidden into people's faces as soon as they found out who she was. But as she looked into Tansy's eyes, Anna saw no trace of that terrible fascination, or – equally hateful – cloying sympathy; only friendly concern. Against all her instincts, she felt herself soften. It hadn't occurred to her that Tansy and Isadora would continue to think about her, care about her, after how she'd behaved. She drew a sharp breath. Apparently, today was her day for making rash, ill-thought-out decisions. 'Did you say you're due for your lunch break? I'm just parked up on St Giles. I could drive us to Isadora's if you know the address.'

Tansy's directions took them to a rambling old house in Summertown. Anna left her Land Rover on the street, and they walked up Isadora's weedy drive where two cars were already parked, a rusty old Volvo and a sleek, silver BMW.

As they got closer, they heard furious shouting punctuated by frantic barking. An irate man in a fabulously expensive-looking suit was yelling through the open front door. 'You're being childish and very unfair to Nicky. She only wants what's best for you. We both do! You're wilfully distorting our point of view!'

'That's Isadora's son,' Tansy said under her breath. 'I don't think they get along,' she added superfluously.

'And you're wilfully distorting my point of view, Gabriel!' Isadora roared from inside. 'So I shall rephrase it in terms that even a soulless weasel like you can understand! I. Am. Not. Dead. Yet! Your gold-digging wife will have to wait!'

'I'm leaving now!' Isadora's son bellowed back. 'But this conversation is not finished!' He turned to leave and looked comically horrified to see the two women awkwardly standing there. His doughy middle-aged face, pinched with fury, showed none of Isadora's dramatic beauty. Mumbling something incoherent he stormed past them to his BMW.

A dishevelled Isadora stuck her head out of the door. 'Do tell Nicky not to hold her breath, won't you!' she screamed at the top of her lungs as Gabriel tore off, spinning his wheels. 'I might just leave it all to a bloody donkey sanctuary!' Having delivered the parting insult, she disappeared back indoors, after shooting a fleeting glare in Anna and Tansy's direction.

. This was exactly why Anna tried to keep her involvement with her fellow humans to a minimum. 'Let's just drop this inside her door and go,' she whispered. On their way back to Anna's car, they'd stopped off at Maison Blanc where they'd bought a box of mixed cream eclairs for Isadora.

'She's seen us,' Tansy said. 'We can't just sneak off.'

'She's upset,' Anna hissed. 'She won't want to see anyone now.' *And for the rest of her life she'll hate us for witnessing such a sordid family row*, she thought, face burning.

Isadora reappeared glowering in the doorway, with her obviously agitated little dog at her heels. 'Well, come on, if you're coming in!' She wore an extraordinary trailing garment, made up of clashing colours and patterns. Without looking back, she marched off down a gloomy corridor, leaving swirls of perfume in her wake, a scent that Anna found she dimly remembered from their first stark encounter on Port Meadow.

Anna reluctantly followed, passing open doors into shadowy heavily-curtained rooms, catching indistinct glimpses of bulky old furniture and artworks inside. Isadora's house smelled of dusty fabrics and damp plaster, mixed with her own foreign-smelling perfume and, increasingly, a powerful and deliciously garlicky smell of cooking.

They emerged in a large light kitchen instantly recognizable as the real lived-in heart of the house. Saucepans bubbled on top of a range-style cooker. A row of graceful arched windows that could have been borrowed from an Oxford college overlooked a wild overgrown garden, where arthritic old apple trees were dropping their fruit among nettles and blowsy yellow daisies. Glancing around, Anna got the impression that Isadora's kitchen was evolving in a similarly organic fashion. Apart from the cooking area, which was scrupulously clean and tidy, every available surface was buried under layers of fascinating clutter.

Seeing that a cupboard door had been left open, Isadora closed it with unnecessary force as she strode past to turn off the gas under the pans.

'We should go,' Anna said, beside herself with embarrassment. 'We're disturbing your lunch.'

'That was for my son Gabriel, and he's already disturbed it! Well, sit down!' Isadora told them brusquely. 'I need a drink. Does anyone else want one?'

'I'd love a cup of tea,' said Tansy. 'Anna brought cakes,' she added enticingly.

'I was thinking more of spirits!' With her back to them, Isadora was hunting through an impressive array of bottles. She selected one, pouring herself a stiff shot. 'I'm sorry for my bad manners, but my son has put me in a rage!' she threw over her shoulder. 'I'll be all right in a minute. Please do sit down.'

Since all but one of Isadora's kitchen chairs were doing double duty as storage for various notebooks, cardboard files and academic journals, Anna stayed where she was. Seemingly immune to social embarrassment, Tansy removed a pile of papers off a chair along with the small erotic carving that Isadora had apparently been using to weigh them down. 'You have this chair, Anna.' Temporarily at a loss, Tansy stood holding the stack of papers, before placing them carefully on the dresser top where someone had abandoned a lavishly wrapped bouquet of visibly drooping hothouse blooms.

'We should go,' Anna mouthed at her.

'No, we need to tell her,' Tansy mouthed back. In her normal voice she added, 'I'm going to borrow that little wicker chair by the cooker, Isadora.' She moved the chair to the table, picked up Isadora's still wild-eyed little dog and sat fondling her ears while Isadora stomped about taking occasional swigs from her glass as she made tea for them.

'Have you got a new admirer, Isadora?' Tansy gestured at the flowers.

Isadora made an irritated face. 'Oh, yes, I forget when those arrived. This silly man keeps sending me flowers. I don't know why. I've never done anything to encourage him.'

'It's a shame to waste them though.' Tansy gently put the dog back on the floor and took the bouquet over to the sink. Finding a suitable knife in the draining rack she hacked off several inches of woody stems as Anna watched, amazed to see Tansy making herself so at home in someone else's space.

'Can I use that gorgeous blue jug?' Tansy asked.

'Yes, of course, darling. Thank you for rescuing them. I know I'm terrible!' Isadora said, not sounding remotely apologetic.

Tansy carried the flowers over in the jug. 'Can you find me a bit of room for these, Anna?' Anna hastily moved an antique sewing box and what she hoped was only a copy of a medieval manuscript, and Tansy carefully set the jug down.

Shunting more objects aside, including a black and silver handled paperknife so lethal-looking that it was possibly a real dagger, Isadora dumped down the mugs and a teapot together with a saucer on which she'd arranged freshly-cut slices of lemon. 'Did someone mention cake?'

Anna belatedly presented her with the box, and Isadora tore it open, immediately seizing on a coffee eclair and taking a large bite. 'Heaven!' she pronounced, closing her eyes. 'No, Hero, get down!' she chided. 'These delicious morsels are definitely not for doggies!' She collapsed into Tansy's wicker chair with a groan. 'Fetch that stool if you need somewhere to sit,' she told Tansy. 'I've taken to writing in the kitchen. So much warmer and friendlier than my study – but I'm accumulating so many notes they're rather overflowing, as you see.'

'What are you writing?' Anna asked shyly.

Isadora's mouth tightened. 'Just a little academic book on courtly love. My son doesn't believe I'll finish it. He thinks it's like Casaubon's Key to all Mythologies in *Middlemarch*.'

Now that Anna was sitting close to Isadora, she saw that her strange trailing garment, which from a distance had resembled some crazy patchwork tapestry, was in fact elaborately hand-knitted. Anna could see a long scarlet thread that had started to unravel from her sleeve. An ornate silver comb jutted out from her wild cloud of hair. She was beautiful, if in a slightly bonkers way, Anna thought. She found herself starting to reconcile the screaming fishwife Isadora with the authoritative woman who had taken charge the morning of Naomi's murder.

'I still feel like we're intruding,' she said.

For the first time Isadora properly looked at Anna. Her aura of smouldering resentment instantly vanished. She patted Anna's hand. 'I'm relieved and delighted to see you, Anna, and I'm charmed that you've brought me these delicious pastries.' She shot Anna the kind of penetrating look that must have sent generations of students diving for cover. 'But I have the feeling this is not just a social visit.'

Anna shook her head. 'We're here because of Naomi.'

'Anna found a message from Naomi on her phone,' Tansy said. 'The police don't think it's significant.'

Isadora gave a strained laugh. 'My dear, you're not proposing we turn—?'

'Absolutely not,' Anna said firmly. 'Look, would it be all right to play you the message? Tansy hasn't heard it yet, and it will make it easier to explain.' She took out her phone and saw Isadora and Tansy trying to prepare themselves to listen to a voice from the dead.

As the message played, a new expression stole over Isadora's face: sorrow mixed with a deep thoughtfulness. Afterwards, she sat in silence, her fingers laced together.

Tansy immediately started hunting in her bag. 'I'm sorry,' she said, pulling out a tissue, 'but that woman should not be dead. It's just – it's just *wrong*!'

Isadora stirred at last. 'Thank you, Anna,' she said quietly. 'Yes, I perfectly see why you can't just let this go. The girl who left that message was not an anonymous victim. She had a life, a life filled with passion and meaning. So much passion,' she added, closing her eyes.

'A life we know almost nothing about,' Anna said. 'I didn't know her very well, but I feel like I owe it to her to find out more about her. At the moment she's like—'

'—a lovely enigma,' Isadora finished. 'The girl with the charm bracelet.'

Tansy nodded. 'It's not like we think we can do a better job than the police. Like we're going to find out Naomi was killed by some opera-loving monk because she'd unearthed some dark secret!'

Isadora gave a little hoot of laughter. 'I think I saw that episode of *Lewis*!' She lifted the teapot and began to fill the waiting mugs. 'I assume you've already thought of googling Naomi to see what she was working on before she died?'

Tansy and Anna exchanged stricken looks.

'That would seem to be the obvious place to start,' Isadora added rather sternly. She gave a weary sigh. 'Then I suggest we do that now.' She rummaged under a pile of academic journals, in the process uncovering a battered spectacles case. 'So that's where my driving glasses got to!' she said, amazed. Additional rummaging revealed a laptop.

It took a while to get Isadora's computer functioning. Then Isadora, possibly the world's worst typist, needed several attempts before she'd successfully entered Naomi's name into the search engine.

Anna had to fight a growing urge to snatch the laptop out of the older woman's hands as Isadora laboriously scrolled through lists of websites, grumpily rejecting them, until her face suddenly brightened. 'Oh, thank goodness, I've found her website.' Isadora did some more clicking and scrolling. 'Now that *is* fortunate! I think I may have spotted our opportunity!' She looked up, her eyes gleaming behind her reading glasses. 'You girls probably don't remember me mentioning that a former student of mine had published a rather important biography?'

Anna nodded. 'Actually, I do. It's about Owen Traherne.'

Isadora blinked at her. 'Anna, I'm amazed you retained that information, given the harrowing circumstances in which you were told.'

'I probably wouldn't have,' Anna admitted, 'but someone at work had just bought it.'

'Sorry, but how is this "an opportunity"?' Tansy asked.

'Because, according to an entry in Naomi's blog, Kit employed her to do his research,' Isadora said. With a creak of wicker, she extracted herself from her chair and went over to her fridge, which served a dual function as her message board. Scattering fridge magnets, she hunted through flyers and invitations. 'Now where did I put it?' she murmured.

Tansy still seemed lost. 'Was Owen Traherne some kind of artist?'

'A poet,' Isadora said, impatiently discarding her dog groomer's business card and a reminder from her dentist. 'Some say a very brilliant one.'

'I remember Jane talking about it at work,' Tansy said, perking up. 'Someone's making a film! They signed Liam Neeson up to play – Owen Traherne, was it?'

'Found it!' Isadora slapped a gilt-edged invitation on the table. 'It's supposed to be a plus-one, but I'm sure I could wangle you both in.'

'Wangle us in where?' Anna said nervously, having spotted the alarming words 'black tie'.

'To the party!' Isadora said, as if this was obvious. 'Owen Traherne's publishers decided to collect all his love poems together in one volume. They're launching it at the Ashmolean. Kit Tulliver was sweet enough to have me put on the guest list. It'll be black tie, of course.' A mischievous gleam came into her eyes. 'You know, it never ceases to amaze me how even a dull unattractive man looks almost handsome in black tie.'

'I still don't understand why—' Anna began.

'If you come with me, I can introduce you to Kit,' Isadora explained. 'He and Naomi will have been working closely together on Kit's book. They must have got to know each other quite well. This is a perfect opportunity to learn more about Naomi! Kit's wonderfully easy to talk to. So! Will you come?'

Anna experienced the unpleasant irony of knowing she only had herself to blame for setting yet another social ordeal in motion, even as she ransacked her brain for an excuse not to go.

'That's a brilliant idea, Isadora!' Tansy said at once. 'Plus, I'd be honoured to come to a posh party with you.' She scanned the invitation. 'Only, I can't,' she said, disappointed. 'A friend is doing a live set at Marmalade that night, and I promised I'd be there.'

'You'll come though, Anna, I hope?' A plaintive note crept into Isadora's voice. 'It would be lovely to have your company. It gets so tedious turning up to these things on my own.'

The thought of being trapped for an evening at the Ashmolean Museum was enough to make Anna hyperventilate. But she knew she couldn't say no. 'Sure,' she said, wishing she sounded more gracious. 'I'll come.'

I don't suppose dogs are allowed, she thought wistfully. It was a new and surprising thought, but Anna felt as if she could cope with almost anything if Bonnie was at her side.

SEVEN

'Did I mention that Kit once tried to get me into bed?' Isadora darted a faintly provocative look at Anna. She had picked Anna up in her ancient Volvo in which a strong smell of petrol mingled with Isadora's perfume and unmistakable undertones of dog. Not Hero, Anna decided; an elderly infirm dog. With a twinge of alarm, she noticed that Isadora wasn't wearing her driving glasses as she craned forward over her steering wheel, peering through the white mist that had suddenly descended on the city, blurring oncoming headlights.

Isadora shot Anna another sparklingly mischievous look. 'I think he thought it would earn him a better grade. Lord knows he needed one!' She gave one of her uncontrolled hoots of laughter, and the tank-like Volvo gave another bucking surge, making Anna surreptitiously grip the side of her seat. She belatedly processed what Isadora had told her. 'Kit Tulliver tried to sleep with you when he was still your student! Seriously?'

Isadora slowed just in time for a pedestrian crossing. 'He was rather a naughty boy in those days.' Anna thought she sounded distinctly fond. 'There's a certain kind of undergraduate, I'm sure you know the type, who comes to Oxford solely with the intention of making useful contacts. They go to parties, join all the right societies, not to mention the wrong societies.'

'You mean like the Bullingdon Club?' Anna said.

'And the rest,' Isadora said, her nose practically level with the windscreen. 'The maddening thing about these kinds of students is that they're often bright enough to coast through their three years here on the minimum of effort. Well, I'll freely admit that I had Kit and his friend Huw firmly in that category. Huw was Owen Traherne's son, by the way,' she added, braking sharply for something that turned out to be a plastic bag. 'But look at Kit now! His book on the *New York Times* best-seller list, glowing reviews in all the broadsheets. Time has proved me wrong, and I couldn't be more delighted!'

'You didn't, though?' For once Anna's curiosity overcame her reticence.

Isadora looked momentarily blank. 'Oh, did I *sleep* with him, you mean?' She gave another delighted hoot. 'Certainly not! There is such a thing as ethics you know! Besides,' she said, a heartbeat later, 'I was *far* too preoccupied with Valentin back then to go bedding my students.' She darted Anna another sparkling look. 'Valentin was the love of my life. I had other loves, obviously, before and after him. But you know the most wonderful thing about my time with him? He came along when I had *utterly* given up hope. So ridiculous! I was forty years old, and in my mind I already had one foot in my grave, when actually my best years were still to—' Isadora broke off, frowning. 'Now cross your fingers we can find a free space somewhere on St Giles.'

There were several free spaces, as it turned out. But as the Volvo was without power steering, it needed a lot of energetic manoeuvring before it was finally parked between the lines.

They set off to walk the short distance to the Ashmolean. Despite, or maybe because of everything that had happened to Anna in Oxford, she still found the city achingly beautiful in all its moods, but that evening with the mist clinging to the ancient golden stone the city seemed more than usually haunting.

Isadora slid an approving glance in Anna's direction. 'You look lovely by the way.'

'I didn't really know what to wear,' Anna confessed. She had popped into Whistles on the High Street to hunt for a suitable dress. She'd ended up buying a sharply tailored black tuxedo jacket and a white silk camisole, which she was wearing with black trousers and a pair of stilettos. She had pulled her hair back into a loose chignon and wore the plain silver necklace she resorted to on the rare occasions when she needed to dress up. Her only nod to decadence was her grandmother's Cartier diamond studs, which she seemed to feel, like cool fire, tingling against her ear lobes.

Isadora had also dressed up for the launch party. Her exuberant hair had been temporarily tamed with combs, exposing giant chandelier type earrings, and she wore a dressy-looking coat in what looked like patterned brocade. Filtered through fog, the street lighting was too hazy for Anna to distinguish colours, but she caught gleams of metallic thread.

'So did you actually know Owen Traherne?' Anna asked.

'I met him a number of times,' Isadora said. 'With both of us moving in the same Oxford circles it was inevitable we'd run into each other. But I wouldn't say I *knew* him or Audrey. Underneath that wild man persona that Owen's publishers loved to trade on, one felt that he was quite a shy, insecure person.'

'Did you ever meet his wife?'

'Three or four times at the most. Audrey socialized even less than Owen. I remember her coming to a reception we held for Owen when he was professor of poetry. Sadly it was just a few months before she took her own life.'

They turned right into Beaumont Street, where Anna was dismayed to see several people in evening dress apparently converging on the Ashmolean. As if she divined her urge to run, Isadora hooked her arm through Anna's.

'What was Audrey like?' Anna asked, dimly noticing that she was somehow managing to keep walking and talking.

Isadora thought for a moment. 'Exquisitely lovely, but utterly elusive – like a beautiful ghost, not quite present. And Owen glued to her side all evening like some grim bodyguard.'

'Someone told me they had a rather tempestuous relationship.'

Isadora gave an astonished laugh. 'That's something of an understatement! Owen and Audrey were the stuff of legends: the brilliant scholarship boy from the docklands who fell in love with the equally brilliant diplomat's daughter. No one could see how it worked, yet through everything that happened – Owen's affairs, all those lost babies, Audrey's constant illnesses – they never ceased loving each other. And it seemed that nothing would or could ever shake that love.' Isadora shook her head. 'Poor man; he never really recovered.'

While she'd been talking Isadora had been gently steering Anna across the street towards the familiar bulk of the Ashmolean. Light streamed out between the sandstone columns illuminating a small knot of guests chatting beside the museum's entrance. 'Thank you so much for coming with me tonight,' Isadora said, taking a firmer grip on Anna's arm. 'Kit's always inviting me to things, but these days I find it such a bore coming on my own.'

'Nice of him to invite you, though.' Anna spoke purely out of politeness since she had a horror of ever being invited anywhere.

'I don't think he does it *entirely* from gallantry,' Isadora said with a sigh. 'The fact is, Kit has been courting me for years.' She saw Anna's face and collapsed into laughter. 'Not for my ageing body, darling! What a thought! You see, at times, my past has been – quite *colourful*, I suppose, and Kit is desperate for me to spill the beans for a book he's writing.' She glanced at her watch. 'How long shall we give it? An hour? I think definitely no more than an hour, don't you?'

The party was being held on the ground floor in the Randolph Sculpture Gallery, a part of the museum that Anna inextricably associated with visits with her school art class. Long and narrow, with a high ceiling, the gallery featured regularly spaced alcoves on either side. These had been painted a deep Georgian red, supplying a warming backdrop to the stark white sculptures displayed within and alongside. Anna had found these statues deadly dull when she was fourteen, and the intervening years had done nothing to change her opinion. It was an odd choice of venue, she thought, for launching a book of erotic love poems.

Apparently thinking along similar lines, Isadora said drily, 'That's the power of Hollywood for you. Not many dead poets get a launch as glittering as this, or live ones for that matter!'

The gallery was already filling up with people that Anna instantly identified as academics and media types, along with a surprise sprinkling of minor celebs. 'That's Richard Curtis,' she whispered in Isadora's ear. 'He makes films?' she prompted. 'I think that's Emma Freud with him.'

Isadora gave the couple a passing glance. 'I suppose she could possibly be a Freud,' she said without much interest. She suddenly gripped Anna's elbow. 'Darling, I don't look too much like some mad old relic do I? No obvious dog hairs? No disgusting bits of spinach between my teeth?'

For the first time it occurred to Anna that the larger than life Isadora might be suffering her own form of stage fright at the prospect of mingling with her former colleagues. Well-acquainted with panic, Anna knew better than to patronize her. 'No *obvious* dog hairs,' she told her, 'and if I had detected spinach I would definitely have mentioned it at an earlier point.'

In a less throwaway tone, she added, 'Actually, Isadora, I think you look impossibly glamorous.' It was true. The lighting in the museum had revealed Isadora's earrings to be set with blood-red garnets, the rich reds and browns of her coat interwoven with glints of gold. But it was some attracting quality in Isadora herself, Anna thought, which really drew your eye.

Isadora seemed to be considering Anna's compliment. 'Impossibly glamorous,' she repeated. 'I may have to use that for my epitaph.' She flashed Anna a distinctly gratified smile. 'Now, shall we grab some of this fizz?' She swiped two champagne flutes from a passing tray, handing one to Anna, and took a long gulp from her own. 'Right,' she said brightly. 'Now we just have to find Kit!'

It had seemed like a feasible plan, sitting around Isadora's kitchen table. Go to the launch party, get Kit alone and ask him to share what he knew about Naomi. But now they were actually here in this crowd of self-important *literati*, it seemed like the kind of ruse Enid Blyton might have concocted for the Famous Five. Judging from the way Isadora had swiftly downed her champagne, she felt the same.

Isadora's slightly hunted expression was suddenly transformed into a beaming smile. 'Etienne! *Quel plaisir de te revoir!*' Towing Anna in her wake, she made her way through the crush towards a wild-haired old man, kissing him enthusiastically on both cheeks, leaving glistening lip-sticked prints. 'Anna, you must meet my old friend Etienne Clement. He's Professor of Philosophy at the Université Panthéon-Sorbonne.'

'And who is this?' Professor Clement twinkled down at Anna.

Isadora completed the introductions then totally confounded Anna by lapsing into French. Anna could hold her own with what she thought of as 'holiday French', but not Isadora's kind of fast fluent excitable French, peppered with what Anna guessed must be the names of rival medievalists.

Anna didn't mind; she preferred to be on the sidelines and was happy to assume the role of appreciative audience. She found herself genuinely enjoying Isadora's delight in her long-lost friend, her giant earrings swinging as she gestured, gestures which were becoming more Gallic by the minute, Anna noticed. Anna sipped at her champagne, politely refusing the various savoury morsels that were being offered around, and was surprised to find her tension ebbing away. She even caught herself imagining telling Kirsty about her evening. Obviously, she'd edit out the tricky detail of how Isadora had come to invite Anna along to the launch in the first place. *Oh, we met at a murder scene. Didn't I say?*

Eventually, an older woman, so elegantly dressed that she could only be Parisian, reclaimed the professor rather forcefully from Isadora and they said their goodbyes.

Isadora helped herself to a second glass of champagne, and they drifted further into the gallery. She seemed to be getting into her stride, smilingly greeting old acquaintances and lingering to talk to others. A tall black man in his thirties emerged from the crowd, seizing both her hands. 'Isadora, it's wonderful to see you!'

'Anna, this is Vincent da Silva, one of my old students,' Isadora said in such warm tones that Anna could tell that the quite luminously beautiful Vincent had been a special, perhaps brilliant, protégé. 'I'd heard you'd since sold your soul to the BBC,' Isadora added, giving him a reproving look. 'And now that I've seen your suit I believe them! Presumably, you've got a couple of camera crews tagging along after you somewhere?'

'Just the one,' he said with a grin. 'Budget cuts! Yes, we're collecting footage for a documentary on Owen Traherne.' He turned to Anna. 'Were you one of Isadora's students?'

She shook her head. 'No, I'm just a friend.'

'So, what do you think of the choice of venue?' Vincent gestured at the increasingly crowded gallery. 'I always think that if these alcoves had more generous proportions and less sculptures they would make a perfect place for assignations!'

'Or assassinations?' Anna suggested, surprising herself.

He laughed. 'You obviously know the academic world quite well!'

After Vincent went off to find his camera crew, Isadora said in a hoarse whisper, 'He's a brilliant and lovely man, but you know he's as gay as a goose!'

Anna frowned at her. 'Why are you telling me that?'

'You responded to him so warmly,' Isadora explained. 'You hardly said a *word* to poor Etienne!'

'Only because I couldn't keep up with your French,' Anna told her.

Isadora looked astonished. 'Were we speaking French? Are you sure?'

'*Absolument*,' Anna said with a grin.

They had almost reached the far end of the gallery. Blackwell's book shop had set up a table piled with vibrant blue and gold hard-backed copies of Owen Traherne's love poems. Publisher's display cards showed blown-up images of the front cover, alongside soft-focus photographs of Owen with a fragile-looking woman that Anna assumed to be Audrey, interspersed with quotations from the poems. By an adjoining table a beautifully dressed but rather grim-faced couple hovered in the place traditionally reserved for the author. Smiling people kept coming up to them clutching their copies of the poems, apparently paying their respects to this uneasy pair of VIPs. The woman's glittering green silk top made her milk-white skin look even paler, Anna thought. She seemed to be avoiding looking at the slight, fair-haired man at her side, though he darted exasperated glances at her.

'That's Owen's son, Huw, and his wife, Sara,' Isadora said. 'Not the most blissful of marriages, as you can probably tell.'

'They seem to be the guests of honour,' Anna said.

'Huw and his wife took on running the Traherne Foundation after Owen's death,' Isadora explained. 'Owen left an extraordinary legacy – scholarships, bursaries, creative writing centres, a stunningly beautiful retreat in Pembrokeshire, which all need to be administered.'

'Sounds like a full-time job,' said Anna.

'I think it is. Huw has pretty much dedicated his life to keeping it all running the way his father would have wished.'

Anna looked at the blown-up photographs of the undeniably charismatic Owen and back to Huw. There was almost no family resemblance, she thought.

'There's Kit!' Isadora exclaimed.

Anna might not have recognized him without Isadora's prompt. Like the majority of book jacket photographs, Kit's had been corny and posed, which might have accounted for his expression: chilly to the point of arrogance. In real life he emanated good humour as he chatted to a skinny girl in a black tunic and leggings, who looked as if she might belong to Vincent's entourage.

'We'll try to grab him the minute she goes,' said Isadora.

While they waited, Anna found herself studying the blow-ups of the cover design that Owen Traherne's publishers had chosen for his anthology of love poems. It was a surprising choice, she thought, with its image of a leafless tree on to which exquisite little paper scrolls had been tied with scarlet ribbons. Though the tree itself was dark and ominous, the tiny scrolls had been painted so that they appeared to give off a mysteriously numinous and alluring light.

Years ago when Anna was travelling through Japan, she'd seen a similar tree in the grounds of a temple, where people came to tie their prayers on to its branches. Other westerners had been delighted by the sight, but Anna had felt saddened by the human suffering she felt seeping out of those countless desperate little scraps of paper.

The sound of tinkling glass shocked her back to the present as Huw's wife snatched up her bag from the table, knocking over someone's glass of champagne and sending it crashing to the floor. 'Oh, Lord, poor Huw,' Isadora said under her breath as Sara Traherne barged her way through the startled guests and went rushing through the gallery towards the street.

Huw quickly excused himself to a dismayed looking PR girl and went to find Kit. Kit murmured something to the girl in leggings, who tactfully melted away. Huw seemed to be apologizing to Kit, agitatedly checking his watch, while Kit listened, clearly concerned, running his hands through his hair. Anna heard Huw say, 'I'd better help her find a taxi. Can you tell the TV people I'll be back in time to do the speech?'

Kit gave Huw a reassuring clap on the back. 'Don't worry. I'll keep everyone warm for you. And tell Sara it was very public spirited of her to come out at all, poor love, when she's feeling so unwell.' Huw moved closer to Kit and said something Anna didn't catch, before hurrying out of the gallery, emanating irritation and stress.

'Now Kit *is* heterosexual and currently single,' Isadora murmured just before they came within earshot.

'Isadora, *stop* it!' Anna hissed.

'And I hear he's a fabulous lover!' she added irrepressibly.
'Kit, *there* you are!' she called. 'We've been looking for you
everywhere!'

Kit turned, and Anna watched him take in first Isadora and
then Anna at her side, so she saw the moment when his expression changed. The cool assessing look in his eyes came and went
so fast as to be almost subliminal, but by then it didn't matter
that he was kissing Isadora on both cheeks and asking warmly
about Anna. Isadora's story about his daredevil past, the fact that
he was a successful writer, his connection with Naomi; everything
had predisposed her to like Kit Tulliver, including Kit himself.
She liked his amiable good-looks, she liked the careless way he
wore his well-cut suit without a hint of a tie, black or otherwise,
but she knew something about Kit now, however much she wished
she didn't.

'Thank God you came to rescue me!' Kit was saying. 'Can I
skulk here with you two for a moment? I am shockingly bad at
these kinds of things. I am hopeless at small talk, isn't that true,
Isadora?'

'It's true! Kit's real forte is piffle!' Isadora's eyes danced with
mischief.

He gave a humorous groan. 'Anna, don't you love how she
managed to slide in that Lord Peter Wimsey reference like a
stiletto into my ribs!' Kit was inviting her to join in their flirty
give and take, but she felt frozen. She didn't want to be this stiff
distant woman, always trapped on the wrong side of a pane of
glass. She didn't want this curse of seeing through people's
disguises into the darkness no one else seemed to see.

She heard her grandfather say, *You don't need more darkness
and suspicion in your life, my darling. You need to learn to trust
again.*

And suddenly she saw herself sitting in Xi'an with Jake
McCaffrey, looking back at him with cold detachment as he
talked about his on-off fiancée. In that instant of shocking clarity
Anna grasped that the expression she had seen on Kit's face had
actually been *her* coldness, *her* wariness, *her* swift clinical
summing up of his worth as a human being, momentarily reflected
back.

She heard Isadora say, 'Kit, I'm sorry if this is distressing, but we wanted to talk to you about Naomi Evans. I believe she was working for you?' And she saw Kit suck in his breath.

'Jesus, Isadora, I'm so sorry. You must think I'm a complete moron. Someone told me you'd found the body. I've just been so caught up with this – *circus.*' Kit's helpless gesture seemed to include the display of books, the BBC crew and the milling guests. His face crumpled with distress.

'It was actually Anna who found Naomi's body,' Isadora said quietly.

Kit's eyes widened. He moved to touch her then didn't quite complete the gesture, letting his hand drop as if he'd sensed her natural reticence. So he was sensitive as well as good-looking, Anna thought and felt her interest tentatively revive.

'Naomi was a wonderful person,' he said. 'When I first met her I thought she was just, you know, a blonde – I know, Isadora, I know! – but my God, what a brain that woman had.' Once again Kit ran his hands through his hair, which was starting to stick up at odd angles.

'She was working with you on Owen Traherne's biography?' Anna said.

'She was my top fact-checker. Kept on top of everything. Dates. Who did what, when, where. All the stuff I'm so bad at. Such a tragedy. An inexplicable tragedy. Although—' Kit checked himself. 'Sorry, I really don't think I can go there,' he said grimly.

'Please finish what you were going to say,' Isadora said.

Kit puffed out his cheeks. 'I'm probably making something out of nothing. Despite my unfortunate resemblance to the great Lord Peter—' he flashed Isadora a self-deprecating smile – 'I have absolutely no detectin' skills! But there are a couple of things that have been bothering me. First, why wasn't there any DNA at the scene of Naomi's murder? It seems especially odd when you think that the monster that killed those other women left *his* disgusting DNA littered all over their murder scenes with what seems like reckless abandon.' He glanced at his watch. 'Damn, sorry, I promised Huw I'd alert the TV people that we'll be running a bit behind schedule.'

'You said there were a couple of things,' Anna reminded him.

His expression clouded. 'I have no actual proof of this, but a few days before Naomi died she seemed very excited about some important new contact she'd made.'

Anna heard Naomi saying, *But oh my God, this is going to be a total game changer, Anna!* 'Do you know what kind of contact?' she asked.

'All I know is that she was convinced this guy could give her unprecedented access into Albanian gang culture. So I'm guessing not the pleasantest person in the world. We almost fell out over it, actually.' Kit shook his head, remembering. 'I told her she should stop and think about what she was getting herself into. Of course, if I'd been a proper friend I'd have insisted she drop the whole crazy scheme. I don't know, obviously, that this has anything to do with her death, but I can't help . . .' Again Kit's face crumpled. 'I just can't stop myself going over and over it. I haven't been able to sleep since I heard.'

Anna knew how that felt. If she'd just left Coffee on the Green a few minutes earlier, decided to walk Bonnie earlier, she too might have prevented Naomi's death.

'Dear Kit,' Isadora said remorsefully. 'I said I didn't want to upset you, and now we have. But when Huw comes back, will you please tell him how much I enjoyed his wonderful foreword to his father's poems. It was an inspired idea to ask someone who knew Owen so intimately, not the usual dry academic *merde*.'

'It's a brilliant piece of writing,' Kit agreed warmly, visibly relieved to return to a less fraught subject. 'Poor Huw, this is such a big night for the Foundation, and just when he needs some support, Sara gets one of her tactical migraines. OK, I'd really better go. Lovely to see you again, Isadora.' He pulled his wallet out of his trouser pocket, extracted a card and handed it to Anna. 'Just in case you think of anything else you might want to ask me about Naomi.' He deliberately met her gaze, and Anna saw a faintly questioning look in his eyes. 'Very good to meet you, Anna, and again, I'm so, so sorry.'

After Kit had gone, Isadora seemed to wilt. 'I'm sure we've been here more than an hour.'

'We've been here exactly an hour and a half,' said Anna, who'd been surreptitiously keeping an eye on the time.

'Well, I've seen at least a dozen people here that I've slept with at one time or another, and I would really prefer not to have to see any more. I suggest we go to the Eagle and Child for a drink.'

'Sure,' said Anna, who had secretly been hoping to go straight back to Bonnie and bed. 'I just want to buy a copy of the love poems for someone. Then I'm ready to go.'

On their way out of the Ashmolean they almost collided with a still-agitated Huw as he hurried back inside.

'You don't mind missing the speeches?' Anna said.

Isadora gave one of her dark laughs. 'My dear, I have heard enough speeches to last me several lifetimes.'

They set off walking back to St Giles in the now thick and swirling mist. The temperature had dropped while they were inside the museum, and they were both shivering in their flimsy clothes.

'You really ought to reconsider my suggestion,' Isadora said. 'I could see how much Kit took to you.'

'There's nothing to reconsider,' Anna said, teeth chattering. 'I'm not looking for—'

'Not looking for what? *Love?*' Isadora was suddenly scathing. 'Only fools go looking for love. Love either comes or it doesn't. Sex, on the other hand—'

'Isadora!' Anna said, her face burning. 'I refuse to talk to you about sex!' After a highly-charged pause, she said in a more neutral tone, 'Isn't the Eagle and Child just for tourists these days?'

'It was my second home in Tolkien's time,' Isadora said loftily. 'With or without tourists I find it a wonderfully comforting place, and with any luck they will have a fire.' Her deep-set eyes had taken on the brooding look that Anna remembered from the row with Gabriel. Suddenly, she looked tired and old.

Anna's brain felt overloaded with sensory impressions, and Kit's mention of criminal gangs had left her confused and disturbed. She hadn't known Naomi long, but she could easily relate to the picture Kit had painted of her, doing everything humanly possible to unearth a dangerous crime ring. She could relate to it except for just one thing. The Naomi Anna had constructed in her imagination was totally devoid of a diva instinct. Her Naomi would have hunted down the facts, care-fully, responsibly, discreetly collecting together all relevant information. Then she'd have tied it all up with a big red bow and handed it over to the proper authorities to deal with. Walking blithely into a den of gangsters looked too much like a death wish to Anna, and if there was one thing she thought she knew about Naomi, it was that she was on the side of life. On the other hand, Anna reminded herself, this piercing insight into Naomi's soul was based on precisely two conversations.

They had almost reached the Eagle and Child when Anna's heart almost stopped as he came loping out of the mist: the boy she'd been pursuing for sixteen years, the boy she came back to find. Seeing him walk towards her, arrogant and alive, Anna felt as if she'd been punched in the stomach, too shocked to call out or even breathe.

A heartbeat later, her brain kicked in. Sixteen years ago this adolescent would have been at preschool. His super-size state-of-the-art headphones hadn't been invented then. Her boy was no longer a teenage boy, any more than Anna was still a teenage girl. Like someone who has almost missed a step, Anna's mistake and her recovery happened in the same electric instant, but she was left shaking, heart pounding. It was as if she'd seen a ghost. A messenger. *Don't forget.*

Isadora looked at her oddly. 'Are you all right?'

'I'm fine!' she said, smiling. 'I'm looking forward to this open fire you promised me!' Anna felt an irrational pang as Isadora instantly accepted her blatant lie.

'That's good!' she said grimly, handing over her car keys. 'Because I intend to get totally and utterly sloshed!'

EIGHT

I sadora delivered on both her promises. Anna had known a few heavy drinkers in her time, and as the empty vodka glasses stacked up she was dreading the moment when this fiercely intelligent woman inevitably crossed the line into maudlin incoherence.

But in some strange reversal of normal laws, excess alcohol only seemed to make Isadora wittier and more lucid, kicking her brain into sparkling overdrive. As she talked and gestured, dark eyes flashing, the actress in Isadora seemed hell-bent on dazzling everybody within earshot. No one came to join them at their fireside table, to Anna's relief, but she could see people becoming drawn in as Isadora described glamorous people she had known and hilarious, surreal or downright dangerous situations she had been in.

She grew slightly huffy when someone announced closing time, but after a little coaxing Isadora allowed Anna to prise her away from her audience and out into the fog. Luckily, Anna had anticipated the effects of cold night air and was ready to catch Isadora at the exact moment she sagged at the knees. Feeling Anna's arm go round her, Isadora lifted up her head and wept.

Anna had to drive the Volvo back to Summertown with a still-weeping Isadora and an ominously flickering petrol light for company. She left Isadora passed out in her bedroom, having placed a glass of water and a waste paper basket within easy reach. Isadora's little dog, Hero, who had followed them anxiously upstairs, jumped up on the bed next to Isadora and lay down beside her, her Marmite-brown eyes alert through her overgrown fringe. Leaving Hero to keep watch, Anna went downstairs to call a taxi.

It was past one a.m. by the time Anna eventually let herself into her own flat. The intensity of her evening with Isadora, on top of her mistaken sighting outside the Eagle and Child, had left her raw and jangling. Then there were Kit's worrying revelations. She'd need to wind down if she was going to get any sleep. Anna popped two chamomile tea bags in the small red teapot she used for herbal tea and poured on boiling water. When her tea was ready, she made herself comfortable on the old leather sofa in her kitchen, rested her steaming cup on its battered arm and sat leafing through the book of love poems she had bought for Kirsty.

With Bonnie dozing at her feet, Anna dipped in and out of the poems, occasionally sipping at her tea. She found the poem she'd recited to Kirsty, and fragments from some of Traherne's other poems came back to her as she read. Anna's memories of her sixth-form studies were hazy at best; Owen Traherne's words had washed over her largely unheeded, along with everything else. But in the lonely small hours, with mist pressing against the kitchen windows and only a sleeping dog for company, she was startled by how much they stirred her.

Carefully holding the book so as not to crease the spine, Anna read, 'Again and again I let myself be lured to that bespelled spring which keeps me forever thirsty and enslaved.'

Only a fool goes looking for love, Isadora had said. Until tonight Anna had not let herself know that she'd been looking. Oh, she knew she could have sex. Any young woman with a pulse could find sex. But no matter how loudly she denied it, it was love, *that bespelled spring*, which Anna secretly longed for. She remembered Kit's questioning look. Kit, who lived in the same city as Anna and was funny and sweet.

At last she forced herself upstairs and into bed, where she crashed asleep until her alarm went off at six thirty.

On the bus into work the next morning, eyes gritty with exhaustion, Anna tried to cheer herself up by imagining Kirsty's surprise when Anna gave her the book. In fact, Kirsty's reaction embarrassingly exceeded her hopes.

'This is such a thoughtful present. I don't know what to say. Oh my God, Anna, this is so perfect.' And to Anna's horror, Kirsty's eyes filled with tears.

'I knew you were interested in Owen Traherne, that's all.' Anna hastily switched on her computer, signalling her intent to get down to work and hopefully putting an end to any unwanted intimacies.

But Kirsty, laughing now as well as tearful, waved away her objections. 'Shush, Anna! You did a really lovely thing. Now you'll have to allow me to take it all in!' And Kirsty continued to perch on Anna's desk, her coppery curls illuminated by the light coming in the window, exclaiming over the woodcuts the publishers had commissioned to illustrate this new edition of Traherne's work.

There was an art to giving presents, Anna thought, and as an unusually (OK, *obsessively*) vigilant people-watcher, she took secret satisfaction in being an insightful giver. But Kirsty had mastered a far more elusive art: the art of receiving. Covertly watching her turning over pages, apparently in a state of bliss, Anna marvelled that Kirsty could make herself so vulnerable to another person.

When Anna logged on to her shared computer she found a flurry of emails waiting. Anna and Nadine had joint responsibility for students coming to Walsingham from outside the UK, and with the Michaelmas term now looming, everyone's anxiety levels were escalating. Anna spent an hour and a half composing reassuring replies to various overseas agencies who were suddenly demanding detailed information relating to student accommodation, airport pickups, visa details etc. Plus it turned out that someone from this year's intake had a disability that no one had previously thought to mention, and Anna had to do some fancy footwork to find him a ground-floor room in halls at what was a ridiculously late stage in the year. She was mentally congratulating herself for pulling off this near-impossible feat (hopefully, there'd be one less Post-it note from Nadine next time Anna came into work) when she received a text from Tansy: *r u free to meet me & isadora 4 late lunch at m'lade?*

Anna immediately texted her acceptance. It was only while she was walking down Little Clarendon Street in slightly hazy sunlight, relishing the quiet of a street that would soon be thronging with cycling dons and undergraduates, that she felt a twinge of panic. How was Isadora going to feel when she saw Anna? If their situations were reversed, Anna would want to jump on a plane to a far distant country and never have to face that person ever again.

But when she took a precautionary peep through the window

of Cafe Marmalade, Isadora was nowhere to be seen. Isadora wasn't there, but to Anna's surprise Sergeant Goodhart was, talking to Tansy in the nearly empty cafe.

Anna pushed open the door in time to hear him say, 'Not a *date* date. Just, you know, a drink or a walk by the river?'

Anna hastily scrolled through her available options. She could slip away now, in which case they might spot her, and thus adding to everyone's discomfort levels, or she could announce her presence before their conversation got any more intense. 'Hi,' she said tentatively, and they both guiltily jumped apart.

Even in faded jeans and a white T-shirt, Sergeant Goodhart looked like what he was, Anna thought – an off-duty cop, and distinctly sheepish at being discovered in close proximity to Tansy. Tansy's face expressed similar confusion. 'Hi, Anna! You remember Liam? Actually, he was just going, weren't you?' she added fiercely.

'That was very subtly done,' Anna commented as they watched the handsome sergeant disappear down Walton Street.

Tansy pulled a face. 'I kind of panicked.' She tugged at her curls then her eyes went wide. 'Oh my God, Anna, Isadora told me about the gangsters. What the fuck was Naomi *thinking*?'

Anna shook her head. 'I can't get my head around it at all.'

Tansy gestured towards a table. 'Sit, sit. Isadora shouldn't be long.'

'Have you actually spoken to her?' Anna asked. 'I mean, you've spoken to her this morning?'

'Yes, when I fixed up our lunch. Why?'

'Did she sound OK?' Anna hedged.

'A bit subdued, maybe. Why, what happened to make you think she wasn't OK?'

Anna gave Tansy a slightly edited version of the end of her evening.

'Oh my God, poor Isadora! Not to mention poor you! Hang on a sec.' Tansy waved Brendan over. 'We're still waiting for our friend. Can you rustle up some bread and hummus to keep us going? Aw, thanks, hon!' Were all Oxford's young men in thrall to Tansy, Anna wondered as Brendan obediently hurried away.

Tansy waited until he'd brought a basket heaped with crusty

slices of warmed-through olive bread and retreated out of earshot before she said, 'What do you think made Isadora so upset?'

What Anna had felt from Isadora as she crumpled into her arms was a terrible grief. She didn't know if she should say this to Tansy though, so she just shrugged. 'Getting old, maybe? Plus, she said she'd seen about a dozen people that she'd slept with at one time or another.'

Tansy raised an eyebrow. 'She actually said "people" not "men"?'

'She definitely said "people".' Anna tore off a piece of her bread and popped it in her mouth.

'Try it with the hummus,' Tansy suggested. 'Seriously, it's so good.' She pushed the little earthenware ramekin towards Anna, and Anna saw that Tansy's nails had been repainted with a pearlescent blue polish sprinkled with tiny gold stars. Like miniature Van Gogh skies, she thought.

Tansy watched Anna slather a crust with garlicky chickpea spread. 'She couldn't have just been upset about the Albanians?'

Anna shook her head. Isadora's anguish had been old, pent up, scalding; the kind of pain it half-killed you to feel. 'The weird thing is she didn't, you know, act upset until the moment I got her out of the pub, then she just . . .' Anna inhaled sharply, letting her sentence just tail off.

'I totally can't drink,' Tansy said ruefully. 'I can't stand that floaty feeling, like I'm losing touch with reality you know? Leo says I'm a control freak.'

'Why do people always say that as if it's a bad thing?' Anna said, perplexed. Why would you *not* want to stay in control, she thought; who else could you trust to keep you safe, if not yourself?

Tansy poured them each a glass of sparkling mineral water. 'I used to do a bit of weed now and then. But I had a couple of bad experiences, and now I'm too much of a lightweight to even do that.'

In her time, Anna had done more than a bit of weed, along with other substances it made her sick to remember. She tried to smile at Tansy. 'We're both lightweights, then.'

Tansy started idly picking pieces of olive out of her bread. Anna could see her thoughts were wandering. 'I've been thinking.

What Isadora's friend Kit said about Albanian gang lords possibly being connected with Naomi's death. You don't think we should maybe check it out?' Tansy shot a glance at Anna then went back to fiddling with her bread.

Anna gave a surprised snort. 'How would we do that?'

Tansy shrugged. 'I might know someone who could help.'

Anna ransacked her brain to think who this someone might be. 'You don't mean Liam?'

'Are you mad!' Tansy looked appalled. 'We can't involve the police with this.'

'Who were you thinking of involving then?' Anna said, bewildered.

Tansy seemed to study her fingernails for a moment, and then she looked up and flashed Anna a grin that couldn't entirely hide her relief at a narrow escape. 'Forget it. No, trust me, Anna, it was a really bad idea, and God knows I've had a few!'

The door to the cafe opened with a crash, and Isadora burst in. Wearing dark glasses and an old mole-coloured trench-coat she looked like a hung-over heroine from the French Resistance. She had bundled her wiry curls into a silk scarf, also mole-coloured. Possibly, she hadn't felt up to dealing with tangles, or colours, Anna thought.

'I need coffee, strong black coffee,' Isadora announced as she dropped heavily into the seat next to Tansy.

'I'm on it,' Tansy said, jumping up. She slipped behind the counter and did something to activate the espresso machine.

Alone with Anna, Isadora briefly lifted her sunglasses, shooting her a beseeching look, before fixing them tremblingly back in place. 'Was I very ghastly? What did I do? No, don't tell me!' she begged immediately.

Now that Anna was actually sitting opposite her, she found that she wasn't embarrassed as much as concerned to spare Isadora's feelings. 'You weren't ghastly. You just told some wonderful stories about being young in the sixties.' This wasn't an out and out lie.

'I didn't tell you that terrible story about Mick Jagger?' Isadora was pressing her fingers to her temples in a way that let Anna know her head was pounding.

'Not that I recall,' Anna said, mentally crossing her fingers.

Tansy came back with a huge mug of coffee and three Cafe Marmalade menus. Isadora began emptying sachets of sugar into her coffee. When she'd reached sachet number six, Tansy's mouth opened in protest.

'Don't say a word!' Isadora snapped. 'It's my hangover. I know what I need!'

The two younger women waited in respectful silence until Isadora had sunk half her coffee. Cautiously removing her dark glasses, she patted Tansy's hand. 'I can probably function now, so long as nobody shouts.' She turned her attention to Anna. 'How much have you told Tansy about last night? About Naomi I mean. Not about me getting drunk.'

Tansy tactfully came to Anna's rescue. 'She hasn't told me much about your evening, have you, Anna? Except for something mad about Naomi having meets with psycho Albanians,' she said, flashing Anna a grin.

'Kit didn't actually use the term psycho,' Anna said. Or 'meets', she added mentally. Despite its swift retraction, Tansy's offer to obtain information about gang lords had left her distinctly puzzled.

'What did he say though?' Tansy asked.

'Anna can fill you in,' Isadora said, closing her eyes.

'He said Naomi was a brilliant researcher,' Anna said, 'and he said that he liked her a lot, but they had a major falling-out about her latest gangland project, and he feels terrible now about not coming down harder on her.'

'That's all he said?' Tansy sounded disappointed. She sighed. 'I suppose it was unrealistic to hope he'd give us something more solid. So how was the book launch? Did you meet anyone exciting?'

Isadora left Anna to narrate the story of how Huw's wife had stormed out minutes before her husband's big moment.

While Anna was talking, she had the feeling Tansy was privately turning something over in her mind. At last Tansy said, 'I'm not sure if you'll think this is really morbid, but people are leaving flowers in Port Meadow where we found Naomi. I thought we could go and take something – not mawkish shit like teddy bears, just flowers. Liam said her body is being taken back to her family in Pembrokeshire, so I thought this was one way we could, you know, say goodbye.'

Isadora opened her eyes to say, 'I haven't been back there since that day.'

'I haven't been back either,' Anna said.

'Nor me,' said Tansy. 'So do you agree this might be a good thing to do? I thought it might be a way of kind of laying her to rest, you know?'

'I think it would be a lovely thing to do,' Isadora said at once. 'How about you, Anna?'

'I'd like to do that too,' Anna said. She wondered if she would have come up with it by herself. She hoped so, but she wasn't convinced.

'Shall we all meet up on Sunday?' Isadora asked. 'That's if everyone is free?'

Tansy and Anna nodded.

'Good, that's settled!' Isadora said, sounding more like her normal self. 'And now I suppose we should have our vegan lunch! What do you recommend, darling?' she asked Tansy. 'My one stipulation is that it shouldn't involve *any* form of tofu. In my current fragile condition, I feel that would be most unwise!'

Anna saw Tansy waiting with Buster as soon as she drove into the car park. Tansy had thrown a leopard-print swing coat over her skinny jeans and was holding an enormous bunch of brightly-coloured flowers that reminded Anna of harvest festivals.

A moment later Isadora's Volvo pulled up. Anna saw Isadora reach into the back of the car, before she emerged with her arms full of russet coloured chrysanthemums. Hero jumped out, wildly excited to see the other dogs. Buster and Bonnie greeted each other with polite interest. Isadora's dog, still half puppy, flew back and forth between the older dogs, exuberantly licking their faces.

Tansy gave a rueful laugh. 'When I pictured us being here in my head it was way more dignified.'

'Shall I put her back in the car?' Isadora suggested.

Tansy shook her head. 'We all have to be here, or it isn't a proper goodbye.' She opened the gate into the meadow. The three women set off a little self-consciously, carrying their flowers, the dogs racing ahead. Overhead, rooks cawed and sullen clouds threatened rain.

'I know this was my idea,' Tansy said. 'But now I'm here, I don't really know how I'm supposed to feel. Does that sound stupid?' In typical Tansy fashion, she was saying what Anna had half-felt but not liked to say aloud.

'It doesn't sound stupid,' Anna said. She wondered if they were all sharing the same thought. If it hadn't been for Naomi they'd still be three strangers, yet here they were tramping over a damp autumn meadow to say goodbye to this woman they had hardly known.

'You've both bought lovely flowers.' Tansy glanced doubtfully at her own offering. 'I took these from Nick and Leo's garden. I just walked around picking everything I liked the look of.' Tansy had included rosemary and rose hips in her bunch, along with late-flowering roses and shocking-pink cosmos. Anna thought Tansy's heartfelt if raggedy posy made her own all-white bouquet look lifeless in comparison.

Isadora brushed her hand over a green spike of rosemary, releasing its scented oil. 'Rosemary for remembrance,' she said softly. 'How perfect, Tansy.'

Long before they reached the spot they could see the sea of cellophane-wrapped flowers left by local people, most of whom had probably not known Naomi, Anna thought; the Lady Di effect. As Tansy had feared there were a few damp-looking teddy-bears. Several mourners had left well-intentioned messages about being taken to be an angel that Anna suspected would have made Naomi laugh. It had rained in the night, scattering raindrops across cellophane wrappings and flower petals like transparent beads. The scene reminded Anna of those eerie double exposures you sometimes saw back in the days when cameras used film; the innocence of flowers and toy bears surreally imposed over the horror of Naomi's last moments on earth. The killer had fled, Naomi's body had been removed, yet the violent act still resonated, unseen but savagely present.

Anna rather awkwardly laid down her flowers, and Tansy and Isadora placed theirs beside hers. Tansy reached into her bag, bringing out a lighter and a white tea light in a clear glass holder. Anna watched her light it and carefully set it next to their flowers.

'Do we have to say anything?' Tansy asked.

Anna shook her head. What could they possibly say?

'It's enough to feel it, darling,' Isadora said.

Anna swallowed. When this little ceremony was over, she and Tansy and Isadora would say their goodbyes and maybe exchange cards at Christmas, because after today there would no longer be any valid motivation for them to continue to meet.

'Would it seem really tasteless of me if I said how stunningly gorgeous this bouquet is?'

Anna followed Tansy's awed gaze, and her eyes widened. The bouquet was three times the size of hers or Isadora's.

'Do you think Naomi's boyfriend sent them?' Tansy suggested.

'I don't think she had a boyfriend,' said Isadora. 'They didn't mention one in the papers, and no grieving boyfriend came forward so far as I know.'

'There's a card.' Tansy crouched down for a closer look. 'It's from someone called Laurie Swanson.'

'Laurie Swanson? Are you sure?' Isadora sounded startled.

Tansy nodded. 'The writing's gone a bit blurry, but you can read the name.'

Isadora seemed perplexed. 'The only Laurie Swanson I know has been a complete recluse for years.'

'This must be a different guy then. Most of his message has run in the rain, but there's a bit about being sorry their connection was so brief and thanking Naomi for listening and being there.'

'Well, whoever he is, he obviously thought a great deal of Naomi,' Isadora commented as they set off back to the car.

'So who was your Laurie Swanson, Isadora?' Tansy asked.

'An amazingly talented composer. People were calling him the next Benjamin Britten. About ten years ago, in the middle of conducting his new symphony in Berlin, he just walked off stage. I heard a rumour that he'd had a massive breakdown, poor man. Still just a baby, really, in his early forties. He hasn't produced any new work since, so far as I know.'

By the time they reached the car park, it had started to rain in earnest.

'Can I offer you a lift?' Isadora asked Tansy.

'That would be great, thanks.' Tansy turned to include Anna. 'I'm really glad you could both come. I feel better that we did this, don't you?'

Anna nodded. 'Much better.' No point trying to put into words her irrational sense of loss, of loose ends that would now forever stay untied. They had started something, the three of them. They just weren't equipped to finish it. There was nothing anyone could do about it, so better just leave it all unsaid. Anna realized she didn't even know where Tansy lived. She'd have to drop off her Christmas card at Marmalade.

Isadora briefly squeezed Anna's hands. 'Goodbye, you darling girl.'

Anna opened the back door of her Land Rover so that Bonnie could jump in. 'I'm sure I'll see you guys around,' she said. She got into her car, gave them a smiling wave and drove away.

NINE

That evening Anna lay on her back on the kitchen sofa wearing her old flannel PJs and a baggy T-shirt, knees bent, a pillow under her head. On the floor next to the sofa was a bowl of sweet 'n' salty popcorn. Now and then Anna threw Bonnie a kernel, though she thought Bonnie enjoyed catching them with a triumphant snap – and, subsequently, crunching them manically – almost more than the actual popcorn. She had her radio tuned to a mellow music station, and Nina Simone was singing 'To Love Somebody'.

Out of all the rooms in Anna's flat, her basement kitchen was the one that said 'home'. It was also the least overlooked, which made it easier to relax. She had installed a small TV and DVD player next to the sofa and had just finished watching *Silver Linings Playbook*. But when she'd checked the time it was only nine forty-five p.m., far too early to go to bed. So she'd switched on the radio, picked up her copy of Owen Traherne's biography and settled down to read Kit's introduction.

She'd bought Kit's book in Summertown after dropping her grandfather back at Bramley Lodge. They'd driven out to nearby Woodstock to the Woodstock Arms for Sunday lunch. By the time they'd emerged from the pub the clouds had rolled away, and Anna had suggested going to Blenheim Palace, a place her grandfather loved. She'd lifted his wheelchair out of the back of her Land Rover, and they'd made a leisurely circuit of the lake known as the Queen's Pool, so he could enjoy the autumn colours twice over, first in the landscape planted by Capability Brown and then reflected back from the millpond still waters.

It had been a good day, Anna thought, what she privately designated as a *normal* day. That's if you edited out the part where she took some flowers to a murder scene and heard a name that for no logical reason had lodged in her brain and refused to go away.

Laurie Swanson. Who was he? And what was he to Naomi

Evans? And what had Naomi done to affect this man so deeply that he had spent the equivalent of Anna's weekly grocery bill on a bouquet to honour her memory? In his message he had thanked Naomi 'for listening', for 'being there for him'. In her group therapy days, Anna had unwillingly found herself in the company of people who used this kind of therapy-speak, but she suspected that Laurie Swanson's words, like his hugely expensive flowers, were the only way he knew to express the inexpressible. He didn't care about being original or even adequate. He was just pouring out his heartfelt gratitude to a valued friend.

Anna shut her book. Not a long-term friend, to judge from his message. But then you didn't need to know Naomi Evans long to want to be her friend. After two conversations with her, Anna had felt that it just might be possible to live the rest of her life as Anna Hopkins. It seemed as if Naomi had worked an equivalent magic for Laurie Swanson, enabling him to open up about a part of his life that he'd felt unable to share with anyone else.

Anna reached down for her iPad, but then helped herself to popcorn instead. The Laurie Swanson who had left Naomi's flowers might or might not be Isadora's reclusive composer. Either way Anna was not (seriously not) going to look him up online. She had gone to Port Meadow to lay Naomi to rest: not Naomi her almost-friend – Naomi's family would have to do that – but the inexplicable evil of her murder. Laying something to rest was like a gentler form of exorcism. You drew a line and told the dark powers: *It's finished!* And then you barred your home, your mind to them forever more, so that you could go on living.

Naomi wouldn't have laid it to rest. The thought made Anna shoot upright as though she'd been scalded, because it was true. Naomi wasn't some Disney heroine, skipping around doing good works. She was a seeker after truth in a world filled with liars. *'Finding stuff out is my drug of choice.'*

But Anna wasn't Naomi. Naomi had not been Anna. Naomi had not squandered sixteen-plus years of her existence in fruitless paranoia. Anna couldn't afford to lose any more years.

A normal day, she told herself. *Just for today, Anna, you will have a normal day.* And she forced herself to return to her

book. Far too twitchy to give her full attention to the text, she
turned to the photographs in the middle of the book. She flicked
past childhood photographs in grim working-class Cardiff, a
teenage Owen, arms folded, stonily staring back at the camera,
followed by the standard Oxford photos: punting, drinking,
Owen as a startlingly feral Oberon in an open air production
of *A Midsummer Night's Dream*, dressed up in black tie for the
May Ball, outside the Exam Schools in cap and gown after his
finals being greeted by a radiant Audrey with a celebratory
bottle of champagne.

Anna tossed a popcorn kernel to Bonnie, taking a handful
for herself before she went back to the photographs. There was
a photo of Owen giving a reading at New York's Café des
Artistes with Alan Ginsberg and other American luminaries of
the time, and another of him reading at Café de Fiore in Paris
while Audrey watched from the sidelines. Judging from the
dates, Owen had been picked up by the literary elite as soon
as he'd graduated. He had also married his beautiful Audrey.
There were pictures of them in the Pembrokeshire cottage where
they'd retreated after their first and only child was born. Anna
flicked past grainy images of Owen chopping wood, striding
along the Pembrokeshire cliffs with his little boy Huw riding
on his shoulders. Their country idyll hadn't lasted long. A few
years later the family were back in Oxford. Anna paused at a
photograph of a tense six-year-old Huw, wearing the uniform
of the Dragon School, the same Oxford prep school where her
younger brothers, Will and Dan, had also been pupils, before
skimming on, vaguely registering faces and places, until a
familiar name stilled her hand.

It couldn't be him. There was no earthly reason that this should
be her Laurie, Naomi's Laurie.

The photo showed a relaxed, sun-burned Owen Traherne
standing with his arms lightly slung around the shoulders of his
teenage son and another boy of similar age. Both teenagers were
barefoot in baggy shirts and ripped denim jeans. A chalked sign
propped against a rickety shack behind them offered freshly
caught lobsters and crab. Pale-yellow sea poppies sprouted among
sand and pebbles. The caption said: *Owen with Huw and school-
friend Laurie. Norfolk.* Anna's attention was pulled back to the

unknown boy. He resembled a wide-eyed fawn, she thought, every nerve quivering and alert.

She shut her book. One minute out of her otherwise normal day. Just one minute, and then she would know for sure and could forget all about Laurie Swanson.

She picked up her iPad, typed his name into the search engine and clicked on 'Images'.

The first picture brought a leap of recognition. It *was* him; older, and unmistakably sadder, but the same sensitive dark eyes, the same expression of alert intelligence.

She scrolled through pictures of the adult Laurie sitting at a grand piano, conducting an orchestra at Snape Maltings during the Aldeburgh Festival, exchanging a joke with musicians during a rehearsal at London's Festival Hall, making music with impoverished Brazilian children. Increasingly spellbound, Anna kept scrolling, though she had no doubt now that the Laurie in the holiday snap and Isadora's Laurie Swanson were one and the same. What the photographs couldn't tell her was if Laurie Swanson the composer was also Naomi's Laurie.

Anna softly tapped her fingers against her teeth. If Laurie Swanson was as famous as Isadora said, he should have an official website. If he disliked dealing with approaches in person, he might employ someone to manage it for him, or someone could have set one up on his behalf. If there was a Laurie Swanson website there would be a contact email. Anna could email him and ask him if he had known Naomi.

OK, maybe three minutes. Five minutes if you included firing off a short email. Five minutes tops. And then she could go to bed knowing she'd done everything possible to track down the mysterious Laurie who had left flowers to honour Naomi's memory.

Dear Laurie Swanson,

I am writing to ask if you are the same Laurie Swanson who left flowers at Port Meadow for Naomi Evans. If so, I think we may have something in common. I knew Naomi for hardly any time, yet she did a beautiful thing for me, just because she thought it was the right thing to do. Now, far too late, I want to be a friend to her in my turn. To this

end, I am trying to find out more about Naomi and about
her life.
    Sincerely,
    Anna Hopkins

Anna scanned her message for obvious typos, pressed 'Send'
and instantly went hot and cold with shame. *Stupid, stupid.* What
was she doing baring her soul to a stranger on the basis of a
rain-blurred message on a bunch of flowers? The website administrator probably wouldn't forward it, she told herself. Even if
they did, the reclusive Laurie Swanson was unlikely to reply. But
she still wished she could take it back.

    Needing a distraction, Anna found the basket she used to store
Bonnie's few canine necessities, took out the bristle brush and
settled down to give her a through grooming. Bonnie loved being
brushed almost as much as she hated being put in the bath,
collapsing on to her side and uttering soft little groans and throaty
grumbles that Anna had initially mistaken for growls. This repetitive task gradually soothed her, and by the time she'd finished
Bonnie's snow-white coat shone like moonlit silk.

    Telling Bonnie goodnight Anna went upstairs to get ready for
bed. She was just spitting mouthwash into the basin when her
mobile pinged, telling her she had an email. *Jake*, she thought.
Her mouth still tingling with peppermint, she padded back into
her bedroom, feeling a pleasant *frisson* of anticipation. Jake's
messages to her were always carefully neutral, yet she could
almost hear his deadpan southern voice filtering through his droll
accounts of missed planes and unlikely travel companions. He
had no reason to keep in touch with Anna, just as she had no
reason to reply. There was nothing in this for either of them, yet
she was already smiling as she glanced down at her phone.

    She froze in shock as she read her one-line email from Laurie
Swanson: *I need to talk to you about Naomi.*

    She hadn't expected him to reply. Her email had been a feverish
last attempt to do her best by Naomi; an attempt she hadn't seriously believed would pay off. She felt slightly sick. It was one
thing to play Internet detective in the safety of her kitchen.
Suddenly, it felt alarmingly real. Swallowing down her nerves
she typed back: *Tomorrow is my day off. Is that too soon?*

She was still clutching her phone when Laurie's reply popped up on her screen. *Can you come now? I live near Wolfson College on Garford Road.* And he gave her his house number.

It was after eleven p.m. Too late to be visiting an unknown man by herself. Luckily, Anna had a solution. *How are you with dogs?*

Bonnie was delighted to be taken out for an unscheduled late-night walk. She pattered along beside Anna, tail waving, enjoying the night smells. Her calm acceptance of their adventure helped Anna to feel less freaked about her forthcoming encounter with a possibly mentally fragile Laurie Swanson. His reply to her dog inquiry had been reassuring. *Love them. Bring as many as you like.* It didn't seem like the response of a devious sex killer.

All the same as she walked up the path to his house she felt her mouth go dry.

She pressed the bell and waited. A light came on in the hall, illuminating elaborate stained-glass panels in the door. After a moment or two, she dimly made out an approaching figure. The door was opened by a short stocky black woman wearing a nurse's pale-blue smock over navy trousers. 'You must be Anna Hopkins,' she said, smiling, and Anna heard the lilt of Jamaica in her voice. 'I'm Paulette. Let me take your coat then I'll show you through.'

That's when Anna realized that it was more than the nervous habits of a recluse that had made Laurie Swanson ask her to come to his house. 'He's having a good day,' Paulette said, lowering her voice. 'That's why he said to come round right away. He never knows, you see, how long a good spell will last.'

'I didn't know he was so ill. You're sure it's OK for me to visit so late?' Though she'd taken them off, Anna awkwardly held on to her parka and scarf.

'Of course, darling! Mr Swanson doesn't exactly keep normal hours nowadays, and it will do him the world of good to see you.' She smilingly took Anna's things.

'I probably shouldn't take my dog in, though,' Anna said, thinking of germs and lowered immune systems.

'You most certainly will!' Paulette said in a mock-stern voice. 'Mr Swanson is totally over the *moon* about seeing this dog. Don't you even think about disappointing the poor man now!'

She led them across polished blue and white tiles and gave a soft knock on a door that stood partly open. 'Your visitor's here, Mr Swanson,' she called, then turned to Anna. 'I'll only be in the next room if he needs anything,' she told her.

The room was lit with the kind of dim soothing light that Anna associated with a child's nursery. The first thing she saw was the raised lid of Laurie Swanson's grand piano faintly gleaming in the lamp light and its wing-like shadow projecting on to the wall behind. Then she caught a slight blur of movement to her left and saw the man in the hospital bed. Anna had tried to prepare herself, but Laurie Swanson's hollow-cheeked face shocked her nevertheless. Then he smiled, and she could see the young, vital Laurie looking back at her. 'Hello,' he said in an amused voice.

There was no established etiquette for this situation; two strangers, one clearly dying, meeting for the first time to discuss the murder of a third. Fortunately, Bonnie had her own ideas about manners. Trotting over to the bed she raised herself up on her hind paws so that her front paws rested on the bed, allowing the sick man to see and touch her. He let out a smothered exclamation. 'This isn't a dog, Ms Hopkins. This is a *wolf*!'

Anna probably would have liked Laurie Swanson anyway, but it was next to impossible, she thought, to dislike someone who responded so warmly to your dog. 'That's exactly what Naomi said the first time she saw her,' she told him, smiling. 'But Bonnie's actually a White Shepherd. I'm Anna, by the way. Bonnie got in first, before I could introduce us properly.'

Laurie slightly inclined his head. 'Thank you for coming, Anna. And please call me Laurie. Forgive me if I don't get up,' he added. 'I can still move around – with a bit of help, but once I'm installed in bed for the night it's a real pain in the arse to get me out again!'

His words were for Anna, but his eyes stayed fixed on Bonnie. He stroked her in the special soft place under her chin, eliciting her happy grumbling sound, then he buried his face in her fur and closed his eyes. 'She smells like peanut butter. My dog Barclay used to smell exactly like that.' He looked up, his face alight with pleasure, so that Anna could see the young fawn-like Laurie. His dark curly hair, his exquisite bone structure, the watchful intelligence in his eyes; all were exactly the same. 'Where did you get this wonderful dog?'

'From the local rescue centre. Before that she was doing a spot of rescuing herself, in Afghanistan.'

'Why does that not surprise me?' Laurie shook his head, smiling. 'Do you know that strange little story *Dean Spanley* by Lord Dunsany? Where he says there are only ever seven exceptional dogs at any one time? Well, Anna, I think you may have found one of the seven!'

Anna watched him fondling Bonnie's silky ears with hands that were prematurely bony and old. An intravenous cannula had been inserted into the back of his right hand; for pain relief, she thought, remembering her grandmother's last weeks of life. But Laurie was still only in his early forties, far too cruelly young to die.

There was an armchair beside his bed. Anna quietly seated herself and was surprised to feel herself relax. Despite the paraphernalia of illness – the unattached drip stand holding its bag of clear fluid (morphine, she thought), the tablets and medicines, an oxygen cylinder trailing tubes – this was a pleasant room; peaceful, even. Lighted candles on the hearth gave the impression of flickering firelight. A scent of white jasmine and mint from a pillar candle helped to relieve an underlying smell of antiseptic. The candles and the three or four shaded lamps gave enough muted light to make out dozens of framed paintings and drawings covering his walls. His bed was littered with pens and sheets of manuscript paper on which he'd been scribbling musical notation, and there was an iPod with an earpiece. Isadora was wrong, Anna thought. Laurie Swanson was still composing.

'I've got cancer of the liver.' Laurie's bony hand paused then resumed its rhythmic stroking. 'They say I could have another six months if I'm lucky, and as I've got a composition to finish, I've decided to be lucky.'

Anna saw no point in offering sympathy; it would just degrade them both. 'What's the composition?'

He shot her a humorous look. 'A requiem. Not my own! That would be just a bit too weird, wouldn't it?' Laurie stopped, his jokey expression gradually fading as he looked down at the sheets of scribbled-on manuscript paper scattered over his bed.

'Ironically, the day after I got my diagnosis, I started writing this.' He lightly touched the score. 'In a funny way it's set me free.'

'Now you just want to live every moment.'

He nodded. 'But you're here to talk about Naomi.'

Anna softly clicked her fingers to her dog. 'Down now, Bonnie.'

Bonnie obediently took herself off to the hearth rug for a snooze.

'You say you didn't know her long?' Laurie said.

She shook her head. 'We only had two conversations. But . . .' She swallowed. She didn't want to cause additional distress to such an ill man. 'I found her after she was killed.'

He closed his eyes, trying to absorb this new shock. 'What a mysterious universe we live in,' he said at last. 'All these invisible threads criss-crossing, and now here we are, you and I, in this room.' He opened his eyes and let out a sigh. 'Anna, I have to tell you that I'm scared the police have it totally wrong.'

'I'm worried about that too,' she told him.

'I have this terrible suspicion that Naomi—' Laurie's voice broke, and Anna carefully looked away until he felt able to continue. 'Oh, damn it!' he burst out. 'I don't know, maybe the meds are fucking with my head! But the day before Naomi died, I told her something that only one other person – one other *living* person – knows. I'm terrified that's why she was murdered.'

Anna stared at him, stricken. 'The night before Naomi died she left me a message,' she said, keeping her voice low. 'She said she'd had an amazing interview with someone and found out something mind-blowing. She said it was going to be a game-changer.'

'It was me. It *had* to be me.' Laurie's dark eyes blazed.

'Who is the other person?' Anna asked in the same low voice.

Laurie looked blank.

'You said only one other living person knew. Who was it?'

His face tightened. 'Eve Bloomfield.'

'Who is she?'

Laurie held up his fingers, ticking them off one by one. 'A bitterly disappointed woman? Owen Traherne's former PA? His fixer? Failed poet? Mistress in waiting? Take your pick.'

'She was in love with him?'

'She worshipped him, and she'd do absolutely anything to protect his memory.

'Including murder?' Anna had to fight to keep the disbelief out of her voice. Laurie was getting increasingly upset. She wasn't sure if he was completely rational. 'You've lost me,' she said in a gentler tone. 'Protect Owen's memory from what? What could he have done that was so terrible she'd have to kill someone to stop it getting out?'

'That's just it. It wasn't terrible at all. It was . . .'

Anna saw tears standing in his eyes. She had tired him out. She was just thinking how she could leave without hurting his feelings when he said, 'There's a box on the bookshelf, on the bottom shelf. Could you bring it over?'

It resembled an outsized wooden jewellery box, decorated in an elaborate mother of pearl design which Anna recognized as Moroccan, with a central star and lesser stars and stylized flowers arranged around it.

'Open it,' said Laurie, visibly trembling. 'Look inside.'

Anna found and released the catch and opened the lid. Inside the box was crammed with letters, cards, little drawings and what looked like several slim notebooks.

'There used to be more,' Laurie said. 'These are the ones I couldn't bear to destroy. Take them out and read them,' he told her. 'Please, I need you to see them. No one's ever seen them, even Naomi.'

Anna tentatively picked one out, a short handwritten note. *'Dearest, darling, most beloved Laurie.'* These endearments were followed by a single paragraph about seeing a young hare in the fields . *'And I remembered the young injured hare you found in Norfolk that time, and how it woke in the night and came to find you in your bed.'* The note was signed *'your Owen'*. Keeping her eyes lowered, and hoping that Laurie couldn't see her startled face, Anna picked another letter at random. It was a love poem. It was *the* love poem. *'Again and again I let myself be lured back . . .'*

'Everyone thinks Owen wrote that to Audrey,' Laurie said.

Anna finally felt able to look him in the eye. 'But it was to you.' She couldn't deny that Laurie's revelation had surprised her. Like Kirsty, Isadora and everyone else, she had bought the

popular myth of Owen Traherne as the rampantly heterosexual
lover-poet who constantly had affairs but always came back –
was 'lured' back – to his beautiful siren-like Audrey. Not so
much a myth as an outright lie, she thought.

'How long were you and Owen . . .?' She didn't know how
to phrase her question.

'Fifteen years,' he said. 'From three months before I turned
sixteen until his death ten years ago.'

Anna did her best to keep her expression neutral as she registered that Owen Traherne had not only had a clandestine gay
love affair, but he'd also had a love affair with an under-age boy.
She couldn't have succeeded though because he said quickly, 'It
wasn't like it sounds. I think I'd always known I was gay, certainly
from my early teens. And believe it or not I never had any illu-
sions about Owen.' Laurie gave a rueful smile. 'Even when I
was a besotted adolescent in the grip of raging hormones I pretty
much knew what I was getting into. I'd grown up around that
man, Anna. I knew he was a selfish egomaniac, that he drank
too much, that he was careless with his own talent, that he'd
been spoiled – paralysed, really – by all that early adulation he
had from the critics when he was just starting out. But I loved
him. I loved Owen body and soul.'

Laurie held her gaze, willing her to understand. 'And OK,
part of me hated that he was too weak, too attached to his image
to acknowledge our love in public. But in another way I didn't
care, because when we were together it was like this private
magic world that just the two of us inhabited together.' He shook
his head. 'I know I must sound like the deluded other woman!
But I believe I had the best of Owen. Everything that was good
and fine in him, everything he'd hoped and dreamed he would
grow up to be, when he was enduring his shitty childhood in
that grim back street in Cardiff, came alive in him again when
he was with me.'

'But how could you bear to keep your relationship hidden for
so long?' Anna asked.

'Owen believed that it would kill Audrey if she found out.
She'd always been emotionally fragile. Then, after she died, you
know, the way she did—' He briefly closed his eyes again before
continuing. 'Their son Huw went off the rails for a while, and

Owen was worried that telling him would tip him completely over the edge.'

'But you think Eve knew?' Anna says.

'She had to know!' Laurie said angrily. 'She controlled his diary. I think she thought she controlled his life. She made all his travel arrangements, she knew where he was and when and with whom. In her head I think she saw herself as closer to him even than Audrey.'

'But if she knew about you and Owen, how could she ever believe—?'

His face twisted with distress. 'Oh, I was just the queer boy, an aberration, didn't count. She's unstable, Anna. I've seen her lose it. You know she actually accosted Naomi?' He passed his tongue over his lips. 'Sorry, mouth's getting dry.'

Anna poured him water from a jug so he could drink, and then replaced the glass on his nightstand. Casting around for a less distressing topic she said, 'I had to study some of Owen Traherne's poems for A level. I don't remember much from my English lessons, but I do remember those poems, they were so strong.'

He nodded. 'At his best he's up there with Heaney and Hughes.'

'Have you got a favourite poem of Owen's?'

'"The Tree of Sorrows",' Laurie said without the slightest hesitation.

'I think that's in the collected love poems,' Anna said, remembering the ominous tree with its tiny shimmering scrolls instead of leaves. 'I was at the launch,' she explained.

'I heard they were publishing them all in one collection,' Laurie said. 'I find it interesting though that they categorized "The Tree of Sorrows" as a love poem.'

'You don't agree?'

'Let's just say it's not the kind people read at weddings,' he said with a wry grin. 'I set it to music, actually,' he added. 'I might play it for you one day if you come again.'

'I'd like that,' Anna said.

They fell silent for a few moments, then Anna asked, 'How did you come to know Naomi?'

'She'd seen pictures of me with the Trahernes on family holidays and figured out that I'd been a school friend of Huw's. My parents were mostly overseas, and Huw's house in Oxford had become like my second home. Anyway, about eighteen months ago Naomi tracked me down. She was hoping I might be able to offer a new slant on the Trahernes for Kit's book. I refused.' He pulled a face. 'I'm sure you can understand why.'

'Yes, I can,' she said very softly.

'Then it became increasingly obvious that recent symptoms I'd been trying so hard to ignore weren't another manifestation of my long-term anxiety disorder or whatever my psychiatrists called it. On top of everything else I was genuinely physically ill. Unfortunately, by then it was too late.'

'I'm sorry,' she said, and meant it from the bottom of her heart.

'Don't be.' He smiled without a trace of self pity. 'It turns out that being close to death brings a certain unexpected clarity. It hit me that Kit's book was out there pedalling all these lies about Owen – who he was, what his writing was about. Both Owen and Audrey are dead. Huw is an adult now with a wife of his own – who absolutely can't stand me, by the way.' He grimaced. 'Though, to be honest, after our teens Huw and I had already started to drift apart.'

'Because you had to keep your relationship with Owen secret?' Anna said.

'That was a contributing factor,' Laurie said with a sigh. 'But after Audrey killed herself, there was a period when Huw was extremely vulnerable, and I suspect I was a painful reminder of happier times. He got in with a rather unpleasant crowd. I'm sure you know the type – over-indulged, over-privileged, avid for any new thrill or sensation. Anyway, soon afterwards, he met Sara and became the pillar of shining rectitude that he is today, but ever since then . . . Fuck, completely lost my thread,' he said abruptly. He passed his hand across his eyes.

'You were telling me that dying brings new clarity,' Anna said quietly.

He flashed a tired but humorous smile. 'Not so good for the short-term memory though, apparently! But yes, I'd been basing my life on the premise that my relationship with Owen had to be hidden at all costs from people who would otherwise be badly hurt. Then it dawned on me that there was nobody left to be hurt.'

'Is that why you got in touch with Naomi? You wanted the world to know the real Owen.'

'No. Christ, no! It was more like I was desperate to share it with one other person. That way it wasn't just some story in my head. I needed one other person to know it was real.'

'Weren't you, I don't know, worried Naomi might go public with yours and Owen's story? I mean, something like that could have made her career, and who could blame her?'

'That was the wonderful thing about Naomi. Researcher or not she had complete integrity. She knew when a secret had to be kept.'

'She was an amazing person,' Anna agreed warmly. 'You know, she did this lovely thing. Did you feel those little scars Bonnie's got under her coat? Naomi had only just met me, but she offered to do some digging around, and she found out that Bonnie used to belong to a soldier – a Navy SEAL, actually – who was serving in Afghanistan. She got hurt trying to protect a small child.'

Sensing that she was being talked about, Bonnie ambled over to them, before collapsing with a contented sigh at Anna's feet. 'Past her bedtime,' Anna said. 'Probably past yours too?' she suggested.

'Let me tell you this one last thing,' he begged.

'OK, then we really must go and let you rest.'

Laurie took a breath. 'After Naomi's third or fourth visit, Eve was lying in wait for her. I mean literally skulking in the bushes. She started ranting about how Naomi wanted to dirty Owen's name with "that perverted filth". She'd already refused to cooperate on the biography with Naomi and Kit.'

'Because she considered Owen was hers?' Anna suggested.

'Fuck knows,' said Laurie. 'Naomi just jumped in her car and drove off, leaving her ranting. Next time she visited she asked me what Eve could have meant, and that's when I told her. Owen loved me, and I loved him. I wasn't just the quirky bachelor people asked to dinner just to make up the numbers. I was in a passionate relationship with another man for over fifteen years. Along with music, Owen was my life.'

Anna said, frowning, 'I can see why you might suspect Eve. But she must be in her sixties at least—'

Laurie cut her off. 'I know! I sound like a ridiculous old queen!

I don't have a shred of evidence. It's just this horrible gut feeling that won't go away. All I know is Eve threatened Naomi, and now Naomi's dead.' His lower lip trembled. 'I'm not asking you to go to the police. I don't even know what I'm asking.' He lay back on his pillows, fighting tears. 'I'm being pathetic, sorry.'

At that moment Paulette knocked and came in. If she was dismayed by the sight of Laurie weeping, she hid it well. She said softly, 'Mr Swanson, darling, you need to get some rest now.'

'In a minute,' he promised. 'I need to ask Anna something.' He dashed away his tears. 'I need you to keep this box for me, Anna. Paulette, could you please find a bag so Anna can carry it home? Then I'll rest for as long as you like.'

'So you say,' Paulette said in a disbelieving voice, but she went to find a bag.

Anna was stunned. 'I can't take something so precious. You don't even know me.'

He managed a smile. 'Naomi met you how many times?'

'Just twice,' Anna said.

'But she felt the kind of instant connection that made her willing to go out on a limb for you? I trust that, and I trust Naomi.' Laurie closed the lid of the box, and she saw his hands tremble. 'I need these to be safe, Anna. If I die and Eve gets her hands on them . . .'

Seeing he was on the verge of breaking down again, Anna said quickly, 'I'll take them because you asked. But if you decide you want them again, I'll bring them straight over, day or night. Is that a deal?'

'I might pretend I want them.' Laurie's face was suddenly drawn with pain. 'Just to trick you into bringing your beautiful Bonnie to visit me.'

'You won't have to trick me,' she told him. 'I'll bring her back to see you very soon, I promise.'

As Paulette showed her out, Anna said, 'Is he as bad as he looks?'

'I won't lie to you, darling. He's bad. But he's got his requiem to finish, that's keeping him going at the moment. And he hasn't needed any morphine so far today, so you picked a good day. I'm glad you came,' Paulette added with genuine warmth. 'I know he's tired himself out talking, but I could see you'd put his mind to rest about something.'

Anna was surprised and touched. 'If that's true I'm glad.'

Walking back to Park Town carrying Laurie's box with his precious papers, Anna felt that she had made a new friend. Laurie had trusted her with a secret that he had felt honour-bound to keep all his adult life, and he'd done it within a few minutes of meeting her. Maybe she could be this woman with the dog who had finally learned how to make friends?

And this was all because of Naomi Evans. Because of Naomi, all these new people were suddenly being pulled into Anna's orbit: Tansy and Isadora, Jake, Kit and now Laurie Swanson. As she walked through the dark silent streets with her White Shepherd at her side, Anna found herself imagining that the energy which had once been Naomi had not, after all, been destroyed on Port Meadow. Like an exploding star, the energy of her passing was still expanding, touching all their lives, reshaping their stories. It was thrilling and also frightening because Anna didn't know where it was going to end.

TEN

She shot up in bed gasping and shaking. Her room was pitch dark, the kind of darkness that's so dense it almost has a taste. Anna fumbled for her phone so she could see the time. She'd been asleep for five minutes max. She could still feel the blast of heat as Laurie Swanson's box and everything in it went up in a sheet of white-hot flame. Her heart pounded in her chest. It was only a dream, but it had shown her something that her conscious mind had overlooked: the incendiary nature of Laurie's secret. Suppose Eve Bloomfield got hold of those papers, or some mercenary media hack? Anna knew what it was like to have tabloid newspapers hounding you. She didn't think they'd take pity on Laurie's frailty, any more than they'd had pity on a traumatized teenage girl.

She swung her legs out of bed. She took her flannel robe from its hook on the door, pulled on a pair of soft wool socks and hurried downstairs. When she turned on the light she was ridiculously relieved to see Laurie's box unharmed exactly where she'd left it on the kitchen table.

Bonnie's dark-rimmed eyes appeared to be tracking Anna's movements as she heated milk in a pan, stirred in spoonfuls of drinking chocolate and poured everything into a flask. But Anna wasn't convinced she was genuinely awake, as her White Shepherd often slept with her eyes partly open. 'Want to keep me company?' she asked, picking up the box and the flask.

One hundred per cent awake now, Bonnie bounded out of her basket and followed Anna upstairs and into her study, a room she had never been allowed inside. She had a quick sniff around then settled down in her favourite sphinx position, interested and alert as Anna switched on her printer and her desktop computer. Anna removed Owen's letters and cards from the box, leaving the notebooks till last.

Although Laurie had invited – *begged* – her to read his letters, Anna had no desire to go pawing through other people's love

lives. She just wanted to scan everything on to her hard drive.
That way if something happened to the originals, there would at
least be copies. But as she scanned the papers that represented
everything that was most precious in Laurie's life, a passage
jumped out:

> I remember that first time, the light of a midsummer
> morning, catching fine gold hairs on your arms so that you
> looked as if you'd been dusted with pollen. I still couldn't
> believe what you were offering. And so it was you who
> made the first move; you shyly reached for me and—

Cheeks burning, Anna hastily turned to the next page and found
an explicit, though exquisite, drawing of an obviously adolescent
Laurie. This was flammable stuff all right. It didn't bother her
that Owen had belatedly discovered he was gay. It did disturb her
that he'd had sex with an under-age boy. Just a few weeks under-
age it was true, and if Laurie had been experimenting sexually
with someone his own age – Huw, for instance – Anna wouldn't
have batted an eyelash. But Owen had been in *loco parentis* to
Laurie while his own parents were overseas. Owen was Laurie's
friend's father and a well-respected poet. Yet he'd described their
first encounter as if *he* was the shy fumbling virgin and Laurie
the strangely knowing boy who had initiated it.

Laurie had told Anna he knew what he was getting into when
he fell in love with Owen. Thinking of some of the things she'd
got into at fifteen, she doubted it. Had he genuinely appreciated
the devil's bargain he'd made? That he'd be forced to live a lie
for the rest of Owen's life – and beyond? Anna wondered if,
having given up so much for Owen, Laurie had felt the need to
rewrite history, making something magical out of something that
was actually exploitative, sordid and cruel.

But then Anna would come across a passage of such naked
vulnerability that she was moved despite herself:

> With you I could be beautiful and innocent again. No, not
> 'again'. Nobody who grew up in my household could be
> either of those things. You gave me back my original face,
> Laurie. You gave me back my body and with it my soul.

Anna no longer knew that she was tired. She was only aware of the whirring of the scanner and the gradually diminishing pile of pages, punctuated by reviving swigs of hot chocolate. At four a.m. she started on Owen's notebooks. The first notebook initially seemed to consist only of rough jottings, phrases, ideas for poems, observations from the natural world, small sketches. But five or six pages in, it had turned into an unofficial diary that Owen had started confiding in when work or family kept him away from Laurie.

> Do you remember that afternoon when I had to pick you up from school? It was the first time I'd really talked to you alone. You'd received a letter from your father, haranguing you about your future, that music was no career for a Swanson. You just poured it all out. Your face was white, pinched. I felt such rage at this blind blustering bullying man, and I had this shocking and overwhelming need to protect you from all future hurt. That was the day I began to love you.

The last notebook was only half full, its scrawled entries often incoherent. Anna suspected Owen had been drunk when he'd written most of them. He talked about his guilt about Audrey, his son, his inability to write. His publisher was waiting, increasingly impatiently for new poems for a long delayed collection. He felt he was being punished – for betraying his family with his muse, Laurie. Laurie, a successful young composer by this time, seemed to have given him good advice.

> Laurie wants me to go to some writers' retreat in the States. He says I've made a kind of false god out of my younger self, the golden boy poet. He says I'm trying to re-enact my past successes instead of writing from my guts. 'You need silence. You need birds and trees and rivers. Then you'll hear the poems singing in your head the way you used to do.' The power of his belief in me almost brought me to my knees. I felt that I would give anything to be the man he described, to shed that fraudulent public persona and be reborn as the man and poet I always—

Something – Anna thought it was red wine – had been splattered across the last few words, rendering them illegible. Laurie had told Anna that Owen had never found the courage to come out as his lover. But in his last entry she felt Owen's desperate longing to be worthy of Laurie's love.

She closed the notebook and sat down on the floor of her study, holding the notebook against her robe. Her head ached. A police car went wailing down the Banbury Road, then the silence closed in again. It was beginning to get light. She felt increasingly disturbed, and she didn't understand why, except that this all felt too desperately *real* in the way the Albanian gang threat had not. It was painful to admit, but even her own traumatic memories were gradually being subsumed into a kind of fiction. She clung to them because it was all she had left.

But Laurie was here and now. She needed to decide what to do with his secret papers. She had thought she might talk to him about storing the originals somewhere secure like a bank. But Paulette had told Anna she'd seen him on a good day. Next time she visited he might be zonked out on morphine, or his illness might take a turn for the worse. When she thought back, she realized that Laurie had given her his papers like someone who needed to be free from a heavy burden. He had handed this huge responsibility over to Anna, and she wasn't sure if she could deal with it alone. She knew she couldn't drag her grandfather, her usual go-to person, into this. But she thought she could ask Tansy and Isadora. For one thing they were already involved. They were both open-minded women who didn't shock easily, didn't worry about convention. She checked the time. It was only five a.m. Much too early to call.

Anna's eyes were hot and gritty from lack of sleep, but her mind was buzzing, her entire body thrumming with adrenalin. *Tired but wired*, her therapist used to call it. There had been a girl in Anna's therapy group who was compelled to cut herself when her demons became too all-powerful to bear. Anna thought she'd been lucky in that she'd found a less violent coping strategy. And she had decided to offer it as a shared tool to help Laurie. This thought exhilarated and terrified her. She flew across the landing to find her phone, firing off a one sentence text to Tansy before she could lose her nerve. Then she sat down at her computer and typed the first name into the search engine. If Tansy and Isadora accepted her invitation, she wanted to have everything ready and waiting.

They arrived in the early evening after Tansy had finished work for the day. Tansy had freed her curls from her waitress's topknot and was carrying a distinctive Marmalade carrier bag. She had texted Anna saying not to bother with food as she'd bring left-overs from the cafe. Anna hadn't liked to say she hadn't even thought of bothering with food. Isadora, dressed in some kind of fringed Navajo blanket over wide-legged trousers, had brought two bottles of red wine.

'Come in, please,' Anna said, knowing she was supposed to put her guests at their ease, but feeling so freaked she could barely even smile. Anna never invited anyone to her home. Her last visitor (not counting Jake, who had somehow slipped under her radar) was the lady who came to do the home check for Bonnie. Anna had cleaned manically for about a week beforehand. She'd felt as if her entire life depended on giving an Oscar-winning performance as a responsible future dog owner. She had that same desperate do or die feeling tonight, but with the added terror of complete exposure because this wasn't a performance. Tansy and Isadora were going to see the real Anna, a person almost nobody had ever got to meet.

'We're in here.' Anna showed them into the sitting room. There was a stunned silence as the women took in the murder-board she'd set up bang in the middle.

'Holy shit,' Tansy breathed. 'I thought only serial killers had these!'

'I'll explain about that in a minute,' Anna said, carefully avoiding their eyes. 'But first, can I get anyone a gin and tonic?'

In the icy grip of panic she could barely remember why she'd invited them. Her private and public lives were converging. Her entire world was about to implode. She vaguely heard Isadora exclaim, 'Bombay Sapphire, one of my favourite gins. Do let me pour them, darling. I'm the gin and tonic queen.'

And Tansy asked, 'And can you just point me in the direction of your kitchen so this food can be out of the way?'

Anna and Isadora made polite conversation while Tansy went

away and returned. They all found somewhere to sit and sip their drinks. They were being far more polite with each other than normal, but as the minutes ticked past it slowly dawned on Anna that no one was about to die simply from being here with her – not tonight, anyway.

She started talking, relieved to hear her voice sounding almost like her usual self. 'OK, I should probably tell you why I've asked you to come round. The thing is, I went to visit Laurie Swanson late last night.' Anna pressed on through their surprised exclamations. 'I managed to track him down on the Internet. It was your composer, Isadora. He lives in North Oxford, and he's very sick. In fact, he's dying. Anyway, he told me something – something he's had to keep secret for more than half his lifetime.' She swallowed. 'He said he'd only told one other living person. He told Naomi the night before she was killed.' She saw their shocked expressions, but kept on talking. She needed them to know everything she knew. 'Before I left he gave me that box.' She pointed to her coffee table where she had deliberately placed it for them to see. Exhibit A.

'Inside, there are letters and drawings that Owen Traherne sent to Laurie over the years, plus some of his old notebooks. I got a bit freaked about having them here in my house – you'll understand why in a minute – so I scanned them all on to my hard drive. I also copied some of his material to show you.' She handed them each a printout. 'I'm sorry to be so school teacherish, but there's too much stuff to just explain.' She took a breath. 'I know I can trust you not to let anything you read here go beyond this room.'

She made herself sit quietly. She wanted Isadora and Tansy to form their own opinions about the contents of Laurie's box. She heard Isadora's sudden sharp intake of breath, then saw her go over to mix herself a second gin and tonic.

Tansy seemed to be counting on her fingers. Anna heard her whisper, 'No *way*.'

Isadora knocked back a good third of her second gin, then set her glass down on Anna's hearth. 'It's not often that I'm lost for words, Anna, but I am utterly stunned by what I've read here today.'

'You never suspected that Owen was gay?' Anna said.

'Never *once!*' Isadora said emphatically. 'I have the most *phenomenally* efficient gaydar, and I had absolutely NO idea that Owen was anything other than one hundred per cent heterosexual. I do remember a drinks party at Somerville and hearing whispers that he might be having an affair with his secretary. But one was *always* hearing whispers of Owen's affairs,' she added carelessly. 'One never took them at all seriously because everyone knew that Owen always went back to Audrey.'

'Tell Tansy what you told me about Audrey,' Anna said.

Isadora frowned. 'What did I say?'

'That she was beautiful but—'

'Oh, that! Yes, she was almost completely absent. Like Sleeping Beauty waiting for the prince to wake her with a kiss. Of course now, with hindsight, one wonders whether if she had married a less conflicted man . . .'

'Did you ever meet Owen's secretary?' Tansy asked.

'Several times,' Isadora said.

'What was she like?'

'A cross between Wallace Simpson and Cruella De Vil,' Isadora said promptly. 'One of those brittle calorie-counting women. Mouth like a scarlet slash.'

'I've printed out a picture,' Anna said. She went over to the montage she had carefully constructed. 'As you can see, I've put up pictures of everyone I can think of whose lives touched Laurie's and Owen's.'

After Tansy's initial nervous reaction, she and Isadora hadn't said another word about the murder board Anna had created using a whiteboard propped up on an old easel of her grandfather's. She wasn't sure if this was because they were too polite, or because they were too alarmed. Either way, it was feeling increasingly like the metaphorical elephant in the room.

She took a deep breath. 'This is the only way I know to make sense of all this stuff in my head. I have to put everything where I can physically see it, so I can literally put my finger on each and every possible connection. For instance, this is Eve Bloomfield, who Isadora was just talking about.' Anna lightly touched Eve's picture. She had found two photographs: one of a younger Eve from the time when she'd been a budding poet in New England, and another of her after she'd turned into Cruella De Vil. The younger Eve had long dark hair that fell over the shoulders of her black Juliette Gréco style polo-neck sweater. Her soulful dark eyes suggested wounded intelligence mixed, Anna thought, with secret longing.

The second picture showed an older embittered Eve, her severely bobbed hair dyed an unnatural black, looking up at someone or something just out of shot. A younger woman in that pose might seem appealingly vulnerable. Eve just looked disturbingly untethered. Her scarlet lipstick only heightened the impression of someone who was inexorably coming undone. Anna had connected both pictures to Laurie's and Naomi's photographs with a whirling vortex of crayoned arrows.

'I don't know, myself, if Eve is capable of murder. But Laurie says she's completely unhinged when it comes to Owen or his reputation. So, OK, even Laurie's admitted that his meds might be clouding his judgement, but I stuck her on the board because I believe she represents a possible threat to Laurie's mental state during his last months of life.' She traced along an arrow to Laurie's photo. 'This is Laurie Swanson, who I went to see last night,' she said for Tansy's benefit. She'd chosen the picture of him playing music with the street children in Brazil. She chose it because it showed him both as a musician and someone capable of adventures, not permanently in Owen's shadow.

Tansy and Isadora had come over to study the photographs.

'Who are these two?' Tansy said.

'That's Owen's son Huw and his wife Sara,' Anna said.

Tansy ran her finger lightly over the montage, finally stopping at Naomi. Anna had taken the picture from one of Naomi's social media pages. It showed her at a fancy dress party dressed as Groucho Marx.

Anna's mouth was suddenly dry. It scared her that she couldn't tell what the others were thinking. She picked up her glass and found it empty.

'Let me fill you up, darling,' said Isadora.

'I know we agreed we'd lay it to rest . . .' Anna began.

'That was before you spoke to Laurie,' Tansy said immediately.

'And before you found out what Naomi was so excited about,' Isadora added.

So they didn't think she was nuts. Anna felt sufficiently encouraged to continue. 'Basically, what I want to know is: what now? Might Laurie be right, or even half right? Might his secret life with Owen have a bearing on Naomi's murder?'

'It certainly suggests a new motive,' Isadora said.

'So you don't think I'm just being paranoid then?' Anna asked anxiously.

Tansy said, 'Ever see that movie *Strange Days*? "It's not about are you paranoid, but are you paranoid enough?"'

'I loved that movie,' Anna said.

'Can we please eat soon?' Tansy asked plaintively. 'I'm starving, and the gin is making my head really swimmy.'

Downstairs in Anna's kitchen, Tansy quickly microwaved any dishes that needed reheating, while Anna fetched cutlery and plates, plus serving bowls for all the leftover salads. Tansy had already uncorked Isadora's wine and found where Anna kept her glasses. 'OK, everybody! Sit down and help yourselves.'

Anna was surprised to find she was ravenous. After a while she glanced up from her plate to find Tansy watching her expectantly. She seemed to be waiting for Anna to say something, so she said shyly, 'This is wonderful food, Tansy, thank you.'

'You're welcome! I never catered a murder investigation before.' Tansy pulled a face at Anna. 'Look, I'm really glad you asked us round, but I've just worked a double shift, so I'm going to have to go home to crash in about an hour. So is it OK if we continue talking about why we're here while we eat? Because I think I know the perfect person to help us.'

'No,' Anna said firmly. 'You can't involve Sergeant Goodhart.'

'Why not? I think we can trust him, even if he is a cop.'

'No!' Anna repeated, and this time her voice had an edge. 'This material is too sensitive to share with anybody else. It would be like stripping Laurie's life naked.' *And Owen's*, she thought. She had risked trusting Isadora and Tansy, but she couldn't expose Laurie to Sergeant Goodhart or to anyone else when there'd be no guarantee his privacy would be respected. Anna laid down her fork, her appetite suddenly gone. 'We did our best for Naomi,' she said, trying to soften her voice. 'We tried to lay her to rest and just succeeded in stirring up even more questions. But Naomi's dead and Laurie is still alive, and he's alone and ill! He's the one who needs our help now.'

'You mean it's down to us?' Isadora sounded dismayed.

'Laurie hasn't got anybody else,' Anna told her. 'He only ever had Owen, and Owen's dead. If he's right about Eve, even if there's only a one per cent chance that Owen's mad, sixty-plus PA attacked Naomi, we can't risk not helping.'

'I suppose . . .' Tansy's voice trailed off.

'What?' said Anna.

'Being sixty-plus needn't put someone totally out of the frame. Eve could have paid someone to – you know.'

'You're not suggesting it was a contract killing?' Isadora sounded disbelieving.

'Why not?' Tansy said. 'If it was a professional hit that might explain why there wasn't any DNA.'

'If Eve did have Naomi murdered, Laurie might be next on her list,' Anna said.

At the moment she made it, her comment seemed to follow naturally from Tansy's talk of hit-men; then she mentally replayed what she'd said and felt herself go hot and cold. She sounded deranged! She was a deranged woman who created murder boards and put them on display; as if that could keep Laurie safe! As if Anna had ever had any influence on the world or its chaotic events!

'What are you thinking, darling?'

Startled, Anna glanced up to see Isadora watching her with concern.

She swallowed. 'I sound like I'm treating Naomi's murder like it's part of some kind of game. I don't want to do that. I don't mean to be disrespectful to Naomi's memory.' Anna knew she was really asking to be reassured about all those other things that Isadora and Tansy couldn't and wouldn't ever know – her cupboard of horrors; her life.

Isadora leaned forward. Her voice was quietly passionate. 'No, this is something real, my darling, something big. I haven't slept properly, you know, since we found Naomi. I can't forgive myself that we arrived too late to save her. This is the only thing I can do for Naomi now – and for myself.'

Tansy said softly looking at Anna. 'Everyone carries secret

stuff around. Things we wish we could change.' There was a long, highly-charged silence, then in the same soft voice, Tansy said, 'Aren't you ever going to tell us about what happened?'

She can't ask me that. No one's allowed to ask me that, Anna thought. Then she felt a rush of relief, as if an invisible knot had come undone, and she thought, *Why not?* They had to trust each other. If they couldn't be their real selves, they'd be lost.

She made herself meet Tansy's eyes. 'I haven't slept for twenty-four hours. It'll have to be the short version.'

Tansy just nodded. Isadora pushed her plate away and rested her elbows on the table, her fingers interlaced. Anna went to sit on the floor beside Bonnie, her back to the French windows. She started to talk, careful not to look at their faces.

'When I was sixteen I was angry all the time. I hated my parents. I hated Oxford. I did a lot of stupid, self destructive things. One day I stormed out after a row. Back then I saw storming out as like my basic human right. I didn't care that it was my little sister Lottie's sixth birthday. I was so wrapped up in myself, I didn't even bother to let anyone know where I'd gone. I went to Natalie's house. Her mother pretty much let her do what she liked, and we got really stoned. Then I borrowed some clothes from Nat and we went out clubbing. I was hoping Max would be there. Any energy I had left over from being angry I spent thinking up ways I could accidentally run into Max. At last he showed up, and we left the club together. We spent a couple of hours getting stoned in his car. Then we had a fight about something and I stormed off.'

Anna shot a glance at the women and forced herself to keep talking. 'I walked all the way back to our house in North Oxford. Someone had tied pink balloons to the handle, and I remembered it was my sister's birthday. I let myself in with my key. I tiptoed upstairs in the dark. I'd decided to get into bed with Lottie so I could tell her happy birthday. I smelled of booze and dope. I was completely off my face. Lottie's door was open. I could see the glow of her night light.'

Anna took a shaky breath before she went on. 'It was the kind of night light that has fairy-tale cut outs. Lottie's had a castle and a princess and unicorns. I walked in and I could – I could see all these cute fairy-tale figures revolving around the room, and then I saw all the blood, dark-red blood, splashed over the walls and soaking into her little flowery quilt. I couldn't make sense of it. I ran out, and I crashed into someone on the landing. I said, 'Dad!' But it wasn't my dad. It was somebody who didn't belong in our house. He had a knife.' Anna's hand went to her stomach. 'I managed to get away. I ran out of the house to find help. But it was already too late. Everyone was dead.' She gave a tight nod. 'That's what happened.'

That's why Anna didn't have friends or lovers. Once she'd spoken the truth out loud, she couldn't bear the sight of them. But when she finally dared to look into the women's faces, it came to her that if either of them had told her the story she had just told them, she would have looked every bit as shocked and distressed as they were looking now.

'Now will you help me help Laurie?' she asked.

ELEVEN

'I'm just saying, I'm not entirely comfortable that you can find out people's private information via these sinister kinds of websites,' said Isadora. Anna shifted her mobile to the crook of her neck while she hunted for her purse. She could hear water thundering into Isadora's stainless steel sink, followed by the clattering sound of her antiquated electric kettle starting to heat up. Further off, Hero gave a short sharp bark. 'Shut UP, Hero,' Isadora bellowed.

'I'm not remotely comfortable with it,' Anna almost snapped as she paid for her take-out coffee. She had adopted the morally convenient viewpoint that these websites existed; she couldn't un-invent them, and they might help her turn up the information she craved. But Isadora's instinctive distaste rattled her more than she liked to admit.

Isadora's voice softened. 'I know, darling. I do understand that we have to live in the world as it is. Is that a police car going past?'

'Ambulance,' Anna corrected. 'I'm on my way to work.'

'Think of me later at the dentist.' Isadora's tone turned plaintive. 'Mr Ashtiani is so handsome, and he has the most perfect teeth. God knows what he thinks of my terrible old gnashers. Take my advice, darling, and never get old. All the good stuff is behind you, and there is nothing but *utter* humiliation ahead.'

'You're only in your sixties!' Anna reminded her.

'My *late* sixties,' Isadora said in a voice of doom.

'It's just a number,' Anna said, gratefully taking a hit of her scalding latte. 'Seriously, you've got plenty of good surprises still to come!'

'It's very lovely of you to say so,' Isadora said, unconvinced. 'Though I must say my life has become considerably less dreary since I met you and Tansy,' she added, with that characteristic frankness which always took Anna's breath away.

Anna ended her call and carried on down the Cornmarket,

sipping at her latte. She'd reached the stage of sleep deprivation where she needed a constant input of caffeine just to walk in a straight line. She'd been too wired to sleep last night. She'd taken a huge risk and was still expecting it to blow up in her face. In the end, Anna's 'murder board party', as Tansy kept calling it, had gone on till late. After their meal, they'd gone upstairs with their coffee, and Tansy had seemed to forget all about her need to go home and sleep. She'd tucked herself comfortably into a corner of a sofa, making increasingly off-the-wall suggestions for ways to protect Laurie. Anna couldn't remember how or when Isadora's 'sinister websites' had entered the conversation. She had been slightly miffed to find out that Tansy not only knew all about the Dark Net, but also how to access it. Between them they had tracked down Eve Bloomfield's contact details. Tansy had promptly put the address into her phone and said, 'I'll get on this tomorrow. I'm off work all day. I'll ask my mum if I can borrow her car, then I'll drive over and see what I can sniff out.'

'Are you sure that's wise?' Isadora had asked.

'Why not! I've always wanted to go on a stake-out.' Tansy had been aglow with excitement and alcohol, also possibly the sugar-loaded chocolate brownies Anna had offered around as a nod towards dessert.

'It's just that if Eve really *did* murder Naomi, it might be wiser not to go alone. I'd come with you, darling, but I've got various appointments tomorrow.'

Tansy had given a scornful snort. 'I might be a vegan, but I know how to fight nasty if I have to, Isadora, trust me!'

Remembering this conversation as she turned into the High, Anna flashed back to a traumatized Tansy vomiting into a hedge. She was finding it hard to get a proper fix on Tansy Lavelle, the vegan waitress who understood the intimate workings of the Dark Net and talked about 'fighting nasty'.

But then how much did Anna's new friends really know about Anna? She thought of everything she'd held back last night. Some things were too evil to be told. Her grandfather had told her that after his own father came home from the killing fields of the First World War he never spoke of it again. He was protecting his wife and his two little boys the only way he knew, Anna thought, and refusing to contaminate their home – their futures

– with the hellish knowledge he'd brought home. Instead he had elected to keep it all locked inside: his guilt and shame, his fear and shock. That way it stopped with him.

As usual Anna stopped in at the porters' lodge. Mr Boswell beckoned her up to his counter. 'I've been looking out for you,' he said in a low voice. 'Ms Costello came in as white as a sheet. I don't know what's up with her, but she looks like she could use a friend.' His pallid features had flushed with concern.

Anna heard her phone ping inside her bag. 'She's probably going down with something. But thanks for telling me.' The poker-faced porter wasn't normally given to overreacting. On the other hand, Kirsty wasn't given to having dramas at work. Nadine, on the other hand . . .

Postponing the moment when she'd have to encounter Nadine's latest Post-it explosion, Anna read Jake's text as she hurried under the ancient arch into the college gardens.

Looks like I'm coming to Oxford sooner rather than later. Any chance you can meet me for a drink?

Anna felt the confused churning that started up every time she tried to think about Jake McCaffrey. That churning was surely a warning in itself? Telling her there were just too many complications – and that's before Anna had factored in the depressing story of the not so ex. She mustn't let this man breeze in and out of her life like some southern-voiced Romeo. She would say a firm no to drinks, she decided, and after that she'd stop replying to his texts, no matter how entertaining.

She toiled up the stairs to the admin office. Unusually, the door was closed. She opened it and found Kirsty silently sobbing at her desk.

'Oh, I'm sorry,' Anna said, hastily backing out. 'Do you want me to go away again?'

Kirsty half-raised her head as if to say something, but only let out a defeated wail, like a small furry animal that had got itself caught in a trap.

'I'll make you some coffee. No, tea!' Anna corrected quickly. Her grandmother had been a believer in sweet tea for any form of human distress.

Kirsty made a weak flapping gesture.

'You don't want tea?' Anna translated. 'Why don't I pop out

and get us both some real coffee?' It would be her fourth this morning, and it was only nine a.m. She'd be lucky to have any functioning kidneys at this rate.

For the first time Kirsty sat up. She was exactly as white as Mr Boswell had described, except for her eyes which were so red and swollen that she must have been crying all night. 'I found some pictures on Jason's phone,' she said hoarsely. She jumped up from her desk. 'I'm going to be sick!' She fled across the landing, and Anna heard vomiting sounds. After a while she came back, watery eyed and trembling. 'Sorry to be so gross. I was hoping I'd stopped.'

Anna kept a small bottle of mineral water in her messenger bag. She fished it out, unscrewed the top and set it on Kirsty's desk. 'You might just want to take a few sips to start with,' she suggested. 'Then tell me about Jason's pictures.' Anna was vaguely alarmed at this super-competent version of herself who could go without sleep for nights yet still cope with a vomiting fellow human.

Kirsty obediently took a couple of sips. 'I knew something was wrong,' she said miserably. 'I've known for ages, though he always denied it. I don't know why I decided to go looking for evidence. I think I just couldn't stand to let things drag on the way they've been.'

'The pictures,' Anna prompted her.

'Recent selfies of him naked with his ex girlfriend, also naked,' Kirsty said miserably. She saw Anna's expression. 'I know, really classy.' She sipped more water. 'You know Jason isn't Charlie's real dad?'

Anna shook her head. It didn't seem like the best moment to say that she had often wondered how such a doughy looking young man could father such a sparklingly mischievous little boy.

'He was really lovely to him until we got married. He was lovely to both of us. Then, almost overnight, he started resenting him, you know, like he just couldn't forgive him for being so little and needing me.'

'He was jealous,' Anna said.

Kirsty didn't hear. 'If Charlie has a bad dream in the night and needs a cuddle – any time he takes my attention away from

Jason, basically – Jason has a total melt down. I keep telling
him, he's just a little boy, Jason, and he just says he's got to
learn! Oh, fuck, Anna, my life is such a mess!' She started to
cry again.

'I'm going to make us both a cup of coffee,' Anna said.
Instant coffee was vile, but she couldn't leave Kirsty in this
state, and today she'd take caffeine in any form she could get.
She arrived back with the steaming kettle just before Paul, the
senior administrator, came in, wearing his usual mud-brown
V-necked sweater over a tired plaid shirt and worn corduroy
trousers and generally looking like he'd just teleported back
from Comic Con.

Paul instantly registered Kirsty weeping at her computer.
Instead of beating a hasty retreat, as most men would, Anna
thought, he said anxiously, 'Kirsty, what's wrong? Is Charlie
OK?' Behind his glasses his eyes were wide with concern.

'You tell him, Anna,' Kirsty choked. She ran out with her hand
over her mouth.

Anna quickly shut the office door, though she doubted that
Kirsty really needed to vomit a second time. More likely she
couldn't bear to have to repeat her sorry story to her boss, however
sympathetic. 'She found pictures of her husband with his ex,'
Anna told him, keeping her voice down. 'Naked pictures,' she
added, to make Kirsty's predicament crystal clear.

Paul whipped off his spectacles, as if he was alarmed she
might actually make him view the pictures. 'Good God,' he said,
appalled. 'She's not planning to stay with the little shit, is she?'

She shook her head. 'I don't know. I've only just got in, and
she was too upset to tell me very much.'

Paul sat down on the corner of Kirsty's desk. 'Naked selfies,'
he said in a disgusted voice. 'Where's the mystery in that?'

'You'd have to ask Jason.' Anna couldn't quite believe she
was having this conversation with her boss, a man whose private
life she knew nothing about, except that he was into something
nerdy like war gaming or historical re-enactments.

The door opened, and Kirsty came in blowing her nose on a
ragged piece of toilet paper.

'I'll take you home,' Paul offered.

'I don't want to go home!' Kirsty wailed. 'I can't be in that flat all by myself. I'll go bloody mad.' She sank into her chair and covered her face. 'Oh fuck, this is all my fault!'

Paul whipped off his glasses again. 'How is this *your* fault?'

'It must be,' she said pathetically. 'Or why would he have gone running back to Claire?'

'Because he's an ungrateful, immature wank—' Paul saw Anna vehemently shaking her head and clamped his jaws together.

Anna didn't have much personal experience of break-ups. You had to make relationships before you could break them up. But she had worked in offices and been party to a lot of break-up conversations, so she knew that while it was OK for Kirsty to criticize Jason, it was too soon for her to permit anyone else to join in.

Giving Kirsty's shoulder an awkward squeeze, Paul left the office, discreetly closing the door on the female turmoil inside.

If she were Kirsty, Anna thought, she'd prefer to be left alone to deal with her misery. If she were Kirsty she wouldn't have been able to face coming into the office full-stop. Her dread of exposure, of letting anyone see her messy vulnerability, would have outweighed everything else. But Kirsty had opted to come to work, and Anna felt she should say something comforting, however banal. 'Look, I'm going to send some emails now,' she said. 'But I'm here if you need me, OK?' *Yep, that was banal, Anna*, she thought and was surprised by Kirsty's tearful nod.

'Thank you,' she said. 'That means a lot.'

This morning Anna had to fine tune arrangements for a seminar that was going to be given by a controversial female academic from the US who believed that schools should stop teaching children IT and teach them philosophy from primary school . onwards. The BBC and also a German TV network were going to be filming, and Nadine had left Anna a more than usually daunting to-do list. With part of her mind on a white-faced Kirsty while she worked, Anna vaguely registered a busy succession of pings before Kirsty said in a depleted voice, 'Someone seems very keen to get in touch with you.'

'Oh, God, I forgot!' Anna dived for her phone and found a dozen or more texts from Tansy Lavelle, private investigator, now parked outside Eve Bloomfield's house in East Oxford and clearly increasingly bored. The most exciting thing she'd witnessed so far was a row in Eve's next door neighbour's front garden between the neighbour and her teenage daughter: *She started pulling up her daughter's top to cover her cleavage, & the daughter was pulling it back down, shrieking, 'Get your hands off me, you jealous cow!' Pure daytime TV!*

'What's funny?' Kirsty asked her. 'I could do with a laugh,' she added with a watery grin.

'Just a silly text,' Anna said. 'Actually, I've been wondering if you'd let me take you out for lunch.' In fact, the idea had just popped into her head. 'You probably don't feel like eating,' she said, over Kirsty's protests, 'but it would do us both good to get out of the office for a bit.' It's what Tansy or Isadora would have done, she thought. It didn't feel entirely natural to make the offer, but Anna liked herself slightly better for having made it.

They went to the Grand Cafe because it was nearest. Supposedly on the site of the first ever coffee house in England, the cafe was popular with tourists. Anna loved it regardless, not so much for its marble pillars and gold leaf, but because it was the first place she had ever ordered a cocktail.

She shared this with Kirsty in the hope of distracting her with lighter topics.

'What were you, sixteen?' Kirsty said at once.

'Fifteen,' Anna corrected. 'But I looked eighteen easily.' *Eighteen going on thirty*, she thought.

'Did you feel impossibly sophisticated, like you should be posing with a cigarette holder?' Kirsty asked.

'I totally did!' Anna said. 'I had a Strawberry Daiquiri, and my friend Nat had a White Russian.'

'And did you feel drunk, like, *immediately*?'

'From the first sip,' Anna said, laughing. She had other memories involving Natalie, but this was one of the better ones, and she was glad she'd been able to make Kirsty smile, if only for a moment.

After Anna had read aloud from the Specials board and mentioned casually that she thought she'd have the soup of the day, Kirsty decided that she might risk a few spoonfuls herself. 'And the crusty bread,' she told the waiter. 'My granny used to break toast into tiny bits for me and dip it in my soup when I was ill,' she told Anna, when he'd gone away with their order.

Anna nodded. Her grandmother had done the same. 'It's not like proper eating then.'

Then, when their order came, Kirsty surprised them both by falling on her food as if she was half-starved. 'I was too churned up to eat last night.' She immediately pulled a face. 'Don't let's talk about me though, or I'll start crying again and make an arse of myself. Let's talk about you. I bet your love life is way more interesting than mine.'

'I suspect it's a lot less interesting than you think,' Anna said, 'though . . .' She shook her head. 'You really don't want to hear about it.'

'No, I really do!' Kirsty said at once. 'You're not in a doomed love triangle are you? Like in those incredibly hot paranormal romances?'

Anna laughed. 'No, but I have met these two very different men—'

'Oh my God, and you can't choose between them!'

Anna shook her head. 'It hasn't got as far as choosing.'

But you hope it will?' Kirsty suggested.

'Oh, Kirsty, I don't know what I hope.'

'Then I'll help you. I'm brilliant at other people's love lives. Tell me about these two very different guys, and I'll tell you which one is the best.'

Anna set down her soup spoon. She knew this was just a game, a way of taking Kirsty's mind off her troubles, but she felt the same silly frisson she remembered from teenage conversations with her girlfriends. 'Well, there's this American guy who had my dog, Bonnie, before me. He rescued her, actually, in Afghanistan, then sent her back to Oxford to live with his aunt. He's a Navy SEAL, or he used to be. He's helping to run some kind of international security business now. He's funny, good-looking in a rough around the edges way.'

'He rescued your dog and now he's a potential *boyfriend*! Anna that is, like, *the* most romantic "how we met" story *ever*. Just imagine telling that to your children!'

'Whoa!' said Anna, laughing. 'Before you get me married and pregnant, let me tell you the drawbacks.' She ticked them off on her fingers. 'He doesn't actually live in this country.'

'Damn,' Kirsty said. 'He still lives in the States. Tricky.'

'Plus he has an ex. Or rather a not so ex.'

'Stay away from him,' Kirsty said immediately. 'I mean it, Anna. Unless you have a Teflon-coated heart those kinds of non-committed guys are lethal. I should know.' Her expression wavered for a moment, then she said brightly, 'Who's the other guy?'

Anna took a breath. 'Well, he's English, *extremely* good-looking.'

'Not rough around the edges?'

'Unless you consider Hugh Grant to be rough around the edges,' Anna said.

'We're talking pre sex scandal Hugh Grant?'

'Yes, *Four Weddings and a Funeral* when he was still cute. He does that same gently self-mocking thing.'

'Only posh people do that,' Kirsty commented. 'So I assume he's posh?'

'He is,' Anna admitted, 'but not annoyingly so. He's good with people. He dresses well, but makes it look like he's just casually thrown it all together, and he's charming, successful, *available.*'

'Same country?'

'Same city,' Anna said.

'This is the right guy, Anna. I can *feel* it,' Kirsty said fervently.

Anna could feel herself blushing. She had completely reverted to her teens. 'I've only met him once. But I did get the feeling he was attracted to me. Funnily enough—' She was about to tell Kirsty that she'd just been describing the man who'd written Owen Traherne's biography, when the waiter came back with the desserts menu.

'Just coffee, I think,' Anna said.

Kirsty excused herself to go to the Ladies and Anna checked her phone to see how Tansy was progressing. To her surprise Tansy had sent a slightly blurry picture taken from outside Eve Bloomfield's house, showing Eve emotionally flinging her arms around another woman. The second woman had her back to the camera, but Anna was almost positive she was Sara Traherne.

She immediately called Tansy. 'What's going on?' she said when Tansy answered.

'I lost them! I'm so sorry,' Tansy said.

'You *followed* them?'

'Of course,' Tansy said, 'or what was the point of me staking her out for hours and hours? Anyway, this car pulled up, and I recognized Sara slash Sarah from your murder board. She went to Eve's house. Eve came out. They hugged on the step, all very kissy-kissy, touchy-touchy. Then they drove off in Sara slash Sarah's's car, so I thought I'd trail them.' She gave a rueful laugh. 'I lasted ten minutes. Got caught in an epic traffic snarl up around the Cowley Road and totally lost sight of them.'

'Oh, you poor thing!' Anna tried to sound sympathetic, but she couldn't help being tickled at the picture of Tansy grimly pursuing her suspect down the Cowley Road. 'So you're not going to be applying to be a full-time PI any time soon, then?'

'Not if I have to do my investigating in my mum's car,' Tansy said, laughing. 'I'd have done better on my stepdad's ride-on lawn mower!'

A few hours later Anna was walking briskly through the city centre. Soon it would be dark when she left work, and tonight there was a distinct chill in the air, 'Will you be OK?' she'd said as she and Kirsty stood on the pavement outside Walsingham, poised to go their separate ways. Kirsty had given her a subdued grin. 'I'm looking forward to seeing my little boy's face. I'm trying not to think beyond that. Where are you going now?'

'I'm going to drop in on a friend.' She'd had an impulse to take Laurie a small gift of some kind. She didn't plan to stay; she had to get back for Bonnie. She just wanted Laurie to know that she was his friend.

She had decided to buy him something tiny but delicious from Maison Blanc. It was only after she'd walked inside and been confronted with display cases filled with an exquisite array of French patisserie that she wondered if his illness was too far-advanced now for him to manage solid food.

'I would buy him *macarons*, Madame,' the male assistant suggested after Anna had explained her dilemma. 'Our *macarons* are as light as feathers and also beautiful to look at. Even if your friend cannot eat, I think he will love that you have brought them.'

Anna walked to Laurie's house, carrying the beribboned box

filled with the delicate pastel coloured *macarons*. She'd been
amused by the theatrically Gallic assistant, a bit *too* theatrical,
she thought, to be the real thing. She'd have to take Isadora
in, she thought, to test him! Anna's thoughts returned to Kirsty.
It seemed unlikely that she and Jason would be able to sort things
out. Maybe Kirsty would ask Jason to leave? That's definitely
what Anna would do. Then she found herself pondering Tansy's
surprise capture of Sara and Eve. It wasn't surprising that these
two rather chilly women knew each other, but the apparent intensity of their connection was.

She walked up the path to Laurie's house and saw a woman
coming out carrying a worn canvas tote bag. When she saw Anna
heading towards her she looked wild-eyed with alarm. 'Nobody
can come,' she recited carefully. Her accent sounded vaguely
middle-eastern. 'I am very sorry to tell you this.'

'I don't want to disturb Mr Swanson if it's a bad time,' Anna
explained, 'but I'm a friend of his, and I wanted to leave him a
little gift.'

The woman shook her head. 'You can't see. Nobody can come.'

'I don't have to come in,' Anna said, thinking she didn't
understand. 'But could you maybe give these to the nurse for
Mr Swanson? And say Anna will come back to see him another
time.'

The woman shook her head, almost frantic. 'Nurse gone.
Nobody can come. I am very sorry to tell you this.' She started
to weep.

Anna felt a chill trickle through her as it slowly dawned on
her what this distraught woman was trying to tell her. 'Has Mr
Swanson died? But the doctors said . . .'

'Not cancer,' the woman said quickly. 'Poor man kill self. This
why police say nobody can come.' She stretched out her hands,
as if she believed herself solely responsible for this terrible event.
'I am so very, very sorry for this.'

The world turned to white noise. Anna pushed the box of
macarons at the person she could no longer properly see and
stumbled back to the street. She started to walk, but only managed
a few steps. She couldn't breathe. She had to take off her scarf
or she'd choke. She ripped it off, gasping for air. Fixated on
saving Laurie's love letters, she had failed to save Laurie himself.

There must have been signs. Signs she had missed. She had hardly known Laurie Swanson, and now she never would. The pain of this new loss almost brought her to her knees.

Still half blind with shock, she set off walking. Her movements felt jerky and puppet-like, as if she no longer had a centre of gravity. Feeling as if she might tip over at any moment, she walked and walked until she got to the Banbury Road, but at the last minute, instead of going home to Bonnie, she instinctively turned towards Marston Ferry Road and north to Summertown. Once she had to stop to lean against a wall. But she knew where she was going now. Not home. She had no home. She had tried to make a home of her own, but it had all been pretence: the pretty china, the fairy-tale wolf. She needed to be somewhere real, somewhere safe.

But when she reached the top of the weedy drive, Anna came to a faltering halt. The rusty old Volvo wasn't there. She rang the bell and battered on the door. But nobody came to tell her that it wasn't Anna's fault that everyone she'd ever cared about ended up dead.

TWELVE

'Anna? *Anna*?' Isadora was bending over her, rubbing her hands. 'I suddenly saw you in the headlights. For a moment . . .' Her voice became brisk. 'Let's get you off this cold step.'

Anna managed to say, 'I didn't know where else—'

'Well, I'm very glad you came to me.' Isadora helped her to her feet. 'How long have you been waiting?'

It could have been minutes or days; she had no idea. 'What time is it?' Her voice was a raspy whisper.

Isadora checked her watch. 'Almost eight.' Her hand moved protectively to her cheek. 'A dear friend took me out for champagne. We have this mutual arrangement to cheer each other up after some particularly grim procedure.' Anna heard faint but frantic barking. 'In a *minute*, Hero!' Isadora called irritably. 'I'll just let her out of the car, then we'll go inside.'

In a series of time lapses, Anna found herself inside Isadora's musty smelling hall, standing numbly in her kitchen then being pushed gently into the small wicker chair as a soft blanket was wrapped around her shoulders.

'Laurie Swanson's dead,' she forced out through chattering teeth. 'He killed himself.'

Isadora went very still. 'The poor dear man,' she said softly at last. She thought for a moment. 'You're shocked, and you're chilled to the bone. I'm going to run you a lovely hot bath.'

She guided Anna up the stairs and into a turquoise-painted bathroom with an old claw-footed bath, pitted and stained with limescale. Isadora put in the plug and turned the hot tap on full. Somewhere far off, pipes began to judder and bang. Eventually, a cataract of scalding water surged out. 'I have oceans of hot water, so use as much as you like,' Isadora said. Above the washbasin mismatched Victorian tiles depicted ornate ferns, lilies and roses. There was a huge gilt-framed mirror which, like the walls, was becoming dewy with condensation.

The rest of the walls were filled with paintings, drawings and framed cartoons.

Isadora touched a small oil painting that showed a tiny white Jack Russell with brown-tipped ears. 'This is Dido, my dog before Hero. I had to have her put to sleep. I begged the vet to do the same for me, and the stupid man thought I was joking.' Isadora went to a low wooden cupboard on which various expensive bath products were set out. She selected a deep-blue bottle. 'This is my current favourite,' she said. 'It contains damask rose, patchouli, pomegranate oil . . .' She continued to list exotic ingredients, making them sound like a poem or a spell. Anna could feel the older woman's voice firmly pulling her away from the dark place, lulling her – *willing* her – into a world of warmth and safety.

Opening the bottle, Isadora liberally sloshed the scented oil into the water that came thundering and frothing from the tap. 'I'll leave it here in case you need to add more,' she said. 'I don't believe one should *stint* on bath oil!' She disappeared for a moment and came back with a violent-paisley-patterned bath towel that might have been new in the 1960s and an extraordinary Chinese looking robe. She dropped them both on the kind of cork-topped stool that Anna remembered from her grandparents' bathroom. 'Now I'll leave you to have a lovely long soak.'

Anna lay in the bath, letting the hot, scented water gradually penetrate into her chilled bones and looking at the little white dog that Isadora had loved so much she'd wanted to die with her.

When the water grew cool, she climbed out of the tub and unsuccessfully attempted to dry herself on the thin, balding towel. In the end, still damp, she numbly wrapped herself in the robe. She must have gone looking for Isadora, or else she was waiting on the landing, because the next thing she knew, Isadora was helping her to a high curving bed and covering her over with a large quilt that smelled of dust and mothballs. 'Now you are not to worry about anything, my darling, do you hear? Just sleep. I'll go and get Bonnie for you.'

Isadora had brought Anna's bag upstairs. Anna managed to remove her spare key from her key chain before she was sucked down into a black, bottomless sleep.

She woke in darkness, totally disorientated, sensing but not able to see her unfamiliar surroundings.

For sixteen years, any awakening after a deep sleep involved a rapid reassembling of herself and her losses. *That is who I used to be. This is who I have to be now.* But this time, as Anna surfaced, the new horror of Laurie's death felt like a punch in her lower belly, physically doubling her over.

She shakily groped around until she found a switch. The lamp cast a thin circle of light, leaving most of the room still in shadow. She peered at her watch. Seven fifteen. Isadora hadn't come home until after eight. At seven fifteen Anna had still been huddled on the step. She had actually slept right through till morning, an achievement so rare she couldn't remember the last time she'd pulled it off.

She slipped out from under the quilt and went across to the window. Pulling back one of the heavy curtains, she found herself looking out on to a dark street, lit by an orange street lamp.

Seven fifteen *at night*. She had slept for almost twenty-four hours.

Bonnie, she thought, then went dizzy with relief as she remembered Isadora's promise to drive over and get her. Seeing a large bottle of mineral water on the bedside table, Anna opened it and gulped down half of it before she stopped to catch her breath. Her bag had been left beside the bed. She found her phone and hastily switched it on. Since her missed call from Naomi, Anna had taken to checking her phone first thing in case either her grandfather or the care home had been trying to get in touch. Anything could happen to a nearly ninety-year-old man in twenty-four hours. But nobody had left a message. Today had been her day off, luckily, so there wouldn't be any problems with work.

Someone – Anna guessed it was Tansy – had left a clean white T-shirt and a soft grey hoodie neatly folded on a chair. She put them on over the dark-grey trousers she had worn to work the previous day. She couldn't find her shoes, so she padded out on to the landing in her bare feet. She could smell cooking – onions, garlic and spices. Voices floated up.

Anna used the bathroom, scrubbing her teeth with her finger and some of Isadora's toothpaste, and made her way down to the kitchen. She felt so dazed that she half wondered if she was still dreaming. Her feeling of unreality intensified when she pushed open the door to see Jake McCaffrey sitting with Tansy at Isadora's kitchen table. The table had been swept clean of its normal chaos, revealing gleaming pine boards. Lit tea-lights flickered in pretty-coloured glasses.

Bonnie had been lying sprawled across Jake's feet. As soon as she saw Anna her tail started to thump the floor in greeting, gaining power and impetus with each new thump. 'I told you she'd be here soon,' Jake informed the dog.

The shock and pleasure of seeing him almost undid her – the cornflower blue of his eyes, those fine crinkles at the corners, the sudden smile that illuminated his normally guarded face.

'How the hell did you get here?' she said shakily. He was wearing a dark-olive polo shirt and blue jeans. His leather jacket was casually thrown over the back of his chair. Like always he smelled fresh and clean, though she hadn't been able to identify any particular cologne or product.

Bonnie came over to be stroked, showing no resentment at having been abandoned for a day and a half. Anna bent to fondle her, grateful for the chance to hide her burning face.

'I found him on your step, darling, just as I was leaving with Bonnie,' Isadora called. 'So I brought him home with me.' She was standing over her range cooker, stirring a vast pan from which wonderful Middle-Eastern aromas rose. On the back of the stove a second huge pan steamed gently under its lid. Hero watched all these preparations with interest from the small wicker chair, her eyes bright behind her fringe.

Isadora looked shamefaced. 'Unfortunately, having perfectly remembered the code for your alarm on the way in, I had totally forgotten it by the time I came out, so I do hope there weren't any burglars lurking.'

'I'm sure there weren't,' Anna said. She had absolutely no memory of giving Isadora the code. She must have been completely out of it. 'What were you doing on my step?' she asked Jake.

'You didn't answer my text,' he said calmly. 'So I thought I'd come over and ask you in person.'

His voice still made her go weak at the knees. She sat in the nearest chair, which happened to be next to Jake. She passed her hand over her face. 'Sorry, I forgot all about it. It was quite a full-on day.' She felt his big hand move to cover hers.

'Seems to me you're having quite a full-on month,' he said quietly.

Anna let her hand rest in his for a moment before she pulled it away. 'Thanks for the clothes,' she said to Tansy.

Tansy's half-smirk let Anna know that she'd registered the hand touching, but she just said, 'No problem. Oh, look at your Bonnie!' she added, laughing.

Bonnie had succeeded in squeezing herself through the narrow gap between Anna and Jake's chairs. Joyfully waving her tail, she looked from one of them to the other with a rapturous expression, as if she might be going to burst into song.

'Supper won't be too long now,' Isadora said, sprinkling fresh green coriander over her pan. 'There are a few nibbles, everyone, if Tansy wouldn't mind setting them out.'

'You haven't been here since last night?' Anna asked Jake over an ecstatic Bonnie.

He shook his head. 'I just came back with Isadora to look in on you, make sure you were all right. Today I had a bunch of stuff to do with Mimi's estate. I arrived about an hour or so ago, and Isadora kindly asked me to stop and eat with you guys.' He gave her his lopsided smile. Americans were supposed to have blinding white movie star teeth, but she liked that Jake's front tooth had that small but visible chip. He hadn't lived that kind of perfect American life. If it hadn't been for Mimi he might not have survived at all.

'If you'd slept any longer, darling, we were going to send him up to wake you with a kiss,' Isadora threw over her shoulder.

'Shame you didn't mention that a little sooner,' Jake told her mischievously, but when he turned back to Anna she saw concern in his eyes. 'Seriously, how are you holding up?'

She shook her head. 'I can't believe I didn't see it coming. I mean, I was with him just two nights ago. And he seemed so wonderfully – I don't know – at *peace*. And I mean about *everything*; his illness, his love for—' Just in time, Anna stopped herself.

'It's OK, Jake knows,' Tansy said quickly. 'Isadora was so upset about you last night that she kind of let the cat out of the bag.'

'Oh, right.' Anna felt a prickle of unease. What else had they told Jake while she was sleeping upstairs?

'I won't go blabbing,' Jake reassured her. 'But I can leave if that would be more comfortable for you guys? It's obvious you've got a lot going on.'

'That won't be necessary,' Isadora called from the cooker.

'We want you to stay, don't we, Anna?' Tansy said.

'Of course!' Anna gave Jake what she hoped was a neutral smile. 'For one thing we need someone to help us eat all Isadora's food.' Isadora would be hurt if Jake left, and Laurie was beyond being hurt now by tabloid hacks or any other ill-wishers.

Bonnie had settled herself under the kitchen table with her head resting on Anna's bare feet. If she looked, Anna knew she'd see Bonnie's snow-white rear end sprawled across Jake's size twelve shoes. Like it or not, she and Jake were connected by this dog, just as surely as they were separated by the Atlantic. It was like some kind of unsolvable riddle. Anna remembered Kirsty's warning and told herself it was better that way.

She noticed Jake frowning at her, almost as if he'd read her thoughts. But he just said, 'So when you saw Laurie the night before he died, you didn't get, like, an obvious suicide vibe off him?'

Anna shook her head. 'Just the opposite. It was like he'd totally accepted everything his life had dealt him, good and bad. He begged me to come back with Bonnie – he *loved* Bonnie! He said she was one of the seven exceptional dogs. It's from a book,' Anna explained to Jake. For a moment she saw Laurie's face, his amused delight as he wondered why dogs always smelled of peanut butter, and felt a fresh pang of loss. She had to swallow before she added, 'He was composing a requiem.'

'Oh, lord, not his own, I hope.' Scooping up some of her sauce on her wooden spoon, Isadora tasted it with a thoughtful expression.

Anna gave her a wan smile. 'Laurie made the same joke. He said he'd made up his mind to live long enough to finish it.'

Tansy came over with a platter of various kinds of meze. 'I never met Laurie,' she said, 'but I've been thinking about him a lot since we read those letters. He must have been despairing after Owen died. Didn't you say he had some kind of breakdown,

Isadora? I guess after he lost Owen there was nobody left to turn to. Nobody he could trust, anyway.'

Anna nodded. It might not have been his intention, but by swearing Laurie to secrecy about their relationship, Owen had effectively separated his lover from anyone else who might be a real friend and equal and therefore a potential threat to Owen. 'He talked about being the quirky bachelor people invited to make up the numbers,' she said.

'So he must have been fucking lonely,' Tansy said. 'And then finding out he was fatally ill, having to be cared for by strangers . . .'

'I know all that,' said Anna. 'And I could make a good story about how a dying man – a recluse, a secretly *gay* recluse – finally feels able to cut himself free from the unbearable burden his life has become.' She shook her head. 'It's just that after my evening with him, I can't believe it.' She rubbed at her temples. 'OK, maybe I just don't want to,' she admitted.

'People don't necessarily seem suicidal just before they commit suicide.' Isadora opened the oven and pulled out an enormous blue tagine, followed by a smaller yellow one. The scent of richly spiced lamb joined the other delicious kitchen smells. 'I've had depressed friends who seemed positively euphoric just before they ended their lives. I suppose it's partly relief to have resolved that appalling internal conflict.'

'OK, I'm not you, Anna, but if it was me and someone gave me their precious secret papers, and then, almost immediately, you know—' Tansy did a graphic mime of cutting her own throat. 'I wouldn't want to think it was suicide either.'

Isadora turned off the back burner, then snatched up a dishcloth and removed the lid from the steamer. She tipped a stream of yellow couscous from the steamer into a brown earthenware dish.

'You want me to bring some of that incredible-looking food over here?' Jake asked, jumping up.

Isadora gave him a grateful look. Not just for his offer of help, Anna thought, but for diverting their attention away from Laurie's lonely death to her lovingly prepared feast.

Tansy was directed to fetch the plates from the warming drawer, and Anna set out place mats while Jake and Isadora carried the food to the table. Isadora swept a last critical glance over her table, checking that everything was present and correct: the mound of fluffy couscous spiked with almonds, raisins and preserved lemon; some kind of stew with meatballs; the two tagines – Isadora had made one with beans for vegan Tansy; and a pile of flatbread keeping warm under a cloth.

'Sit, eat! Eat *lots*,' Isadora told them, 'or poor Hero will be eating couscous for breakfast for the rest of the week. As you see, I am incapable of cooking in moderation.'

'Moderation isn't really a word I associate with you, Isadora,' Tansy teased.

Anna found she was famished. For a few moments everyone just concentrated on their food.

'The last time I ate Moroccan food this good I was in Marrakech.' Jake gave Isadora his crooked grin. Like their hostess he had opted to bypass his cutlery, scooping up his food with his bread.

She was delighted. 'You've been to Marrakech?'

'Yes, ma'am. A couple of times now.'

Isadora launched into a description of backpacking through Morocco in the 1960s and how wonderful and unspoiled it was then.

Anna remembered how Jake had joked that you could drop him out of a plane and wherever he came down he would immediately make himself at home. She stole a look at him, this surprising American, sitting at Isadora's kitchen table in exotic North Oxford, chatting easily with three totally different women, and he did indeed seem quietly at home. She wondered if you could hope to learn that kind of ease after a certain age; if it could maybe rub off on you, if you were around someone like Jake for long enough. It was a tempting, bitter-sweet thought.

Jake turned to Anna. 'You're looking a better colour for getting a little food down you,' he commented. He had rested his hand next to hers on the table, and she could feel that effortless male vitality emanating from him.

'I *feel* a better colour,' she said, trying to match his easy tone. 'This is wonderful, Isadora, thank you so much.'

'I love cooking for people,' Isadora said. 'I really should do it more.'

After they'd finished their meal, Isadora brought them mint

tea in Moroccan tea glasses. Their talk meandered from a recent incident at Marmalade, involving a health-conscious mother and a food-phobic small child, and then to Isadora's son, who had always been picky about his food. 'Now he's just picky!' Isadora said with one of her great hoots. 'Poor Gabriel, I think he was always secretly in training to be an accountant!'

Jake asked after Anna's grandfather, and she told him of her attempts to get him to agree to exhibit his work. Isadora wanted to hear more about his paintings, but as Anna launched into a detailed description, she had the feeling that Tansy's mind was elsewhere. 'I'm being really self indulgent,' she apologized quickly. 'It's a good thing I'll never have children. I'd be showing off their pasta collages to strangers on the bus!'

Tansy looked mortified. 'You weren't boring me, Anna! Your grandfather sounds amazing. I just – well, I don't know if this is a good time to talk about this, but I've been doing a bit more research, and I kind of need to tell you guys about it.'

'What does "a bit more research" mean?' Isadora asked suspiciously, just as Anna said:

'You didn't chase someone down the Cowley Road again, did you?'

Tansy turned to Jake. 'Just to give you some background, I should explain that my first and only attempt at a stake-out turned out to be a major non-event.'

'Who were you staking out?' Jake asked with interest. Anna could see him rapidly revising his first impressions of Tansy.

'A total nutter who threatened Naomi and Laurie,' Tansy said, 'but like I said, it was a non-event of epic proportions. Then suddenly Laurie was dead, and poor Anna—' Tansy tugged on a loose curl as she struggled to put her thought processes into words. 'Anyway, I felt like I should be doing more to help,' she summarized, sounding slightly defensive. 'So I went online, and I did some digging around about Owen and Audrey Traherne.' Tansy reached into her tote bag and pulled out a file. 'I just wanted to see what was out there. Fill in some of the gaps.' Her hand hovered over the file. 'This really isn't the right moment, is it?' she said anxiously.

'I'd like to see,' Anna said quickly, though she doubted that anything Tansy had found would give them the answers she craved.

Tansy took out a few printouts which she had neatly stapled together and passed them around. The information seemed to be a mishmash of old news clippings, mixed up with entries from the kind of literary blogs that specialized in backbiting. She'd found a description of an infamous literary party at the Trahernes where a furious but stone-cold sober Audrey had emptied a jug of rum punch over her drunken husband's head, whereupon Owen had immediately poured a bottle of red wine over her, ruining the Dior evening dress that he had bought her especially for the occasion. Their fight had escalated until they'd had to be physically separated by some of the other guests. There was a story about Audrey being found barefoot and disorientated in Stoke Newington and taken to a psychiatric unit for assessment. There were stories from Owen's later years, mostly involving drink. He had been arrested for hitting a man in a Dublin bar. He had publicly insulted a fellow member of a literary panel.

It made depressing reading, Anna thought. Far from filling in the gaps, these gossipy snippets offered only a lurid caricature of a marriage from which any real truths had been edited out in favour of spite and sensation.

Isadora obviously felt the same. She compressed her lips together. 'Owen Traherne was not an amiable drunk,' she said coldly. 'But he was not Richard Burton and Audrey was not Liz Taylor, whatever these vultures would like us to think.'

Tansy placed her two hands protectively on her folder. 'I brought some other stuff,' she confessed. 'But I chickened out about showing you. I still don't know if I should show you.'

'What kind of stuff?' Isadora said, still frosty.

Anna saw worry and embarrassment flit across Tansy's face. 'I can't explain it, really. I just had this feeling that I had to keep digging until I turned something up. So there are these Internet sites? Like, death tribute sites?'

Jake sat back in his chair. 'You're going to have to explain that to a poor southern boy.'

'And to an elderly academic,' Isadora added with one of her dark laughs.

'I know about them,' Anna said, feeling the need to help Tansy out. 'When someone famous dies, their fans get hold of police info, autopsy photographs and reports, that kind of thing, and put them up online as some kind of bad taste tribute.'

'To merit a tribute site, they have to be, like, famous *and* charismatic,' Tansy explained. 'The kind of dead people that myths grow up around.'

'Ah, I get you. Like Tupac the rapper,' Jake said. 'Or JFK, right?'

Tansy nodded. 'And James Dean, Marilyn Monroe; you get the picture. Well, it seems that Owen was like the rock star of the poetry world and his wife Audrey was beautiful but also incredibly unstable. That kind of volatile combo gets some people incredibly overexcited for some reason. Anyway, I found some material connected with Audrey's suicide . . . This is a bad idea,' she said interrupting herself. 'Why did I ever think—?'

'I want to see it,' Anna said.

'Does everybody else agree?' Tansy said uncertainly.

Isadora gave a weary sigh. 'If you must.'

Jake looked doubtful, but he nodded. 'Sure.'

Tansy slid out some grainy black and white photographs.

Anna felt Jake go very still. Jake McCaffrey must have seen hundreds of dead bodies in the course of his military career, some reduced to little more than shreds of meat. Anna doubted that the crime-scene photograph of this physically intact dead woman would shock him very much, which meant that something else about this picture had jolted him.

Isadora's hand went to her mouth. 'Put them away. Sorry, Tansy, I understand that you only want to help, but I don't see how we're helping Laurie or anyone by looking at these dreadful images of poor Audrey. Images nobody was ever intended to see.'

Tansy's face crumpled. 'Oh, shit! I forgot you actually knew Audrey.' She scrabbled to get the pictures back in her folder.

'No!' said Jake.

They looked at him, startled.

'What?' said Tansy.

Jake rubbed his hand across his face, and Anna heard the faint scratch of stubble. For the first time she saw that he was tired. 'Well, like Tansy here, I felt kinda sick about what happened to

Anna last night, and so I have also been doing a bit of – *research*.'
He shot Tansy a comradely grin.

'*Why?*' Anna said, confused. This had nothing to do with Jake.

'Hey, it wasn't a big deal. In my work I have to access all kinds of information. The only difference is this time I asked someone to get me some intel from your Thames Valley police.'

'You hacked the *police*,' breathed Tansy. 'You could get yourself into some serious trouble.'

He shrugged. 'I doubt it. My guy is good at getting in and out without anyone knowing. I wasn't going to tell anyone about it, but having seen that picture of Audrey, well, I feel like I should come clean.' He went out into the hall for a moment and came back with his tablet. He flipped back the cover. 'You might not want to look, Anna,' he said soberly.

Isadora and Tansy came to stand behind his chair. Anna heard Isadora catch her breath.

'OK,' said Jake. 'There are several of these from slightly different angles.'

Anna made herself look at Laurie's empty-eyed corpse. Everything in her wanted to deny that it was him; the vital, living Laurie was still so vivid in her mind. There were crumpled sheets of paper on Laurie's floor, music paper, which someone, a policeman or a paramedic, had trodden on. She could see Laurie's scribbled notation showing through the dirty prints from someone's shoe.

'You OK?' Jake asked her.

She gave a tight nod. 'Show me that photo of Audrey again.'

'Oh, *fuck*,' Tansy whispered. 'How weird is that?'

The similarities were chilling. The invalid's feeder cup was placed at the same angle as the elegant champagne flute by Audrey's bed. Stranger still, each corpse seemed to be pointing a lifeless finger, almost accusingly, at an open book.

'I don't understand,' Isadora said.

'I'd say we're looking at two possible scenarios,' Jake said. 'Either your friend Laurie deliberately staged his suicide to echo Audrey's, or someone else did it for him.'

Anna felt her arms break out into goosebumps. 'Are you saying someone helped Laurie to choreograph his death-bed scene in some kind of weird homage to Owen's wife?'

He spread his hands. 'At this stage, I'm just speculating, throwing some theories around. But it's not impossible that someone came into Laurie's house, after the event.'

'Someone he knew, you mean?' Isadora said. 'Someone who knew about Laurie and Owen?'

Tansy's eyes went wide. 'You seriously think someone broke into Laurie's house, found him lying dead and deliberately re-arranged his death bed so it was like a near-perfect echo of Audrey's? That's the kind of thing psychopaths do in movies.'

Jake shrugged. 'I'm just saying, after seeing those pictures, we shouldn't rule anything out.'

Nobody spoke for a moment, then Tansy said, 'Eve sounds like someone who is mad enough to do something like that.'

Isadora drained the last of her mint tea. 'We should go to the police.'

'And tell them what?' Anna said.

'About the similarities between the pictures.'

'If we went to the police, we'd have to tell them how we got hold of the pictures of Laurie,' Tansy reminded her.

Isadora closed her eyes. 'Catch twenty-two,' she said softly. 'The infernal paradox. Just when we really have to go to the police, we can't go to the police.'

'And I'm responsible for landing you in it,' Jake said. 'I'm sorry.'

'Don't be,' she said. 'There's no way anyone could have anticipated this.'

'I never thought I'd have to be involved in these kinds of fucked-up things.' Tansy was tugging at her stray curl, stretching it out and letting it go. She seemed to have forgotten about Tansy Lavelle fearless PI and reverted to the shocked girl Anna had first met on Port Meadow. She'd said something similar then, Anna remembered.

'It would be different if you could come up with some hard evidence,' Jake said. 'At the moment it's just feelings and hunches. You need something solid if you're going to take it to the police.'

'What if we could prove that Eve had been threatening Laurie in some way – that she was responsible for pushing him over the edge?' Isadora said.

'Then surely the police could get her for stalking?' Anna said.

Tansy sat up. 'It's a shame we can't access her emails and social media accounts. I bet we'd find a ton of incriminating stuff.'

Anna shifted in her chair. 'I could do that.'

'Anna!' Isadora said.

'Hey, if it gets the job done,' Anna said defensively.

Jake shook his head. 'I don't want any of this coming back on you. Like I said, I know a guy who can get in and out again without setting off any alarm bells. Seriously, we call him "the ghost".'

'Suppose we're wrong? Suppose our feelings and hunches all turn out to be wrong?' Isadora said. 'Then we've invaded that woman's privacy for no good reason. Then *we're* the criminals.'

'But at least we'd know,' Tansy said. 'We could cross Eve off our list.'

'On the other hand we might just end up with a new and more impenetrable mystery,' Isadora said gloomily. She attempted a laugh. 'Sorry, darlings, I think I'm getting tired.'

'Me too,' Jake said. He stood up and held out his hand to Anna. 'Come on, kid. I'm taking you home. I have a plane to catch tomorrow morning, and you need to get back to normal.'

They said their goodbyes in the hall. Jake stooped to kiss Isadora on the cheek. 'Ma'am, your hospitality is out of this world. I'd like to return the favour one day and cook you some real southern-style buttermilk fried chicken.'

'Is that what your mother used to cook for you?' Isadora asked.

'No, ma'am,' Jake said, smiling. 'My mom wasn't exactly famed for her cooking. But my Aunt Mimi knew how to cook that dish to perfection.' He turned to Tansy. 'No more going off and playing detective on your own,' he advised.

Jake drove Anna and Bonnie back to Park Town in his hire car. *My mom wasn't exactly famed for her cooking.* Jake had smoothed the awkward moment over so quickly, he'd scarcely missed a beat, but Anna had felt it, felt the jagged edges of a memory too dark to be approached.

'I'll come in with you,' he said as they pulled up outside her house. 'Isadora said she didn't reset the alarm. I'd like to make sure everything is OK.'

She gave a tired laugh. 'Are you going to "secure my perimeter"? Isn't that what you military people say?'

Sitting close to him in the dark, she heard the smile in his voice as he said, 'That's right, but it sounds a lot more appealing when you say it.'

It was suddenly hard to look at him. Compared to Jake, other men Anna had known seemed like boys. Jake's brand of masculinity was unequivocally grown-up, and that attracted and scared her both at once.

She waited in the hall while he checked around. It was an unfamiliar sensation, being taken care of by a man. She told herself she was only allowing it because she was too disheartened and vulnerable to protest, and anyway she wasn't going to see him again.

He came back upstairs from her kitchen. 'Perimeter secured,' he said, saluting. 'Bonnie's already curled up in her basket. She's promised to keep an eye on you for me.'

Don't, Anna thought. *Don't be nice and funny and caring when you're only going to leave.*

'Good night, kid,' Jake said softly, looking down at her. 'Remember to set the alarm, won't you?' He hesitated, searching her face for something which he apparently didn't find.

A moment later he'd gone.

Anna reset the alarm because she always reset the alarm. She didn't need a man to tell her how to take care of herself, a man who lived on the other side of the ocean.

She snapped on the sitting room light, saw Laurie's smiling face on her murder board and immediately snapped it off again.

Her flat felt cold, bleak; a home without a heart. She pictured herself trying to sleep in that bare, unfinished room and knew that – tonight, anyway – she couldn't do it. Not alone.

Bonnie, Anna thought, but she must have actually spoken her name aloud because her White Shepherd immediately appeared at the top of the stairs. The look on her face was a comical mix of surprised and hopeful. She gave a cautious wag of her tail. 'Just for tonight,' Anna told her. 'Don't get used to it, OK?'

She waited till her dog had followed her into her bedroom, then she closed the door and started getting ready for bed.

THIRTEEN

'Can't your family help you?' Paul said.

Kirsty shook her head. 'They all worship Jason,' she said miserably. 'Especially my mum. She's so grateful to him for rescuing me from unmarried motherhood that she won't hear a word against him.' Her skin had broken out, and she had enormous shadows under her eyes. Even her coppery curls had lost their glow.

Paul had invited Kirsty and Anna to lunch in Walsingham's ancient oak-panelled buttery. Outside, wind and rain battered the mullioned windows. Occasionally, a sodden leaf whirled by. Apart from a lone don and a small group of postgraduate students they were the only diners, sitting at one of the long highly polished refectory tables, as tens of thousands of college members had done over the centuries.

The food – salmon *en croute* and steamed vegetables – was good, but no one was giving it much attention. Kirsty's marital troubles had reached crisis level, and Jason had issued an ultimatum, giving her two weeks to find somewhere else for her and Charlie to live. Unfortunately, Jason's was the name on their lease.

Anna glanced at her watch. Jake would be in the air now. She'd spent hardly any time with him, yet some merciless recording device had logged every quizzical smile, every fleeting touch and was now replaying them on permanent shuffle. For reasons that would probably require months of therapy to unravel, the memory that cut the deepest was the image of Bonnie joyously looking from one of them to the other, as if her broken universe was being magically reassembled in front of her eyes. *You're ridiculous*, she thought. Kirsty was about to be made homeless. Anna was supposed to be helping her come up with solutions, not moping like some lovesick teen.

She heard Paul saying, 'Can't you talk to your dad?'

Kirsty gave a tiny shake of her head. 'My dad says he doesn't believe in taking sides.'

'How can there be a *side*!' Paul said, outraged. 'Jason is making you and Charlie *homeless*!'

'Talk to Citizen's Advice.' Anna brought herself back with an effort. 'They'll tell you your rights.'

'And you and Charlie *do* have rights,' Paul told Kirsty, grim-faced. 'No matter what your husband wants you to think.'

Kirsty gave another more vehement shake of the head. 'I couldn't stay after this. It's like he's ripped off the latex mask and I've seen the sick immature bastard underneath. I don't want that person around me or my little boy. It's just crap timing that I'm looking for basic-type rented accommodation just as all the students are coming back.'

Paul turned to look out of the window though nothing could be seen through the driving rain. 'Things might work out,' he said vaguely. 'Sometimes life surprises you.'

'So I've discovered,' Kirsty told him, with a flash of savage humour.

Part-way through the afternoon, Anna was composing an email to the visiting American academic who was turning out to be something of a diva when an email popped up from Paul saying he needed a discreet word. Mumbling an excuse to Kirsty, she crossed the landing to Paul's office, wondering if she was about to get the sack. 'Have I done something wrong?' she asked bluntly. 'I know Nadine and I don't always see eye to eye.'

Paul looked startled, then whipped off his glasses. 'Oh, I *see*! Because I asked you to be discreet. No, this has absolutely nothing to do with your work – which is exemplary, by the way. It's actually to do with Kirsty.'

Anna was puzzled. 'So shouldn't you be talking to her?'

He shook his head. 'I don't want to seem to be . . .' He seemed to search for words. 'Cashing in.'

She frowned. 'Cashing in how?'

'Like some dirty old man who also happens to be her boss.' He saw Anna's perplexed expression and said gloomily, 'I'm making it worse, aren't I?' He took a breath. 'I've got somewhere Kirsty could stay till she and Charlie sort themselves out. Well, as long as she needs, really.'

'That's wonderful!' Anna almost asked him why he hadn't mentioned this over lunch. 'Where is it?'

'That's the problem,' Paul said anxiously. 'This probably makes me seem quaintly unadventurous, but I still live in the same house where I grew up.' He relayed this information as though he was used to people thinking this wasn't a very manly thing to do. Anna had known, in fact, because Kirsty had told her. Paul's mother had been ill for some years, and he had stayed at home to give her the necessary support.

'Towards the end of her life my mother became quite disabled,' he explained. 'So we built on a single-storey annexe where she was able to live reasonably independently. It's not palatial, but there are two bedrooms and a big sitting room, and there's a courtyard garden where Charlie could play.'

'That sounds perfect!' Anna said. 'You should tell her.'

'You don't think she'd feel – you know, compromised?' Paul flushed deep red. 'I mean, I'd be living next door.'

'I don't see why. So long as everything's drawn up legally. Seriously, go and tell her now,' Anna said. 'She'll be over the moon.'

'Everyone's been telling me I should let it out or sell it off,' Paul said. 'But my mother only died last year, and I couldn't seem to get my head around a stranger living there. But I don't think I'd mind Kirsty and Charlie.' He gave Anna his diffident smile. 'It has its own entrance. Kirsty wouldn't have to see me at all if she didn't want. She's having such a horrible time, and I'd hate her to think that I'm—'

'She wouldn't,' Anna said quickly, to spare him further embarrassment. 'But it's good of you to make the situation crystal clear.'

'So do you think you could ask her?' he said hopefully.

'If you like, but wouldn't you rather ask her yourself?'

He shook his head. 'This way, if the idea fills her with horror, she doesn't have to try to be polite.'

Anna flew back to give Kirsty the good news. 'He says you and Charlie can stay there for as long as you need. If you're interested, he can show you around after work.'

Kirsty stared at Anna as if she had suddenly started speaking in tongues. Her eyes slowly filled with tears. 'Sorry,' she said, gulping. 'I think I might need a moment to take that in.'

'He says you won't be in each other's pockets. You and Charlie will have your own garden and your own private entrance.'

Kirsty blew her nose. 'I can't believe it. I feel as if I'm dreaming. I just—' She stopped herself.

'You're wondering why Paul felt he had to go all around the houses?' Anna suggested.

Kirsty nodded. 'He knew all this when we were having lunch. Why didn't he just tell me then?'

Because the poor man is mad crazy in love with you and doesn't think he stands a chance, Anna thought. 'I think, as he's your boss, he didn't want to seem to be exploiting your vulnerability,' she said, which was also true.

Kirsty's hand went to her mouth. 'Oh my God, how sweet is that?'

'He's a really scrupulous guy,' Anna said.

Kirsty shook her head. 'He's like a knight in a story!' Her lips curved into a half smile. 'A sweet, geeky knight with terrible taste in knitwear!'

'You should go and tell him,' Anna said. 'About the house, I mean. Best not to mention his knitwear!'

Kirsty disappeared across the landing. Anna returned to her to-do list as rain lashed at the windows. Outside, the weather seemed to be whipping up into a gale.

At the end of the day, Paul and Kirsty left the office together so they could pick Charlie up from his nursery on their way to look around the annex. Anna stayed at her desk for another half hour, hoping the wind and rain would ease off, then decided she'd have to brave the storm.

Out in the high street, the air was full of the sound of water, pouring out of overflow pipes and gurgling along the gutters. A gust of wind caught Anna's umbrella, blowing it partly inside out. It took a few moments of wrestling before she got it under control. Slightly breathless, Anna set off towards Carfax Tower and her bus stop. She heard a female voice say, 'I need to talk to you.' A woman stepped out in front of her, grasping her by the arm. With a clutch of fear, Anna recognized Eve Bloomfield.

She was soaked through, her wet hair plastered to her head.

In the greenish light of the storm, her pale face seemed almost luminous. Her mascara had run, making sooty tracks on her cheeks. Isadora had compared Owen's secretary to Wallace Simpson, but at this moment she looked more like one of Tolkien's murderous ring-wraiths. Anna remembered Laurie's fear that Eve was capable of killing someone. At this moment she was gripping Anna so tightly that her overlong finger nails were actually digging into her flesh. Anna smelled alcohol on her breath. With a swift jerk of her arm, she released herself. 'What do you want?'

'To open your eyes, you stupid meddling girl! He took you in, just like he did that slutty researcher girl. The poor sensitive little queer.' A gleam of malice lit her eyes. 'I bet poor innocent Laurie didn't tell you he was responsible for finally tipping Audrey over the edge! He didn't tell you she actually caught him and Owen *at* it?'

Anna quickly stepped back, lowering her umbrella, partly to prevent it tearing itself apart in the howling wind, but mostly to keep Eve at a distance. The weather had driven everyone off the street. Rightly or wrongly, Laurie had believed Eve capable of murder. If she produced a knife now there'd be nobody to see, nobody to hear Anna's calls for help. Raindrops, hard and stinging as hail, hurled themselves at her face. 'Laurie Swanson's dead,' she said clearly and firmly. 'Everyone involved is dead. You should just forget about all of them or it's going to drive you mad,' she added, though she suspected her advice was several years too late. Eve looked as unhinged as they come.

'Audrey was never a strong woman, mentally or physically.' Still in the grip of her internal narrative, Eve carried on as if Anna hadn't spoken. 'But Owen was her first and last love. To know that he and that boy . . .' She gave a shudder. 'Well, I'm neither sorry nor surprised he killed himself,' she said with sudden venom. 'Presumably, the shame and guilt of his disgusting little life had finally caught up with him.'

Two drenched tourists ran past, a boy and girl, exclaiming laughingly in Japanese.

Anna could feel cold rain trickling down inside her collar. Her trench-coat was only supposed to be showerproof, and like her trousers it was completely saturated.

'I tried to tell that Evans girl, but she wouldn't listen,' Eve said, switching to a more reasonable tone. 'Don't you make the same mistake.'

'You mean the truth about Laurie?' Anna said, confused.

'Not *Laurie*,' Eve almost spat. 'The poems. *The love poems*,' she almost shouted when Anna obviously didn't understand. 'The poems everyone thinks he wrote for Audrey!'

'I already know about the poems,' Anna said. 'Laurie told me.' She was desperate to get back home and stand under a hot shower, yet something kept her out in the wind and the rain.

Eve gave a scornful laugh. 'Laurie Swanson couldn't tell you who wrote them because he didn't *know*, you stupid girl. Nobody knew except for Owen and me.'

Anna felt a tingle of shock followed by disbelief. '*You* wrote them?'

'I was a published poet once,' Eve said. 'A good one, not that anyone remembers. But I didn't write those poems for publication. I wrote them because it was the only way I knew to bear the pain.'

Anna had to push her dripping hair out of her face. Even her eyelashes were dripping. 'I don't think I under—'

'The pain of loving Owen and knowing I could never have him!' Eve's face contorted with some private emotion. 'But then after Audrey – you know – Owen couldn't write. I could see it was killing him. There was so much pressure on him to produce a brilliant new collection. So I gave him mine and told him he could do what he liked with them.'

'And he *took* them?' Anna was appalled.

For the first time Eve smiled. 'Oh, yes. I'd offered him a way out, you see. Some he changed quite radically. Others he used as springboards for ideas of his own. A few he left exactly as they were, which I regard as a great compliment.'

'But didn't you mind?' Anna said, trying to stop her teeth chattering.

Eve looked at her as if she was insane. 'Why would I mind?'

'Because he stole your work and was lauded for it.' *Not to mention getting paid for it.*

'Owen didn't steal my poems, you ridiculous girl! I *gave* them! I'd have done *anything* for Owen.' Eve's eyes blazed.

'I'd have torn my heart out of my body! And it worked! It got him writing again. My poems helped to spark his genius into new life. For a short time, I was his muse.' She gave a humourless laugh. 'So you see, things aren't as simple as Laurie Swanson painted them. To borrow from police terminology, he was the perpetrator, not the victim. The Trahernes took him into their family, and that little pervert destroyed it as surely as if he'd set fire to their house and burned it down.' Her face twisted. 'Poor, poor Huw.' For a moment words seemed to fail her. 'If Owen could have loved me, we could have made a real happy family for that boy,' she said, shaking her head.

Anna felt a pang of pity for this deluded woman. Even though Owen was in love with another male, more than twenty years his junior and his son's school friend, even though he was prepared to pass off another poet's work as his own to preserve his image in the eyes of the world, even though he was a selfish, cowardly fuck-up, Eve Bloomfield still saw him as the charismatic genius of her girlhood dreams. With just a little airbrushing here and there, she, Owen and Huw could have made the perfect family.

A bus went by, sending water spraying in all directions.

'I am going to go now before we both get pneumonia,' Anna said, attempting to break the strange spell that Eve was exerting over her.

Eve seemed to be gazing mistily at something only she could see. 'They say the children of lovers are always orphans,' she said softly. 'I'd hoped Sara would heal him. She tried. But it's so hard for Huw to trust people now, you see?' She turned her misty unseeing eyes on Anna. 'There was no love for him in that house, only obsession. Audrey's obsession with Owen, and Owen's for—' She quickly stopped herself, as if even uttering Laurie's name made her sick to her stomach.

'But you still loved Owen,' Anna heard herself say. 'Despite everything.'

Eve gave a gasp, as if she'd been lost in a dream and Anna's words had shocked her awake. She passed her dripping hand across her face. Her eyes held nothing but pain. 'Yes, I still loved him. I loved him from the very—' Without another word, she turned and fled across the High, vanishing behind fast-moving veils of rain.

Thirty minutes later Anna was standing under a scalding hot shower, thawing out the chill in her bones. She felt deeply disturbed. There had been a strange hallucinatory quality to her encounter with Eve which had prevented her from asking obvious questions. Such as: how the hell had Eve known of Anna's connection with Laurie? And, more alarmingly, how did she know where Anna worked? Laurie had said Eve had been spying on Naomi. Had she been spying on Anna too? Could Eve have seen Anna the night she visited Laurie? Almost as disturbing was Eve's claim that she had written or provided some material for Owen Traherne's later love poems in the newly published anthology.

Anna had lived among the mentally damaged at a time when she herself was damaged, and she knew that somebody's insane delusion, if it was presented with absolute belief, could completely rock your sense of what you thought you knew to be real. Eve's twisted version of Laurie, undoubtedly tainted by sexual jealousy, not to mention rabid homophobia, was nevertheless causing Anna to doubt, very slightly, her own instinctively sympathetic response to him. But, much as Anna would have liked to write Owen's assistant off as a mad, malicious old woman, she found that she couldn't, not completely. In amongst Eve's wild accusations, Anna had detected a disturbing ring of truth.

By the time she had finished drying her hair, she had thought of someone who could help her get her facts straight. Kit Tulliver knew the Trahernes, so by association he probably knew Eve. He'd written a book about Owen. He should know, if anyone knew, if there was any truth in what Eve had told her. She found Kit's card in her study where she had left it and rang his mobile.

He didn't answer right away, which gave her too much time to ask herself what she was actually hoping to gain by getting in touch with Kit. Was she trying to compensate for what had happened – or rather what hadn't and couldn't happen – with Jake? She was still anxiously pondering this when Kit answered in a slightly muffled voice.

'Anna!' he said warmly when she'd introduced herself. 'What a lovely surprise! Could you just hang on a sec? I seem to be inadvertently talking through a towel. Ah, that's better! I was only thinking about you a few minutes ago and thinking that I must get in touch. Are you still in Oxford?'

'Yes, still in Oxford.' She had forgotten how warm and funny Kit could be. She could feel her lips curving into a smile as she pictured him trying to talk through a towel.

'I've just come back from a long tedious day in London where I got totally soaked. Hence the towel,' he added, 'in case you were wondering. I hope you're calling to arrange for us to meet up?'

'In a way,' Anna said. Kit's direct style of flirting was making her blush. 'At the book launch, you said I could talk to you, if I felt I needed to.'

'About Naomi.' His voice became serious. 'Yes, of course, and I meant it.'

'Well, this isn't about her directly, but it is kind of connected with her.'

'OK, let me think for a minute. I've literally just walked in through the door, so I'm in urgent need of dry clothes and a hot meal. Could you meet me in Browns, say, in about half an hour? We could have drinks and something to eat?'

'OK, yes, I'll see you there.' *Half an hour.* She was still wrapped in a towel! Bonnie would have to miss her second walk, Anna thought guiltily. She felt slightly giddy. Kit had given the impression that he'd been having a really bad day until she brightened things up with her phone call.

Anna put on fresh make-up and dressed with care. She gave herself a swift head to toe glance in her full-length mirror and felt satisfied with the overall effect. Her narrow black trousers, cropped to the ankle, looked good with her short leather jacket and simple black flats. She left her hair loose, wound a soft grey pashmina around her neck and set off to drive into the city through the rain.

Everything had been arranged so quickly, there hadn't been time for Anna to be nervous, but at some traffic lights she had a moment of cold panic. Would Kit Tulliver have been so charming if he'd known that Anna had recently had a complete meltdown on Isadora's doorstep? Jake had seemed to take it all in his stride, but would Kit? *Stop it,* she scolded herself. *You're just going for a meal with a nice man.*

Kit had reached Browns before her and secured them a table. He spotted her coming in and rose from his seat, kissing her lightly on both cheeks. 'Well, you're worth waiting for!' he said with warm approval.

You too, Anna thought. He looked – and smelled – wonderful.

Kit had already ordered them a bottle of red, and Anna let him fill her glass. 'Only one,' she told him, 'since I'm driving.'

'I need meat,' Kit announced, scanning his menu with comical ferocity. 'I'm hankering for some kind of medieval Robin Hood dish, but I'm not confident of my chances.'

'You could have the wild boar and chorizo burger,' Anna suggested. 'That's *almost* medieval – if you pick out the chorizo and throw away the brioche bun. And the pea shoots. And the rocket salad,' she added. 'You'd be extremely hungry, but I imagine Robin Hood and his Merry Men went to bed hungry all the time.'

Kit laughed. 'You're more subversive than you look!'

'Am I? So exactly how subversive do I look?' she asked demurely.

He glanced down at his wine for a moment, then looked directly into her eyes. 'I think my answer would depend on how closely I investigated,' he told her, straight-faced.

'Damn all you Oxford men and your academic rigour,' she said, laughing, but for the second time that day she felt her cheeks go rosy.

A girl came to take their order. Anna chose the crab linguine. Kit went for pork belly and mash with apple brandy. The girl went away smiling to herself. You could tell that Kit had charmed her to within an inch of her life. Anna knew how that felt. She was spending the evening with an attractive and available man; a man who made it clear that he was equally attracted to her. Everything about Kit Tulliver was so easy, she thought gratefully as she allowed him to pour her another half glass of wine to drink with their meal. 'So what's happening with the movie?' she asked. 'Is it all going ahead?'

'So my agent tells me,' Kit said cheerfully.

'And is it true they're signing Liam Neeson to play Owen?'

He laughed. 'Ah, that's interesting, I hadn't actually heard the Liam Neeson rumour. Last thing I heard they were trying to get

Daniel Day-Lewis for Owen and Scarlett Johansson was being put forward as the perfect choice to play Audrey.' He gave a rueful laugh. 'In other words, Anna, your guess is as good as mine. I'm just the writer, after all, so I'll be the last to know!'

Slightly intoxicated by this conversation, Anna ate her meal almost without noticing. When the dessert menu arrived, she tried to refuse, but Kit insisted on ordering profiteroles to share. 'Bring two spoons,' he told the girl with a grin. 'We'll start at opposite ends and duel it out! Oh, and two espressos.'

'Not for me, thanks.' It was the first time he'd put a foot wrong, but it had jarred.

Kit must have heard the sudden frost in Anna's tone because his smile faded. 'Sorry, am I being one of those annoying alpha males?' Reaching across the table he gently moved a strand of Anna's hair from her cheek. 'It's just that I can't help wanting to look after you. Also,' Kit added with his disarming grin, 'I did genuinely think you would want coffee!' And his grin, together with the pleasant frisson from that fleeting physical contact, instantly banished her irritation.

'So what did you want to ask me about Naomi?' he said when they were alone again.

Though it was for exactly this reason that Anna had got in touch, she immediately felt tongue-tied. By this time their meal had taken on the flirty ambience of a successful first date. To bring up her concerns now felt tasteless to say the least. But while Anna was reluctant to ruin what had been until now a very pleasant evening, for Laurie and Naomi's sakes she had to finish what she'd started. She took a breath. 'When we spoke at the launch you were concerned that Naomi had got herself mixed up with the criminal underworld and that she was possibly killed because of that.'

He nodded. 'I remember.'

Anna felt her nervousness growing, but there was no going back now. 'It's just that a few things have happened recently to make me wonder if Naomi's killer might have been someone a bit closer to home.'

Kit sat back, still holding his coffee cup. If anything he seemed to become more relaxed and attentive. 'I see,' he said, 'or rather, I don't quite see yet, but please do go on.'

She swallowed. This was proving harder than she'd thought. 'So much has happened over the past few days. I don't really know where to—'

'Start wherever it makes the most sense to start,' he said sympathetically, and Anna had a sudden flashback to the police interview room with Inspector Chaudhari on the morning of Naomi's murder.

'OK,' she said, trying to think, 'then I'll start with finding Laurie's bouquet on Port Meadow.'

She heard Kit draw a sharp breath. 'Did you say Laurie?' He made an apologetic gesture. 'Sorry, I was brought up never to interrupt, but if you're talking about Laurie Swanson, who has just—' He passed his hand across his face. He looked almost ill with distress.

'I'm afraid I was talking about that Laurie, and now I've upset you. I'm sorry.'

'No. Well, yes,' Kit corrected. 'It's always upsetting, obviously, when someone you know kills themselves, but I also wanted to make absolutely sure I hadn't misunderstood and you weren't talking about a completely different Laurie who is still alive and well.'

'No,' she said, swallowing. She still ached about Laurie.

'Huw is inconsolable, of course.' Kit shook his head. 'I was in Paris when it happened, unfortunately, promoting *The Boy in the Blue Shirt*, so I was no bloody use at all.' He rubbed his face. 'Owen was very much a second father to Laurie, you know, so Laurie and Huw were practically brothers. After Laurie's breakdown though, things were never really right between them. I never did understand why that was, and I don't think Huw did either.'

Anna was just remembering Laurie's very different take on his and Huw's relationship when Kit added unhappily, 'But even though Huw was obviously bewildered, he never stopped caring for Laurie. And now another part of his past has just gone forever.' He drained the last of his coffee, setting down his empty cup. 'Please go on, Anna. I promise I won't interrupt again. I know this must be hard for you.'

Kit kept his promise, listening in silence while Anna talked. She told him how she'd been moved but also intrigued by the message Laurie had sent with his flowers. 'In the short time I knew her, Naomi sort of changed my life. I had the feeling she'd done something similar for Laurie.' She explained how she'd tracked Laurie down and been invited to visit with Bonnie. As she talked Anna noticed she was swiftly editing out parts of her and Laurie's conversation as she went along. She completely omitted any whiff of Laurie's love affair with Owen, which meant she also had to leave out how he'd given her his box of papers to keep safe. She couldn't explain why, but now that it came to it, Anna felt reluctant to expose Laurie's secret life to Kit. Obviously, she couldn't mention the bizarre similarities between Laurie and Audrey's suicides either, since this was information she wasn't meant to have. Feeling that she was skating along on ever thinner ice, Anna said, 'But here's the thing that's really bothering me. When I talked to Laurie, he told me that Eve Bloomfield had confronted Naomi outside his house, seeming quite unhinged, he said, and apparently she also made threats against Laurie.'

Kit rocked back in his chair as if he'd received a physical blow. 'Shit,' he said, half to himself. 'And now they're both dead. That is actually extremely disturbing, Anna. You don't think Eve could possibly have—?'

'I don't know what I think,' Anna told him. 'That's really why I wanted to talk to you.' She described how Eve had been waiting for her outside Walsingham and had claimed authorship of Owen's love poems. 'I mean, you knew the Trahernes, so presumably you know Eve? Could there be any truth in it, do you think?'

He shook his head. 'I very much doubt it. One thing you should know about Eve – she's notorious for her histrionics. She's an attention seeker, always has been. The only difference now is she's too old and bitter – and, let's face it, too bizarre – to get the male attention she craves. There's no way she can prove she wrote those poems, and she knows it.' Kit drew a much-needed breath. 'Sorry, as you can tell I am not a big fan of Eve Bloomfield. You know she refused to give us any help with Owen's biography? You'd think she'd have jumped at the chance to give the world her version of Owen, but no!'

'I suppose – if she's loved him unrequitedly for all those years, she just wanted to keep her version of Owen for herself,' she suggested.

Kit's expression instantly softened. 'What a very sweet girl you are, Anna Hopkins. You make me feel quite ashamed of my own base and selfish character. Look, I really appreciate you telling me all this. I think I should go and have a private talk with Eve. Apart from anything else, if she's becoming as dotty as you say, she should probably be getting some kind of help.'

'Thank you,' Anna said. 'Thank you for listening and for your time. Now I really should go so I can take my poor neglected dog out for a last walk before bed.'

'What kind of dog?' he said at once.

'A very beautiful one with a mysterious past,' she told him, laughing. She felt almost as if she was watching herself, a witty young woman in a movie, a woman who was confident of her charms. Being with Kit somehow set her free; free to be a different, lighter Anna.

As they left Browns, she felt the pleasant pull of the unmistakable sexual tension that had been building throughout the evening. So when he leaned in to kiss her on the lips it felt natural to respond. Kit was a good kisser. He'd presumably had a lot of practice, she thought, remembering Isadora's shameless matchmaking. She was enjoyably aware of the light pressure of his hand touching the small of her back. Anna had rested her own hand against the front of his beautifully-cut tweed jacket. She caught a delicious whiff of his aftershave as she closed her eyes. Kit smelled subtly expensive, wonderfully kissable.

And totally wrong. She stepped back, flustered. She wasn't sure, but she might have very slightly pushed him away. 'I've had such a lovely evening, thank you,' she said politely.

If Kit was dismayed he was too well-bred to let it show. 'The pleasure was all mine,' he said without missing a beat. 'I hope I've helped. And I promise to let you know what I find out.'

As she watched him walk away, she was already pressing buttons on her phone.

Tansy answered at once. 'Hey, Anna, what's up?'

'I need to tell someone about my rather weird day. Do you think you can bear to listen?'

FOURTEEN

The rain had almost stopped, but the wind was still wild, sending ragged clouds scudding over the city as Anna drove to the Jericho address Tansy had given her. This turned out to be a former industrial building of some kind, now stylishly converted into a home.

Tansy opened the door, accompanied by Buster. 'Wow, you look gorgeous!'

'Ditto,' Anna said, smiling.

Tansy looked down at herself in surprise. She had wrapped herself in a brightly-coloured Fair Isle cardigan with a fleecy lining. Her skinny jeans were tucked into fleecy boots. 'I'm basically trying to keep warm,' she said as Anna followed her into the house. 'I've been soaked through three times today!'

A steep flight of stripped wooden stairs led directly up from the hallway. The artworks on the walls were mostly old black and white photographs. Anna followed Tansy up to the landing with Buster frisking alongside. At the top was an ornate chest on which was displayed an old-fashioned gramophone with a horn.

'What an amazing place to live,' Anna said. 'What did this building used to be?'

'An old Victorian corset factory,' Tansy said with a grin. 'Nick runs his graphics business from a studio at the back.' She ushered Anna into a high-ceilinged open-plan space in which living, eating and relaxing areas were suggested by arrangements of furniture and art objects rather than imposed by walls and doors. Anna looked around with approval bordering on envy. Industrial conversions often seemed soulless, but Nick and Leo had succeeded in turning the small factory into a genuinely comfortable – as well as aesthetically impeccable – home.

'Did your friends do this all themselves?' Anna asked.

'I don't think they did the plumbing and wiring, but everything else,' Tansy said. 'Shall I make us both some herbal tea before we get settled?'

She disappeared into the kitchen, leaving Anna with Buster. Having sniffed Anna's trouser hems to his eventual satisfaction, he sat at her feet with an expectant doggie grin. It was strange to think that this woolly poodle and Bonnie both belonged to the same species. Buster looked so different in every way to her elegant wolf-like Bonnie.

'Are Nick and Leo both artists?' Anna asked as Tansy came back in, setting a tray down on the hearth.

'Just Nick. Leo runs that artisan bread shop in the covered market. They supply all the bread for Marmalade.'

'He and Nick must have worked hard, building up successful businesses and doing up this place,' Anna said.

'Too hard they'd say now.' Tansy perched herself on the arm of a sofa opposite Anna. 'Leo had a cancer scare,' she explained. 'They decided it was a wake-up call. That's why they're taking this trip. Leo says it's going to be the gay version of *Eat, Pray Love*,' she said with a laugh. 'Nick says he just hopes it doesn't turn into *Thelma and Louise*!'

'It's a great place to house-sit,' Anna said. 'How long will your friends be away?'

'Another six months then it's back to the real world of minging house shares. I had this pathetic fantasy that I'd run into Mr Right while I was walking Buster. Actually, the way things are going, I might settle for Mr Almost Right.' She gave Anna a wry smile.

'I just spent the evening with Mr Almost Right,' Anna told her. 'Kit Tulliver invited me to dinner at Browns.'

'You went on a date with Kit Tulliver!' Tansy sounded scandalized.

'Not intentionally,' Anna said.

'How can you *accidentally* go on a date?'

'It's hard to explain,' Anna said.

'Sounds a bit suss to me,' Tansy teased.

'You know what's weird? I'd been kind of hoping he'd kiss me, but when he did—' Anna let her sentence hang.

'No chemistry?'

'Until he kissed me I'd have said there was tons. But then—'

'But then *bleargh*!' Tansy said with a sympathetic shudder. 'It's such a let-down when that happens. Though I wouldn't have thought you'd need to go looking for extra chemistry, having seen you and Jake the other day.' She pretended to fan herself.

'There isn't a "me and Jake",' Anna told her.

'If you say so, sweetie.' Tansy jumped up from her perch and poured out straw-coloured chamomile tea into two mugs, handing one to Anna. 'So tell me about your weird day that ended in an accidental date with Mr No Chemistry.'

Anna told Tansy about being waylaid by Eve. Tansy listened wide-eyed, pulling on a straying curl and occasionally interrupting with comments like, 'Shit! No WAY!' or, 'Oh my God, the homophobic bitch!' But when Anna reached the part where Eve claimed to have given Owen her love poems to him, so that he could publish them as his own, she said uncertainly, 'That *can't* be true! Can it?'

'I don't know,' Anna said. 'I get the feeling Eve Bloomfield has spent a lot of her life feeling disparaged, most of all by the man she loved. By giving away her poems to Owen, I think it was like she'd ridden in on her white horse to save him, but also surpassed him at the same time.'

'She sounds like a bloody scary woman,' Tansy said with a shiver. 'So is that why you contacted Kit?'

'I wanted to know if he'd heard any rumours.'

'But he hadn't?'

Anna took a sip of her hot tea. 'No. And he had no idea that Eve had made threats to Naomi and Laurie. He was really shocked, in fact. He said he's going to talk to her, try to get to the bottom of it.'

Tansy looked alarmed. 'You didn't tell him everything, did you? I mean, about the autopsy reports.'

'Of course not,' Anna said. 'And I didn't tell him about Laurie and Owen, or about Laurie's papers. Kit really can't stand Eve,' she added. 'He thinks she's a compulsive attention seeker.'

'Do you think that's true?'

Anna put down her cup. 'I can't help thinking there's a grain of truth in there somewhere.'

'Maybe we should go and talk to her?' Tansy suggested.

Anna felt a rush of something like relief. 'Seriously?'

Tansy shrugged. 'She's obviously got a story she needs to tell, and no one else seems to want to listen. We could go right now.

It's better if there's two of us,' she added, 'in case she goes postal again and tries to pull a knife.'

'At least we don't have to worry about being rude turning up unannounced,' Tansy said as Anna drove them to Eve's house in Blackbird Leys. 'Seeing as Eve accosted you in the first place. Seriously though,' she added anxiously, 'what shall we say when she asks why we've come?'

'I think we should say what you said,' Anna said. 'That we want to hear her side of things.'

They arrived outside the small town-house that Tansy had staked out a couple of days previously. Anna thought of Owen Traherne and his beautiful houses. After all her years of devotion, Eve had ended up living in this cramped little house with neighbours who held screaming matches outside her door. Someone had abandoned a rusty fridge and an old sofa in one of Eve's neighbour's gardens. A group of youths hurried by, their faces obscured by their hoods. Anna could smell the familiar sweet stink of dope.

They walked up the path, and Anna pressed the buzzer, but no one answered.

'I can't see a light, can you?' Tansy tried to peer through the grubby sitting room window.

'She might have just passed out,' Anna said. 'She reeked of alcohol this afternoon.' She kept her finger on the buzzer for longer this time, then she rapped on the front door.

A woman came out of the neighbouring house. 'She's not here.' Her voice had a strong Oxfordshire twang. 'Someone came to pick her up in a car about an hour ago.'

'Oh, OK, thanks,' Tansy said, just as Anna said:

'Did you see who came to fetch her?'

'A big bloke I've never seen before,' the woman said.

Anna and Tansy exchanged glances.

'What kind of big bloke?' Tansy asked.

The woman wrinkled her nose. 'The kind you don't want to get too close to. I didn't get a good look, but he sounded Eastern European. I work with some at the factory. He sounded like them, like he'd got fistfuls of nails in his mouth. Sly buggers the lot of them. I don't know why this government—'

'Thanks for your help,' Anna said, cutting her off before she could get into a rant about immigrants.

They hurried back to the car. Neither of them spoke until they were inside with the doors closed, then Tansy turned to Anna with an incredulous expression. 'Do you think he was Albanian?'

'I don't know.' Anna felt thoroughly confused.

'Shit – you don't think she's been kidnapped?'

Anna shook her head. 'No, it's got to be a coincidence. He was probably just a friend.'

'He didn't sound like a very pleasant friend,' Tansy pointed out.

'They'll suit each other then!' Anna said, hoping to make her laugh. She felt Tansy was blowing things completely out of proportion. 'Maybe she found him on a special website?'

Tansy immediately covered her ears. 'Euw! One of those disgusting fuck buddy websites for old people!' But after her burst of hilarity, she went quiet again.

They drove back to Jericho in silence. Once, Anna glanced across at Tansy and saw her staring straight ahead, lips pressed together as if her thoughts were too complicated or unhappy to share.

Anna was welcomed home by a rapturous Bonnie. 'I know, I know,' Anna soothed her, feeling pangs of guilt. 'I am a rubbish dog owner. Let me just grab your lead and we'll go for a quick walk before bed.'

The streets of Park Town were wet and shining after the heavy rain. The high winds had brought lower temperatures, and the air was chill but fresh. Anna felt herself starting to unwind as she walked along with Bonnie, letting her sniff at every lamp post and wheelie bin in compensation for being left alone for so long.

Somehow she found herself outside the gates of the Dragon School, where Laurie and Huw had both been pupils. Anna's brothers, Dan and Will, had also been pupils there. The familiar sign, with its golden dragon, gave her a bitter-sweet pang. Under the seated dragon was the school's Latin motto in letters of gold. *Arduus Ad Solem*; striving towards the sun.

Anna's younger brother, Will, a natural rebel, had instantly distrusted that motto. 'Someone should tell them about Icarus,' he'd protested to their father. 'Icarus strove towards the sun, and he crashed to earth in flames!' She closed her eyes and saw Will's brown eyes glinting with mischievous delight at having found a way to challenge the world of adults, if only for a moment; her funny, bright, maddening little brother, who never had a chance to strive for the sun, or to become the wonderful man he was born to be.

Next morning Kirsty came into work bubbling over with excitement. Her visit to Paul's home had been a big success. She told Anna that she'd been inwardly bracing herself for a possibly gruesome apartment where a dying woman had spent her last days. Instead she'd found herself walking around a light, spacious dwelling. 'And you know the strange thing – it felt so *happy*, Anna!' Kirsty had accepted Paul's offer to let her rent it for an initial six months and was now searching the Internet for an affordable man with a van to help her and Charlie move their belongings.

Anna worked on till her lunch break, when a text from Tansy popped up on her phone: *Couldn't stop thinking about this Eve thing. Going to London tonight, hoping for some answers.*

'Whatever that means,' Anna said under her breath.

She left Kirsty talking to a possible van man and went out to pick up some groceries. She was just walking into the covered market when she got a call from Isadora. 'Darling, I really think this business is driving us all mad. Did you know Tansy's shooting off to London to question someone who might know more about this – I think rather far-fetched – Albanian connection? Have you any idea what she might be up to?'

'Absolutely none,' Anna said, making her usual queasy detour around the butcher's shop where dead partridges and hares hung limp and bloodstained from steel hooks. She heard Isadora take a breath.

'Anna, I am faced with something of a dilemma. The other day when you were dead to the world, I heard Tansy on the phone talking about something I wasn't supposed to overhear. I believe there's someone in her past who at one time posed a real danger, someone she's made strenuous efforts to cut out of her life.'

'And you're worried that's who she's going to see?' Shocked by Isadora's words, Anna had come to a halt, forcing annoyed shoppers to weave around her. She had sensed something was wrong last night, but she couldn't imagine why Eve's unknown Eastern European male had sent Tansy hurtling off to London to meet some dangerous man – Anna assumed it was a man – from her past. Why was she risking herself on this mad mission, which as far as Anna was concerned was pure fantasy? You never really knew what was going on in another person's mind, she thought. Even someone as sweet and innocent as Tansy Lavelle.

'I'd gladly go with her to make sure she's not getting herself into hot water, but I have to attend a dinner at my old college. Do you think you could go along and keep an eye on her?'

'Of course I'll go.' Anna suppressed a sigh. 'I'll drive her.'

She texted Tansy as she joined the queue at Ben's Cookies. *I'll pick you up after work. I'll drive. You get to choose the tunes.*

Inevitably, there had been an accident. A lorry had overturned, and the London-bound carriageway of the M40 was gridlocked for miles. Anna was forced to creep along in the slow lane. Beside her Tansy sat huddled inside her leopard-print coat, picking agitatedly at her nail polish. Apart from commenting, 'Does Bonnie like travelling in cars? Buster always gets sick,' she'd hardly said a word since Anna had picked her up. Mindful of what Isadora had told her, Anna just let her be. She knew better than to try to talk Tansy out of whatever hare-brained scheme she was hatching. She would just let it play out and hope she could help to pick up the pieces afterwards.

Unlike Buster, Bonnie was a seasoned traveller, and she was over the moon to be included on Anna and Tansy's road trip. Anna caught glimpses of her each time she glanced in her rear-view mirror, snowy ears pricked, dark-rimmed eyes shining.

Eventually, the traffic eased and Anna was able to put her foot down. Tansy took out her mobile phone. Hooking it up to Anna's car stereo she selected a playlist. The chilled sounds of Big Calm filled the car. 'I thought you'd be more, like, old school.' She flashed a wan smile.

'You were right,' Anna said, though it was hard for her to think of Morcheeba as 'old school'.

Tansy went back to picking at her nail polish, and Anna concentrated on driving, wondering how it was that music could comfort and sadden you at the same time. She'd been so ridiculously young when she bought that CD.

'There are some cookies,' she said, 'if you're hungry.'

Tansy shook her head. The playlist ended, and Tansy didn't move to select a new one.

They were approaching London's outer edges, and Anna was starting to feel nervous. 'You'll have to tell me which part of London I'm heading for,' she said, just as Tansy said, in a voice sharp with tension:

'Have you heard of someone called Frankie McVeigh?'

Anna gave a surprised laugh. 'I might be old school, but I wasn't born under a rock! You'd have to be brought up on a desert island not to have heard of Frankie McVeigh.' He was right up there with the Kray twins and Ronnie Biggs the Great Train Robber; except, unlike Ronnie Biggs, Frankie McVeigh had never been formally charged. The tabloids hinted at evidence going missing, crucial witnesses being mysteriously spirited away; whatever the reason, nothing ever finally stuck to Frankie.

'You want to go west,' Tansy said abruptly. 'Follow the signs to Ladbroke Grove.' She was sitting forward in her seat now as she issued directions, ash-pale with tension. 'Park here,' she ordered at last.

Anna parked, cracking open a rear window for Bonnie. 'Guard the car, OK?' she told her dog.

After Oxford, London seemed scruffy and grim: bins overflowing with fast food detritus, bits of rubbish blowing down the middle of the road. People on the street walked fast, avoiding eye contact.

'Where are we going?' Anna asked Tansy.

'Not far.' Tansy set off at a fast clip.

Anna had forgotten the constant exhausting rumble of London's traffic, the way the air already felt used up before it reached her lungs. They crossed over a couple of streets, passing Asian- and Caribbean-owned off-licences and grocery stores.

Tansy came to a standstill outside a Chinese restaurant sandwiched between a betting shop and an Afro-Caribbean barbers.

The name of the restaurant was The Jade Pagoda. A glance through the window between dangling Peking ducks, violently red and complete with heads, told Anna that this was the kind of authentic Chinese eating place patronized mainly by other Chinese. There was one European customer sitting alone, shovelling in rice Chinese-style from a bowl held up to his mouth. When she saw him, Anna felt all the tiny hairs stand up on her neck. She knew this man. Not from real life, from TV news bulletins. She pulled Tansy away from the window before he could see them. 'Jesus, that's *him*!' she hissed. 'That's Frankie McVeigh!' She had a sudden appalling thought. 'Tansy, please tell me we haven't come to see this terrifying man? I was willing to go along with this, but—'

'He's my dad,' Tansy interrupted in a flat voice.

'Frankie McVeigh is your dad? Jesus *Christ*, Tansy!' Anna saw Tansy freeze. 'Sorry,' she said quickly. 'You just took me by surprise.'

So this was the dangerous somebody that Isadora was so worried about Tansy letting back into her life. Not some abusive lover, as Anna had anxiously assumed, but her own father, who also happened to be the head of an infamous criminal dynasty. Drug trafficking, bribery, gambling, arms dealing, assault, extortion, fraud, prostitution, murder; Frankie had done it all. In his time, Frankie had been known to associate with Yardies and Colombian drug cartels, as well as the Russian and Albanian Mafia and, it was rumoured, the Triad. Then a big robbery had gone wrong, after which Frankie McVeigh's nefarious dealings seemed to come to a halt, though various body parts belonging to the gang member who'd informed on him were later found floating in the canal.

'Listen to me, Anna,' Tansy said urgently. 'Let me do the talking, OK? Whatever he says to you, if he offers you the moon and the stars and your own private nightingale to sing you to sleep, don't let yourself get sucked in. He's a clever bastard, my dad, so we'll just go in and out. No friendly chit-chat. We go in, we get the info, and then we're gone.'

'What info?' Anna said. 'You do realize I haven't a clue what's going on!'

'About Eve and the Albanians,' Tansy said, as if this was

obvious. 'Promise me you won't listen to him, Anna,' she begged, and Anna could hear real panic behind her words.

Anna had never been a big hugger, but just at that moment Tansy looked so scared that she might have risked it if she hadn't been afraid that would totally finish Tansy off, so she just said firmly, 'I promise.'

'Just in and out, remember?' Tansy's face had gone taut with stress.

Anna nodded. Tansy pushed open the door.

Frankie McVeigh saw them the minute they walked in. He looked in better shape than he'd looked in the news photos, Anna thought. He set his rice bowl down. 'Maxine!'

'Hello, Frankie,' Tansy said coldly.

Anna followed her past Formica-topped tables, over to Frankie's solitary corner. The restaurant was strictly canteen-style, no ornamental dragons or smiling Buddhas. More of the startlingly red Peking ducks hung from hooks above the counter. Stainless steel trays filled with noodles and vegetables in sauce were keeping warm. The smells wafting from the kitchen made Anna's mouth water. No one looked up to watch as they walked past, but she seemed to feel eyes boring into the back of her head. It was ironic, she thought, remembering all the social situations she'd avoided over the years, that she had actually invited herself along to this awkward, possibly dangerous father-daughter reunion.

Tansy's father stood up, smiling, opening his arms wide. Tansy immediately folded hers.

'Come on, sweetheart, don't be like that! Give your old man a hug.' Frankie's accent was pure London filtered through a smoker's rasp. Tough and stocky with a strong Irish jaw that was faintly stippled with designer stubble, he looked good in his flawless white shirt, well-cut charcoal grey jacket and jeans. He was surprisingly youthful-looking for a man who must be in his sixties.

Tansy pulled out a seat for Anna and sat down next to her. 'You do know I didn't come here to play happy families with you, Frankie? You actually remember the reason I'm here? One woman has been murdered, and another woman might be missing. For all we know she's dead now too.'

Anna was slightly alarmed to notice that their fantasy of Eve's blind date had escalated to kidnapping and possibly murder. But now that she knew Tansy's father was Frankie McVeigh, her friend's irrational fears were suddenly given a more credible context. In Tansy's past life, unexplained disappearances probably hadn't ended too well.

Frankie McVeigh abandoned the pose of exuberant dad reuniting with his long lost daughter. Letting his arms drop to his sides he returned to his seat. He gave a curt nod to Anna. 'Who's this?'

'A friend,' Tansy said before Anna could answer. 'She drove me here.'

'Your friend got a name?'

'Not as far as you're concerned,' she flashed back. 'You think I want you knowing who my friends are, or where they live? I know what happens to people who get close to you, remember.'

'No, you just think you know,' he rasped. 'You only know what your mum told you, and she's a tiny bit biased. If you'd let me tell my side just—'

Eyes blazing, Tansy didn't let him finish. 'Don't you fucking dare,' she warned. 'Don't you dare try that tired old story about Mum. I knew he'd do this,' she said to Anna. 'He never bloody changes.'

There was a highly-charged silence, during which Anna could hear the distant metallic clashing of woks and someone shouting, apparently angrily, in Cantonese.

Tansy and her father stared stonily at each other, neither of them willing to be the first to look away. At last Tansy stirred in her seat. 'You said you'd find something out for me,' she reminded him in a taut voice. 'Well, did you? Or was that just you being the Don, as usual?'

He threw her an injured look. 'I made inquiries for you, yes.'

'And what did you find out?'

'I'm not happy about this, Maxine,' he burst out. 'I know you're not a little girl any more, but there are certain kinds of vermin that you don't want to go stirring up with a big stick, know what I mean? These mafia Shqiptar geezers are evil bastards. Drug trafficking, people trafficking, robbery, arms dealing, extortion, murder; they're into it all.'

'Sounds a bit like your CV, Frankie,' Tansy said, quick as a flash.

Frankie McVeigh gave his daughter a reluctant grin. He wrote an imaginary number '1' in the air; one point to Tansy. 'Just like her mum,' he told Anna. 'Sharp as knives, both of 'em. Can I order something for you two lovely girls? No? Pot of jasmine tea?'

Tansy just waited him out, grim-faced. Anna thought she caught a flicker of hurt behind his eyes. 'Take these plates away,' he told a passing waiter irritably. 'My daughter's put me right off my food.'

When the table was clear and the waiter had gone, Frankie abruptly returned to business. 'I put the word out, but so far I'm coming up empty,' he admitted. 'I think this is a clear case of Occam's razor. Sometimes the most obvious solution is the right solution. If you want my opinion, the Oxford Ripper looks good for Naomi's murder. From what I can find out, none of the Albanians had a problem with her and none of them has ever heard of an Eve Bloomfield.'

Tansy unhooked her shoulder bag from the back of her chair and stood up. 'Thanks,' she told him. 'Thanks for the information.'

Again that flicker of something in his eyes, hurt mixed with hope. 'No need to go rushing off,' Frankie said. 'How's your mum? Keeping well?'

'I appreciate you doing this,' Tansy said. 'But now we're done. This was not me holding out the olive branch. You won't be seeing me again, Frankie.' She gave him a curt nod then started making her way back past the tables, and Anna followed.

Tansy had almost reached the door when Frankie called after her. 'Just one last thing before you go. Ever heard of a woman called Sara Traherne?'

FIFTEEN

Anna saw the lights of London thin out in her rear mirror, eventually dwindling to nothing. Keeping to the speed limit, she drove in a kind of trance, overtaking and switching lanes, just wanting to get home. Beside her Tansy leaned her head against the passenger door, emotionally drained after her fraught encounter with her dad.

Tansy had been right to warn Anna against Frankie McVeigh. Consciously or not, he had known exactly how to manipulate them. Anna felt as if she no longer knew what to think about anything now, including Tansy. Things that had never quite added up were starting to make a very different kind of sense.

I never thought I'd have to see anything like this, she'd said that morning on Port Meadow.

That must have been the promise Tansy's mother had made when they ran away from Frankie for ever: no more violence, no more blood, no more lying about what your daddy does for a living, no more jumping up in terror when the phone starts to ring in the night . . .

Tansy's mum's courage had paid off. She'd made a new life for them both. Tansy Lavelle, formerly Maxine McVeigh, had grown into a law abiding person who cherished her friends instead of leaving them floating in the canal. But violence and blood had followed her, just like they'd followed Anna.

She stole a glance at Tansy. Her eyes were closed as chaotic lights and shadows from the motorway swept across her face. She looked so fragile that Anna was suddenly mortally afraid for her. In case Tansy was genuinely sleeping she made her voice soft as she said, 'Tansy Lavelle suits you much better.'

Tansy immediately shifted in her seat. She gave Anna a wan smile. 'Lavelle was my gran's name – my Trinidad gran. I chose Tansy myself. My mum said I could be whoever I wanted now.' She did a dark laugh. 'My first choice was Beyonce, but my mum vetoed that! I'd met this girl on holiday who was called

Tansy, so I named myself after her.' Anna heard her swallow. 'I
was twelve years old. I thought if I had a beautiful name maybe
my life could be beautiful too.'

Anna kept her eyes on the road, but she could hear that Tansy
was close to tears.

'Why did I just put myself through that? I feel like I've been
dragged through the shredder, and we still don't know if
anything's happened to Eve. I feel *so* stupid.'

'What are you talking about, you daft vegan?' Anna said,
giving her a brisk pat on the knee.

'Making you drive us to London and back, all for nothing.'

'You didn't know it was going to be for nothing,' Anna pointed
out. 'And you didn't make me. I offered. I want answers just as
much as you do.'

'We didn't get answers though, did we? For all we know
Frankie's lying through his teeth. It's all about power with my
dad. If he can make out he knows something we don't, it gives
him a reason to slither back into my life.'

'You think he was lying about Sara Traherne?' Anna asked.

Tansy sat up in her seat and pulled off her ponytail band. 'I'd
like to believe he was, yeah.' She ran her hands roughly through
her loosened curls. 'Fucking Frankie!' she burst out. 'He's totally
done my head in with all that stuff he came out with.'

'Mine too,' Anna said. After what she'd seen at the book
launch, it wasn't a big stretch to imagine that the Trahernes'
marriage might be in difficulties. But the story Frankie had told
was like something out of the Sunday tabloids.

According to Frankie's source, the Trahernes' marriage had
been in trouble almost from the start. Two years ago, Sara had
become so unhappy that she'd gone completely off the rails,
drinking, gambling, doing hard drugs then secretly siphoning off
money from her father-in-law's foundation both to feed her
cocaine habit and pay off her mounting debts.

Frankie had hinted that Sara had at one time sunk so far as
to take part in sexual activities which he said he absolutely
refused to describe in the presence of his daughter. If Frankie's
story had ended there, Anna would have found it easier to
believe. Privileged and well-educated people *did* go off the rails
and end up in the Sunday tabloids. And if Sara had been caught

stealing to feed her addictions she might have shared their fate. But she'd been rescued in the nick of time by a very singular white knight.

Tansy's dad had narrated this part with relish, describing how Sara's debts had come to the attention of a man called Dritan Lika, the head, or 'Krye', of an Albanian gang that operated out of Oxford. Frankie knew this to be gospel truth, he'd said cheerfully, because it was Dritan himself who'd told him. 'He's a ruthless bastard,' Frankie had said, in his London rasp, 'but he took a real shine to this posh bird for some reason, and it seems she's took a real shine to him. Anyway, long story short, Dritan found a way to help her out of her difficulties, and as a result him and her have got quite close.' He'd flashed them a meaningful look to make sure Tansy and Anna grasped his inference. 'Last time I talked to him, he reckons she's just waiting for the right moment so she can leave and be with Dritan.' He'd let out a gusty laugh. 'You know what he told me "Dritan" means? It means "light". I think old Dritan fancies himself as a bit of an avenging angel, deep down!'

Frankie had told them that Dritan had personally assured him that the Albanians had nothing to do with abducting Eve Bloomfield, if that's what had happened, or with the death of Naomi Evans. 'And Dritan said to tell you – if your Naomi was writing a book about gangs in Oxford she never approached him or any of his men about it. He seemed a little bit miffed, actually. Bit of a narcissist, our Dritan, like most career criminals.' He'd shot a lightning glance at Anna to see if she'd clocked his use of psychological jargon.

When Anna and Tansy had finally left the Jade Pagoda more than an hour after their first attempt, Frankie had followed them out into the street.

'Maxine, wait!' The raw emotion in his voice had stopped Tansy in her tracks. 'I miss you, girl,' Frankie had told her huskily. 'I miss you, and I miss your gorgeous mum and them blistering put-downs of hers. I was a fool, and Christ knows I've paid for it. I don't expect you to believe me, and I don't blame you for not believing me, but I've changed, darling. I've learned what's really important. I was so bloody happy that you'd actually asked me for help! And if ever – *ever* – you're in trouble and you need your old dad for anything, *anything* at all . . .' He'd had to stop, fighting for self-control.

Tansy hadn't said a word. She'd set off back to the car at a fast march, not looking at Anna. When they'd reached the Land Rover, Anna had silently let Bonnie out and walked her briskly around the block, to give Tansy some space and so her dog could stretch her legs before they set off on their journey home.

No wonder Tansy feels shredded, Anna thought now. She felt shredded, and Frankie wasn't her dad. Seeing the sign for a service station up ahead, she put on her flashers and slipped into the inside lane to pull off the motorway.

'Why are you stopping here?' Tansy's voice was sharp.

'My car needs diesel,' Anna said, 'and I need caffeine.'

At first Tansy insisted she'd rather stay in the car, then reluctantly agreed she could use a pit stop. As they crossed the car park Anna noticed Tansy looking around her with obvious anxiety. They found the ladies' washroom then emerged back into the starkly lit concourse. Apart from Starbucks and Burger King all the concessions were closed. A young woman in a stained Burger King uniform was wearily wiping down one of the tables.

'I bet they have this exact lighting in the hell dimensions,' Anna said.

'And this exact waitress, poor thing,' Tansy said, watching the girl trudge to the next food-littered table. 'Wonder what she did to end up in service-station hell?'

A young couple were taking it in turns to plead with their screaming toddler. The air smelled of coffee and fries and slightly burned sugar. Other travellers were dotted about the space. At least, Anna assumed they were all on their way somewhere, not just creepy types who liked hanging out in service stations late at night.

Anna bought them both coffees from Starbucks and carried them back to the Burger King concession, where she ordered herself a Whopper and fries. Then they found a table as far as possible from the screaming little girl.

'I had totally given up caffeine until I met you,' Tansy said plaintively. 'Not to mention whatever dodgy trans fat these have been cooked in,' she added, helping herself to a handful of Anna's fries.

'Is there, like, a vegan confessional you can go to and be absolved so you can start again with a clean sheet?' Anna asked her.

Tansy laughed, then her eyes immediately filled with tears. 'Sorry,' she said shakily. 'I seem to be on a bit of a knife-edge.'

Anna pretended to be concentrating on her burger until Tansy seemed more composed, then she said, 'I was thinking in the car, and I might have figured out how Kit's Albanian gangster fantasy came about.'

'How?' Tansy said in a tired voice.

Anna took a bite of her burger. 'Think about it,' she said after she'd swallowed her mouthful. 'Naomi spent a lot of time with the Trahernes doing research for Kit. Maybe she stumbled across something that made her suspect this dark side to Sara's life? And maybe by then she was already thinking about writing her book on criminal gangs. So when she found out about Sara's connection to Dritan Lika, maybe – I realize this is a lot of maybes – but *maybe* she thought she might as well approach him for help getting first-hand material with her book? So Kit was right that Naomi was thinking of going to Dritan, but wrong to think she'd be putting herself in danger. Dritan Lika doesn't sound like a pleasant character, but he's not, like, a rabid dog – and anyway, he'd probably have seen Naomi as Sara's friend, don't you think? Plus, from what your dad says, Dritan would have been thrilled to be included in her book.'

'But Kit couldn't have known that,' Tansy said, light dawning.

'No. So, completely understandably, when she was found murdered, his mind immediately went to evil gangsters. So Kit's shocked and panicky, plus he's gone into a major guilt spiral about not being a good friend to Naomi—'

'And how he should have foreseen this exact catastrophe etcetera,' Tansy suggested.

'Exactly like you do when someone you care about dies.' Anna pushed her Burger King bag out of reach, to stop herself from eating the last congealing bit of burger. 'And you and I totally bought into it. Kit's guilt and paranoia has had us jumping at shadows, seeing kidnapping and conspiracies and I don't know what else.'

Tansy's eyes went wide. 'Fuck, Anna! Sara and Eve are friends! Eve probably knows Dritan. He could have been the bloke who picked her up from her house!'

Anna nodded. 'He could have just been picking her up to go out somewhere. Sara could have even been in the car.'

Tansy briefly buried her face in her hands. 'I'm such a muppet!' she said from behind her fingers. 'Of all people I should have known better.'

'What do you mean "of all people"?'

'I'm a fucking gangster's daughter,' she hissed. 'I hung out with criminals for the first twelve years of my life. And my dad and his mates did some terrible things. But they did normal things too, took their wives and kids on holiday, they even had a weird kind of loyalty to each other.'

'A code of honour,' Anna suggested.

'Don't know if I'd go that far,' Tansy said with a flash of black humour. 'What I'm saying is criminals might be like the dregs of the human race, but they're still human. They're not all mad psychopaths, like in the movies. And I *knew* that, yet I went jumping feet-first into some *Daily Mail* type yarn about evil Albanians.' She took a sip of her coffee, and Anna could see her thinking something through. 'Do you think Huw knows about Sara and Dritan?'

Anna thought back to the evening at the Ashmolean and Sara's dramatic exit. 'It would be terrible for him if he did. Poor guy. Always living in his father's shadow. Now on top of that he's having to keep up appearances in public with Sara. Imagine how much fun that must be if he knows she's on the verge of leaving him for some tattooed thug.' She saw Tansy's face. 'OK, so I don't actually know Dritan's got tattoos,' she said with a grin, 'but he's got to be more macho than poor Huw.'

'Why does everyone always say "poor Huw"? As if he's been fatally harmed or cheated out of his rightful whatever,' Tansy said irritably.

'Because he *has* been cheated,' Anna said. 'He's obviously had a crap life. His mum killed herself—' She struggled to communicate her impression of Owen Traherne's only son. 'You know those photos of First World War poets? The way you can already see in their faces that they're not going to come back from the trenches? That's Huw.'

Tansy drained the last of her coffee. 'I suppose my dad did help us solve one mystery tonight. We've finally solved the mystery of the Albanian non-connection!'

Anna laughed. 'Come on. Let's get back on the road.'

As they came out into the chilly night air and headed back to the car, Anna noticed Tansy quicken her step. 'I hate service stations late at night,' she confided. 'I had a bad experience in one once.'

Given what Anna now knew of Tansy's early life, if she described something as a 'bad experience', that's exactly what it had been.

Without prompting, Tansy started to describe what had happened. 'I was driving back from Scotland. I'd just ended a relationship with this hopeless guy. Don't ask,' she added, pulling a face. 'I stopped off at a service station. It must have been about three in the morning. Anyway, this guy obviously saw I was on my own and followed me out to my car. I got away, luckily.' She shot a look at Anna. 'You'll be glad to know I gave him a few nasty gashes on his face to remember me by.'

'I hope they got infected,' Anna said grimly.

Tansy tried to smile. 'Yeah, but it totally shook my confidence. For months I kept imagining someone was trying to break into where I was living. I literally slept with the kitchen knife under my pillow. I even signed up for a kick-boxing class.'

'That's why I took five years of Krav Maga – Israeli self defence,' Anna said.

'When I first met you, Anna, I felt like we were from totally different planets . . .' Tansy let her sentence trail off.

Anna remembered feeling the same about Tansy. She had seen her as inexperienced and naive, yet all the time she'd been carrying this burden. Before she turned the key in the ignition, Anna said, 'You could have told me, you know.'

Tansy didn't need to ask what she meant. 'How could I? After what happened to you and your family?'

'Your dad didn't murder my family in cold blood,' Anna said.

'No, but he did some – some really bad things, and he paid other people to do bad things.' Tansy wrapped her arms around herself. 'It would have been like telling you that I was from the same evil fucked-up world that – that ruined your life.'

Anna wanted to say something to comfort Tansy, but she couldn't think of a single word that wouldn't sound fake. She drove to the pumps and filled up with diesel.

As they pulled off the slip road, Tansy said, 'Do you ever feel like, no matter how hard you try to wash the crap of your old life away, people can still, you know, detect that whiff? I do try to be a good person, but I'll always be my father's daughter.' Tansy's voice gave a wobble. 'I am, you know! I take these mad chances. My stepdad calls it my "kamikaze" side. Take today. I suddenly go tearing off to London because I've got this . . . *fixation*, or whatever, that Eve's been abducted by Albanians.'

'It wasn't so ridiculous,' Anna said, pulling out to pass an ancient Renault Clio being driven at about forty miles an hour. 'People *do* get abducted. Statistically, a small percentage must be abducted by Albanians.'

'And I always get involved with rubbish men,' Tansy said miserably, as if Anna hadn't spoken. 'I daren't get involved with good men like Liam Goodhart because I'm scared how they'll react once they know the real me. It's like however hard I work at being Tansy, my default setting is always going to be bloody Maxine.' She darted a look at Anna. 'Sorry, I always get morbid when I'm tired. Feel free to slap me any time.'

'I don't want to slap you, but I am a bit talked-out.' Anna managed to summon a smile. 'Find a good music station,' she suggested. 'Old school as you like.'

'Can we have talk radio instead?' Tansy asked. 'I listen to it sometimes when I can't sleep.' She searched through the available stations, eventually landing on Radio Oxford.

Anna also listened to talk radio sometimes when she couldn't sleep. The anonymous bee-like murmur felt like proof that the world was still turning. It was like dozing in the back of the car at night when you were a kid, hearing the monotonous ebb and flow of your parents' voices discussing subjects that held absolutely no interest for you and was comforting for precisely that reason.

Tansy tensed. 'Did he say Inspector Chaudhari?' She hit the volume button in time for them to hear the rest of the newsflash, telling them that a member of the public had phoned the Thames Valley police with important new information. As a result, they had now formally charged a suspect believed to be the so-called Oxford Ripper and who had admitted responsibility for the spate of local murders. The newsreader read out the names of the murdered women. To their astonishment Naomi's was among them.

Tansy looked wild-eyed. 'Oh my God, Frankie was right! I can't believe it.' She pressed her hands to her cheeks. 'I don't know if I want to laugh or cry.'

'Nor me,' Anna said. The horror of Naomi's unsolved murder had hung over them since the day they met. Now it had been solved at a stroke, and it was a complete anticlimax.

In the end Naomi had just been another young woman in the wrong place at the wrong time. There was something depressingly random about this which Anna didn't feel up to examining. 'The university authorities will be happy,' she said, striving to be upbeat. 'Leaving home is scary enough for young girls without a serial killer on the loose.'

'Yes, totally,' Tansy said. 'But this should be a good thing, right? So why doesn't it feel like a good thing? Doesn't it make you feel very slightly insane?'

Anna didn't feel able to say that she would love to feel only very slightly insane. She wanted to scream at the top of her lungs that now absolutely nothing in her world made sense. Anna didn't need a therapist to tell her that her obsessive need to make sense of Naomi's death had its roots deep in her own bloodstained history. Turning detective had been her way of dealing with experiences too unbearable to deal with any other way. But Tansy Lavelle was different. Despite her criminal dad, maybe even *because* of him, Tansy had learned to bring a kind of luminous integrity to everything she did. Tansy's mum had helped to make that happen when she'd taken her daughter away from Frankie and Frankie's life. And then along came Anna with her obsessions and her murder boards and suddenly Tansy was going on stake-outs and accessing autopsy photos online. Anna didn't want to be that person who had dragged her back out of the light into the shadows.

When they pulled up outside the converted corset factory, Anna said, 'Next time we get together we should do something that doesn't involve murder boards.'

Tansy faked wide-eyed amazement. 'You're suggesting we do something just for *fun*?'

'Yes, like go to see a movie or a play.' If Anna shut her eyes she could still see the motorway with its constantly shifting lights. She was suddenly so tired that she could have crawled into the back with Bonnie and crashed out there and then. Yet once she got home she wouldn't be able to sleep.

'Rambert is coming next month,' Tansy said. 'I'll get us tickets if you like.' She looked pleased and excited. 'Did you ever see that Rooster ballet?'

'I loved that ballet,' Anna said. 'I love modern dance.' She had a sickening sensation of falling as she remembered all those other times that she'd resolved to do the things that happy healthy humans do and how it had ended.

Tansy yawned and stretched. 'So, just to be clear, you still want to be my friend even if we're not being the dog walking version of *Charlie's Angels*?'

'Never tell anybody this, but I did secretly enjoy us being the dog walking *Charlie's Angels*,' Anna said, 'but I don't think it's good for our mental health; yours, mine, or Isadora's. As for being friends . . .' She looked away for a moment. 'I don't have a lot of experience of being anyone's friend in normal adult life.' She gave Tansy a cautious smile. 'But I'm willing to give it a shot if you are.'

Tansy already had one hand on the door handle as Anna added, 'Talking about normal and adult. You should give Liam a call. Just tell him about your dad. He can handle it.'

'You think?' Tansy said wistfully.

'I know he can!' Anna took a breath. 'Tansy, what you did today was really brave.'

She stiffened. 'I'm not scared of my dad.'

'I know that. But I think you're scared you might turn into him, or get sucked back into his world.'

Without warning Tansy threw her arms around Anna. 'I know we met in such a terrible way, but I'm so glad I met you.'

'Me too,' Anna said, gently detaching herself. 'Me too.' If someone had talked to her like this when she was Tansy's age, Anna thought, she might have turned out differently. She might have made a proper life for herself instead of just wandering through a recurring bad dream.

Back home, Anna fed Bonnie and threw some dirty clothes into her washing machine. She was hungry, but it was too late to cook proper food so she made herself French toast and ate it in front of the TV.

Though she was sitting quietly in her kitchen with her dog at her feet, somewhere inside she was still driving through the dark. Anna put her hand against her chest and felt her heart speeding. She'd first felt it in the car: the fear that she was in danger of losing her grip on what was real. The last few weeks had left her strung-out and depleted. She had to be careful or she'd make herself ill, as she had done before.

Anna admitted to herself that she was never going to give up her searches for the person or persons who had come into her parents' house that night and slaughtered everyone they'd found inside. She wasn't going to chop up her cupboard of horrors and set it on fire. She couldn't. Not until her family's killers had been brought to justice. But nor could she be everybody's favourite caped crusader.

Anna had to take her own advice to Tansy and take a step back. While it was terrible that Laurie was dead, she had to try to accept that he may have actually taken his own life. Though it might seem macabre, it was not impossible that Laurie had styled his suicide as an especially melodramatic way of telling the world that he was Owen's partner and lover just as much as Audrey.

Anna put her plate in the dishwasher and went upstairs. She switched on a lamp nearest the sitting room door and saw the murder board she'd created.

'I thought only serial killers had these!'

She stopped to study the faces in the photographs, then walked to her fireplace. Kneeling by the hearth, she took kindling and screws of paper from a basket and set a fire. When the tiny flame from the match had caught and the kindling was burning, she added small logs, then slightly bigger logs, and sat watching, holding out her hands to the flames, waiting for the moment when her fire put out real heat.

Her father had taught them all how to light fires, just as he'd insisted they all learned to swim. In that way he'd hoped to keep them safe from two of the world's oldest dangers. The third danger he couldn't possibly have anticipated.

Anna rose from her knees and went back to the murder board. One by one she removed the photographs. They didn't need it. Nobody had ever needed it. When the board was empty she carried her collection of pictures back to the fire. Squatting by the hearth she gradually fed them to the flames, watching as they started to curl at the edges; Naomi's laughing face, Laurie playing music with the street children, Owen and Audrey, Eve, Huw and Sara. If she'd had a picture of Dritan Lika she'd have burned that too. She stayed watching even after they had all burned down to ash.

SIXTEEN

It was the first Tuesday after Michaelmas and the new term had begun, bringing a storm of inquiries and complaints from staff and students to Anna's desk. On the first day of term the control board had gone down in one of the lecture theatres, making it impossible for lecturers to link their laptops with the screens. Three of the IT guys were off work with flu, and Nadine had put up the backs of the remaining two as only Nadine could. As a result, Anna had come in to work to find the electrics still weren't fixed. She was eventually able to soothe everyone's ruffled tempers, but in the meantime the Nietzsche lectures had to be temporarily reassigned to a different room, which meant notifying everyone involved.

'Looking on the bright side, I can now spell Nietzsche in my sleep,' she joked to Kirsty as they walked through the city centre in their lunch hour, making the most of the sunshine before they had to be back at their desks.

Kirsty laughed. 'I've been here three years and I have to google it every time!'

The students' arrival was an irresistible tide filling the city with youthful energy and purpose. Dons and students were everywhere; coming out of cafes and bookshops, whizzing by on bikes, their short black gowns flapping and flying. Kirsty and Anna watched one glowingly beautiful girl cycle by wearing her gown over denim jeans. She had filled her bicycle basket with bright-yellow daisies and loaves of bread. 'We should photograph her for the Walsingham prospectus,' Kirsty said. 'She looks as if she's starring in a movie about Oxford.'

'They're all starring in movies about Oxford,' Anna said wryly. 'Nobody ever came here before them.'

'Bless them,' Kirsty said as the girl lifted a graceful hand from her handlebars to wave to some friends. 'So good they caught that guy,' she added with a shiver. 'Or that gorgeous creature might have found herself starring in a different kind of movie.'

Anna quickly changed the subject. 'Don't you think it feels weirdly timeless when the students are back? You'd think it would make Oxford seem more modern. But if you edit out everyone's smartphones, it feels like it could be almost any era.'

'That's why I love this city,' Kirsty said. 'It's the closest place I know to Narnia! Oh, did I tell you Paul says I can decorate? He says if I like I can have a twelve-month lease.'

'Do you think you will?'

'It's such a lovely part of Oxford,' Kirsty said. 'Charlie loves his new nursery, and it only takes one bus ride to get there. Also, Paul is charging us super-cheap rent.'

'I'm glad,' Anna said. 'You and Charlie deserved a break.'

'Though I thought we'd blown it the other day,' Kirsty said, pulling a face.

'Oh, no, what happened?'

'Paul has this massive table totally given over to some civil war enactment. I had to go and see him about something, and of course Charlie is immediately fascinated by all these little figures everywhere, and Paul says, "Oh, don't worry, Kirsty, he can't hurt them." And I'm thinking, he's obviously never seen the kind of carnage one three-year-old boy can create!' Kirsty laughed. 'So inevitably Charlie breaks one of the tiny soldiers, and then gets completely hysterical because Jason always got so mad about stuff like that. But Paul's just like, "It's fine, Charlie. That's why glue was invented. We'll have it fixed in no time."'

A group of hefty red-faced young men in grass-stained rugby clothes hurtled by, talking at the tops of their voices as they passed an open bottle of champagne between them.

Kirsty's smile faded. 'Jason's been texting me. He wants me to forgive him.'

'Don't tell me, his ex dumped him?' Anna said, and Kirsty nodded. 'Good!' Anna said, narrowly avoiding a collision with a child's buggy. Her phone pinged.

'So, how about you?' Kirsty asked. 'What's been happening in your life?'

'Nothing much,' Anna said, smiling at her text from Kit.

Bloody students are back. Feel a hundred years old. Fancy meeting a bitter old bastard at the Duke Bar later for a drink?

She quickly sent a text agreeing to meet him. Though she had kept to her resolution to step back, Anna felt she owed it to Kit to put him out of his misery about the Albanians. She couldn't bear for him to spend the rest of his life reproaching himself for Naomi's death because of a stupid misunderstanding. Unfortunately, this meant sharing what she'd learned about Sara Traherne, but she thought Kit deserved to know. It was up to him if he decided to pass it on to Huw.

As she and Kirsty headed back to Walsingham, Kirsty said fervently, 'I could never go back to Jason now. This is the first time I've felt really free to be me – and, Anna, I'm talking about in my whole *life*.'

Anna felt an envious pang. She knew that from the outside she must look like the poster girl for liberated womanhood. She owned her own home. She had no tiny dependent children or unfaithful husbands to worry about. But she was constantly battling impulses and imperatives that had a mysterious agenda all of their own.

The night after she'd got back from London, Anna had eventually given into her compulsion to drive by Eve Bloomfield's house and check if the lights were on and she was OK. She'd felt almost furtive, leaving the house with a sweatshirt pulled on over her pyjamas. It was only when she was turning into Eve's street that she'd remembered that even if she was at home safe and alive, she was likely to be tucked up in bed. But to her relief Eve Bloomfield's lights had been on and, as she hadn't properly drawn her curtains, Anna had been able to glimpse her pacing her small sitting room, apparently talking on the phone. Eve's 'abduction' really had just been a figment of Tansy's overactive imagination.

Anna was startled to feel Kirsty suddenly linking arms with her, apparently oblivious that Anna's attention had been elsewhere. 'It's like that song, "Sisters Are Doin' It For Themselves"!' Kirsty's eyes sparkled, then she gave a naughty giggle. 'Not in a rude way, I don't mean!'

'I know! I always thought those lyrics sounded really suspect!' Anna laughed and surreptitiously disengaged her arm.

A few hours later, Anna was standing in front of her wardrobe trying to decide what to wear for her date with Kit. She took down and discarded various tops, then felt annoyed as she caught herself smilingly remembering a recent email from Jake. He had sent her a photo of the view from his hotel in Stockholm and said he'd been trying to come up with a funny story ideally combining Scandinavian meatballs and Ikea furniture, but had had to give up. '*I did meet a wild pair of nuns on the plane though. I think you'd have liked them.*'

Anna couldn't figure Jake out – either what she meant to him, or even what she really felt about him. But she had been doing a lot of hard thinking, and she'd begun to wonder if part of the attraction was his unavailability. Though she sensed that he liked her as a friend, he had never sent any clear signal that he wanted a deeper relationship.

Since that night driving back from London with Tansy, Anna had decided that if she was going to stay mentally well, certain things had to change. She couldn't live a healthy life unless she made healthy grown-up decisions. Falling in love with an unattainable guy was not a healthy decision. It could only end in grief, and Anna had had enough grief. Kit, on the other hand, had made it clear from the start that he liked her, and he always seemed flatteringly delighted by her company.

Anna stopped in the middle of putting up her hair. Was it healthy and grown-up to enjoy being flattered and flirted with? Her phone rang before she could follow this thought to any conclusion. It was Jake. 'Anna,' he said, when she picked up. 'How are you?'

It was ridiculous how much she loved to hear him say her name. Just an ordinary two-syllable name, yet Jake's voice endowed it with colour and warmth, which if she didn't know better could be confused with real affection. 'Hi,' she said. 'I'm fine. Bonnie's fine. Well, she's fine, but we are having a bit of a situation at the moment.'

'You and Bonnie?' He sounded astonished.

'There are these treats my grandfather has got her addicted to. I only give them to her occasionally because they're so calorific. Now she's figured out where I keep them. First she started sniffing madly around the bottom of the cupboard, then twice now I've surprised her opening the cupboard to help herself!'

There was a short pause before Jake said a little sheepishly, 'I might be to blame for that.'

She laughed. 'How are you possibly to blame?'

'Me and the guys trained her to get us beers out of the ice box. It was like her little party piece. We'd tie a string on the handle, and she'd pull on it with her teeth until the door opened, and then she'd take out our beers one at a time!'

'Well, thanks for that,' Anna said. 'Because Bonnie has now progressed to opening doors *without* string and I'm dealing with the consequences.'

'We had a bit too much time on our hands between ops,' Jake confessed. 'And she was such a smart dog. And it was so much more fun than just getting up and fetching your own beer! Anyway, I'm due at a meeting in a few minutes so I should probably tell you why I'm calling. Our ghost just got back to me, and he came up with absolutely nothing. Eve Bloomfield has sent about ten emails in her life and doesn't even seem to *own* a mobile phone. My guy wondered if she maybe sends her messages by carrier pigeon.'

Anna laughed, enjoying the image of Eve in full make-up sending pigeons winging into the air from her narrow little house in Blackbird Leys.

She could hear traffic and other exterior sounds competing in the background. Jake must have left his hotel. 'My taxi just showed up,' he said. 'So before I go, tell me what you're up to. Are you off out partying tonight with the girls?'

Anna could see herself in the mirror holding her phone to her ear and was dismayed to see that her expression didn't so much as flicker as she told him a lie. 'Nothing so exciting,' she told him coolly. 'I'm just about to go downstairs to heat up some soup, then I'm going to finish reading my book.'

Jake's voice was breaking-up against the noises from the street. 'I'm missing you, kid. Hope to see you before too long and catch up with you and Bonnie.'

Anna went back to making up her eyes. Jake's phone call was a perfect example of Reasons Not to be Silly about Jake McCaffrey. He had only called to update her on his ghost's unsuccessful hacking activities and to ask about Bonnie. Even if she went back over their conversation with a fine toothcomb,

Anna knew she wouldn't find one iota of romantic content. *You and Bonnie*, she thought irritably, accidentally poking herself in the eye with her mascara wand. It was always, 'You and Bonnie.'

As usual the Duke bar was crowded, and it took Anna a few moments to spot Kit. Officially called the Duke of Cambridge, it was a lively venue on Little Clarendon Street. The walls were painted anthracite grey and hung with pictures of Edwardian men on bicycles and framed pictures of botanical and butterfly specimens, presumably chosen for their vintage feel. Long curving leather sofas took up most of one wall. The Duke felt timeless but intimate; a world of its own. The press of people felt less claustrophobic than it might have been, thanks to the glass dome that had been set into the roof and which at night was illuminated by a cleverly-placed chandelier. Looking up, as a temporary respite from scanning the faces of strangers, Anna could make out vague shapes of rooftops and chimney pots and a full, almost rosy-coloured moon sailing in an apparently cloudless sky.

Suddenly someone moved at the bar, and Anna saw Kit waving and smiling. She started to make her way to him, trying not to step on people's toes, but when she looked for him again in the crowd he had turned away, apparently talking to someone beside him. She heard his warm laugh rise above the talk and laughter. 'Sorry I'm late,' she said slightly breathless as she reached him at last. 'I had trouble parking.'

He always looked so good, she thought. Somehow Kit made being Kit Tulliver seem at once effortless and immensely enjoyable. She smiled up at him just as Kit said, 'Anna, darling, come and meet Huw! I've told him all about you, and he's been longing to meet you.' Only then did she recognize the man standing beside him at the bar.

As she and Huw exchanged pleasantries, she thought that finally meeting him was like seeing a fictional character come to life. Without intending to, Anna, Tansy and Isadora had collectively created a character for Owen's son. *Poor Huw.* Now here he was with his oddly unmemorable features, nursing his glass of spirits and smiling at her with an expression that, with the best will in the world, Anna found hard to interpret as a longing for her acquaintance.

With Huw present Anna couldn't bring up the subject of Sara

and Dritan. But Kit must have told Huw that they'd talked about Laurie's death, she thought. So after they'd taken their drinks to a slightly less crowded part of the bar, she said hesitantly, 'I was so sorry to hear about Laurie Swanson.'

For the first time Huw's slightly fixed expression wavered. 'It was a terrible shock,' he admitted. 'But I think Laurie's suicide showed immense courage. *He* decided, not the doctors, or the hand of fate, how and when Laurie Swanson made his exit from this world.'

Anna hadn't noticed at the book launch what a beautiful voice Huw had. It was almost an actor's voice – resonant and authoritative, and far deeper than she'd have imagined could emerge from such an unprepossessing frame.

'Hard on the people Laurie left behind though.' Huw stared off into space, his face bleak. 'I've known him since I was seven years old. He's woven through almost every one of my boyhood memories.'

Anna thought of the many losses Huw had suffered; now his friend was dead and Huw would go to his grave never knowing why Laurie had to distance himself the way he had.

'Tell Anna about Laurie's memorial,' Kit prompted.

'Yes, yes, the memorial.' Huw seemed to shake off sad memories. 'For obvious reasons, the funeral is just going to be very quiet, but we're planning a big memorial at the Sheldonian. I know Kit would love it if you were able to be there, Anna.' Huw glanced at his watch. 'Shit, I'd better get back to Sara. We've got a business dinner to do with funding.' Once again he was the fraught man she'd seen at the Ashmolean, trying and failing to keep all the plates spinning.

Kit and Anna watched him go hurrying out into Little Clarendon Street.

'Those people over there are just leaving,' Kit said. 'If we're quick we might get a corner of a sofa to ourselves.'

As soon as they were seated, Kit said in a low voice, 'That poor guy. Now Huw will never know why Laurie cut him off like he did.'

Anna didn't say she'd been thinking the same thing. Laurie's reason for dropping Huw felt too private, too painful, for her to even touch on.

Kit took an appreciative sip of his wine. 'Don't say anything to Huw,' he said, 'but I actually went to see Laurie after he'd got that terrible diagnosis. Maybe Laurie told you?'

'Actually, no, I don't think he did.' Laurie hadn't mentioned visits from Kit or anyone else. She'd had the impression he'd withdrawn totally from all normal social contact.

He shrugged. 'I knew if they didn't sort it out before Laurie died they'd never have the opportunity, and I thought that would be a fucking shame.'

'That was a really lovely thing to do,' she said.

'Huw's my friend,' Kit said. 'I was concerned about the effect Laurie's death would have on him. Rightly, as it turns out. Now on top of all that there's all this shit with Sara.'

'Oh, yes, about Sara,' Anna started tentatively.

There was a sudden swell of laughter from the bar, and Kit didn't hear. 'Sara always was high maintenance, but these past months she's been poison. They were ridiculously young, mind you, when they got married. Exactly a week after graduation, can you believe?'

'That *is* young,' Anna said. 'I mean maybe in the 1960s . . .'

'You mean in the 1960s when Owen and Audrey got married? *Also* exactly a week after they'd graduated?' Kit's tone was heavily ironic. He shook his head. 'Can you see a subtle pattern emerging?'

Anna felt a pang of pity. The loss of her family had left her prey to her own destructive patterns. But Huw Traherne's life seemed to have taken on the dimensions of a Greek tragedy. Though he'd spoken admiringly of Laurie for taking charge of his own fate, he seemed to have very little control over his own.

'I don't think Huw even realized, you know, that he was unconsciously following in Owen and Audrey's gilded footsteps,' Kit said with a sigh. 'Like so many people who got sucked into Owen's orbit, poor Huw bought into the whole monstrous myth.'

'You sound as if you didn't like Owen very much.'

'I don't like what he did to Huw,' he said sombrely. 'Huw absolutely hero-worshipped him. On some level he's always been trying to please him. I think that's why Huw has been half killing himself to keep his marriage going, regardless of how appallingly Sara behaves. It's his parents' marriage he's trying to save.'

'Sara is one reason I wanted to see you,' Anna said before she could lose her nerve. 'I've been given—' she tried to find a way to phrase it that wouldn't sound ludicrously melodramatic – 'some rather sensitive information that I think you should hear.'

Kit shot her a mock-wounded look. 'Here am I innocently imagining that I've convinced you of my charms, when actually this is the second – no, actually I do believe it's the *third* – time that you've come to see me with an ulterior motive!'

He had not only kept count of how many times he'd met Anna, but he'd also entertained hopes of charming her. Storing this information away for later, Anna lowered her voice and started to tell Kit what Tansy's father had told them about Sara Traherne.

'Sorry,' he interrupted, 'but how exactly do you know this?'

'I can't tell you that, but it's from a reliable source.' Maybe not exactly 'reliable', she thought, but terrifyingly well-informed. Taking a breath she went on to tell him about Sara's involvement with Dritan Lika. 'So there was an Albanian connection,' she finished up. 'Just not in the way you thought.'

Kit seemed temporarily speechless. 'And you're absolutely sure this is true?' he said at last.

'Pretty sure, yes.'

He looked completely stricken. 'Then why the hell didn't Naomi say anything?'

'I can only think she decided it would put you in an impossible position, being so close to the Trahernes.'

'That's exactly how Naomi would think.' Kit's eyes grew sorrowful, then he tossed back the last of his wine. 'But you were absolutely right to tell me, Anna. I'll tell Huw, obviously, but not till all this publicity madness for Owen's biography is behind us. He's going to be devastated, and he's got enough stress with the funding bid and organizing this huge memorial for Laurie. When it's over, I'll take him away somewhere and tell him then.' His face twisted. 'How could any sane woman pass over a lovely guy like Huw for some thug?'

Anna shrugged. 'I suppose some women are irrationally attracted to thugs.'

'Like those ghastly women who fall in love with killers on death row, you mean?' Kit peered into her glass. 'You've still got half your designer lemonade! Come on, drink up, and I'll get us both a proper drink.'

'I'll just have another Limonata please,' Anna said. 'Driving,' she reminded him.

When he eventually returned with their drinks he said plaintively, 'You know my manners are usually much better than this.'

She laughed. 'I hadn't noticed you being excessively bad-mannered!'

He gave her a grin. 'Thank you – I think! But I have a horrible suspicion that last time we met, I must have talked non-stop about myself. I've just realized that I know almost nothing about you, Anna, except that you own a dog with a mysterious past and are friends with the fabulous Isadora.'

'I can't believe you remembered about my dog,' she said, smiling. She was about to tell him about Bonnie's latest escapade, when he said:

'So, tell me about your life. I don't even know what do you do for a living!'

She briefly considered telling him she worked in admin, but settled for, 'I think I'm one of those sad people who are still figuring out what they want to be when they grow up.'

'Who the hell wants to be grown up?' Kit made his quick comeback sound like a joke, but for the first time Anna thought she detected real unhappiness. 'You know those Bob Dylan lyrics?' he asked. '"I was so much older then. I'm younger than that now"? When I think of the dreams I had as a boy, I could seriously tear out my hair.' He tugged at it to demonstrate, making it stick up in tufts. 'You see, I even have comedy hair!'

Kit always could make her laugh. 'Comedy hair aside, you seem to have grown into a reasonably OK adult,' she told him.

'That's very sweet of you. But in reality I'm just another hack, making money – extremely good money, admittedly – out of other people's achievements. If I was going to write a great novel, I rather think I'd have done it by now, don't you?' He laughed and shook his head. 'I told you, it's all these students everywhere with their shiny unused faces, making me feel old.' He frowned into his glass. 'Time to stop drinking, Tulliver,' he admonished himself. 'Any minute now I'll start blaming my mother.'

'Don't,' she told him, 'or only if your mother did something hideous and Gothic, like dressing you up as a girl or holding you up by your ankles over a pan of boiling chip fat.'

'Christ,' Kit said appalled, '*do* people do those kinds of things? Come to that, does anyone boil chip fat?'

'So I've heard,' Anna said evasively, with a mental apology to the people who had shared these precise traumas with her long-ago therapy group. 'I think you actually enjoy being self-deprecating,' she went on sternly. 'It's part of your "I'm charming-but-harmless" routine.'

He sat forward in his seat. His eyes held a sudden unreadable gleam. 'Is that what you think I do?'

'Yes, I do.' Anna didn't know why being with Kit made her so outspoken. Maybe it was the sexy way he looked at her, as if he was utterly fascinated by her. 'And given what most people in the world have to do for a living, who the hell cares if you never write the great British novel?' she flashed back at him. 'You had enormous respect for Naomi, after all, and she *loved* finding out about people and felt enriched by it.'

'Well, well, well,' he said softly, 'so the beautiful Anna is a glass half-full person, after all.'

'Glass half-full? Me?' she said in surprise. 'I don't know if I even *have* a glass!'

He seemed to think for a moment. 'OK, then, Anna Hopkins.' His eyes met hers in a humorous challenge. 'Tell me something *incredibly* fascinating about yourself that absolutely nobody knows.'

Anna's mind immediately jumped to her cupboard of horrors. She gave a startled laugh. 'Like what?'

'The whole point of this exercise, you enchanting but maddening girl, is that it's something I don't already know.'

'I did get that,' she said, feeling her cheeks go hot, 'but since you've suddenly sprung this on me in a crowded bar, I think you should at least give me an example.'

Kit considered for a moment. 'OK. Well, for instance that, since your childhood, you have had the most extraordinary affinity with bees.'

'Bees,' she repeated.

He nodded, eyes sparkling. 'When you were a little girl, you used to go down to your grandmother's beehives and tell the bees your troubles.'

'My grandmother never kept—' she started to say.

'You asked me for an example, woman,' he interrupted sternly, 'and this is my example! You used to talk to the bees as a child, and as a result bees – all bees everywhere, even enormous, vicious, venomous African bees – love you and would never sting you, not if their very lives depended on it.'

Kit's eyes were so soft and mischievous as he spun this impromptu fairy-tale that, had Anna been a different person, she might have grabbed his lapels and kissed him on the lips there and then. Instead she said coolly, 'Isadora was right about you. Your speciality is piffle.'

'Piffle is my gift to the world,' he agreed solemnly.

When they eventually left the bar, Kit walked Anna back to her car. 'Don't forget to text me your address,' he said, 'then Huw can mail your invitation to the memorial.' He didn't try to kiss her, just touched her cheek very lightly with his fingertips and gave her a smile that felt like a promise.

On Sunday Tansy and Anna had arranged to drop in at Isadora's for coffee. Anna immediately spotted the stylish invitation stuck to Isadora's fridge. 'Do you think you'll go?' Anna asked her.

'To Laurie's memorial? Yes, I thought I'd go. Why, are you?'

'I'm going with Kit,' Anna said a little self-consciously.

'You know why they had to throw it together so quickly?' Isadora said.

Anna shook her head.

'Apparently, Gisela Van Holden is desperate to be there, but she only has this tiny window before she goes off on some world tour.'

'Who's Gisela Van Thingummy?' Tansy asked, unpacking cookies from a plastic box and setting them out on a plate.

'World famous cellist, darling,' Isadora said. She had made coffee for her and Anna and a pot of ginger green tea for Tansy. The kitchen table, cleared for their Moroccan feast, was already disappearing under a tide of books, papers and domestic detritus.

'This memorial is a massive deal then?' Tansy said.

Anna helped herself to a cookie. 'Kit said half the music world is going to be there.'

'That's OK,' Tansy said, putting on a small voice. 'I don't mind being the only person who doesn't get invited to mix with music-type celebs.' She laughed. 'No, seriously, I don't mind! Because guess who I'm meeting as soon as I leave here?'

'Liam Goodhart!' Anna drew a sharp breath. 'Did you tell him about . . .?'

Tansy nodded, eyes shining. 'You were right, Anna. He barely blinked. These were his exact words after I'd dropped my big bombshell. "Your dad's Frankie McVeigh? Thank God! I was beginning to think I had bad breath!"'

Anna and Isadora both laughed.

I'm glad,' Isadora said warmly. 'Liam seems like a sweet man.'

'I agree,' Anna said. 'Not sure why "nice" is used like a four-letter word these days. If you ask me, nice and normal is the way forward!'

Isadora said, 'I've got some news of my own. Not quite as lovely as Tansy's.' She paused for maximum effect. 'I'm going to get a lodger, possibly two!'

Tansy's eyes widened. 'Wow, a big change then. How come?'

'I've agreed a compromise with my son,' Isadora explained. 'Gabriel's been on at me for months to move into something more affordable. He says my house is suffering from appalling neglect, which is true, and that it's becoming too much for me to manage, which is also true. But I told him, "Gabriel, this house holds a lot of sacred memories, including memories of your childhood." I said, "I know you didn't enjoy your childhood very much, darling, and I haven't been the kind of cake-baking mother that you'd have preferred. But this is my home, and I'm not ready to leave. I may *never* be ready." And then Nicky, his wife, who, up until now, I have never really taken to, said, "Why don't you get lodgers? You could put the money towards doing up your house, and I think you'd enjoy having young people around you again."'

'Hey, good for Nicky!' Tansy said.

'Indeed.' Isadora's expression became slightly mischievous. 'Did I mention that I received some beautiful flowers from a very attractive man?' She gestured to an autumnal bouquet in a simple glass vase. 'They actually arrived in the vase! Wasn't that thoughtful of him?'

'Were they from Etienne?' Anna still remembered the obviously enamoured Frenchman at the launch.

Isadora shook her head. 'No, they were from Jake to thank me for my hospitality. That man has such lovely manners.'

'Yes, he does,' Anna said a little wistfully. Jake hadn't mentioned his intention to send Isadora flowers. But that was typically Jake, she thought.

'Lucky Anna,' Tansy teased. 'She's got *two* yummy men after her!'

'In your fertile imagination, maybe!' Anna said.

The phone rang, and Isadora went to take the call.

'Seriously, though, how are you?' Tansy asked Anna. 'I've been worrying about you since we came back from London. You were giving me all this great advice, but it felt like you were almost—' She abruptly changed what she'd been going to say. 'I don't know,' she said anxiously. 'You just didn't seem right.'

'I'm fine!' Anna reassured her. 'I was just tired from driving, and since then I've had a lot of things to sort out.'

Tansy isn't criticizing you, she told herself, even as her heart rate sped up. *She's being a friend*. Friends monitored your expressions and tone of voice. They scrutinized your behaviour to make sure you were on track; that you were OK, that you were acting normal. With the sensation of inner doors and windows protectively slamming shut, she added, 'And I'm really looking forward to us going to the ballet.'

SEVENTEEN

The weather was suddenly unmistakably autumnal. A cutting east wind went right through Anna's flimsy evening dress, making her shiver as Kit guided her through the waiting crowd towards the round temple-like structure of the Sheldonian. Her black shawl embroidered with silver thread looked perfect with her understated black dress, but a coat would have been kinder to her kidneys, she thought.

Despite having grown up in Oxford Anna could count on the fingers of one hand the number of times she'd actually been inside the Sheldonian Theatre where the memorial Huw had organized to celebrate Laurie Swanson's life and work was to be held.

The last time she'd been this close to its doors it had been in morning sunshine with Jake. 'Christopher Wren built this?' he'd said. 'The same guy who built St Paul's Cathedral? He had quite a thing for verdigris domes, didn't he!' In the middle of their discussion of theatres in the round (Jake had been to the reconstructed Globe Theatre in Southwark and been blown away), Anna had turned round and surprised a group of Korean visitors in high-end travel-wear, listening with apparent fascination to her tour-guide spiel.

Tonight this same space was lit by the electric lights streaming from the windows on all three storeys of the Sheldonian as it steadily filled with excited fans and paparazzi.

It had rained earlier, leaving a watery sheen on the ancient pavement. The tremendous outpouring of light from inside the theatre picked up and intensified this slight shimmer, making it seem as if the guests were walking along some kind of celestial pathway, while the fans and members of the press, hungry for a glimpse of Gisela Van Holden or other luminaries of the music world, looked on from the sidelines.

At last Anna and Kit were able to join the slow procession of guests making their way into the theatre. Self-consciously aware of Kit's arm linked through hers, she whispered, 'I feel like a bloody character from Jane Austen.'

'Which character am I, then?' he asked at once, and Anna hissed:

'I didn't say I knew *which* bloody character!'

Inside the doors Sara and Huw were greeting guests as they arrived. Sara was nodding and smiling, playing the part of the loyal wife with a glittering intensity that suggested she'd taken something to help her through the evening. She looked even thinner than she'd been at the launch, and the cosmetic concealer she'd used didn't adequately conceal the dark lines under her eyes. It was weirdly fascinating seeing Sara perform her part, knowing what Anna now knew.

When it was their turn to file past the Trahernes, Anna saw Sara's social smile falter, then, blanking Kit, she shot Anna a look so hostile that it registered almost as a physical slap.

'What did I do?' she whispered to Kit when they were out of earshot.

'I told you, she's a bitch,' he whispered back. 'Just ignore her. Come on, let's find our seats.'

As Anna had explained to Jake, the Sheldonian Theatre was originally designed as a venue for graduation and other academic ceremonies. Graduations had previously been held in a local church, but by the mid 1600s these ceremonies had become increasingly raucous affairs so the then Vice Chancellor had proposed the theatre as a secular alternative.

Looking up at the glowing ceiling frescos with their flying angels and cherubs, Anna decided that the word 'secular' had been interpreted a little differently in those days. The Sheldonian, with its encircling galleries, emanated a timeless solemnity, giving her the shivery feeling she had occasionally felt in lovely Italian churches.

Anna was secretly impressed to find that she and Kit were sitting in the VIP area directly opposite the raised stage where Gisela Van Holden was going to perform. Behind the stage the members of the orchestra had already taken their seats. Anna felt the familiar tingle of excitement as they began to tune their instruments.

Kit discreetly pointed out some well-known stars of the Royal

Opera House and someone from Milan's La Scala. Then an elderly woman behind them recognized Kit, leaning over to talk to him in a drawl so upper class that it was almost a self-parody. How many different Oxfords there were, Anna thought, invisibly contained inside each other like Russian dolls; but this was the first time she'd found herself entering this particular rarefied city within a city.

Kit gave Anna an apologetic glance as the elderly lady continued to hold him captive. 'Friend of my mother's,' he whispered.

The theatre was steadily filling. Anna glanced around, hoping to catch a glimpse of Isadora. Eventually, she spotted her several seats away, talking to a man with snow-white hair and an immense silvery beard. Isadora was wearing something black with flowing sleeves. Anna could see her garnet earrings swinging as she gestured. Anna tentatively raised a hand in greeting, but Isadora didn't see. Instead of completing her wave, Anna reached up to touch the new pendant at her throat. Its metal had felt chilly against her skin when Kit first fastened it around her neck, but her body heat had gradually warmed it.

He'd produced the small box when he came to pick her up. 'I've bought you something,' he'd said, and Anna's heart had given an unpleasant flutter. Anna disliked all surprises, but she had a particular dislike of surprise presents, especially when the giver was waiting for her delighted reaction.

'What is it?' she'd said suspiciously.

'A mouse trap,' he'd teased at once. 'No, of course it isn't,' he'd added quickly. 'All the jewellers had sold out of mouse traps, so I got you something nice instead. Well, I *hope* it's nice.'

Kit had seemed uncharacteristically anxious as she opened the box. He'd watched her unfold the layers of white tissue paper, then smiled with relief as she'd exclaimed over the exquisite little silver bee suspended from its chain.

'I saw it and immediately thought of your magical childhood among your grandmother's beehives, and I couldn't resist,' he'd told her.

It was one of the loveliest and certainly one of the silliest things anyone had ever given her, and she was more touched than she knew how to say. She knew that Kit was an experienced flirt. But he made her feel so . . . She searched for the right words to express the sensations she experienced whenever she was with Kit Tulliver; *cherished*, she thought. He made her feel feminine and desirable. It was a deeply seductive feeling.

Kit turned back to Anna and caught her fingering the little bee. He smiled. 'You really like it? You're not just being polite?'

'I love it,' she told him, 'but you shouldn't buy me presents.'

'Nonsense!' Kit lightly touched one of her diamond ear studs. 'These are beautiful. You were wearing those the first time I saw you.'

'They were my grandmother's.' Despite the chaotic circumstances of their first meeting, Kit had noticed every little thing about her, Anna thought, even her earrings. She felt her cheeks colour, but was distracted by the sight of Isadora waving wildly from her seat.

Moments later, Anna spotted another familiar face in the crowd. It took her another moment to identify Laurie's Macmillan nurse, Paulette, under her spectacular hat. She had done Laurie proud, dressing in the kind of splendour that Anna suspected she normally reserved for church. She seemed to have come alone and looked a little lost and nervous.

Though there was no obvious signal that Anna could see, she felt an expectant stillness descend on the audience. 'They're starting,' Kit murmured.

Huw walked out on to the platform, a slight, fair-haired figure wearing formal black tie, and made a short speech in his beautiful resonant voice. Thanking everyone for coming, he explained that this was to be a joyous yet at the same time solemn celebration of the life of Laurie Swanson, the world-famous composer who was also Huw's much-loved friend from his boyhood. He described how they had first met at the Dragon School where Laurie had been a boarder from the age of eight years old and how he had seemed isolated and forlorn. Huw knew that Laurie's father worked in the Far East and so Laurie only saw his parents in the long summer holidays. A kindly teacher had taken him home for Christmas, but for other holidays he had to stay on in the boarding house with the few other children who had nowhere else to go.

'Like most seven year olds I had little life experience but

extremely sound instincts. I instinctively felt that Laurie was not loved, or even liked, by his parents, and this distressed me more than words could say. However, my father, the poet Owen Traherne, saw that I was upset about something, and he sat me down and made me tell him what was wrong. After I'd told him of Laurie's situation, my father suggested he should come and stay with us for half term. This visit turned out to be the first of many. In his own family, Laurie had always been an outsider, but with us his particular brand of sensitivity and intelligence was not only recognized but also actively enjoyed and encouraged. Laurie quickly became an honorary member of the Trahernes, staying over at weekends and included on family holidays. I like to think that my family played a part in Laurie's eventual, though tragically all too brief, flowering as one of this country's most talented composers in recent years.'

Clearly emotional, Huw seemed to breathe deeply to compose himself before he went on. 'As some of you know, we have the honour to have Gisela Van Holden with us this evening to play for us. Since she literally has a car waiting outside to take her to the airport, I don't intend to hold up proceedings with my boyhood anecdotes. Ladies and gentlemen, Gisela Van Holden!' Holding out his hand, Huw smilingly invited her on to the stage.

Carrying her cello, her long blonde hair pulled back from her face, Gisela Van Holden was even more beautiful than her photographs. Like Huw she was visibly emotional as she explained regretfully that she had to be on a plane to Buenos Aires in four and a half hours. She apologized for dashing in and out, but said she had needed to be here to celebrate the life of a shy, almost reclusive man who nevertheless had had the divine fire of genius in his soul and whose music she had loved and revered for many years. 'The piece I am going to play is the first one of Laurie Swanson's compositions I ever heard. It is called "The Lost Shapes of Water".'

To Anna's shame, she hadn't yet listened to any of Laurie's compositions, afraid that it would be the kind of dissonant postmodern music that her grandfather disparagingly referred to as 'post-tune'. She had liked Laurie so much that it would seem like a betrayal if she disliked his work. But his cello piece had a haunting recurring melody which pierced her to the heart. The audience listened with rapt attention, and when Gisela Van Holden finally lifted her bow, tenderly stilling the strings of her cello, there was a moment of absolute silence before the thunderous applause.

After Gisela Van Holden had taken her bow and run off stage to her waiting car, a succession of composers, conductors and musicians came on stage to sing or play or talk about Laurie and his work. One of the street children he had taught in Brazil, now a professional violinist in the Chicago Symphony Orchestra, described how Laurie, and the music project Laurie had actively championed, had saved him from a life of deprivation in the *favela*.

Listening to so many impassioned accolades, Anna felt a growing awe. She hadn't realized how far-reaching the impact of Laurie's life and work had been. How terrible then, she thought, that Laurie's love for Owen had eventually led him to deny his music to the world.

Towards the end of the concert, Huw came back to the platform to tell the audience about the song they were about to hear and which he said was especially dear to his heart. 'I chose this piece to end the concert, firstly because I love Laurie's exquisite setting, but also because the words are from a poem that my father wrote when he was just starting out as a young idealistic poet and, I suppose, just starting to come to terms with the loss and suffering that life inevitably brings to our door. It's called "The Tree of Sorrows".'

Anna felt her breath catch. She heard herself ask Laurie, 'What's your favourite poem by Owen Traherne?' and his unhesitating answer, '"The Tree of Sorrows".'

A statuesque young black soprano came on stage. She waited composedly for the sweeping opening chords of Laurie's music, drew a breath that made her bosom swell like a songbird's and began to sing. Her voice, like the music, was exquisitely beautiful, and Anna thought she recognized, here and there, broken phrases from Purcell's 'Dido's Lament'. But Owen Traherne's words left a bitter taste. The final verse described a man stealthily leaving the warmth of his sweetheart's bed not to meet with another lover, as you might expect, but to stand transfixed by the flickering shadows cast by an ominous tree. '*Only one tortured shadow is mine, and so I choose it again and again as the feverish world turns and turns.*'

Laurie himself had expressed surprise at the poem's inclusion in the anthology of love poems, she remembered, commenting drily that it wasn't 'the kind people read at weddings'. *Damn right*, she thought. Despite its sorrows, Laurie's life had been about love: his love of Owen (however undeserving, Anna thought), his love of music, his love of dogs and the natural world. Though he had made what Anna considered unwise choices, there was nothing doomed about Laurie Swanson. He had chosen love and he had paid a price, but even in the last days of his illness, she didn't think Laurie had ever seen himself as a victim of fate. So why, out of all Owen Traherne's work, had this darkly fatalistic poem been his favourite?

Anna's face must have reflected her confusion because Kit whispered, 'Are you OK?'

She nodded, but he took her hand and held it for a moment, and his simple gesture of comfort brought her close to tears.

The soprano left the stage to enthusiastic applause, and Huw returned to bring things to a close. He told them smilingly of a fund that had been set up for promising young musicians at the Royal Academy of Music in London and which would be known as the Laurie Swanson Memorial Scholarship Fund. 'Please give generously,' he urged, 'so we can ensure that Laurie's legacy goes on.'

'I'll meet you by the door,' Anna told Kit as the audience began to leave their seats. He looked puzzled, and she explained, 'I've seen someone I need to talk to.'

Anna had spent years of her life second-guessing herself, wishing she'd reached out to people, but rarely following it through. She didn't want to be that Anna any more. She pushed her way through the crowd and found five-foot nothing Paulette clinging on to her hat and in imminent danger of being crushed. 'Hi, Paulette,' Anna said breathlessly. 'I hoped I'd catch you!'

Paulette's face broke into a beaming smile. 'You came to see Mr Swanson that night. How is your beautiful dog?'

'Still beautiful,' Anna said. 'I was so sorry to hear about Laurie.'

'Oh, darling, I was *so* shocked. I didn't see it coming at *all*.' Paulette's voice became more emphatically Jamaican.

Caught up in the throng of people trying to leave the theatre, she and Paulette kept being pushed into each other's personal

space. At one point the diminutive but top-heavy Paulette was
forced up against Anna. 'Sorry about my boobs, darling!' she
said with a laugh. 'My husband says the Almighty designed the
lions and the tigers. He designed the moon and the sun – and
then he made Paulette, the Munchkin! That poor, poor man,' she
added, her smile fading, and after a moment's confusion, Anna
realized she'd returned to Laurie. 'Maybe it all suddenly got on
top of him, darling?' Paulette said sadly. 'Liver cancer is not a
nice way to die. Maybe he just couldn't take any more pain and
loneliness and needed to go back to his everlasting home?'

What a relief to be Paulette for a few hours, Anna thought,
and believe, even temporarily, in an everlasting home. A moment
later she saw Paulette's eyes light up.

'God bless that lovely man! You know he came to see Mr
Swanson?' she told Anna. 'I do my best not to eavesdrop, but I
could tell from his tone, you know, that he was trying to make
everything right between them. He was *so* sweet.'

Anna glanced over her shoulder and saw Kit gallantly shep-
herding the alarming old lady through the press of people. She
was about to agree warmly that he was a lovely man when
Paulette gave an enthusiastic wave to someone over by the doors.
'That's my poor husband looking for me. He can't stand crowds.
I'd better go.' She gave Anna a quick hug, then valiantly set off
towards her husband.

Anna found that she was smiling. Paulette's mention of Kit's
visit to Laurie had touched her to the heart. How good of him to
try to make peace between Laurie and Huw before it was too late.
It was already too late, in fact, but Kit couldn't have known that.
Even if he had gone years earlier, it would still have been too late.
To resume his relationship with Huw after so many years of estrange-
ment, Laurie would have had to lie to Huw by omission, to fake
friendship, in other words, or he'd have had to disclose the secret
of his long love affair with Huw's father, which he could never do.

Kit saw Anna looking around for him and smiled. 'Stay there!'
he mouthed, gesturing towards his elderly companion. 'I'll come
back for you.'

So Anna stayed. The crowd was thinning now, and all at once
Isadora was coming towards her, enormous earrings swinging.
'Anna, how lovely you look! Wasn't that a glorious concert?'

'It was,' Anna agreed. 'I found that last song a bit depressing though.'

'Not a cheery note to end on,' Isadora agreed. 'But Jewish folk tales are notoriously gloomy.'

'Is that where it comes from, a folk tale?'

Isadora nodded. 'An old Hassidic teaching story.'

'Have you read it?' Anna felt a childlike impatience to know what it said. Somewhere in the darkness of this story there had to be a kernel of light and hope, surely, or Laurie couldn't have loved it so much?

'I have, but years ago,' Isadora said, just as her distinguished looking companion caught her up. 'You can probably find it online,' she called to Anna as he bore her away, no doubt for an intimate dinner for two.

'Finally!' Kit said, arriving at her side. 'That was worse than a rugger scrum! Poor old Lady Bracknell was nearly knocked off her feet.'

Anna felt her eyes widen. 'Lady Bracknell, seriously?'

'No, but she might as well be!' he said, laughing. 'My parents always said that if Oscar Wilde had met her first he'd have put her in *The Importance of Being Earnest* instead of Augusta Bracknell.' His expression became sober. 'Huw just asked me if you and I could join him and Sara for a late supper. It means putting up with Sara, unfortunately, but I know it would mean a lot to Huw.'

'Of course I'll come.' Anna was hungry apart from anything else, but more than that she was intrigued by Sara Traherne and this was an opportunity to study her at close quarters.

An hour later Anna was sitting opposite a stony-faced Sara as Huw and Kit swapped anecdotes. Sara had virtually ignored Anna since they'd arrived at Gee's, the iconic North Oxford restaurant that exactly resembled a beautiful glasshouse. While everyone else tucked in to their food, Sara just picked at hers but drank steadily throughout the meal.

Anna guessed it was partly to compensate for his wife's hostile silence that Huw had embarked on his mildly scurrilous stories about his undergraduate days. Several involved Kit. After the third or fourth of these, Sara set down her glass with a theatrical *thunk.* 'If I have to hear one more tedious anecdote about your golden fucking youth . . .' Leaving her threat unfinished, she seized an almost empty bottle of red wine, tipped the dregs into her glass and knocked them back.

Between courses, Anna left the table to go to the ladies' cloakroom. When she came out of her cubicle she saw Sara standing in front of the mirror reapplying her lipstick, something which seemed to be taking all her concentration.

Quickly washing and drying her hands, Anna went to join Sara at the mirror. Huw's wife immediately fixed her with an aggressive female stare that took Anna right back to her short-lived teenage clubbing phase. It gave her the exact same sinking feeling she'd felt then.

Keeping her eyes blearily on Anna, Sara seemed to be struggling to articulate some enormous grievance. 'Did you think I wouldn't find out!' she exploded at last. 'Well, *did* you?'

'Find out?' Anna felt a flicker of real fear. Sara was very drunk now, and Kit had several times described her as unhinged.

'You've been poking about in my private business, you interfering judgemental bitch.' Taking an unsteady step towards her, Sara pushed her face right into Anna's, her alcohol-laden breath making Anna's nostrils flare. 'You have no idea what you're dealing with. None!' She frowned, as if she'd lost her thread, then her expression cleared and she jabbed her finger into Anna's chest. 'So let me give you some free advice.' She swayed on her feet. 'Don't play with fire! Unless you – you enjoy being burned! Now fuck off and leave me in peace!' She hastily disappeared into a cubicle.

Humiliated and shaken, Anna had to return to the table where Kit and Huw were still reminiscing. Huw's tiredness had apparently dropped away as he relived happier times with his friend.

'Huw's been telling me all these wonderful stories about Laurie,' Kit said as she sat down beside him. 'I knew he was a musical genius, but it turns out he was a bit of a Doctor Dolittle too. You know, talked to the animals!'

'I'm sorry I missed it,' Anna said.

'Tell her the one you just told me,' Kit said to Huw. 'You're going to love it, Anna.'

Still reeling from Sara's assault, Anna did her best to be a responsive audience as Huw repeated his story.

'As you know, Laurie often spent school holidays with my family. We had a cottage we went to in Norfolk, surrounded by open fields. Often when we were out walking, we'd see hares. Dad had a dog in those days, a springer spaniel, and it loved to chase them, but of course it didn't have a prayer of catching a full-grown hare. Then one day this spaniel – her name was Jess – found a young hare in the lane. It must have been hit by a car. My dad insisted we had to leave it. If you've read his poetry you'll know he was very big on nature taking its grim and bloody course,' he added with a laugh. 'But Laurie wouldn't have it. He had this way of going completely white in the face when he felt passionate about something. "I'm taking it back to the cottage," he told my father. "So it knows that some humans can be kind." Well, we could all see that Laurie was absolutely set on saving this hare. So my dad gave one of those weary adult sighs, and Laurie carried this limp little body back to the cottage. Laurie and I made it a nest out of a box and an old blanket and put it in our room. And it just lay there, panting with distress, and I heard my mother telling my dad, "You should have left it in the hedge. It's going to die in the night, Owen. Imagine how broken-hearted that little boy is going to be then."' Huw stopped to take a quick swallow of his wine.

Anna seemed to be the only person who had noticed that Sara still hadn't come back from the cloakroom. Maybe she'd passed out? Or she could have slipped out of the restaurant when no one was looking and hailed a taxi to take her back to Dritan?

'Anyway, bedtime came,' Huw said, resuming his story. 'And this part of my story is a little embarrassing, Anna, because it involves a night light. Even at eight or nine years old I was too afraid of the dark to sleep without one. So you have to picture two little boys sleeping in their beds, with a night light flickering on a chest of drawers and this young hare lying apparently close to death on its piece of blanket. And then something, a small movement, woke me, just in time to see the hare sit up in its box and pull down one of its long ears to wash it. Then it went lolloping over to Laurie's bed and jumped up on to his stomach.'

'Can you believe that, Anna?' Kit said.

She smilingly shook her head.

'I saw Laurie's eyes fly open,' Huw went on. 'I don't think either of us dared to breathe. Then, very slowly and gently, Laurie sat up, and the hare climbed right up on to his chest and began to sniff all around his face with absolutely no fear. And Laurie whispered, "It *knows*. It knows I saved it." And I actually believe it did.'

It was a charming story, but Anna had found it almost unbearable to hear Huw talking about his old friend with such affection. She knew the truth, the unpalatable truth, about Laurie and Huw's father, and as she smiled back at Huw she felt like Judas.

Sara returned looking extremely white. Huw said they were both bushed and should probably head home to bed. Though Gee's was only a couple of streets from Anna's flat, Kit insisted on driving her to her door. Sitting beside him in the car, nervously fingering Kit's silver bee, she felt a creeping despair. She'd been invited for a civilized dinner at one of Oxford's most desirable restaurants and ended up being threatened in the toilets.

Tansy was right. She and Anna must give off some unsavoury pheromone. No matter how hard they tried to break with their pasts, people could sniff them out. Sara had smelled Anna's brokenness, she'd smelled her hurt and shame, and like a jackal she'd attacked.

'You seem a bit subdued, love,' Kit said as he pulled up outside her house. 'Did Sara say something? I was concerned when I saw her following you into the loo. She has a tongue like a viper when she's been drinking.'

'She didn't say anything,' she lied. 'She just asked what shade of lipstick I was wearing.'

'That's good.' Kit gently tilted her chin, so that he was looking directly into her eyes. His expression was so tender that it made her ache. 'I'd hate for her to have hurt you.'

She'd told Kit she didn't know which Jane Austen character she felt like as she swept into the Sheldonian on his arm. But that had been another lie. For a brief unguarded moment she had been Elizabeth, arm in arm with her Darcy. Only, Anna bet that nobody had ever followed Elizabeth Bennett into the women's toilets and called her an interfering, judgemental bitch.

'Thank you so much for supper and bringing me home,' she managed. Before Kit could move to kiss her, she quickly got out of his car and fled inside.

EIGHTEEN

When Anna returned home with Bonnie next morning after their walk, she longed to stay home with her dog, watching old Katharine Hepburn and Spencer Tracey movies. The sordid end to her night out had left her feeling bruised and grubby, and she just wanted to hide from the world. But it was Sunday morning and she and her grandfather had a long-standing date to see Turner's later paintings at the Tate. So she dropped her dog-walking clothes into the hamper, showered, changed, made-up her face and drove to Bramley Lodge to pick him up.

Two and a half hours later, as she took her grandfather around the exhibition, she felt her depression lift. Turner's paintings had helped, but it was really her grandfather she had to thank. On the drive down he had wanted to hear all about Laurie's memorial. He'd quickly spotted and admired Kit's pendant, which she was still wearing, then immediately asked if she'd heard any more from Bonnie's previous owner; 'Your American admirer,' as her grandfather called him. 'And do Kit and Jake know of each other's existence?' he'd asked slyly.

'Well, no,' she'd admitted, and found herself blushing and laughing.

And somehow she'd found herself telling him about Sara's drunken outburst. She hadn't gone into details. Her grandfather didn't need to know about Dritan or Frankie McVeigh. She was glad she was driving because she could keep her eyes fixed on the road while she was pouring it all out.

'There's a reason people used to call it the "demon drink",' he'd said when she'd finished. 'It was the booze talking last night, not Sara, and today, assuming she even remembers what happened, she's probably filled with self-disgust. She sounds like a deeply unhappy woman.' He stopped talking while Anna negotiated a tricky roundabout then said huskily, 'It makes me happier than I can say, Anna, to see you going out into the world again. Don't let that woman's problems drive you back into yourself.'

He'd understood, she thought now as they halted before a painting of a seascape which seemed on the point of dissolving into light and fire. He'd understood exactly how low, how *wrong* Sara had made her feel. Her grandfather, on the other hand, had always had the power to steady her, to lift her up, reflecting Anna back to herself as someone worth knowing, worth loving. Even if his version of Anna was not the true one, she could feel herself flowering in the warmth of his love and approval. Her life wasn't like he thought, but for a few hours she could enjoy the pretence that it was.

Her grandfather was still gazing at the painting. 'You know how John Ruskin described Turner?' he said, turning round to Anna. 'He said he was "an archangel packed into the squat body of an eccentric cockney"!'

She smiled. 'Good quote.'

'Isn't it?' he said, eyes shining.

'Ready to move on?' Anna was becoming aware of an impatient queue of people building up behind them waiting for their turn to view the painting.

He nodded. 'Yes, thank you, darling.'

She was just about to wheel her grandfather on to the next painting when she saw a familiar figure walk into the room. 'Did you know Desmond was coming?' she asked, surprised.

'Desmond's here?' Her grandfather peered around Anna, but couldn't seem to see the larger than life Rasta. 'Are you sure it's him?' he asked doubtfully. 'I mean, Desmond isn't someone you can easily miss!'

It belatedly dawned on her what the problem was. 'You're too low down.' And there were too many ill-mannered people looming over him, she thought grimly. 'Hang on!' Anna quickly wheeled him around. 'Is that better?'

'Oh, it *is* Desmond!' Her grandfather broke into a delighted smile.

He was already striding towards them, silver dreadlocks flowing over the shoulders of his ancient leather jacket. 'Look who it is! My friend the culture vulture,' he said, laughing. 'And you've brought your beautiful granddaughter with you.'

The two men had met at a local class on the history of art and instantly clicked. Still handsome in his late sixties, Desmond radiated enthusiasm for art and life, and Anna's grandfather found him a welcome relief from the non-stop recitation of woes that passed for conversation amongst the majority of residents at Bramley Lodge.

'Who's calling who a culture vulture?' he teased. 'So what do you think now you're here?'

'This stuff is good, man,' Desmond said, 'but I can't take it all in at one go or my brain starts to swim, you know? I like to sit in front of one painting for a while, let it soak in, then go away, drink some coffee and let the magic go to work undisturbed.'

'I wish my art teacher had thought like you,' Anna said, smiling. She was remembering a school visit to the Uffizi where the teachers had seemed hell-bent on forcing them to view as many works of art as humanly possible in the time available. 'Talking of coffee,' she added, 'shall we go to find a cafe somewhere?'

'Or a bar, maybe?' Desmond suggested, eyes glinting.

They found a pub by the river and ended up staying on for lunch. When they eventually parted, Desmond made them promise to come to his house the following weekend for a proper Jamaican slap-up meal. 'And if your grandfather thinks he's man enough, I might even break out my bottle of white rum,' he told her.

'That sounds like a challenge to me,' Anna's grandfather said.

Anna's phone pinged. She'd had a text from Kit: *Hi, beautiful bee girl. Couldn't have survived last night without you. Would love to wine and dine you next weekend if you're free?*

'See that smile?' Desmond said to Anna's grandfather in a loud whisper. 'Any time a young woman smile like that, there is *always* a man involved!'

That night as she lay in bed reading, Anna's mind was still whirling with light-drenched Turner skies and landscapes. In fact, despite her strenuous efforts to concentrate, Turner was currently winning out over Owen Traherne's biography. Though she liked Kit Tulliver, the man, she sometimes found his writing hard-going, and her mind kept wandering back over her day.

She'd enjoyed seeing her grandfather sparring with his rascally friend. George Ottaway had lots of life in him still, she thought. But it must be humiliating to go from being the kind of man who had hiked up mountains with energy to spare, to someone who was so dependent on others. As care homes went Bramley Lodge was a palace of privilege. Even so, Anna found herself grinding her teeth when she heard how some of the carers spoke to him. She wasn't sure who she hated more – the ones who talked down, or the impervious-seeming ones, all falsely breezy and brisk.

Her grandfather's wits were as sharp and steely as ever, yet today as she'd wheeled him around the exhibition, and later when they were in the pub, people had looked through or over him, as if he was some kind of elderly child. Though his wheelchair offered freedom of a kind, it also reduced him to a non-person; a Munchkin, she thought, thinking of pocket-sized Paulette. Even wearing heels she barely cleared five feet. Anna had an inadvertent image of her helplessly buffeted by the people around her. Then Anna saw herself turning around, arching her neck and eventually seeing Kit in the crowd.

She sat up, letting the book slide to the floor.

Paulette was too short. Just as her grandfather in his wheelchair had been too low down to see Desmond through those tutting Turner fans. She couldn't have seen Kit, not from where she was standing. But if Laurie's nurse hadn't seen Kit, who had she seen?

Anna forced herself to replay the scene in slow-motion. It was true Kit had been there in the crowd, but someone else had been between him and Paulette, effectively blocking her view.

Once again she replayed the memory, watching Paulette break into a reminiscent smile as she caught sight of Laurie's visitor. Then she played it again, only this time without editing out the person standing next to Kit. 'God bless that lovely man,' Paulette had said. Anna had assumed she'd meant the man who had come to Laurie's house 'to put things right'. And that *had* been who Paulette had meant, but she'd also been referring to 'the lovely man' who had just spoken so beautifully about Laurie at his memorial. She'd been talking about Huw Traherne.

Anna felt her heart rate speed up. She had mentally erased him from the crowd. She'd seen him, but immediately discounted him because Huw wasn't supposed to have visited Laurie. It was *Kit* who'd gone to see him. Kit had told her that Huw and Laurie hadn't talked for years. If Huw had lied about that, what else had he lied about?

She flashed back to Frankie McVeigh at the Jade Pagoda: '*Sometimes the most obvious solution is the right solution.*'

Anna was sitting on the edge of her bed now, tugging at her hair. She'd allowed herself to be fatally distracted by gangsters and mad personal assistants when all the time she'd just needed to ask herself one simple question. *Who stood to gain the most from Laurie's death?*

This question naturally led to a second and equally disturbing question, one she'd never previously thought to ask. Had Laurie and Owen really succeeded in concealing their relationship from Huw? Laurie believed they had, but how likely was that in the real world? Family secrets are like splinters. Sooner or later they work their way out. Eve had said Audrey had caught Owen and Laurie having sex. Huw's was a famously dysfunctional family. Who knew what Huw had seen or heard, or what the mentally unstable Audrey might have told her son?

Anna buried her face in her hands, the light-drenched Turner skies replaced by a succession of images of Huw. Huw at the book launch; in the Duke bar; at the Sheldonian holding Laurie's concert together, the concert which he had organized and which had left him visibly exhausted. Oddly remote, permanently stressed, beautifully-spoken Huw. Could someone, *anyone*, let alone a manifestly fragile man like Huw, get up on stage in front of the great and good of Oxford and talk about his old friend with such obvious emotion if he had cold-bloodedly murdered him weeks before? And at Gee's, that sweet story about Laurie and the hare; Huw had told it with such tenderness that for the first time she'd felt herself almost warm to him.

If he'd been faking she'd have felt it, wouldn't she? Unless he was a consummate actor?

But if Huw *was* implicated in Laurie's death in some way, why would he have staged a suicide scene that so closely mirrored his mother's?

It was long past midnight, and there was no chance now that Anna would be able to sleep. She put on her flannel robe and her warm socks and went downstairs to make a pot of chamomile tea as Bonnie watched sleepily from her basket. She perched tensely on her kitchen sofa, snatching sips of still-scalding tea. Suppose, just suppose, that for all the false twists and turns and mistakes, Anna's instincts had successfully led her to the man who had murdered Laurie? Suppose it really was Huw? Then where did Sara Traherne fit in, if she fitted in at all?

You didn't need a degree in couples counselling to see that there was something deeply dysfunctional about the Traherne's marriage, but might they still be acting as a team? Despite her affair with Dritan, might Sara still have a vested interest in shoring up the profitable myth of Owen Traherne as the charismatic Antony to Audrey's Cleopatra? They stood to make a pile of money if the Hollywood blockbuster got made. But if it got out that Owen had had sex with his son's under-age school friend, the movie wouldn't get made, and the Trahernes' empire and everything Huw had worked for would collapse in ruins.

The chamomile tea was not having a noticeably calming effect. The more Anna tried not to think about her suspicions, the more she couldn't stop. She took her mug to the sink and rinsed it. She could go back to bed and listen to talk radio until she fell asleep, which would possibly be never, or she could find some other way to get through the night.

She'd thought of texting Tansy and Isadora with her discovery, but immediately vetoed this plan. It wasn't as if she had real proof. It was more like a feeling, a kind of all-pervasive nausea. That ominous slipping, falling sensation she'd felt when they were coming back from London had never quite gone away. What if her sudden obsession with Huw Traherne was a symptom of her returning illness?

Fetching her iPad she went to sit on the rug by Bonnie. Anna's dog looked up at her with soulful eyes. Petting her White Shepherd with one hand, Anna did an Internet search for Huw Traherne with the other. She'd searched for information on the Trahernes before, but this time she tried different criteria. At first she just got the usual screeds of PR concerning the Traherne Foundation.

OK, gloves off, she thought. Deleting her current search Anna entered the words 'Huw Traherne scandal' into the box.

She skimmed through pages where the words 'Huw' or

'Traherne' or 'scandal' were randomly highlighted, such as: *'The level of support for the arts in this country is a **scandal**,' says **Huw Traherne**, son of famous poet Owen **Traherne**.*

Halfway down the third page she was surprised to see her search terms pop up in someone's blog. She clicked on the link because there was no point doing a search if she didn't chase up likely leads, but as she started to read she let out a moan of protest that made Bonnie sit up in concern. 'A conspiracy nut,' Anna explained in disgust. The blogger had 'proof' of an elitist secret society of Oxford undergraduates dedicated to drink, drugs, decadence and very likely other behaviours beginning with the letter 'D'. Then she saw something that made her freeze.

'Oh, shit,' Anna said. She ran her hands through her hair. '*Shit!*'

NINETEEN

The coroner's verdict on Aidan Rose had been suicide, 'while the balance of his mind was disturbed'. There had been no suggestion that another person or persons might have been implicated in Aidan's lonely downward spiral. But the anonymous blogger (had he been Aidan's friend, Anna wondered, or a concerned sibling or other family member?) insisted Aidan had been the victim of a sustained bullying campaign which had led to him taking his own life part-way through his second year. Acknowledging that Huw Traherne was not the only student involved, the blogger was adamant that he'd been the main instigator, stepping up his persecution to such a pitch that, broken and demoralized, Aidan was driven to take an overdose.

As she read and reread the ugly accusations, Anna felt increasingly light-headed, as if she was being sucked out of the mundane physical world into some horrifying dimension where nothing was too terrible to be true.

She remembered Isadora confessing, as she drove through the mist, that she'd initially pegged Huw and Kit as the kind of undergraduates who came up to Oxford to join the right societies, 'not to mention the wrong societies'. But then he'd met Sara and become a reformed character.

Anna quickly typed Aidan Rose's name into the search engine, misspelling Aidan three times because her hand was shaking both from excess adrenalin and fear of what she might find. In fact there was pitifully little to show for his nineteen years on earth. There was a heartbreaking photo of a bespectacled Aidan in the college gardens, proudly wearing his cap and gown and a white bow tie. Anna guessed it had been taken in his first term when he was still aglow with his achievement. A working-class boy from Newcastle on Tyne, he had delighted the teachers at his comprehensive school by getting a place at Magdalen College.

Anna found a brief mention of the tragedy in the *Newcastle Evening Chronicle*. Aidan Rose had also been name-checked in a Sunday broadsheet, one of those perennial articles about the high risk of depression amongst less privileged Oxbridge students and how they should be offered counselling as a matter of course. That was all. Unlike Huw Traherne, Aidan Rose was not connected to anyone of note, and so he had simply vanished into the statistics of those undergraduates who turned out to be insufficiently robust to cope with the rigours of an Oxbridge education.

Anna pulled up a photograph of Huw Traherne. Why did she always have that tragic war-poet association? Huw's father, who *was* a bona fide poet, had looked like a scruffy countryman, a man's man, someone with a dog at his heels and a hip-flask in his pocket. But Huw was now in his forties, and his face still had the unlived-in look of a boy whose world had imploded before he'd had the chance to grow up. People interpreted this look as intolerable disappointment and stress – *poor Huw*. But Anna didn't think it was either of those. It was something else, she thought, studying his face; something he kept hidden.

Had Huw found out about his father and his school friend, then swiftly pushed this devastating knowledge out of sight? Then, when Owen died, had Huw found some bizarre relief in promoting the life and work of a largely fictional father, the heroic father Huw had wanted and needed, the father he *should* have had? Until Laurie shared his and Owen's secret with Naomi . . .

Anna felt her breath catch. For a moment she'd seen another hated face overlaying the pixels that made up Huw Traherne's image. She tried to tell herself it was just her tired brain playing tricks. But by then it was too late. The old compulsion had been triggered. She saw herself flying upstairs, unlocking the cupboard doors, scrawling her pain across the picture of that other privileged white boy; anything to relieve the pressure mounting inside.

But somehow this time she was able to make herself wait it out, and when the worst had passed she found that she'd decided to phone Isadora. Isadora had known Huw when he was up at Oxford. She would have heard if he'd been involved in a scandal. Just in time, though, Anna thought to check her mobile. It was only three a.m. What was an OK time to call someone to tell them you had possibly uncovered a murderer? Was eight a.m. too soon?

Too tired for rational thought, but too wired to unplug herself from the Internet with its addictive allure of instant answers,

Anna started doing random searches. She looked up Sara Traherne and discovered that she had also lost her mother, in a car accident in her teens. The daughter of an eminent heart surgeon, she'd been educated at St Paul's School for Girls and read English at Somerville College where she'd got an impressive first. Had the motherless Sara seen a fellow orphan in Huw? Eve had said she'd hoped Sara's love might heal him. What exactly had she thought Huw needed to be healed from?

Anna was going round in circles, and she still had to get through another five hours before she could decently phone Isadora. She suddenly thought of another search she could do to kill time. She could look up the folk tale that had provided the inspiration for Owen Traherne's perplexing poem, 'The Tree of Sorrows'.

She found several versions of this rabbinical teaching story and printed one off to mull over later. It went like this:

> Once upon a time, God became aware that his people had fallen out of love with his Creation. To start with they'd had nothing but praise for the beautiful world he had given them to live in, but now all they did was bemoan their sufferings. So in his infinite compassion, God created a giant Tree where for just one day humans could hang up these same sufferings, like washing left out to dry. The thought of handing them over for even twenty-four hours made everyone dizzy with excitement. People were queuing all night. Everyone wanted to be first to be rid of the oppressive conditions that had dogged them all their lives.
>
> Miraculously, the Tree had just enough room for everyone's woes, and for an entire day, everybody felt as peaceful and innocent as humans were originally designed to be.
>
> But all too soon the day was ending and it was time to shoulder their detested burdens and limitations once again. Seeing everyone's long faces, God suggested that they should walk around his vast Tree of Sorrows until they found something that suited them better. The people thought this was a wonderful idea. They walked round and round the tree, enthusiastically peering into the branches, determined to find a set of sufferings that were more congenial.
>
> Next morning, God came by to see how his new

arrangement was working out. To his dismay, every single
human had reclaimed his own sorrows.

A therapist could have endless fun interpreting that story, Anna
thought grimly as she fled upstairs carrying a litre bottle of
mineral water. Did people fall obsessively in love with their
sufferings like the unfaithful lover in Owen's poem, even as they
longed to be rid of them? Anna's sorrows were so much a part
of her now. How would it feel if she could just shrug them off
like a worn-out coat and hang them up for twenty-four hours –
or forever? Who might she be without them? *Nobody*, she thought
bleakly. Owen's poem had depressed her because it was true.

Anna pulled sweat pants and a running vest out of a drawer
and put them on. Tugging her hair through a scrunchy she went
into her study, switched on her running machine and began to
run. With breaks for water she ran for the rest of the night. What
was the point in asking who Anna would be without her sorrows?
This was who she was: this thirty-something woman desperately
running from nowhere to nowhere, all because she couldn't bear
the terror that overcame her when she stood still.

At six a.m. Anna stepped off her running machine, draped a
towel around her sweating shoulders and called Isadora's number.
'I'm sorry, I know it's early,' she said, breathless from fear as
much as from running. 'I hope I didn't wake you.'

'Not at all!' Isadora said, as warmly as if her friends phoned
her at dawn all the time. 'Hero already did that an hour ago by
throwing up on my bed! Poor little thing, I think she's got some
kind of bug. So I'm up drinking coffee till it's time to call my
vet. So, darling, what's got you so agitated that you're up and
awake at this appalling hour?'

'I wanted to ask if you remembered an undergraduate called
Aidan Rose.' Isadora must have met thousands of students. Anna
anticipated a long pause as she went hunting back through her
memories.

But she said immediately, 'Yes, I remember Aidan. I didn't
know him personally, but one of his friends was in my tutorial
group. It was absolutely tragic what happened.'

'I tried to look him up online,' Anna said, 'but there's hardly
anything.'

'There wouldn't be, darling,' Isadora said. 'It was rather hushed up. Quite wrongly in my opinion.'

'You mean the college authorities hushed it up?' Anna was sitting on the floor in her study. Outside her window it was reluctantly getting light. She swallowed. 'I found this blog. The writer thinks Huw Traherne drove Aidan to kill himself.'

Isadora sighed. 'I'm afraid there might be some truth in that story. This might sound fanciful, Anna, but the first time I met Huw, I felt that he was deeply damaged.'

'Because of his mother committing suicide?'

'My feeling is that Huw's problems pre-dated her suicide. It's just that afterwards they became more apparent. He had – episodes. Once he physically attacked one of his tutors because he thought the tutor had said something detrimental about his father's writing. The tutor was a known drunk though, so Huw narrowly escaped being sent down, despite breaking the poor man's jaw.'

Anna heard the surprised trill of a bird as an electric light came on somewhere. 'Do you know who else might have been involved in the bullying?' she asked. 'I mean, was Kit?' She hated asking, but just now she didn't feel she dared to trust anyone.

Isadora sounded appalled. 'No, *no*. Never! If anything, Kit was Huw's Jiminy Cricket, trying to keep him grounded. It was really Kit and Sara together who helped him stay on track. If it wasn't for them, I doubt he'd have even scraped a pass.' Anna heard her take a gulp of liquid. 'What's this really all about, darling? Why are you digging up these sad old stories?'

Anna pictured Isadora wrapped in an exotically patterned kimono, bushy hair uncombed, doing her pouncing academic's look. 'Oh, you know me, the obsessive midnight googler,' Anna said carelessly. 'I'm having one of my insomniac phases that's all.'

'So this hasn't got anything to do with Laurie?'

'Absolutely not,' Anna assured her. 'Didn't Tansy tell you? I've officially resigned from detecting. Just one more thing though before I go – why didn't you tell me about Huw before?'

'About the scandal? I think that would have been most unethical of me, as well as unfair. It was a long time ago. Huw changed, like we all do. God knows I've made some terrible mistakes in my time, and I would hate for people to still be throwing them in my face.' She stopped for breath. 'Sorry, I didn't mean to rant.'

'That's OK,' Anna said. 'I've got to go now. I hope Hero gets better soon.'

'I was thinking of going into town after she's seen the vet,' Isadora said. 'Would you like to meet for lunch?'

'Another time,' Anna said quickly. 'I've got rather a lot on just now.' Promising to arrange something very soon, she rang off and went to shower and change.

Three hours later Anna walked into the offices of the Traherne Foundation. Her plan, if you could call it a plan, had come into her head as soon as she'd looked up the Traherne Foundation's website and seen that their head office was in Central Oxford. Once she had this information she knew she had to go there to talk to Huw. She had to know if Huw had gone to see Laurie. The compulsion overwhelmed her need to hide and conceal.

She found the Foundation's offices up a smart cobbled alleyway almost backing on to the Museum of Modern Art and at the top of a steep flight of stairs. The building dated back to the Georgian era, but the offices inside were airy and open-plan. Anna could smell fresh coffee and new paint. A low bookshelf was stocked with collections of Owen Traherne's poems, some translated into different languages. The leather sofas looked expensive and comfortable. As offices went, it was pleasant.

The young woman at the reception desk was busy on the phone, so Anna went over to look at the large black and white photographs on the walls. All the pictures were of Owen except for a portrait of a touchingly young Owen and Audrey. With her long hair falling over her shoulders, Audrey looked as if she'd just that minute hitch-hiked back from some hippy festival. The photographer had posed them in a country lane, white and frothy with May blossom, making it seem as if Nature herself had decided to give them a wedding.

The girl at the desk finished her call. But before Anna could state her business, she saw Sara hurrying towards her. Dressed in faded denim jeans and a navy sweater, she was as skinny as an adolescent. Anna could see the sharp edge of her collarbones as she took a breath. 'You should go now,' she told Anna in a low voice.

Anna felt her stomach go into a slow dive. For the first time she understood that Sara was more than just bitter and unhappy. She was scared.

'I mean it, Anna, just go,' Sara pleaded.

'Well, this *is* good timing on your part!' Huw arrived beside them, smiling his usual taut smile. 'Sara was just making coffee, weren't you, darling?'

Sara nodded and smiled, but her eyes signalled, *Run!*

'No coffee for me, thanks,' Anna said. 'I'm here because I want to clear something up.' This was not how she'd meant to begin, but with Huw standing just a few feet away her nerve-endings were sparking like loose wires. She resisted the urge to touch her cheeks, which were suddenly burning.

'That sounds very mysterious,' he said, still smiling. 'Should I be sitting down?'

'Did you go to see Laurie?' Anna heard her voice shake. 'Did you go to his house before he died?'

The smile was instantly wiped from Huw's face. 'I didn't even know where Laurie was living,' he said brusquely. 'We hadn't spoken for years.'

'Laurie's nurse recognized you at the memorial,' she said, fighting for calm. 'She said you came to his house. She heard you talking.'

'Then Laurie's nurse, whoever the hell she might be, is mistaken,' Huw flashed back, and Anna felt his cold fury like a physical force in the room. Not disappointment, not stress, she realized in that moment, but a raging need for control, a need that would stop at nothing.

Huw was hiding something, she was completely sure of that now.

'You knew, didn't you?' she said, playing a hunch. 'You knew about Laurie and your father!'

She saw him go paper white around his eyes. 'That's it!' Huw's voice was like a whip. 'I want you to leave this building *now*.'

'Oh my God, you didn't even ask me what I meant! What did you *do*?' she hissed at him. 'What did you do to Laurie?'

'Get out!' Huw ordered. He was shaking with rage. 'Get out before I call the police.'

'Go ahead! Because that's where I'm going next!'

The police station was just a few streets away. She ran all the way, heart thumping, a wild euphoria rushing through her. She wasn't mad. She'd been right to suspect Huw. She hadn't been able to find the person or persons who had murdered her family, but she could do this. She could put this right.

Bursting through the doors Anna pushed to the head of the small queue of people waiting to talk to the duty sergeant, ignoring their protests. 'I've got to talk to Inspector Chaudhari,' she demanded, breathless.

'I'm sorry, miss, but you'll have to wait your turn,' said the sergeant.

'I can't!' she almost yelled. 'I think I know how Laurie Swanson died!'

But the stolid sergeant held his ground. When it was finally Anna's turn, he told her with polite regret that Inspector Chaudhari had left the building some time ago. He couldn't say when he'd be back.

Anna took one of the moulded plastic seats. Pressing her trembling knees together, she prepared herself to wait. Her heart was hammering like a rabbit's. *It's OK*, she told herself fiercely. She just had to keep it together a bit longer. She could keep it together for Laurie. After that it didn't matter if she fell apart. It wouldn't matter.

At last Liam Goodhart appeared. He smiled, but it wasn't, Anna felt, a completely convincing smile. 'The sergeant says you have important information about Laurie Swanson?' he said.

She sprang up. 'Yes! Yes, I do! Is Inspector Chaudhari here?'

Liam led her downstairs to an interview room. Anna thought it was the same one, but maybe there were dozens of featureless rooms down here. She took a chair and Liam leaned against the wall, and they waited in uneasy silence for Inspector Chaudhari to join them.

When he walked in, he exchanged a private look with Liam, and she felt a jolt of fear. She had burst in babbling about Laurie. They thought she was nuts. Anna couldn't blame them. She even looked nuts. She was so freaked that one of her knees had taken on a jiggling life of its own, and she was fighting a losing battle to keep it still.

In her panic Anna started to pour out what she'd discovered: that Huw Traherne had been seen visiting Laurie; that he'd needed to silence this man, his father's secret lover, before the news could get out and wreck his Foundation. Or that's what she tried to say. But she couldn't seem to get her thoughts in any kind of order. Like startled birds they scattered as soon as they'd formed. 'I've got evidence,' she heard herself say over and over like a mad bag lady. 'Please, you've got to believe me!'

When the wound-up spring inside her had finally run down, and Anna had stopped talking, sick with humiliation, Inspector Chaudhari made a quick note of something on his phone, then he passed his hand over his thick black hair and gave her a look that somehow combined concern with reproof. 'Mr Traherne has just called the station. Your accusations have made him extremely upset. I am therefore giving you an official warning not to go round to his home or to his offices or to try to contact him again.'

Her hands flew to her head. Too late she remembered that this was the classic pose of the mentally unwell and returned them to her lap. 'But what if he killed Laurie?' she said in a pleading voice.

The inspector drew a breath. 'Anna, listen, however strongly you feel, you can't afford to go throwing these kinds of serious accusations around.' He gave her a long look. 'Not with your history.'

Anna felt her blood drain from her face. When she was seventeen, a restraining order had been taken out against her by the family of a boy she'd believed partly responsible for the deaths of her parents and siblings. She'd been wrong. She'd been off her head. She wasn't wrong this time, but to the inspector she would always be that teenage girl whose disturbed ramblings they still had recorded somewhere on their files.

The inspector went on to say a few other things. She was tired and upset. It might be time to think about talking to a professional counsellor, get some help. Anna could hear the sympathy in his voice, the kind of tone you might use to soothe a skittish pony. Summoning the last of her strength, she opened her mouth to plead one last time, then was overcome by a sense of utter futility.

'My sergeant will show you out,' the inspector said.

When they reached the reception area Anna was bewildered to see a tense-looking Tansy waiting by the desk. 'I called her,' Liam said. 'I thought you might need a friend.'

Like a humiliated child, Anna waited as Liam handed over his car keys so Tansy could drive her home. Exhausted and wrung-out, she followed Tansy out to the car.

As Tansy drove, she kept darting anxious looks at Anna. 'I feel so terrible about this,' she burst out at last. 'Liam said he took the call – you know from that arse Huw?' She took a breath. 'Remember when we came back from London? You said we just need to be normal?'

Anna didn't see the point of saying that this was normal for her.

When they arrived outside Anna's door, Tansy said, 'I don't feel happy about just dropping you off, but I've got to return Liam's car then go back to finish my shift.' She flashed Anna a grin. 'When I left, Julie looked as if she was about to have a stroke, so it's not all bad news!'

'I'll be fine,' Anna muttered. She felt sick with shame. 'Thanks for the lift.'

'Isadora's got some big dinner party tonight,' Tansy said, glancing at her watch, 'but if it's not too late – actually, even if it is – we'll pop over and make sure you're OK.'

Anna shook her head. 'No, don't worry. I just need to sleep.'

To sleep and also to sever every last connection to the outside world. Though cutting her connections wasn't going to be a problem, she thought wearily as she let herself into her flat. She caught herself unconsciously fingering Kit's pendant. She wouldn't let herself think about Kit Tulliver. She'd blown it for all time with him. No matter how much she tried to explain, she knew he would never forgive her for publicly denouncing Huw.

She went down to her kitchen where Bonnie was already waiting expectantly at the foot of the stairs. Anna knelt beside her. Wrapping her arms around Bonnie's solid warmth, she buried her face in her snowy coat. *At least I've got you*, she thought. *No matter how mad people think I am, I've got you, you sweet, beautiful dog.*

TWENTY

Despite what she'd said to Tansy, Anna didn't take herself off to sleep. She daren't. That she wouldn't actually dissolve into sea foam like the Little Mermaid, just because she'd relaxed her vigilance for an hour or two, made no difference. If she let go now, she was afraid she'd fall all the way to the bottom, and this time she might not be able to fight her way back up.

Instead she filled a bucket with hot water, found kitchen cleaner and an abrasive pad and made herself clean the fronts of her kitchen cupboards. She did it through a fog of tiredness and misery, but the important thing was that she did it. Cupboard by cupboard, door by door she was restoring order to her life. Her therapist had been right. The repetitive chore made Anna feel . . . not normal – she was several miles to the left of normal by now – but as good as it was possible to feel now that her last chance of 'normal' had gone swirling down the plughole.

Eventually, she'd worked her way round to the cupboard where she stored Bonnie's forbidden treats. Bonnie's repeated assaults had left a Jackson Pollock spatter-effect of grubby paw marks. Seeing Anna scrubbing away at her special cupboard, her White Shepherd casually ambled over with a hopeful glint in her eye. Dogs were such ridiculously hopeful creatures. 'No way!' Anna told her sternly. 'You'll get treats when I say, or you will have a waist like a – dog with no waist.'

Bonnie lay down with a disappointed sigh, but kept her eyes pointedly on Anna, the dispenser of treats and walks.

Encouraged by her gleaming cupboards, Anna decided to tackle her grandmother's china. One by one she lifted down the eggshell thin cups and plates, hand-washed them in warm soapy water, rinsed and dried them and returned them to their original positions on her shelves. Anna must only have been eight years old when her grandmother had decided she could finally be trusted to help with this near-sacred task. At that age Anna had still been a trusting open-hearted child, seeing magic in everything. Before puberty hit and turned her into every parent's worst nightmare.

'*Don't*,' Anna told herself sharply. She looked around for another mindless task. *Bird feeders*. She hadn't checked them for days. She took bags of peanuts and sunflower-seed into the garden and refilled the half-dozen or so feeders. Until now she hadn't even noticed what kind of day it was. She'd been too obsessed with Huw. For the first time she properly registered the overcast skies. Fitful gleams of sunlight came and went through the thinning leaves. A smell of bonfires drifted to her on the breeze.

By the time she'd filled the last and smallest feeder, a blackbird and several blue-tits were queuing up along the fence, waiting for her to leave. She walked back into the kitchen just as her landline started to ring. She checked the caller's ID, in case someone was calling from Bramley Lodge, and recognized Jake's number. At the last possible moment she snatched up the phone. 'Hello?'

'Anna, I wasn't sure if you'd be home. How's it going?' The sound of his warm southern voice saying her name was so good that she had to close her eyes. 'I had a gap between meetings. Thought I'd find out what our girl's up to.'

'Where are you?' She wanted to be able to pinpoint him in time and space.

'Where am I? Hold up! Let me look out the window – I think it's Berlin. Yes, yesterday was Zurich, so today has to be Berlin.'

'Sounds like a hectic schedule.' She tried to sound upbeat, not like a hysteric who'd accused someone of murdering his father's gay lover.

'Yeah, well, hopefully we'll get a few good contracts out of it, then I can decide where I'm going to be living for the next few years. So how's our treat thief? Attempted any more break-ins?'

'Actually, she's just been watching me remove her mucky prints from the crime scene,' Anna said. 'She might have been experiencing a moment of guilt, but I think it's more likely she was hoping I'd open the cupboard and give her a treat.'

He laughed. 'So that's Bonnie. How about you?'

'Me?' She felt herself falling. Jake's innocent question had pulled the rug out from under her, and underneath there was just – terrifying space. 'I'm – I'm actually not very – I'm – I'm sorry!' To her horror she heard her voice rising like a child's as she fought and failed to contain the storm that had been building for so long.

She fumbled for the button that would sever the connection. She could hear him saying, 'Anna? Are you still there?' And she just stood holding the phone, listening to his voice saying her name, as if he was her lifeline.

'It's OK,' he said softly. 'It's OK, sweetheart. You're gonna be OK.' Jake sounded concerned, but he didn't sound dismayed. Maybe that's why she could finally tell him the truth.

'I'm not OK, Jake,' she almost whispered. 'I'm a mess.'

And then she told him about the night that had turned her into this messed-up person. She didn't tell him everything, she wasn't sure if she even remembered everything that had happened, but it wasn't the cleaned-up version she'd told Isadora and Tansy. She described finding her little sister Lottie in her blood-soaked bed and colliding with someone on the landing who had stabbed her, then stumbling, half-falling, downstairs, clutching at her stomach with both her bloody hands. And as she told her story, she was seeing the sixteen-year-old Anna, she was feeling her mindless terror and the stinging pain from her stab wound, running frantically from the house where her parents and her two young brothers lay dead. They had been brutally slaughtered, their bodies scarcely recognizable, as though the killer's primary need was to punish, tearing into their soft innermost parts like wolves, except that wolves kill for food or to defend their young, and there was no sense to this killing, none at all. And each time she thought she'd reached the end of the horror, there was more, until she felt like her own entrails were being dragged out and exposed.

'The police suspected everyone,' she said. 'Kind normal people who'd babysat me and my brothers, and whose kids came to our house for sleepovers; people we'd been on holidays with. Then the tabloids jumped on board, digging up dirt about my parents' sex lives, my dad's finances. I was a suspect at one time, even though I'd been stabbed . . .' Anna's hand went instinctively to the puckered little scar. 'I knew some bad people in those days,' she said, her voice faltering. 'They thought I'd brought them back to the house, to get money for drugs.'

It was like hurtling along on some kind of confessional rollercoaster. It was terrifying, and compulsive, her sudden violent need to be heard by this man. But after a while she noticed that, though Jake was listening with close attention, he showed absolutely no sign of surprise. She sat down abruptly on a nearby stool. 'You knew,' she said flatly. 'Did Isadora tell you?'

'She told me some.' Jake sounded matter of fact. 'There's quite a lot about you online.'

'I don't – as a rule I don't tell—' she started.

'Why should you have to?' he said. 'It's nobody's business but yours.'

'Yet you looked me up,' she said, very quietly.

'True, but I had a vested interest.' His voice was suddenly so warm that it felt as if he'd put his arms around her. 'Also, I admit that it had occurred to me that, if the day was to come when you decided you could trust me to know you a little bit better, it might be helpful to arm myself with some basic facts.'

She caught sight of her reflection in her kettle and was surprised to see tears streaming down her face. As soon as she saw them she could feel them slipping down her cheeks, running into the neck of her sweater. How long had she been crying? She swiped the tears away. 'I did a terrible thing today,' she told him. 'I think I've blown it with Isadora and Tansy.'

And Kit, she thought, touching the silver bee at her throat. It was strange; for a while Kit had seemed like the more realistic possibility. But she could never have talked like this with Kit Tulliver. She couldn't say how she knew. She just understood, deep in her bones, that it was true.

'Why do you think you've blown it?' Jake asked.

She told him about Laurie's mysterious visitor and how Anna had worked out that it had to be Huw. Then she described what she'd found out about Aidan Rose and how she'd confronted Huw in his office, then rushed straight to the police, given a prize-winning performance as a nut-job and been told to have nothing more to do with the Trahernes. Almost worse than her failure to convince the police of Huw Traherne's involvement in Laurie's death was emerging from the interview suite to find an embarrassed Tansy waiting to take her home. It wasn't the first time Anna had been picked up from a local police station in disgrace, but that only made it more, not less, humiliating.

When she'd finally run out of words, Jake stayed silent for so long that she was convinced he'd terminated the call in disgust. 'Hello?' she said in a panic.

'Still here,' he said cheerfully. 'Just thinking about a bunch of stuff.'

She'd forgotten Jake's lengthy pauses for thought. She waited and eventually heard him take a breath.

'OK, here's the first thing,' he said. 'I don't believe there is anything on this earth that could permanently damage the connection you've got with those girls. You met them at a murder scene. Y'all have been through fire together, and these are not the kind of friendships people just throw away. Trust me on that, OK?'

'OK,' she whispered.

'Second, you need a break. You need to take time out, get away from all of this for a while. How would you feel about taking a trip somewhere with me?' he added, so abruptly that she almost dropped the phone. 'I've got to come back to see Mimi's solicitor in a couple of days, and I'd been thinking of driving up to the Lake District. That day we had in the Cotswolds really made me want to see more of the English countryside. There's a lakeside hotel in Ullswater that takes dogs. I could book us a couple of rooms. A few days of peace and quiet, mountains and lakes, wood fires, good food, long country walks with Bonnie for your chaperone – what do you think?'

She nodded dumbly, then realized Jake couldn't see her. 'Yes,' she managed. 'Yes, I'd like that.'

They talked for a few minutes longer, then Jake had to go and meet some possible future clients.

After Anna had ended the call she opened Bonnie's cupboard and gave her a treat because she needed to celebrate with someone, and who said dog owners had to be one hundred per cent consistent? 'We're going on holiday,' she told her, 'with your Jake!'

Having crunched up her treat in double-quick time, Bonnie gave the short sharp bark she used when she was excited.

'I *know*!' Anna said. She didn't understand how it had only taken a single phone conversation with Jake McCaffrey to restore her perspective, nor did she care exactly how he'd worked his magic, only that it had worked. An hour ago her life had been over. Although, her previous misgivings about Jake still applied; he presumably still had a not-so-ex. He was still based on the wrong side of the Atlantic. But just at this moment none of these things seemed nearly as important as the compelling fact of Jake himself. She had never felt such an intense connection with a man – and they had never even kissed! *But I'd like to*, she thought, and she felt her skin flush as she imagined other things she'd like to do with Jake.

But right now she had an overwhelming need to crawl into her bed. She went up to her bedroom, pulled off her boots, fell on to her bed fully-dressed and gave herself up to sleep.

When she woke it was pitch dark and she felt more rested than she had for days. She checked her phone and saw that it was half-past midnight. She'd slept for eight or nine hours! She'd have been tempted to turn over and sleep some more except that she was suddenly famished. She showered, quickly towel-dried her hair and slipped into her flannel robe. She was just tying up the belt with sleepy fingers, wondering without much hope if there was anything in her fridge that could be made to resemble a late-night snack, when she heard a loud 'clunk' from the kitchen. 'I can hear you, you know!' she called. 'If you're messing up my clean cupboards, there'll be big trouble!'

She padded out on to the landing in her bare feet, not bothering to turn on the light. She could see her way to the stairs by the glow from the street lamp outside the window. She had taken two or three steps, when she felt her right foot almost skid out from under her. She'd stepped in something warm and wet. Now that she looked down she could see it, a glistening liquid trail. The dog flap must have malfunctioned as it had occasionally done before. Anna had been dead to the world for hours, and Bonnie hadn't been able to get out.

She groped for the light switch so she could assess the extent of the puddle and whether any rugs were involved. For a moment she stared down, unable to process what she was seeing, then with a moan she backed away from the ominous pool. But it was too late; her feet were covered with blood.

The hall was suddenly rushing away from her like smoke. *It was happening again*. She flashed back to Lily's blood-soaked bed. The sticky black-crimson mess, the same ferrous tang making her nostrils flare.

Sick and shaking, Anna somehow dragged herself back to the present. This wasn't then; it was *now*. Whatever this was, it was real and new.

She forced herself to look further down the hall and felt her heart almost leave her mouth as she saw the huddled white shape lying near the front door. *Bonnie*.

Anna scarcely noticed that she had to walk through her dog's blood to reach her. She was just suddenly crouching over her, fighting down waves of shock and nausea. Someone had stabbed her in her side. Fresh blood was still flowing, staining Bonnie's snow-white coat. She was panting with stress and fear. The instant she felt Anna bending over her she made a valiant effort at wagging her tail, almost breaking Anna's heart. That was the moment when she knew just how much she loved her brave beautiful dog. 'You'll be OK,' she told her, putting all her love and belief into her voice. 'Everything's going to be OK. Just try to hang on, and I'll get help.'

But why would someone break in and hurt Bonnie? And how had they got in?

She hadn't set the alarm. She'd been such a mess when she got home that she hadn't set the bloody alarm. Lulled into a childlike illusion that Jake had somehow made the whole world safe, she'd slept while someone had broken into her house and attacked her dog.

She heard a floorboard creak. Still in a crouch, she whirled around, fists raised, adrenalin surging through her veins, to see Huw Traherne standing over her with a bloodied knife.

In her heightened terror it felt as if floodlights had turned on in her brain, and she saw him, the real Huw, his veneer of humanity ripped away.

'You're causing me *much* too much trouble, Anna,' he said in a bored voice. Reaching down, he grabbed her by her shoulders. He was far, far stronger than she'd thought. He partially lifted her off the floor, then slammed her into the wall sending an agonizing pain shooting through her collar bone and jarring every last bone in her body. The force of the impact sent a picture crashing to the floor. Winded and bruised, Anna tried to sit up, sucking in her breath as tiny shards of broken glass stung her palms. For the first time she saw Laurie's box by Huw's feet. She started to struggle towards it, but Huw was too fast.

Pulling her up by the front of her robe he pinned her shoulder to the wall with his free hand. A heartbeat later, she felt the sharp point of a knife being pressed to her throat a few millimetres above Kit's pendant. For a moment she was confused by the unnatural waxy whiteness of his hands, before she realized he was wearing gloves.

There was a kind of slowed-down dreamlike rightness to it. This was how Anna's story was always supposed to end. She was meant to have died along with everyone else. She'd just had to wait sixteen years to get what she deserved. Once it would have been a relief. A few months ago she'd have begged him to get it over with, to just kill her, put an end to her long lonely nightmare and be done.

But when Anna looked up at this pale, normal-looking man who had killed Laurie, she understood that she couldn't just submit, not without a fight. She couldn't leave Bonnie to bleed to death all alone.

'Aren't you going to scream and struggle and beg?' Huw sounded almost petulant. Without warning he pushed the point of the knife under her pendant in a short, sharp upward thrust, and she felt the silver links snap. The broken chain slithered from her neck, carrying Kit's little winged bee with it. She instinctively moved to save it, but he slapped her hand away. 'You stupid cow! You have no idea, have you?'

'I know you killed Laurie!' she flashed back, surprising herself with the sound of her own voice. In dreams her vocal chords were always paralysed. In dreams she was still sixteen.

'Oh, that. I *had* to do that,' he said carelessly. 'I couldn't just let him ruin everything. Laurie Swanson and my mother almost destroyed my father's reputation once before. I couldn't let him do it again!'

'Laurie and your mother?' Anna said blankly. She could feel Huw's rage vibrating through the knife and into her flesh.

Huw was still talking. 'I did go to see Laurie; you were right about that. He was pathetically pleased to see me, said he'd never meant to hurt me.' He laughed. 'Creepy little pervert. Even so, I'd almost made up my mind to let him live. Didn't see the point of taking stupid chances, not when Nature was already fucking him up the arse! And then, on my way out, that little black nurse with the huge tits thanked me for coming to see him. She said it did him good to have visitors. She said this lovely young woman had come to see him the other night with her dog. She could tell Mr Swanson had liked her because he gave her that beautiful box he kept his special papers in.'

Huw slightly shifted position, and Anna felt the pressure from the knifepoint ease. 'I asked her if this lovely young woman was anyone I knew,' he said, 'and she told me your name.' He gave a short laugh. 'I guess she was off sick the day they did the security module!'

'So you went back and killed him.' Anna could smell Huw's subtle sandalwood aftershave, a smell she'd always loved until now.

'He was three-quarters dead already. It wasn't hard!' For a moment he sounded like a sneering little boy. 'I had some creative fun with his death bed though.'

'To make it look like your mother's suicide?' The words jumped out.

Huw stepped back, still pointing the knife, genuinely shocked. 'How could you possibly know that? That wasn't in the papers!'

'It must have been,' she said quickly, 'or how would I know?'

'True,' he admitted. 'You're not nearly devious enough to be able to access that kind of information.'

Anna wondered if he'd registered the crucial space he'd left between them. She could knock away his knife now and run to Bonnie. But then he'd just come after her and do to her what he'd done to her dog.

'My mother didn't commit suicide, anyway,' Huw said carelessly. He looked down at the knife in his hand, and she saw his coldly knowing smile.

Anna's brain refused to take it in. It was horror piling on horror. She thought of Audrey, luminously beautiful in her hippy smock. 'You *killed* her?' she said numbly. 'But . . . she was your *mother.*'

'I had to. She didn't give me a choice.'

Anna thought she heard a movement behind her. *Bonnie!* She was still alive! *Hold on*, she told her silently. *Just hold on, and I will get us out of this.*

'My mother had been seeing a new therapist,' Huw said. 'I imagine you know quite a bit about therapists yourself, don't you Anna?' he added spitefully. 'Well, this particular therapist was big on family openness and sharing. Some might say *over-*sharing.' He gave another of his cold laughs. 'So one day, shortly before I'm due to go up to Oxford, my mother announces that she and my father had both been living a lie, and she had given him her blessing to go and live with my best friend Laurie. She said she was going to move to London and it would be a fresh start for all of us. Didn't give a flying fuck about the effect it would have on me, what they were doing to me. *Of course* I had to kill her.' His face twisted with hatred.

He still hadn't tried to close the gap. If Anna ignored the throbbing pain in her shoulder, and the fact that she was only wearing a short robe with nothing underneath, she could unbalance him by hooking her foot around his ankle and sending him crashing to the floor.

'Women, Nature's biggest disappointment,' Huw said, in an almost sing-song voice. 'You're all mad manipulative bitches. Take Sara, telling me I was the man of her dreams. I'm stuck with the barren bitch for now, sadly.' He shot Anna a vicious smile. 'Happily, I'm not stuck with you – or not for much longer!'

To Anna's bewilderment, Huw dropped the knife, kicking it away from him. He slid something narrow out of his pocket, something that glinted under the electric light. With a clutch of fear she saw that it was a syringe. 'Sedative to keep you quiet later on,' he explained coolly. 'But it's not time for you to meet your maker just yet.' Without turning his head, he called in a bored voice, 'Isn't it your turn now?'

In childhood nightmares people Anna had trusted in waking life – good, kind, familiar people – suddenly turned on her with unmistakably evil intent. When Kit stepped out of her sitting room, calm and smiling, it felt so exactly like those dreams that she thought her heart would stop. Snapping a pair of latex gloves in place, he bent down to pick up a tiny object from the floor, holding it out to her on his palm. It was the silver bee.

'You really didn't remember it, did you?' He saw her bewilderment and shook his head. 'I thought girls noticed little fripperies like that! It came off her bracelet in the struggle,' he explained. 'I kept a few for souvenirs.'

Naomi's charm bracelet. Anna remembered the cold burn of the metal against her skin as Kit fastened the charm around her neck, and the horror almost made her black out.

'Such a witty, prickly, faux enigmatic girl, aren't you?' Kit said with a sigh. 'Yet when it came right down to it, such a complete fucking pushover! Admit it, Bee Girl, my little present totally charmed the pants off you! Assuming you wear any, that is? From where I'm standing, I'd say probably not! Huw and I both look forward immensely to finding that out, don't we, Huw?'

Behind her, Anna heard Bonnie start to keen, the same high-pitched sound she'd made that morning on Port Meadow. *She knows I'm in danger.*

Anna felt blank with shock. She'd known something was wrong with Huw. But she hadn't let herself see the rottenness in Kit. Seduced by his flirty humour, the fact that he'd come so warmly endorsed by Isadora, she had let herself be played like a gullible teenage girl.

'She's not quite so witty now,' Kit said to Huw in fake disappointment. 'I think it's finally penetrated – if you'll excuse the tasteless metaphor, darling!' He flashed his smile at Anna, the smile she'd once found so appealing and which now seemed as predatory as a cruising shark. 'I'm not *really* into screwing women when they're unconscious, by the way,' he added casually. 'That's more Huw's thing. I wouldn't have minded a crack at Naomi though, in other circumstances. But DNA is such a bloody passion killer!' He laughed. 'Imagine my surprise when that local nutter claimed responsibility for doing her as well as the others!'

Numb from Kit's betrayal, Anna's brain could only process what he'd told her in successive shock-waves. Kit Tulliver had murdered Naomi. Then he'd gone back to his life as if nothing had happened. Taking a life was nothing to Kit, she understood then. Anna's life would be nothing. She might have been able to fight Huw, but she couldn't fight them both.

'Poor baby, we've scared her out of her wits!' Kit said, amused. 'Don't worry,' he told Anna. 'You'll feel nicely relaxed after we've shot that stuff into your veins.'

'How do you think you'll get away with it?' Anna said, finally rediscovering her voice. 'No matter how careful they are, people always leave DNA behind.'

'I didn't with Naomi,' Kit said.

Huw sniggered. 'Oh, come on, mate, you've got to admit you got seriously lucky with that one!'

'Besides, Anna, you and I were practically dating, and who knows what else?' He mimed a grotesque pelvic thrust. 'It's perfectly reasonable that I, or even my best friend Huw, come to that, could have been in your flat.'

Huw let out a snort of laughter.

They were like adolescents, Anna thought – crude, lecherous, over-privileged adolescents. At some point they must have recognized something in each other, she thought – something demonic and depraved. Huw had always lived in his father's shadow. He'd even lost Laurie, his friend and almost-brother, to Owen. He must have felt he had no control whatsoever over his life. And then he'd found a new, darker brother in Kit.

'Kit can tell you we always get away with it. My fucking mother.' Huw shot Kit a look. 'That pathetic little oik, Aidan.'

'Still trying to pay you back for that one, mate,' Kit said carelessly. 'I'd have been sent down!'

Behind Anna's back, Bonnie had been painfully inching along the floor. Anna only knew this when she felt the unmistakable warmth of her dog's body pressing against her bare foot. Bonnie's soft keening intensified, an eerie sub-vocal protest that was impossible to ignore.

'For fuck's sake, shut up!' Kit yelled at the dog. He directed a kick at Bonnie's head, and she let out a yelp of mixed terror and pain.

When Anna saw Kit hurt her helpless dog, a red mist filled her head and she launched herself at the knife. Kit quickly snatched it up and came towards her, grinning.

It was then that she remembered. She *had* seen the real Kit: that cold look in his eyes at the book launch. She'd felt it again when she kissed him. Some primitive part of Anna's brain had instantly smelled out what he was. But she had overruled it because she wanted to be happy and normal, to fall in love and be loved.

Anna felt it surge through her like a lightning strike, a sudden furious will to live. She had the optimum space now to execute the flying kick she'd learned from her Krav Maga instructor, so that's what she did, sending Kit sprawling and knocking the knife from his hand. 'Did you say you like us to struggle?' Anna asked him, before briskly head-butting Huw in the face. By this time a furious Kit was scrambling to his feet. Before he could get his balance, she spun around, kneeing him viciously in the groin.

The men were blocking her path to the front door so she fled down the stairs. She'd escape out through the back. She'd run to Dana to get help.

Downstairs all the lights were blazing. Her kitchen smelled of cold air and autumn leaves. The wind had blown them in through the open French windows. That's how Huw and Kit had broken in.

She heard someone pounding down the stairs behind her. Anna hurled herself towards the open doors, but Kit threw himself on top of her in a rugby tackle, knocking all the breath from her lungs. 'No you don't, you little bitch!' he hissed. She felt a sharp pain as the needle punctured her thigh. Kit sat back on his haunches, still getting his breath back. 'Go ahead,' he invited. 'Run! I won't stop you. And Huw can't. You broke his fucking nose!'

Anna started to crawl towards the doors on hands and knees that were fast turning to jelly. She was almost there when she heard a low, drawn-out, unmistakably evil growl.

Still on her knees, she turned to see a terrifyingly transformed Bonnie, ears flat to her head, her upper lip curled back showing wolf-like fangs dripping long strings of saliva. Covered in her own blood, she was the dog of nightmares as she sprang at Kit's throat, snarling.

Cursing, Kit staggered back, but Bonnie was too weak from blood loss to sustain her attack, and he was able to fling her from him, sending her crashing into Anna's dresser. Her grandmother's precious cups and saucers flew up into the air. Bonnie slid to the floor in a rainbow of broken china where she lay totally still and silent.

Nobody was going to come to save her, Anna thought. She had fought them with all her strength, but it wasn't enough. But at least she and Bonnie could die together.

Anna began to crawl towards her dog's limp unmoving body. She had almost reached her when she thought she heard people yelling upstairs. 'Don't actually shoot him, darling!' a familiar voice called. 'Just clock him hard with the barrel!' An ominously loud thud followed.

If this was a hallucination it was a shared one, because Kit made an instant dash for the doors, but Anna somehow grabbed him by the ankles, bringing him toppling down.

She was still grimly hanging on to him when someone came thundering down into the kitchen and she heard Tansy yell, 'Stay right there or I'll shoot you in the bollocks, you disgusting bastard!'

Anna's vision was starting to blur, so she couldn't be sure what was real and what was due to the effects of the drugs, but she thought she saw Tansy pointing a gun at Kit with a shaking hand. Isadora was talking into her phone and simultaneously brandishing a nearly-full bottle of Bombay Sapphire over Kit's head like a club.

Using the last of her strength, Anna managed to curl on to her side, so that she and Bonnie were nested together like spoons. Resting her head against her dog's warm lifeless body, she stroked her tenderly, and then, completely spent, she closed her eyes.

Strangely, instead of stopping, her hallucinations shifted into a new and gentler octave. She felt a fleeting touch against her eyelids, like a ray of winter sunlight, and she thought she heard Naomi say softly, *It's all right, Anna. Your friends came to save you.*

Then the tide came rushing in and carried her away into the dark.

TWENTY-ONE

The grave was so small.

A short distance away, a robin perched on a nearly leafless branch, producing a stream of crystalline sounds for no other reason than that it was alive. The sky was a misty watercolour blue. She could hear church bells and the sound of a distant train.

The last time she was here it had been for the funeral, and she'd been so heavily sedated that it almost felt as if it was happening to someone else. It had been a hot, cloudless summer's day, and that had felt jarring and wrong, as if mass murders only happen in midwinter. There had been people sobbing and clutching each other for support, people she didn't even know, and, in the background, press photographers snapping and police watching.

Sixteen years ago. Half Anna's lifetime. Now the mossy old churchyard was steeped in peace. A giant holly-tree was already covered in scarlet berries. In the new year snowdrops would come up in green and white drifts among the headstones. Thanks to her friends, Anna would be here to see them. She still didn't know what to make of her strange visitation in those moments before Kit's sedative had overwhelmed her. Had she really been visited by Naomi? Or had it just been Anna's personal version of her, the part of Anna that had needed to change and reach out, the part of her that, despite everything she'd lost, still wanted to live?

Like a half-remembered song, that longing to be truly alive, to rejoin the world, had first tentatively made itself felt after she'd moved back to Oxford, Anna realized now. She'd told Jake she'd gone to the rescue centre to find a dog because she was scared to be alone in the house. But that hadn't been the whole truth, since Anna had only recently understood this herself. Secretly, Anna had hoped that getting a dog would change her life. And it had! She had found a murdered woman and almost been killed herself, but in the process she had exorcized demons and found good friends who cared about her.

She hadn't brought flowers. In her mind her brother would still always be nine years old, and nine-year-old Will had not been big on flowers. She was here at his grave because she had woken with the realization that today should have been his birthday, so she had bought helium balloons in his favourite colours and secured the ends of their strings with a hefty but handsome stone she'd taken from her garden.

'Do you think Will would like them?' she whispered, stepping back, and the snow-white dog beside her immediately came alert. Anna reached down to pet her silky ears. Yesterday, the vet had given Anna permission to remove the hated lampshade device from around her White Shepherd's neck. The stitches had all been taken out, and though Bonnie was still moving cautiously, her wound was healing well. Like Anna, Bonnie was one of life's survivors.

The robin was still singing, its tiny throat throbbing as it poured an increasingly intricate song into the air. 'Channelling Mozart,' Anna said softly, and she smiled to herself because she had finally solved a small but persistent mystery.

After the horror of that night, and after Isadora and Tansy came back with Anna to her flat to help clean up the mess, she'd found the contents of Laurie's box strewn across her study. Owen's diary, the one he'd been using before he died, had been hurled across the room. It was one of a line of specialist diaries made by Moleskin, especially loved by writers and artists because of the addition of an inside pocket for small memorabilia, tickets, photographs. The night that Anna had scanned in Laurie's papers she'd been too tired and panicky to pay proper attention. The actual diary had ended halfway through with Owen's protestations of love for Laurie. It hadn't occurred to her that there was anything else to find. But as she picked up the diary from where it had fallen, she'd felt something rustle inside. She knew it was silly, that it might just be a long-forgotten shopping list, but it felt like a final message from Laurie.

Heart beating, she'd pulled out a yellowing sheet of A5 paper, worn into creases from being constantly unfolded and refolded. It was a poem written in Owen's handwriting. It was titled 'The

Tree of Sorrows (II)' and it was dedicated to *My Darling Laurie*. In the poem, Owen revisited the image of the sleepless lover in the first version. This man was older and a little wiser, but equally unable to shut his mind to the sorrows that haunt the Tree outside their window. There is so much suffering: his own, his parents', the world's.

But instead of sneaking from his bed to be alone with his pain, the man takes his lover out into the winter's night, where they defiantly make love against the trunk of the Tree of Sorrows. When dawn comes the lovers find themselves in a landscape that is utterly transfigured. The Tree, together with all the trees for miles around, has burst into simultaneous blossom. There are other miraculous happenings. Prison bars buckle and break under the sheer weight of fruiting vines. The old become young. All the birds begin to channel Mozart. Owen's poem was meant for Laurie's eyes only, and it was playful, passionate and silly. Whatever Anna's private misgivings about their relationship, this was the poem that Laurie had loved best, with its message that his and Owen's love was infinitely more powerful than the dark forces ranged against them.

With a final flurry of notes, the robin flew off, and Anna turned to look for her friends. The two women had taken their dogs to the older part of the graveyard, keeping a tactful distance until they were needed. Anna could see Isadora peeling back a spray of ivy so that she and Tansy could read the name on a weathered headstone.

Anna gave them a wave, and they walked over to join her.

For a moment, the three women silently contemplated the balloons Anna had brought for Will as they tugged at their strings in the breeze. Then Tansy gave Anna a sideways look. 'You know Kit told the police I had a gun? Liam told me.' She gave a mischievous laugh. 'Luckily, they didn't believe him! Liam's like – but she's a vegan! What are the chances she'd go marching into her friend's house waving a shooter?'

'He didn't *really* say "shooter"?' Anna said.

'No, he actually did,' Tansy said. 'I told him he watches too many Guy Ritchie movies!'

The charges against Kit Tulliver and Huw Traherne were so serious that they'd both been remanded in prison pending their trial. Sara had apparently left the Traherne's marital home. Anna suspected she was with Dritan, but she could have gone away with Eve until the media frenzy had died down. Nobody knew for sure, just as nobody knew who would take over the running of the Traherne foundation.

They set off walking back to the car, taking it slowly because of Bonnie. The women had talked together several times since that night, but still found themselves needing to go over and over what had happened; a kind of informal therapy, Anna thought. It was novel and comforting, not to be dealing with her latest trauma completely alone.

'So what have you done with your dad's "present"?' she asked. 'Did you send it back?'

Tansy just gave her an enigmatic smile.

'I almost wish we'd shot him,' Isadora said fiercely, 'or at least smashed that bloody bottle over his head – Kit Tulliver, I mean,' she explained. 'I still feel so terrible about him, Anna. I let myself be completely taken in, and he could have—'

'He could have, but he didn't,' Anna said, interrupting. 'You and Tansy came and saved me.'

'And you're going to the lakes with sexy Jake!' Tansy waggled her eyebrows suggestively.

'I keep *telling* you, he's booked separate rooms,' Anna insisted, though she privately hoped this arrangement might change.

They had reached the lych gate in the shadow of a yew tree, where the women stopped to attach leads to their dogs.

'Did you ever figure out why your dad sent you the gun?' Anna asked abruptly.

'Apparently, he had a "feeling".' Tansy put ironic air quotes around the word. 'At first I just thought he was playing his old mind games, trying to reel me back in, then I remembered all the times my dad's "feelings" had kept him alive and/or out of jail.'

'And you did sound so strange when you phoned to ask me about Huw,' Isadora explained. 'Then Liam told Tansy you'd gone to Huw's office and accused him of killing Laurie.'

'Not my smartest ever move,' Anna said.

'I'd say a downright stupid move!' Tansy gave Anna's arm an affectionate squeeze to take the sting out of her words.

A few days after Huw and Kit had been taken off in handcuffs, Inspector Chaudhari had paid Anna a visit. He'd explained what he couldn't tell Anna at the time she'd come in with her suspicions. 'We'd just found out that there were significant holes in the so-called Ripper's statement. Things didn't line up. There was no way he could have killed Naomi Evans. And though I wasn't sure who had, I wanted you out of Traherne's way while we investigated more thoroughly.' Before the inspector left, he'd said, 'I wanted to say how much I respect you for fighting for Laurie Swanson the way you did.' Then he'd given her a stern look. 'I also want you to promise me you'll never to do anything that stupid ever again!'

He was a good man, Anna thought, and his words had meant a lot.

Still standing by the lych gate, Isadora was playing their new game of *What if?* 'I keep thinking what if we hadn't come to apologize for not listening to you, Anna.' Her eyes went wide with distress. 'We wouldn't have heard Bonnie making that terrible sound. You'd have ended up like Naomi!'

'Thank God, Isadora still had your spare key,' Tansy said.

Anna still didn't really do hugging, but she briskly hugged the two women who had saved her and Bonnie, then they closed the gate behind them and began walking back along the grass verge to where they'd left Anna's Land Rover.

'Can you drop me back at Marmalade?' Tansy asked.

'Of course. What about you?' she asked Isadora.

'Just take me home, darling,' she said. 'I've got to interview a potential lodger. Anything to keep that bloody wolf from the door!'

Anna opened up the back of her vehicle, and all the dogs piled inside. She could hear Tansy talking anxiously about her own housing problems. When her friends got back from their travels, she'd have to find somewhere else to live. Life was like that, Anna thought. The darkness and uncertainty never really went away, but like the man in Owen's poem, you could make a choice. You could decide to be a sufferer, picking over the bones of old sorrows for the rest of your days, or you could be a lover like Naomi. Anna wanted to be like her. She wanted it with all her heart, but she wasn't sure if it was something she could achieve through willpower. She thought timing might be involved. She might just need more time to overcome her old mistrustful ways.

She was about to get into her car when she heard a familiar ping. Anna quickly checked her mobile and saw that she had a Google Alert. She hesitated, but the habit was too ingrained and so she clicked on the link.

Her friends' voices, the sound of the wind in the trees and other sounds of the natural world cut off. The only sound left was the rush of blood inside her ears.

He was back. He was back in the UK.